# THE FOURTH
# ARCHANGEL

Also by Sharon Butala

**Novels**
*Upstream*
*Luna*
*The Gates of the Sun*
*Country of the Heart*

**Short Stories**
*Fever*
*Queen of the Headaches*

# THE FOURTH ARCHANGEL

## SHARON BUTALA

HarperCollins*Publishers*Ltd

First Edition

Canadian Cataloguing in Publication Data

Butala, Sharon, 1940-
  The fourth archangel

ISBN 0-00-223757-1
Trade Paperback ISBN 0-00-647404-7

I. Title.

PS8553.U73F6 1992    C813'.54    C92-093392-0
PR9199.3.B87F6  1992

92 93 94 95 ❖ RRD 5 4 3 2 1

Neil Locke's readings are from *The Papers of the Palliser Expedition 1857-1860*,
copyright 1968 by The Champlain Society, Toronto; and *The Great Lone Land*,
by William Francis Butler, published by The Musson Book Company Limited,
London, 1924, and in Canada by Hurtig Publishers, 1968.

# ACKNOWLEDGMENTS

I wish to thank all of those people who gave freely of their time and expertise to help me with this book. Kenneth Aitken at the Prairie History Room, Regina Public Library, always knew exactly the information I needed, sometimes before I knew it, and precisely where to find it. Potter Zach Dietrich gave me a tour of the studio he shares with his wife, sculptor Wendy Parsons, lent me a book, and took the time to answer my questions. Beeke Bailey, Carol Bonnett, Rosemary Cowan, Coralie Geving, James Misfeldt, and Milton Skippon all read early drafts and made comments and suggestions, not all of which, I confess, I acted upon. Extension Agrologist Jim Donovan, his assistant Ethel Wills, and fellow writer, lover of the southwest, and forage specialist Don Gayton both answered specific questions and recommended source material. Our local librarian, Betty Ann Huhn, cheerfully provided me with hard-to-locate books. Thanks to all of them for their generosity.

I also wish to thank the Saskatchewan Arts Board for a Senior Arts Grant which enabled me to complete this manuscript.

And most of all, thanks to Peter Butala, who makes it all possible.

# PREFACE TO
# HISTORY

At every moment, things are as they should be.

At the heart of the continent lies a land as intimidating as the thickest forest or any range of craggy, impassable mountains or wet green jungles. It is as solitary as the oceans, in summer subject to dust-storms, storms of thunder and lightning, and heat so intense that life comes to a standstill, and in winter to cold far worse. From the time of the Wisconsinan Glacier only roving bands of aboriginals dared to call it home. It is the Great Plains of North America.

Centuries passed while all around the world, deserts, jungles, mountains, and forests yielded to settlements by Europeans, but the Plains did not. On the Plains there was nothing to build with, no wood with which to make fires, no natural barriers other than distance itself to keep herds from wandering.

In the first quarter of the nineteenth century, habitation of the grasslands all over the world began to take place. This coincided with the age of minerals when substitutes for wood (of which on the treeless plains there was none) in the making of machines and tools began to be developed. In July of 1860, the first patent for barbed wire was given to Leonce Eugene Grassin in France, making it possible to keep animals enclosed within a large area. Thus the building of permanent homes on the Plains became feasible, as did the tilling of the soil.

Settlement of the grasslands proceeded.

# PART ONE

Amy Sparrow is dreaming. She moves to the door of her log cabin, opens it, goes outside to stand under the low, snow-covered eaves. It is night and there is a deep, muffled silence. Snow is banked up chest-high on each side of the door, and before her, glittering fields of snow disappear into the blue-black and hollow distance. It is eerie, but the eeriness has nothing to do with the wildness of the place in which she finds herself, or that it is night. It must be because this is a dream, and though it is winter and she finds herself standing in her nightgown in snow, she is not cold. And everything has been stripped away: the sense of home, of people nearby, of domestic animals in the corrals. She has gone to sleep, stepped out of a hunter's cabin into primeval wilderness, out of time into snow, eternal night and sky inseparable from it.

From out of the deep shadow on her left a coyote appears. It moves slowly toward her, limping on three legs, and as it passes her it turns its head to look directly into her eyes. It is a white coyote – a maimed, white coyote.

Old Man Paslowski is tossing and calling out from his hospital bed. Soon the nurse will come and give him an injection to quiet him before he wakes the other patients in the small hospital. He is restless all these nights and the nurse knows his time is drawing to a close. Of course he dreams; she hopes she will dream too at the end, for who knows what the dreams are teaching him about the place to which he will soon go.

But Old Man Paslowski is far out on the Great Plains, the place to which he came as a boy and which in ninety years he has never once left. He stands alone far out in the prairie grass and wind rustles in his ears.

Indians on painted ponies gallop past, brandishing bows and feathered arrows with hard, glittering tips, white dust roiling up around their horses' hooves. He listens hard and hears the thunder of passing buffalo and sees in the tremulous yellow distance tipis riding the heat waves. The scent of sage fills his nostrils and he is comforted.

The nurse looks down on him with eyes filled with the knowledge of death. Not many more nights, she thinks.

Now cowboys are riding slowly past him, he remembers some of their faces from years before. They ride over the prairie on their tall, strong horses, their clothes worn and dusty, their eyes in their weather-beaten faces the pale blue of the spring sky, and they look outward to places far beyond the horizon. They are searching for water, searching for somewhere cattle can wander forever through endless grassy fields, their bellies full.

But Mr. Hartshorne, a local minister, has fallen into a sleep so deep that though his dream will remain with him all the rest of his life, he will never be able to recall its source. Where did he see it? Was it in a movie? On TV? In a book by some long forgotten – except for CanLit classes – prairie novelist? Grove or Stead? Or Ross or Ostenso? Such a vision only a minister of a Protestant denomination could see. It is beyond the experience or beliefs of Roman Catholic priests, and Christian fundamentalists see such things only in dreams of heaven.

He is driving down the highway between towns – he spends much of his life driving from town to town since the population is so sparse and scattered and churchgoers relatively rare – when just above the line ahead of him where the road should meet the sky, a town appears.

It is suspended in the sky, emerging out of shimmering waves of heat that dissolve the horizon; first, the gently undulating grey highway melts into a zone of wavering yellow grass, then into a belt of deep, violet-blue that seems to hold the hidden beginnings of some other world, and rising out of this is the phantom town. Its neatly painted wooden houses and false-fronted stores, muted and greyed, oscillate gently in the sky, its parchment-thin beige streets spread delicately between the rows of buildings looking as though no human has ever trod on them, and the dusty foliage of the tall old trees wavers lushly between and above the buildings. The scene is animated by the occasional glint of sunlight striking leaves. This is a perfect jewel of a town, quivering palely in the sky above the end of the road.

Mr. Hartshorne sees its beauty with a sense of fulfillment and no surprise. He has no doubt that this town is an earthly one, one built by people and inhabited by them. In fact, he sees a strong resemblance to Ordeal, the town where he makes his home, that village on the wide and lonely plains far away from cities, set in a flat valley bottom where long, deep coulees converge, where a few trees grow and a narrow stream runs by most of the year. Such peace, such pristine beauty. This vision is what lies back of all his labours; God's kingdom come to earth.

————————

# CHAPTER
# 1

Amy could not think what was to be done; she had been this way ever since she'd wakened this morning. She'd left the stove turned on under the coffee pot and had to drive a mile back to turn it off. Before that she couldn't seem to get herself dressed; putting on one garment, forgetting the rest, walking into the kitchen barefoot and in her nightgown with her cotton slacks under it, drifting back to take off the nightgown and put on a bra, then sitting absently on the side of the bed staring at her sandals lying this way and that on the crooked and wrinkled scatter rug. She wondered if she'd remembered to brush her hair. Touching it with her palm and feeling its smoothness, she knew she must have, then recalled viscerally the feel of the cool, tarnished handle of the silver brush against her palm – the brush had been her mother's – and its satisfying tug in her long, sleep-tangled hair.

That was it of course. It was the dream from which she couldn't seem to fully wake. Or was it that she didn't want to? That the ambience of the dream had been at once so compelling and so mysterious that she wished never to wake from it? The silver night, the moon-washed, glittering snow, the sense of limitless space hidden in the hollow, blue-black darkness. Night, winter, the snow banked up to the eaves of the cabin in which she found her dream self. Though it was the farm where she lived, had been raised, yet it was not the farm. Everything had been stripped away: the house she knew, the sense of it as home, of neighbours not far away, of domestic animals nearby in the barn and corrals.

Meditating on it now, she found herself lost again in the wonder of that world, its reality so powerful it washed away the paleness of her shop with its bare wooden walls, its shelves of pottery bowls and mugs and vases, the floor that creaked when she shifted her weight, the gathering heat in the brilliance outside her window that was the town of Ordeal.

It was the coyote that puzzled her; she knew a spirit creature when she dreamt one, knew it in her gut or some other, deeper part of herself for which she had no name, or, if pressed, might have called her soul. She pondered the animal's limping, a strange, yet surely significant thing, the meaning of which she couldn't divine. She shivered, allowing the dream to drop slowly out of sight into the depths where such things lived till, one day, they would unexpectedly reappear, rearranged, suddenly clear and eloquent.

Absently she ran her hand over her hair again, fiddling with the elastic that held it back from her face in a low pony-tail. She went to the window where her dusty display of bowls sat holding the sun in rows. Pat McNamara, Rita Zacharias, Margaret Dubbing, and Eleanor Dumas, four of the town's many widows, were passing by, each waving as they noticed her watching them. They were on their way to Beata Morgan's or Zena Lavender's for coffee, Amy guessed. Sympathy for them touched her and she smiled and waved back even as it came to her with an unpleasant little jolt that she, Amy Sparrow, was by rights one of them too.

The town was full of widows. Despite their years of hard work, their sometimes excessive child-bearing, and frequently the abuse, physical or otherwise or both, which some had withstood, the women of the town outlived the men by a ratio Amy estimated in amazement to be two to one. It was an unacknowledged but basic fact of life in Ordeal, and these women without men formed a little sub-society within the main one, the nature of which only its members understood.

The spell of the dream was at last dissipating, as if the sight of widows forced one back to reality. Amy went back to the counter and leaned against it again. Curious, she thought, running her finger across it and leaving a neat, narrow trail in the white clay dust – I must clean this place up one of these days – curious: imagine a society of widows, women without men, women who married men and had children with them in the full knowledge that they would have perhaps thirty years together and then the women would spend the last third of their lives alone, women who would from birth plan for this sequence of events instead of always being taken by surprise. She tried to picture such a fate for herself – never a man again – but drew back from it, although not before she had seen a glimpse of herself walking alone in her weedy, unkempt yard. And then there's Neil – but she drew back from that too, dubiously.

A car bearing Ontario licence plates passed the window. Another tourist, she thought, and was struck by the lack of curiosity on the driver's face which she had glimpsed for a second. I bet he's a lot younger than he looks, she thought, and remembered the lives of certain people in cities; how they clung to routines for comfort, kept their dreams and their yards neat and tidy, the grass mowed, the children stifled. Not their fault, she scolded herself. What do they know of the tang of wildness in the air, the steady heartbeat beneath the warm earth, the fierce joy of winter? And if they did, how then would they survive from house to car to factory or office building and back again? Such a pity she had for them, a fleeting second during which her heart seemed to open wider and the pain made her drop her head. She sighed. In an hour or so she would have to stop daydreaming, forget her coffee mugs and her bowls, brush the clay dust off her slacks, wash her hands and face, get into her truck and set out for Swift Current and the rally.

She eyed the shelves laden with her work. Coffee mugs and bowls. And don't forget the plates commemorating wedding anniversaries, birthdays, family reunions. The pitchers, the ashtrays. Sometimes her heart clenched like a fist in her chest at the thought of more of them, wouldn't go on, not for another coffee mug, another souvenir candy dish that said *Ordeal* in appalling gold lettering that she had done herself, could blame no one else for. Except there's my need to eat, she reminded herself. They sat, in varying stages of completion, on the shelves that leaned against three of the four walls in her shop, flanking her two potter's wheels – the electric and the kickwheel – her workbench, the shabby wooden chairs she kept for visitors, and the dust-covered counter. She didn't own a cash register.

She thought longingly of the delicate figures she had experimented with in art school, of the rough, finger-pressed sculptures she had made as she searched through the things she was learning to do with clay for shapes that would fit her hands and eyes. She longed, too, to make pots as beautiful and as permanent as the vases, urns, and amphorae of the Greeks, that had lasted twenty-five hundred years and more, or the simple but unforgettably powerful god-statues of Sumeria, more than four thousand years old. Images passed before her eyes: the heartline pots of the Acoma Pueblo Indians of New Mexico, the ceramic sculptures of Joe Fafard. The palms of her hands ached to hold the clay in them. She felt it to be hers to shape, she would shape the images of her dreams, the ones that blossomed in the shadows of her night garden or those that appeared in her heart when she felt Lionel's presence, cool and dark, inside her, and the moon shining on the tall grass and the weatherbeaten, unpainted shingles of her house.

There was a loud rap on her window and, startled, she straightened up. Grant Voth was passing by, had almost vanished by the time she realized what had disturbed her ruminations. He was always in a hurry, rushing into town for parts – no, not parts, you couldn't get parts in Ordeal any more, he must have been over to Crisis – or to straighten out some snafu with taxes or looking for help or God knew what, then rushing back home again. Twenty years before she had gone to school with him, and now he was a married man with half-grown children and a secure position in the community where he had grown up. And she, Amy, was a childless widow who knew herself to be marginal in the very town where she had been born, where she had spent all her life except for her four years away studying art.

This was not the consequence of being the first child to go away and study art; it was that she was the only one who had returned, who stubbornly refused to leave, who, in fact, was doing everything she could to help save the town while Grant Voth raised his children and his calves, cut his hay in summer and fed cattle in the winter, and refused to believe that the world as he had known it could indeed end. Even as it passed, he refused to believe the evidence before his eyes.

She slapped the counter with her hand and dust rose up, tickling her nose, making her sneeze – I really *must* clean this place up one of these days – and she was reminded of the mess in her storeroom at the back and of the load of matching coffee mugs in her kiln that wouldn't be ready till the next morning.

The school bell was ringing faintly two blocks over, letting the children out for recess. In her mind's eye she saw them racing around the schoolyard, playing their incomprehensible and complicated games. She thought of the ballgames now that it was almost summer, was reminded of hockey in winter and of all the other games the kids of the district played with such seriousness: volleyball, basketball, football. She wondered how many of them were secret poets, how many of them cherished longings they couldn't articulate because no one had ever taught them about art and the creative urge or helped them to understand that the restlessness and anxiety they sometimes felt came from the need to create. A hundred years this community has been settled, she thought angrily, and in this, the year of the first millennium's end or the beginning of the second, the best of them are still being stifled by the ignorance of their elders. It made her furious.

But what kind of an example am I, she reminded herself, with my stupid ashtrays and coffee mugs? I could work differently, I know how, I know what art is, I think. And yet I don't do it, and by not doing it I am guilty of a crime against myself and a crime against the people of my community, the children especially.

While she stood, one hip against the counter, still watching out the window but seeing nothing, the door creaked open and she turned, brushing hastily at her hair, checking the fastener that held it back from her face.

"I thought you'd be on the road by now."

Amy smiled, pleased to see Lowell Hartshorne, minister of the Good Shepherd Church on the other side of town. She remembered their last conversation when he had told her about trying to persuade his parishioners to change the name of their church: "I told them we should call it 'The Good Farmer Church' or 'The Good Cowboy Church,' but they either laughed at the idea as absurd, or were scandalized. I couldn't get them to see that 'Good Shepherd' is a metaphor that simply doesn't fit in a place where almost nobody has sheep, where people don't like sheep." When Amy had asked him why he wanted to change the name, he told her he was trying in every way he could think of to get his people to see the church as an integral part of their everyday lives, not as something set apart.

"But," Amy had argued, "I think what people need *is* something set apart: ritual, ceremony, a more powerful sense of the mystery life is. Like the Catholic Church used to be before Vatican Two."

"No, no," he'd said softly, admonishing her. "Every move we make, every breath we draw should be imbued with a sense of its holiness, and of the simplicity of holiness." They had studied each other, each seeing some wisdom in the other's opinion. "Like you," he'd said after a moment, and when she'd stared at him in surprise, he'd added, "Your work, I mean. The way you approach your work."

Flustered again by the memory, she said now, "I've been day-dreaming." He smiled.

"I can't persuade you to come, Lowell?" It was not just that he was needed, but that she felt him to be lonely since his wife's death, despite his spending all his waking hours with people. She saw this sometimes in a kind of longing in his eyes which he always quickly veiled if she looked at him too closely.

"I think not," he said in a brisk way that wasn't like him and that she saw as designed to cover his uncertainty. "I admire your efforts, but I don't think it's my place – not my work, I mean – and anyway, I've another widow to visit."

"Ah," Amy said. Dennis Bound had died the night before, heart attack at seventy, no surprise to anyone. Still . . . "I'll have to go and see Ava myself, tomorrow, I guess," Amy said. "But I'll have to have a long talk with you someday soon about all of this. We need you."

"Yes, surely," the minister said vaguely, re-setting his thick glasses up the bridge of his nose, then wiping at his fringe of grey hair absent-mindedly, as Amy often did with her own thick, long hair. "I met a lot of vehicles on the road here from Crisis heading the other way. It looks like most of the district will be there."

"I hope so," Amy said, looking around for the straw bag she used for a purse. "I'd better get moving. I'd no idea it was so late."

"Ah, you artists," he teased her. "Always in another world."

"Some artist," Amy said, grieved again by her weakness, especially in front of him, who saw so much.

Somewhere on the hot and dusty street outside there was an indeterminate rumble growing louder as it approached. The noise resolved itself into that of a pack of dogs: the sharp yip of a small dog, a terrier maybe, the deeper woof of a Labrador or German shepherd heard over the steady yap-yap and the occasional howl from what might have been two or three other dogs. Amy's eyes met Lowell's in an expression of mutual concern and helplessness. Both turned their heads to watch out the front window as Pastor Uriel Raven passed by, striding as he always did, his head up, his orange hair catching the sun so that it looked as though he were crowned with fire, his pale face set, seeming not to hear or even to notice that he was being followed, as always, by a pack of dogs. The cacophony grew louder as Raven passed the window, then softened, faded, and died.

For a moment both Amy and Lowell were silent with embarrassment. Hartshorne was the first to speak as though there had been no fiery apparition, no doggy heralding of it. "Do you know Neil Locke?"

Amy coloured, startled, and nearly dropped her bag, which she had at last located in the corner next to the row of clay-spattered vats of glaze.

"No. Yes," she said. "I mean, why?"

"He's been in the district nearly a year now and I haven't seen him in church, nor has anybody else – none of my colleagues at the various churches." Given its size, Ordeal was extremely well churched. Since its crime rate was exactly the same as that of any prairie community of its size, the number of its churches was the subject of much joking among those who chose to stay at home on Sunday mornings. "I wondered if you knew anything about him. Should I pay him a visit?"

"I know him a little," Amy said, stalling. "I doubt he'd be very . . . approachable," she finished lamely. "He's quite prickly about things like religion. He thinks it's all pretty silly."

The minister reflected, not looking at her. She saw a wave of something that might have been sadness cross his face, slowly followed by acceptance or perhaps dismissal. He nodded.

"Well," he said, and turned from her, his hand on the doorknob again. "Well, then, it's Mrs. Bound, I guess." He paused, his back to her. "I run out of things to say," he murmured. He went out, shutting the door carefully behind him.

Now, did he come to ask me that? she wondered, or did he have some other reason he'd forgotten? Or did he just stop to say hello? She couldn't put her finger on the reason his question about Neil had embarrassed her so much, or why, in fact, it seemed unthinkable to her that people should know about her relationship with him.

And Lowell would have seen her confusion. He would have filed it away to ponder another time and he would quickly realize she had been seeing Neil.

He would say nothing; he would simply know, and if something happened with Neil that made her need comforting or someone to talk to, he would be there. It angered her that his gentleness and mildness made people judge him as ineffectual and useless. He was neither, and those who had genuinely sought his counsel knew this.

She thrust all of this out of her mind. She had no time to waste if she wanted to make Swift Current in time to take part in the protest. She wanted only to stay dreaming in her shop, sketching, throwing a pot, brushing on glaze. But then, too, she wanted to be part of the struggle to save the community. She forced herself not only to attend meetings, but even to organize them, because she knew that it had to be done or there'd soon be nobody left. She knew herself to be almost alone in her private attitude, which was not even to think about anything but clay, her glazes, her dreams for them, and she assumed ruefully that everybody else must be right in their dreams of glory both for themselves and for their town, and she wrong and missing some vital urge for self-preservation. Perhaps that was why she pushed herself so hard, made a public spectacle of herself in urging others to join her in protest against what was happening to all of them.

Part of her was reluctant; still, she was looking forward to today's speeches, to listening to the people muttering to each other around her, to knowing their responses to the crisis they were all facing: townspeople, farmers, ranchers, Hutterites alike. She dusted half-heartedly at her slacks, then went out of the shop, locking the door behind her, got into her battered truck, and set out for Swift Current.

Standing at the back of her class, Alma Sheridan was fighting to stay awake. More than half of the children were missing, gone with their parents to the rally, which didn't make it any easier, since the ten or so who were left had been rendered lethargic and dreamy-eyed by so many empty desks. She was confident her own relatives would not waste their time on such foolishness. It was scandalous really, possibly treasonous. She believed firmly in hard work and minding your own business and so far this policy had worked well for her and for those close to her. A vulgar entertainment, that was all the rally would be.

"Ricky Pollard," she snapped into the drowsy silence. "Eyes front!" Ricky swivelled slowly around, dropping his eyes to his notebook before she could tell him to. Alma moved up the room on the way to the blackboard, glancing with half-controlled habit out the classroom window as she passed it. Though it was early June, a dwindling bank of dirty snow still pushed up in the corner against the other wall of the school where the sun never shone directly. It seemed to the weary Alma that that snowbank had been there forever, as long as she could bring herself to remember. She saw, too, that finally it was beginning to melt. Next to it a puddle of icy-looking water was forming, reflecting her classroom wall back to her. The sun was fairly high now at ten o'clock and thank heaven it would soon be recess.

She did not know how she would get through the rest of the day. Since so many of the children were missing – even the twenty or so high school students – she suspected (and in the face of her own disapproval, privately hoped) that the principal would get the fifty or so children left into games on the playground for the entire afternoon. She might then even have a cup of coffee in the staffroom where doubtless the other teachers would be wasting their time going on endlessly about the rally in Swift Current. And all the children there too! For what reason she couldn't begin to imagine, with the school buses virtually empty at the best of times. A foolish waste of the already hard-pressed taxpayers' money.

She sighed. Abortions, she was sure, had something to do with it. She winced at the very word, unmarried as she was and in fact still a virgin if the truth were known, which fortunately, she thought, it was not. She was near retirement now, *she* didn't mind if they had to close the school in two years, as the school board had just officially predicted since there was to be no growth in the school-age population. She knew perfectly well there would be no growth. Everybody was leaving, moving away to the city, and the ones who were left behind weren't having babies anymore. Doubtless they were all having abortions in order to keep the birth rate down. It was a wonder, she thought, the Lord didn't strike them all dead: the whole lot of them would have abortions at the drop of a hat, it was no more to them than drowning a litter of kittens. Disgusting. She pursed her lips tighter and sat down at her desk. But she should not even be thinking such thoughts in front of a room of children.

"Belinda, I do not want you to speak unless I ask you to," she said, in her precise, schoolteacher's diction that she had spent thirty-odd years cultivating. "Sit up straight." She could hardly keep her own back straight she was so sleepy, though that was no reason Belinda should be allowed to slouch. Seeing that her steely glance around the room had at least momentarily cowed the small group, she allowed herself a moment's respite, closing her eyes and pressing her palms over them.

And it came over her once more.

She saw the vast expanse of farmland with its tiny, infrequent squares of native grass and her little town resting snugly in the heart of all those billowing acres; she saw the friends and relatives and people she had known her entire life sitting on tractors in their plowed fields, or strolling down the town's narrow sidewalks or weeding their bright gardens or sitting quietly in front of television sets in their small tidy houses. She found herself shouting at them, "Look! Look!" pointing frantically at the enormous purple sky behind and above them that became, as she watched, a tumult of high black clouds roiling toward them as rapidly as in a speeded-up film. But no one would look at her as she ran to and fro, no one would speak to her or acknowledge that she was there screaming into their averted faces, clutching at their just-out-of-reach arms. "Look out! Look out!" she cried again and again, but nobody looked or spoke or even moved, while the seething cloud swept closer and closer.

Then it was on them. No rain, only wind, a black whirlwind of indescribable proportions, moaning, wailing, its whistle and roar drowning out the screams of her people as it swept away their houses, cars, even their fresh, green lawns and red and yellow flowerbeds, blackened and shrivelled and vanished in the instant it touched them. And the people too, it picked them up and swept them away until they dwindled to tiny black specks then disappeared altogether into the storm.

While Alma stood on the post office steps shrieking without sound into the wind, blackness enveloped her. Then she was in a sandstorm, sand stinging her face and arms, pinging up against her robes. Just when she couldn't bear any more of its torment, the air thinned, grew paler, the wind dropped off altogether and she could see that where the town had been there was now only a desert of blowing sand. There was no sign of human presence in any direction no matter how she searched the distance with shielded eyes all the way to the faded, shimmering horizon.

She was engulfed in a wave of desolation deeper and more overwhelming than she had imagined humans could be capable of.

She forced her eyes open, put down her hands and found herself gasping so loudly that all her children were staring at her. Instead of speaking, for she tried and found she couldn't, she rose, and though she knew it to be unprecedented that she, Alma Sheridan, might leave her classroom untended during school hours, she hurried from the room and bent over the water fountain in the hall, trying to sip the foul-tasting water with lips that quivered and refused to shape themselves.

"Alma?" It was the voice of the new young principal whose name she could never remember. The shock of being caught out of her classroom when it wasn't even recess, a breach of professional behaviour she was constantly deploring in other teachers, was enough to bring Alma most of the way back to herself. She straightened hurriedly, all the way up to that unbending, straight-backed posture she had spent years maintaining as the only stance dignified enough for one who called herself teacher.

"Yes?" she said coldly, as though it were not unusual to be caught like this, having left no one in authority with her children.

"Are you all right?" he asked, a little uncertainly, since Alma had seen to it that he was intimidated by her. She turned. He was a short man, and he peered up at her with an earnest expression.

"Perfectly," she replied. "Excuse me, I must get back to my class," as if he were the one holding her up.

"No rush," he said in a friendly tone. "There are so few of them today."

No rush indeed, Alma thought scornfully. Typical of the new breed of teachers with their informal speech and their casual air about the whole business of "interacting" with the young. No rush, indeed. She walked away from him without speaking again, went into her classroom and closed the door, failing to notice the blush that suffused his head from the line of his thick brown hair to the collar of his plaid sport shirt, and the look of perplexity that followed, directed first at her back and then at her closed classroom door.

This couldn't go on. She had first had the dream almost two years earlier. Just once then and not again for quite a long time. Then it repeated itself and began to come more frequently – sometimes with details that were slightly different, but always essentially the same: her trying to alert all the people she had known all her life, their refusal to pay attention to her, the tumultuous descent of the wind-driven cloud followed by the appearance of the desert where the town, farms, and ranches had been.

Whirlwinds in the desert, pillars of fire, she reminded herself, then drew back from the thought, for she was a religious woman, and knew she could have no truck with bizarre or ungentlemanly manifestations of the Divine Spirit. Divine Spirit indeed, she told herself scathingly, but a stab of fear went through her and goosebumps rose on her forearms and when she got control of herself she saw her class – to a child – was staring at her again, so she had to rap her knuckles hard on the wooden desk to make their eyes drop in unison back to their work. And yet she wondered, even as she dismissed the idea, if the fact that this was the year the century turned was somehow causing the dream.

The bell for recess rang and though the children hastily shut their notebooks and grabbed the edges of their desks with their hands, eyes fixed on her, not one of them even half-rose before she gave them the signal that said they might proceed in an orderly fashion out onto the playground. When they had gone, she sat at her desk again and stared at her daybook, open in front of her, without seeing any of the notes made in her precise, small handwriting.

She hadn't gone to sleep till six that morning and her alarm had gone off at seven, the time when she always rose, though since she had never overslept before the alarm had never been allowed to ring. And this was the third time this week alone. This simply can't go on, she thought, knowing even as she thought it that she had no idea how to stop it.

Maybe she should swallow her pride and return to the doctor, this time to tell him the truth, that dreams caused her sleeplessness. She dismissed the idea at once. Too many people were involved: the receptionist, the nurse, the doctor himself, the waiting room full of people she knew. Something about a visit to the doctor, if it was out of the general run of things – dysfunctioning gall bladders, weak hearts, sick colds, broken legs – always leaked out and was around the community in a flash. No, a lifetime here had taught her that there were no secrets, and she could not bear to think of the people she'd been raised with, gone to school with, and the ones she'd taught thinking that she, Alma Sheridan, was losing her mind.

Nor could she go to the pastor. Good man that he was, he'd only tell her to pray, and hadn't she done that and then done it some more? It occurred to her to wonder if God wanted her to have these violent and terrifying dreams, but she instantly squelched the thought. Certainly not. It was the kind of thing the god of infidels and barbarians and Roman Catholics might do, but never her God. Unless He was punishing her. This thought made her pause and her heart fluttered for a second at the base of her throat, but no matter how earnestly or how long she racked her brain and then searched her soul, she could not discover any sin deserving of such harsh correction.

Nor Flora, either. She couldn't go to Flora, who'd married her cousin Herb, and who'd been her friend from the time they were children and who had stood by her in the past: the time she had lost her temper with that dreadful McKenzie boy and struck him with a ruler, raising a welt on his ear and breaking his glasses, and his parents, quite dreadful themselves, had threatened to sue or have her fired; the time she had gotten into a quarrel with eventually the entire Voth family over failing one of the dull-witted Voth children; all those times when she and Flora were children themselves in the dim and faraway past and Flora had defended her from bullies and tried to show her how to be like other children, insisting she be included in games she would otherwise have been left out of.

This would be too much even for Flora. She would be quite simply scandalized and disgusted (and who could blame her) that a member of her family had a hidden secret life – worse, dreams that refused to be held in check and that spilled over into Alma's day-time life. Look at what had happened at Thanksgiving dinner last fall when Jessie, Val's new young wife, had started to tell them all about some peculiar dream she had had. Everyone had been embarrassed and Flora herself had started talking about something else over Jessie's voice, so that Jessie, puzzled, then hurt, had blushed and kept silent all the rest of the evening. Though Jessie, too, come to think of it, was as likely to have resorted to abortion as any of them. Flushing foetuses down the toilet, throwing them out with the dishwater. Childless, and the two of them married now for two, no three years.

She sighed deeply. If she had been the crying kind she would have cried now. Was there no one who would share this burden with her? For Alma knew, with a relentless certainty that gripped her deep inside, that these were not ordinary nightmares, that they were not caused by eating pickles or watching television or staying up too late. They sprang from other than the usual place of dreaming; they sprang from some source that seemed to her to be outside her own mind, and as they grew more insistent, she could tell they were not dreams at all, but . . . but what? Here her agitated ruminations always failed her, for she could not accept that they were more than dreams or other than them. It was too terrifying; it was godless.

She turned her face to the window through which the warm sun had begun to shine and the cries of the children in the yard outside reached her ears. It was a sound she had been within range of for so many years that she seldom heard it any more, unless it changed in tempo or volume or intonation in a way that told her that someone had been hurt or that instances of bullying had gone beyond the normally allowed bounds. Today she listened as if the high, wild cries of the children might carry a message for her. Two older girls passed under her window chattering eagerly together. She couldn't see them, but their voices reached her, the words broken, the bits drifting upward through her open window and into her classroom.

She thought of the weekly newspaper, the new column that everyone laughed at yet everyone read. She wondered how many of those who laughed were among those who wrote to it signing themselves with aliases. She imagined them secretly poring over *Dear Madeleine's* replies. She had been privy to a few serious discussions among women as to the reasons for and the validity of *Dear Madeleine's* advice. Maybe I should write to her, she thought, then stopped, shocked at herself.

The very idea! she scolded herself, but the letter was already shaping itself in her mind: "Dear Madeleine, I have terrible dreams at night that frighten me very badly. . . . " Should she? The idea seemed undignified in the extreme. It simply was not something that the Alma Sheridan who had taught school in this town for nearly forty years should even be thinking of doing. And yet, where else had she to turn?

Comforted a little by this half-made decision, she rose and went to stand at her classroom window looking out over the small, stony schoolyard, at the children hanging from the tires suspended by chains or swinging on the swings or playing scrub far off in the opposite corner of the grounds. She was a relative – by blood or by someone else's marriage – to maybe a quarter of them if you bothered to trace out all the connections. She watched the children speculatively and not without disapproval.

It seemed to her that no one any longer knew how to raise children and that this was one of the reasons the community was in such disarray. Even though she led a sheltered life and had never married, rarely sat in the café, or danced at wedding dances, she felt she knew her community. How better to know it than through knowing the children? To see them grow from frightened kindergarteners to swaggering grade twelves. To see how their families grew and changed and how they saw the world, made evident to her by the things the children, deliberately or inadvertently, told her, or failed to tell her. The signs of confusion and loss were everywhere.

Everyone was spoiled, parents too, hopelessly spoiled, she thought. Always looking for greener pastures, for bigger rewards. Nothing, it seemed to her, satisfied any more, nothing was good enough, or simply enough. In the early days things had been different, somehow their society had held together, had a coherency that all understood, and now things were not the same. There was discontent, there were splits in the society, a hierarchy had developed based on money that had not been there when all of them were young. Then there had been a mutual sense of purposefulness. Now the core was gone.

Teach them, Lord, she prayed. Save them from themselves.

# CHAPTER
2

Val and Jessie Sheridan had driven to the huge field where the provincial high school track meet was held each year and where the rally was to be staged. Two blocks before they reached it Val had to slow down, sometimes coming to a a complete stop to let people heading toward the field cross the street in front of them. He began searching for a place to park, but half-tons were parked bumper to bumper around the field's perimeter, and behind the trucks, all down one long side, a row of tractors was pulled up onto the edge of the grass. Two of the tractors towered over the others, four-wheel-drives the size of small houses, the one a Big Bud, the other a bright green Steiger. Inside their cabs would be air-conditioning and all the latest in computerized equipment, and Jessie noticed Val giving them an appraising glance.

He had to park across the highway where a row of motels were strung out, their parking lots emptied now of the previous night's occupants and not yet filled up with today's patrons. They got out and stood for a moment, side by side, looking across the highway to the great field on the other side. The tracks for racing, the jumping pits filled with sand had been obliterated under a thousand pairs of feet and the few bleachers on one side were packed with people. The field was a moving sea of bodies, mostly men, and dozens of kids raced in and out among the adults. Bobbing above the heads of the crowd were a few white squares with black lettering on them. At the end of the field nearest Jessie and Val a wooden platform, it looked like the floor of a grain bin, had been pulled into place by a big red Versatile tractor that had been parked to one side. Several microphones on stands clustered in one corner of the makeshift stage.

Jessie stood uncertainly, having intended to stay only a little while before taking the truck to go shopping downtown or over at the mall, but now, seeing the unexpected size of the crowd and the handful of young cowboys with guitars moving onto the platform, thoughts of shopping vanished. She could feel Val's eagerness, some not-quite-explained tension in his arm as he placed it across her shoulders, urging her to cross, then holding her back as a rig heading west roared past them, kicking up dust even off the blacktopped highway. They ran across the road, forded the dusty wide ditch, and came up onto the field next to the platform.

Now Jessie could read the lettering on the signs closest to them. The one on her right said *Remorse* and the one on her left *Solitude*, both names of towns near Ordeal. So Ordeal must be on the right. She and Val turned simultaneously in that direction without speaking and in a second Jessie had to run a few steps to catch up with him, first avoiding two little boys who raced past her, and then nearly tripping over an older man, wearing a Banvil cap, who'd abruptly decided to sit down on the grass directly in front of her.

Behind them there was an ear-piercing whistle from the public address system. It moderated to a howl that slowly died away, followed by a crackling so loud it produced winces on the faces of the people Val and Jessie were passing. Then, too loudly, a male voice wished them a good afternoon.

"Starting right on time," Val remarked. All around them as they hurried down the field people turned their faces to the platform.

"We're going to start with a little music while people are still arriving. It should help you get in the mood," the speaker said, the

28

volume less ear-splitting now. People began to move together, clustering behind the signs naming the towns from which they had come, and to sit shoulder to shoulder on the dry grass.

"Over there," Val said, changing direction so abruptly that he bumped into Jessie, then he put his arm around her again, guiding her to a few familiar faces among the many people she didn't know standing or sitting on the grass behind the *Ordeal* sign.

"Over here, Val," people beckoned to them.

"Come and sit with us," Amy Sparrow called, and patted the grass beside her, so that Jessie, pleased to have been paid some notice, moved to the edge of the inner group of women and small children. The bigger kids were playing tag on the grass at the edge of the field.

"I didn't expect anything this size," she said, plopping down and arranging her skirt over her legs.

"Isn't it a terrific turnout?" Amy said. "I don't think anybody expected this many people would show up."

"Really great," Jessie said, glancing around. "I was going to go shopping, but when I saw all these people, I thought this might be interesting." Amy glanced at her, a speculative expression in her eyes, then looked away.

Val stood at the front of the group greeting men who, as far as Jessie knew, he saw every day. They weren't grinning and making small silly jokes in their usual way, but were straight-faced and sober, clasping hands with a faintly embarrassed look and an air of ritual. Jessie frowned, wondering what the reason was for such solemnity. She looked around at all the people near her and for the first time noticed they weren't smiling either as they stretched to see what was happening on the platform far down the field from them. She looked back to Val for reassurance, staring fondly at his wide shoulders and trim hips in his clean, snugly fitting Levis. He wasn't a tall man, and she had always been attracted to tall men, but he was handsome, sexy even, all her girlfriends at college had said so. He had his back turned to her, but she could see before her his clear brown eyes with the straight black eyebrows and the way his hair grew into curly sideburns that she was always after him to keep trimmed. If it weren't for those sideburns you could hardly tell him from a city man. Although today he fitted right in, looked like this was where he belonged.

"Still," Amy said, "I'd hoped to see certain families here . . ." Her voice trailed off and Jessie glanced at her, puzzled. Amy, too, was sober, frowning as she studied the backs and shoulders of the men seated in front of them, their heads turned toward the singers at the end of the field. She'd be pretty if she wore make-up and dressed up a bit, Jessie thought. Even if she is at least thirty-six or thirty-seven. The way she wore her hair, pulled back in a low pony-tail, made her look younger, but Jessie could see the tell-tale wrinkles at the corners of her eyes. She was dressed in the only way Jessie had ever seen her, in faded cotton slacks and a cotton blouse, and there were dusty smudges on them, too white to be field dust. A little blonde streaking in her hair would make a world of difference.

But her hands . . . Jessie was startled anew whenever she noticed Amy's hands. They were strong-looking, the veins on the backs unusually prominent, and she had long fingers that ended in nails she kept short and blunt. Not feminine hands at all, though Jessie had to admit they didn't look any worse than the hands of the women who'd been first farmers' daughters and then farmers' wives. She glanced proudly at her own nails, grown to an attractive length, carefully shaped, and covered with shiny pink polish.

"Are you one of the organizers?" she asked Amy, just to say something. Amy nodded, though she didn't speak or look at Jessie so that Jessie, intimidated by Amy at the best of times, wished she hadn't asked her that particular question, since it must have consti-tuted prying. Would she never understand these people? And Amy had an air of quiet dignity and unruffleable calm that Jessie, who recognized a touch of unacceptable flamboyance in her own charac-ter, envied. After all, Amy was said to live alone on the farm where she had lived with her husband. Why would anyone want to live alone, Jessie wondered, especially on a farm? And why had Amy not married again? But wait, wasn't she said to be Neil Locke's girlfriend? Jessie started to look around for Neil, but realized that, first, she'd never seen him and wouldn't know him if she did, and second, judging by his reputation as a sour recluse, there was no way he'd be here anyway. She fidgeted. Everyone seemed to be talking to someone else or to be listening intently to the boring country music coming through the loudspeakers. After a moment, she leaned forward and tapped the farmer sitting in front of her, whose face was vaguely familiar, on the shoulder.

"Where are they?" she asked.

"Who?" he responded, apparently surprised she had spoken to him, rearranging his Buctril M cap to keep the sun out of his eyes.

"The Premier and his cabinet," she said, surprised in her turn.

"Oh," the man said. "Cabinet meeting's not supposed to start till two, so he ain't likely to come over here before maybe two-thirty." He laughed, a sour sound. "After they've had time to talk it over and figure out they'd better show up." Another farmer, wearing a light windbreaker with *Monsanto* embroidered on the shoulder, sat down heavily beside him. Instantly the first farmer turned to him and away from Jessie, ignoring her as if he hadn't spoken to her.

The chairman was speaking again and Jessie craned to see what was happening on the platform. A group of five young men, white shirts and white Stetsons dazzling in the noon sun, were arranging themselves at the microphones which had been moved into a line across the front of the stage. They put their guitar straps over their shoulders, grasped their guitars and began to sing. Gradually the crowd quietened.

*I'm a simple country boy, Lord,*
*A cowboy of the plains,*
*I gave up my life of drinking*

*My godless rodeo ways,*
*For the promise of Your coming*
*And the glory of Your ways.*

Their combined voices echoed and blended pleasingly, though the song seemed to Jessie peculiarly inappropriate.

"Who are they?" Jessie asked Amy.

"I think they call themselves the Righteous Riders for the Lord," Amy said. "Haven't you heard of them?" Jessie shook her head no.

"They're rodeo cowboys," Amy explained, "but they're born-again Christians. They don't sing anything but so-called Christian music." Jessie strained to get a better look at them. Young, hand-some, with trim, athletic-looking bodies and an air of cleanliness that even from this distance bordered on the painful.

"Who's minding your studio?" Jessie ventured, unable wholly to assimilate the Righteous Riders and judging it better to ignore them.

"I closed it for the day," Amy said. "I wanted everybody to come." Two more businesses had shut down in the town in the last year, leaving the community without services in two more areas. And so this rally, Jessie realized, for the first time recognizing that it had a serious purpose, might be justified as more than entertainment. She had a moment when she felt glad she was present, and much to her surprise, almost a social activist. This last thought struck her as ridiculous, then embarrassed her, and then made her feel proud.

Val had moved from the front line of their group to a place a few feet ahead of Jessie, next to his father, Herb, who had wandered over from the crowd on the opposite side of the field. A new woman had come too, and after nodding and smiling at Jessie and the rest of the women, she sat down with the men. She was their MLA, a sturdy middle-aged farm woman wearing a dark, wine-coloured pantsuit and a Pool cap to keep off the sun. She seemed right at home among the men and, Jessie noticed with amazement, they seemed accepting of her.

Suddenly Val got up from where he had just sat down, went to the MLA, and squeezed in beside her. While Jessie watched he put his head close to hers and spoke into her ear. She listened intently. Then Val stood and went back to his original place. The Righteous Riders for the Lord had moved off the platform now, and there was scattered clapping from the crowd which had been only half listening. Now a tall, lean man jumped onto the platform and went to the centre mike. Jessie recognized him from short clips on the evening news from Swift Current, though she couldn't remember what organization he headed.

"As you all know," he began, "the Premier and his cabinet are having a travelling cabinet meeting right across the street from us. We've sent a messenger over to them, to tell them we'd like them to send over a representative to talk to us. Until somebody comes, though, we've arranged for a series of speakers who'll speak about the issues that have concerned us enough that we've gathered together here today. It's the year 2000, ladies and gentlemen! We can't go on the old way any longer – and that's why we're here!" The crowd cheered and clapped while another man who'd been standing at the edge of the platform climbed onto it and went to the mike.

The sea of people sat or stood patiently, silent now, waiting expectantly for what would come next, the warm spring sun shining on their capped heads, reddening their already reddened necks and faces.

"I'm Mike Murray and I'm with the NFU."

"National Farmers' Union," Amy said to Jessie in a low voice. The crowd sighed, muttered, and shifted, then fell silent again. He was an older man, tall and flat-stomached, slow of speech. The sunlight glinted off his glasses, and he took off his cap (he was too far away for Jessie to read the label on it) and wiped the sweat off his forehead with his forearm.

33

"Our farmers are going broke, losing their places, leaving to get lost in the cities. Is the government doing anything significant to help us?"

"No!" everybody shouted.

"Our small towns are drying up and dying because we're losing population so fast that there's nobody to buy things in our stores and the stores are going broke and closing. The fewer services a town has, the fewer people will want to live there."

"Atta boy, Mike, you tell 'em," somebody shouted. A few people clapped and whistled.

"Is the government doing anything to help subsidize the stores enough that we can keep essential services? No!" he shouted, this time with the crowd. "Instead they're closing down our small-town hospitals, our schools, and they're busing our kids further and further every year so they spend less and less time on their home places learning how to farm, and now – and this is the last straw – they've closed many of our post offices!" The crowd moved angrily and confused shouts of agreement rang out. "Are we going to let them get away with it without a fight?"

"No!" the crowd bellowed.

"What are we going to do about it?" The crowd's reply was broken and uncertain, an unintelligible, mixed series of shouts. Jessie turned to look at her neighbours and saw that they looked puzzled and angry, glancing in frustration at one another, searching for the right answer.

"Protest!" the MLA, who sat in Opposition, shouted, and all around her people took up her cry.

"Protest! Protest! Protest!" The speaker got down off the platform to thundering applause.

He was followed by two more speakers, both men, their short messages much the same, and the crowd grew louder and more vehement in its replies.

When the third speaker had finished and the crowd was no longer passive, but agitated, moving restlessly, and freer with their shouts to the speakers, their calls changed spontaneously from agreement to, "Where's the Premier? We want the Premier!" The chairman climbed back onto the stage and held up his arms for quiet.

"Our messenger isn't back yet," he told the crowd. "Be patient a while longer. While we're waiting . . ." shouts of "Boo! Boo!" . . . "we'll have one more speaker." Another man, Jessie thought, resignedly.

But the people had stopped paying attention. A coherent muttering had begun that swelled into a cry that moved through the crowd, growing in volume as others took it up: "Where's Tommy Douglas! Find us a Tommy Douglas!" It turned into a rhythmic chant: "Tommy Douglas! Tommy Douglas! Tommy Douglas!" Through all this the new speaker, a short man, adjusted the microphone, straightened his hat, hitched up his pants. Slowly the cries faded and the silence melted into a loud mechanical hum from the mike. His round belly hung over a large, silver belt buckle that sent out streaks of brilliance as the sun caught it. His pale-blue suit looked too small for him and was wrinkled at the elbows and baggy at the knees, and his dark tie, hanging over a white-shirted front, was askew. He took off his hat, an old-fashioned straw hat, signless, and began to speak in a soft voice. The crowd strained to hear, a few voices called, "Louder! Louder!" but even they were silenced when they realized he was praying.

"Lord," he murmured, "bless those of us who are gathered here today in our righteous purpose which is to save our little communities and our dying towns which you know full well, O Lord, are good places for us to raise up our kids and to live out our lives as good, Christian people, hard-working and God-fearing."

"Jesus Christ!" the older farmer sitting on Jessie's right mumbled to the man next to him. "It's that fool, Havoc." One of the farmers sitting ahead of him spoke over his shoulder: "Shhh!" Somebody else muttered angrily, "Harold's no fool!"

"Hah!" the first farmer said, and there were more hisses for silence. Jessie strained to hear. Now that he had everybody's attention, the speaker raised his voice.

"Lord, I would that You'd give to me the gift of prophecy so that I could speak up and speak to these people, tell them what the future holds for them, tell them what they need to do. But we know, oh Lord, every one of us here knows that if things have gone wrong, we have to take our share of the blame." The crowd shifted uneasily, but remained silent. "We are the ones who weren't satisfied with Your bountiful prairie, with the grass and the sky. We are the ones had to have Cadillacs and six-bedroom houses with five bathrooms, we are the ones . . ."

"Hey, Harold," a man's voice from far up the field shouted, "I hear *you* got a Cadillac!" People began to laugh, and heads still bowed for prayer lifted and swivelled to see who was heckling.

"We are the ones stopped going to church on Sundays, stopped paying our tithes to Your Christian church, we are the ones forgot to pray. When we received Your bounty, did we even stop to give thanks to You, O Lord?"

"No!" a few voices replied, and "Praise the Lord!"

"Praise the Lord indeed!" Harold Havoc shouted, raising both hands to the sky, his belt buckle beaming one brilliant flash of light out to the crowd so that people turned their heads away, blinded.

"Hey, Harold, you got something to say, say it!" a farmer bellowed, and the man sitting next to Jessie yelled, standing as he shouted, "Yeah, say it, Harold!" Jessie glanced at Amy, unsure how to react to all this. Amy was watching the speaker intently, but her expression, though not exactly one of agreement, had a – could it be – a gentle touch? God, Jessie hoped this didn't mean Amy was religious. But Havoc was bellowing on now, and she was reminded of Val's eight-thousand-dollar bull that was keeping them awake nights, roaring out the early spring down in the corral.

Slowly Havoc lowered his arms and the crowd stopped moving, stopped shouting. It waited. Havoc leaned into the mike. Everyone could hear him draw a deep, amplified breath.

"Remember the past?" he asked, his voice soft again. There was a breathless feel to the air: everyone was silent. "Remember when you were a kid on the farm? Remember when there weren't no cabs on our tractors? Or even farther back when there weren't no tractors? Remember when a day on the land really meant a day on the land? And your father came in black with the dirt of the field that fed all of you ground into his clothes and all the creases of his skin? Remember when every one of you came home from school to do your chores? Feed and water the horses and turn 'em out, feed the chickens, water the pigs, fork the manure out of the barn onto the stoneboat, do the evening milking?"

The crowd was silent, its mood turned soft. Then a farmer shouted, "Remember burning cow chips for fuel cause you couldn't afford coal?"

"Remember malnutrition?" a woman's voice called, cracking with fury. "Remember rickets and scurvy?"

"Remember patched pants and no shoes to go to school in?" someone else shouted. "And worms?"

"What are you gonna do about it?" the MLA shouted to the speaker far up the field on the platform. All around her people took up the cry, "What's your answer Harold? Tell us what to do!" The cries grew louder, nobody was listening any more, but turning restlessly to one another, muttering angrily. A few weak "Praise the Lord"s drew derision.

"Let the Premier help us! Never mind the Lord!"

"Where the hell's the Premier?"

"I'll tell you what to do about it!" Havoc was shouting now and there was something in his voice that quieted the angriest among them so that once again there was quiet and the great strain of waiting. "Rein in your greed!" His voice thundered through the tense air, bounced off the scoreboards and the high cabs of the four-wheel-drive tractors, swirled in around the women's skirts and the men's dust-covered cowboy boots. Next to the platform the Righteous Riders for the Lord had dropped to their knees and lifted their arms to the sky. "Come back to God's green earth, to nature's bounty that ain't yours to exploit!" Even the gulls that had been wheeling over the crowd emitting raucous cries had perched along the tops of the cabs of the tractors and on the billboards advertising Ralgro and Esso Fuels, as if to listen. Harold drew in another breath and lowered his voice.

"Ladies and Gentlemen, we got an election coming up soon, and I'm here to tell you that this election's our chance to change the way things are. It's our chance to remember our Christian values, to remember the Christian way of life of our grandparents, of those brave pioneers who settled this place, and to show we intend to change, that we intend to stop being the pawns of agri-business and of the devil. That we intend to remember once again who we are, who we've always been – Christian yeomen! Sons and daughters of the soil!" Clapping and shouts of agreement burst out of some of the people, while others shuffled their feet nervously, feeling, perhaps, that they ought to agree, but resenting something about Harold's message.

"I'm Harold Havoc!" he shouted. "And I'm the leader of the Sons and Daughters of the Soil Party and I urge every one of you to get out and vote for me if you want to see this prairie green again!"

"Can you make it rain?" a quavery old voice cried out nearby, but it was lost in the whistles and shouts of the main body of the crowd. Havoc had raised his arms skyward again, tilting his head back so his straw hat fell off and his belt buckle sent out a series of blinding streaks of light – purple, red, gold.

"Praise the Lord!" he bellowed, and for a second it seemed there might be an answer from the highest, most brilliant layer of the sky. Then Havoc turned and walked off the stage, a short, stout man in a rumpled blue suit, hatless in the relentless sun.

"God's green earth!" one of the women behind Jessie said angrily into the hush, not lowering her voice. "We haven't had a blade of green grass in the last ten years! It's been nothing but drought and drought and more drought!" She sounded as if she might cry and her husband hushed her, embarrassed.

"Drought and grasshoppers," another woman said. "And wind."

"Politicians can't make it rain," the old man hidden in the crowd called, but it wasn't loud enough to be heard by many. Jessie stretched, trying to see Val. He was listening to the conversation between two men beside him and she saw a strained look around his mouth and a tenseness in his shoulders she hadn't seen before. Beside her Amy drew in a deep breath and expelled it slowly.

"Wow!" she said, smiling at Jessie, who was rendered speechless, half-frightened and half-exalted by the whole business.

"Is he . . . right?" she asked Amy. She thought vaguely of the shopping she'd hoped to treat herself to, but the picture was fading. She hadn't realized how serious everybody would be, how serious things were in the community. Val never said much, and though her in-laws never talked about anything else, she'd discounted it as more of the older generation's constant mindless harping on the Depression, an event that, she kept wanting to remind them, had happened more than sixty years ago. Or had she simply not been paying attention? Amy was studying her gravely.

"Partly," she said finally, ruefully. "But he's one of those with his eyes firmly fixed on the view in the rearview mirror." Jessie recognized the quote but couldn't remember where it had come from. "He's a backward prophet," Amy said, laughing now. "He prophesies backward."

The sun's heat was growing stronger by the minute, a crackling, dry heat that parched lips, made men pull down their hats more securely and women fan themselves with any piece of paper they could find. The chairman had returned to the microphone, but many of the people had gotten to their feet and were stretching and chattering to each other so that he had to call loudly for their attention.

"Here's the situation, folks!" he called. "Our messenger is back and he says the Premier and his cabinet aren't there, that they're nowhere to be found, and that the motel owner made them leave the premises. But Jim thinks the Premier *is* over there hiding somewhere and that the cabinet is there too, and they just don't want to come out and talk to us." Heads began to turn back to him when he delivered this message; first murmurs, then angry shouts rang out from one end of the field to the other. Jessie turned her head and caught a glimpse of a Mountie parked in front of the tractors at the edge of the field. He was talking into the microphone of his car radio.

"Hold on! Hold on!" the speaker called. "Here's what we better do. We'd better all go – in an orderly fashion, slowly, not running – across the highway and gather in the parking lot outside the motel. Maybe if the Premier looks out and sees so many of us standing there waiting patiently for him to speak to us, he'll come to see that he has to have a word with us. He'll realize that he can't get out of here unless he talks to us." The crowd began to move toward the platform, a little uncertainly, nobody wanting to be first. Everybody around Jessie had stood and Jessie dodged between two of the farmers to stand by Val.

"Now," the speaker said, "quietly and in an orderly fashion. Remember, we're going over there to remind the Premier of our democratic rights to be heard and of his duty to speak to us – the taxpayers, the people who put him in office."

A front line of sorts had formed, and people were falling in behind it, moving across the ditch in a steady stream and up onto the highway where cars and trucks travelling across the country screeched to a halt to let the procession pass. Val began to move too, and the MLA fell back a little so she was walking beside them.

"Good day for a rally," she said to Val, studiously, casually, it seemed to Jessie. "I don't believe I've met your wife." Val, who had not even looked at Jessie up to this point, seemed to come back to himself from a distance where he had been lost in thought. He apologized, and introduced Jessie.

"Nice to see you here," the MLA said.

"It's nice to meet you, Mrs. . . . ."

"Vera, call me Vera."

"Is this going to do any good?" Val asked, interrupting, grim again. Vera shrugged and smiled, though Jessie saw that her pale green eyes remained humourless and steady.

"Can't hurt," she said, and Jessie wanted to laugh, would have if Val hadn't been holding her arm so tightly, refusing to look at her. She couldn't figure out what was wrong with him.

Across the highway, the Premier and his cabinet, behind sheer curtains, watched the crowd flow toward the motel where they were conducting their meeting in an upstairs suite.

"They look pretty riled up," the Premier remarked to his Deputy, who stood beside him.

"They want us to save them," the Deputy said, his voice full of contempt. "They're out of their minds if they think we're going to."

"You know, Mr. Premier," an older man seated at the table behind them said, "we could still save them if we wanted to."

"Are you crazy?" the Premier asked. "We're just getting the farm community cut down to size. We've driven out almost all the weak ones. Why would we want to save them?" He shook his head in disgust. "World markets are in terrible shape, competition's getting worse all the time, subsidies have to be so high they'd break our treasuries. Family farming's over; it's a whole new ballgame." He sat down in an easy chair and stretched out his legs comfortably. "Looks like we'll have to wait 'em out. So tell us, how could we save 'em?" The older man didn't move.

41

"To begin with, we could legislate farm size. Nobody could own more than a section."

"They'd never stand for that," the Premier said, laughing. "That's what Nasser did in Egypt – and they assassinated Nasser." Laughter went around the room. "Anyway, people here in the Palliser Triangle would starve on a section, this land's so poor."

"We'd have to give them a guaranteed income then, and we'd have to legislate what land could be ploughed up and what couldn't."

"You really *are* crazy," the Premier said with feeling.

"Then we'd start slowly shifting over to markets for domestic needs only, get out of the foreign-market squeeze entirely, try to become self-sufficient in cereal crops."

"We need the cash flow," the Premier said. "The world needs our durum."

"Seems to me," the Deputy said, sitting down too, "that we're talking about poverty again."

"They're not so rich right now," one of the others remarked. He was ignored.

"We'd outlaw the use of farm chemicals next. In the long run they do more harm than good. Then we'd institute price controls on farm machinery. Get those input costs down."

"Sounds like socialism to me," someone who hadn't spoken before said. "I thought we'd finally gotten rid of all the farmer-socialists by the time Tommy Douglas died. All those ones who set up the Co-ops and the Credit Unions and the marketing boards."

"I thought we had too," the Premier said ruefully. "Give us another couple of years, all the rabble-rousers will be broke and long gone from the farms."

"I tell you," the man whose remark about poverty had been ignored said again, "we're talking about a rural population living in poverty."

"I'm trying to make a point here," the older man said over the murmurs of agreement running around the room. "If you could only own a section of land, if grain prices were fixed, if your income was guaranteed at a certain level so that you knew you'd never be able to get rich, who'd want to farm?"

"That's right!" and "Yeah!" filled the room. The older man raised his voice to be heard.

"Only those who really *do* want that way of life," he said. "The businessmen would find some other way to make money. Only the real farmers would stay. And that's the point." The others were listening now and he lowered his voice again. "That would be the test of all that rhetoric about farming as a way of life, wouldn't it? If what you really wanted was to live out there in nature, tilling the soil like grandpa used to do, then you'd stay. We'd see if there'd be anybody left out there."

"Forget it," the Premier said, still easy. "Governments can't afford to provide services to isolated places miles from anywhere any more. No more school buses, no more grid roads, no more rural electrification . . ."

"People could live in towns and drive out to their places. We could afford to service towns – they'd come back to life," somebody else said, but voices of protest were rising all around the room.

"You're nuts!" "Talk about Utopia!" "You're talking about turning back the clock."

"I'm not talking about merely turning back the clock," the older man protested, but nobody was listening, the room was in turmoil.

They had been milling around the parking lot for a good hour now and the crowd was thinning out. Jessie's legs were aching from standing. She longed to go sit in the truck, she had lost track of Amy, and now all she wanted to do was to get out of here, to go home. She leaned against a lamp post, her hands behind her back, at the edge of the crowd, and saw how it had diminished. People were crossing the highway in droves now, going slowly back to their parked vehicles. She saw one of the big tractors starting its ponderous way down the city street, belching black smoke, and the man who had chaired the meeting was moving among the crowd now with a steady look that was tinged with worry, stopping to speak to men and women here and there, apparently encouraging them, discussing what to do next. When the crowd parted for just a moment, Jessie saw the two Mounties standing at the double doors that led into the motel lobby. Obviously they had been stationed there to keep the crowd out. Above their heads the curtains at a second-storey window twitched now and then and she could see the shadowy figures of several men moving about the room.

She searched the crowd for Val and saw him finally off to the far side by their truck, his back to her, deep in conversation with the MLA. She hesitated, watching them. They were so intent that she felt shy about interrupting them, but she slowly pushed herself away from the lamp post and walked toward them.

They were leaning against the truck box, their heads bent as though they were staring at something lying on its bottom while they talked, each sending the occasional brief glance toward the other, then quickly looking away. Jessie approached quietly.

"I figure I can hang on one more year," she heard Val say. She stopped dead.

"That bad, eh?" Vera said.

"Worse," Val said. "I figure I owe a quarter million easy, probably more. And if I don't get a crop again this year, we're gone." He paused, looked back down at the truck box, then turned his head away from Vera out toward the prairie on the edge of the city. "It'll kill my father." Vera said nothing. "That's why we gotta get a moratorium on farm debt. Just five years, that's all. Just long enough for me – for us – to get back on our feet again."

"That'd only help a few," Vera said. Behind her, Jessie was paralysed with shock. Val spun around abruptly, as if he had divined somehow that someone was standing behind him. When he saw Jessie, he opened his mouth to speak, but no sound came out. Vera looked quickly from one to the other, then quietly moved away without speaking, disappearing into what was left of the crowd.

"How did this happen, Val?" Jessie asked in a wail she couldn't seem to control, that, even as she tried to control, she felt was justified. She turned her head away from him, looking out the truck window toward the fields they were passing, though she didn't see them. "I thought we were well off. I thought there was lots of money."

"There was," Val said. "It just wasn't ours."

"Whose was it?" Jessie asked, her voice flat, knowing the answer.

"The bank's. I borrowed it."

"How is it that I didn't know about it?" She turned to him, angry now.

"I didn't hear you ask about it," he answered, angry too. "Remember that time between our graduation and the wedding when I came home to help Dad seed?" He refused to look at her but seemed to want an answer from her. She nodded. "The government had a deal out to help young farmers get started. I told you about it." Jessie tried to remember, but couldn't, except that vaguely, somewhere during that exciting time, he had talked to her about money. But she was about to graduate from university, she had a wedding to plan, how could she have been expected to pay attention? "I talked Dad into going with me for the full amount – three hundred and fifty thousand –" Jessie gasped, "– at 8 per cent. Things looked good then," he argued, as if she'd spoken. "Prices were way up, we'd had good crops. How could I know this was going to happen?"

"Three hundred . . ." She turned her head angrily toward him. "Is that what built our new house?" Val stared straight ahead through the windshield at the highway unfurling beneath them. "So that's why you wanted to come to this rally." She wanted to say more, much more, but her shock was so great that no words she could form seemed quite the right ones. She wanted to cry; she wanted to get out of the truck and go as far away as she could get; she wished she had never met Val.

Val suddenly seemed to deflate. He took one hand away from the steering wheel to push his Hoe-Grass cap back from his forehead, and the tension went out of his lean body, that till this moment she had loved wholly, without question.

"There's nothing else left to save us," he said. "Only political action, if we can get the government to move."

"Us!" Jessie found herself shouting, relieved even to discover anger. "*Now* it's *us!*"

"You just don't understand," he said, no longer angry himself. "You're a city girl. There's no other way for a new farmer to get started, unless his old man is rich, or has the good sense to die so the son can inherit the place. If I wanted to farm and you know I wanted to farm," now he was angry, "I had to borrow the money to do it!"

"But your dad . . ." Jessie began.

"He couldn't just hand the place over to me. He and Mom still have to eat," Val said. "And it won't support two families at the best of times, never mind during one of these endless goddamn droughts. I had to buy it. And the only way I could was to borrow the money."

Silenced by the logic of this, Jessie sat motionless.

"Still," she said finally, sounding sulky even to herself, "you should have told me." Now, even as she spoke she was no longer listening to herself, was beginning to see what this really meant, how it would change their lives.

"You dope," he said, patient now. "How could you not have known? Where the hell do you think I got the money?" She didn't answer, not even bridling at the injustice of this, while visions of disaster and shame passed before her. They drove in silence through Crisis, the town next to Ordeal. He hit his fist on the steering wheel once, smartly. "You saw the letters from the bank! You handed them to me!"

"I thought they were just . . . statements or something." She had begun to cry at last, but silently. She wiped tears from her chin before they trickled onto her dress. "But you never said a word. You just took them. You didn't even open them in front of me." He glanced at her, but she stubbornly wouldn't look at him. What would she tell her parents? Their friends from college? Would they have a home at all? But worse: how could he have let her go on believing everything was fine? As if it were no affair of hers?

She felt her heart might be breaking. She waited for his touch, his hand on her knee, or for that special voice he used when he wanted intimacy with her. Nothing. She glanced at him. He drove with his hands clenched into fists around the steering wheel, his face set. She felt then his turmoil, felt the emotion he was struggling to control washing out from him toward her, saw that it was all he could do to keep quietly driving the truck down the road.

The green "Ordeal" sign rose up and fell away. Val's skin was grey and for the first time she saw that he would not live forever, that he, too, would age, was aging in front of her. She reached out carefully and touched his knee. Abruptly he swerved to the shoulder, braking hard as he did so. They screeched to a halt, Jessie putting both hands against the dash, her seatbelt tightening painfully against her shoulder. He shoved the gears into park, opening the door at the same time, jumped out, hurried around to the side of the truck while she watched in horror, and vomited into the sparse, dust-covered grass of the ditch.

# CHAPTER
3

Faith had left the city in the early morning, before even its earliest risers were stirring, but she had stopped now and then to look at an interesting plant growing in the ditch, to study the sky, or simply to sit in the car with her hands resting on the deliciously soft leather cover of the steering wheel and think through whatever new idea had popped into her head. And she intended to spend the afternoon at Saskatchewan Landing enjoying the lake and the park.

She had already taken one twenty-five-mile detour to visit an historic site, the marker for which she had seen on the highway. Whenever she worried about the length of time it would take her, at this rate, to reach her destination, she reminded herself of her resolve, of her refusal any longer to let conventions dictate to her how she would live her life. And the day – this day, the one she had chosen as the first of her new life – was pale, clear, and beautiful, the air lilting with springtime, light and warm and scented. It seemed a shame to drive through it when walking was the only way to catch each second.

But her new car was a joy to drive. It was the first one she had ever owned, the first she had ever gone out and bought herself, chosen it herself too, even the colour, which Neil would hate, a red as vibrant as fire, as vibrant as the new life she felt coursing through her veins. She had sold the house Neil had signed over to her when he left – Neil didn't know she'd done that – she'd sold it and moved into an apartment. She'd put most of the money into the bank until she knew what she wanted to do with the rest of her life, and with the remainder she'd gone out and bought herself this wonderful car, this dream car. It was the first time in her life, other than the time she'd refused to see Neil when he'd come to visit her, and that, she admitted ruefully, had been as much out of weakness as it was out of strength, that she had acted as an adult. No, she corrected herself: as an autonomous individual. She relished the syllables and relived the thrill of saying to the delighted salesman, "I want that one," and then writing out the cheque, as though she did that sort of thing every day of her life.

My life, she thought, sobering – what life? It seemed to her that all her past, from the time she was a little girl until yesterday when she had bought the car, was only a bad, ugly dream from which she was finally waking. If Neil – no, she had vowed to stop allowing Neil inside every thought, Neil wasn't her husband any more, Neil wasn't her life, her life was her own now – but if Neil knew her as she was now, would he want her back?

No, he wouldn't want her back. He had wanted her in the first place because she was weak and childish and needed him and his strength, relied on him, loved him unquestioningly with every atom of her soul. Until he got tired of that. Until she got tired of it herself, though she hadn't realized it until he'd left her. She shuddered thinking of the terrible time that followed – *terrible* wasn't a strong enough word: hellish, nightmarish, agonizing. She shook herself, found herself roughly pushing back her hair with one hand, forced herself to stop.

And yet, here she was driving her brand new car to the little town where he'd decided to make his home without her. Her new life would not be new, she told herself fiercely, until she had bearded the lion in his den. She was at last her own person; she would face the man who had loved her and betrayed her, she would accept even her share of the blame, she would tell him her news, and then she would go on to the end of her journey.

"Absolutely not," Neil Locke was saying to Amy Sparrow. It was evening, though still fully light, and he was sitting at his desk in the small house he had bought on the outskirts of the town. Amy stood across from him in her faded and smudged cotton slacks and blouse, leaning against the door frame between the living room and kitchen.

"You don't have to say anything or do anything. Just come, just be there to show your support."

Neil stood, went to the old horsehair couch he'd rescued from the dump after he'd left the city, and sat down on it, stretching his long legs out in front of him. Amy came and sat beside him, but at the far end, where she knew he couldn't reach her without moving himself. "Our rally in Swift Current got people excited . . ."

"Even if it wasn't exactly an unqualified success," he interrupted wryly. She ignored him.

"We don't want that sense of possibility to die away."

"Strike while the iron is hot." He couldn't help mocking her. "No," he said. "I don't want anything to do with it. I don't care if they keep their stupid post office or not. I don't care if their stupid school closes. I don't care if every last one of them loses his farm. What do I care about farms? They've done nothing but damage this country, and besides, farmers brought this disaster on themselves." He paused to tamp down his rising anger. He hated to have Amy see him lose control. "Besides, even if I wanted to, what could I do?"

"I don't know," she said, her voice gone soft. "I don't know if there's anything you can do, even if you wanted to. But the thing is, Neil . . ." When she called him Neil, he had to listen, it was the note that came into her voice when her feeling for him showed, a hint of huskiness normally missing, a special tone that spoke of their silent times together in the darkness. ". . . the thing is, this town is shutting down. This beautiful, small, historic town. People who have never lived anywhere else in their lives, or their parents before them, are going to have to leave here, go someplace else, be like immigrants in their own country for the rest of their lives. Displaced people . . ."

He sighed, not wishing to argue, but unwilling to accommodate her.

"You mean, become like two-thirds of the rest of the world's people? They're far too smug as it is. Let them learn how the rest of the world lives." Amy tossed her head, and he saw that he was making her angry. "I'm not going," he said, keeping his voice gentle. "It is absolutely no use to ask, and it only spoils things between us." He turned to her, reaching out, stretching to touch her and not quite able to reach her. "Come and sit closer to me."

"I have to get down there," she said, but she turned her face toward his and even in the interior gloom he could see her giving up her anger. He persisted.

"Just for a minute."

"We're starting in half an hour," she said, but she was moving nearer to him. "You have a doctorate, Neil. People respect that. You *chose* to come here to live."

"Then they're damn fools," he said, angry again, dropping his hand from the side of her face. But she lifted it, surprising him, taking it in both of hers and pressing it to her cheek, then she put her lips to his palm, and they slid together on the prickly horsehair sofa as his arms went around her and hers around him. Their mouths met, held.

When she pulled away a moment later and stood, her face flushed, her blouse twisted, shaking her long legs to straighten her pantlegs, he said, "I can hardly imagine my life without you any more, Amy Sparrow," then said it again for the sound of it, for the peculiar, lovely sound of it.

"Oh, you scientists," she said irrelevantly, "you're all madmen."

"Come back when the meeting's over."

"The neighbours will talk," she said, her blouse straightened, her hair neat, the colour gone from her cheeks.

"I don't have any neighbours up here on my hillside," he said, "and if it really matters to you, you can park your truck behind the shed at the back. Nobody from down below can see it there." She had gone to the doorway.

"I'll see how late it is when it's over. I have a batch in the kiln that I have to get out in the morning and another commission for a dozen coffee mugs."

He laughed. "Why do you do that shit?" he asked. "You're an artist."

She moved uneasily. "You know I have to support myself," she said. "And you know I can't work if I don't get any sleep. But I better go." He watched her disappear into the kitchen, heard the back door shut, then rose and followed her. She was already driving away in her battered old truck, down into the warm spring evening, the light beginning to fail in the valley below.

When she disappeared from view in the tall trees that lined the streets of the town below, he went back to his combination living room and study – the house had only three rooms if you didn't count the bathroom – and sat down at his desk again.

Butler's *The Great, Lone Land* lay open before him, but he stared at it, not seeing it, his mind on Amy. He was trying to locate the source of the uneasiness he always felt when he thought of her, even when he was with her, and even as he was filled with pleasure at her skin, her long, slender legs, the quietness in her brown eyes. He reminded himself that he had given up everything and left the city to be solitary. He had cast off all their claims on him – his parents', his friends', his university's, his wife's – in order to be free to do the best work, the work of finding himself. Instead, he had found Amy and, though he had tried, he couldn't give her up.

He looked down at Butler, turned the book over, read a line. The print wavered and dissolved and he was back on the prairie again, where he had been at sunrise, on the last big area of native shortgrass still left in the west. He went there several times a week, it was the reason he had come here to live, and it brought him the solace that nothing else could. Each time he stayed a few hours by himself listening to the few birds, the insects, seeing the occasional coyote, deer, antelope, and watching the sky. When he was there, that sense of uneasiness that was always otherwise with him at last flattened out, smoothed itself into a speck on his mental horizon, allowed him peace. On the prairie, it seemed, he knew with certainty what was important and what wasn't.

He sighed, looked down at his book again, pushed himself away from the desk and went to the window where he stood staring out without seeing anything. They had destroyed the prairie, ploughed it up, tried to make it into something it wasn't before they had any idea what it was. In a couple of years he doubted that even that one big field would be left. It sickened him to think of it; if they did that, he promised himself, he would leave, go to the pampas of Argentina, or the steppes of Russia. Still, he thought ruefully, if he sometimes had the feeling that the heart of the grassland eluded him, it might not be that it held back from him, but he from it.

And that was why he was reading Butler: not to write a paper, not to argue or criticize, not for any reason he could put his finger on, but out of his unmet need to know everything there was to be known about this place he had picked, out of all the places on the globe, to settle in.

And Butler, who had travelled the west in and around 1872, was a constant surprise to him, a military man who was also a gifted writer, and who even more surprisingly put into words something of what Neil, more than a century later, himself felt.

. . . Around it, far into endless space, stretch immense plains of
bare and scanty vegetation, plains seared with the tracks of countless
buffalo which, until a few years ago, were wont to roam in vast herds
between the Assineboine and the Saskatchewan. Upon whatever
side the eye turns when crossing these great expanses, the same
wrecks of the monarch of the prairie lie thickly strewn over the surface. Hundreds of thousands of skeletons dot the short scant grass;
and when fire had laid barer still the level surface, the bleached ribs
and skulls of long-killed bison whiten far and near the dark burnt
prairie. There is something unspeakably melancholy in the aspect of
this portion of the NorthWest. From one of the westward jutting
spurs of the Touchwood Hills the eye sees far away over an immense
plain; the sun goes down, and as he sinks upon the earth the straight
line of the horizon becomes visible for a moment across his blood-red
disc, but so distant, so far away, that it seems dreamlike in its immen-
sity. There is not a sound in the air or on the earth; on every side lie
spread the relics of a great fight waged by man against the brute creation; all is silent and deserted – the Indian and the buffalo gone, the
settler not yet come. You can turn quickly to the right or left over a
hill-top, close by, a solitary wolf steals away. Quickly the vast prairie
begins to grow dim, and darkness forsakes the skies because they light
their stars, coming down to seek in the utter solitude of the blackened plains a kindred spirit for the night.

It made shivers run down his spine to think of it; how only a
little more than a hundred hears ago the prairie had seen destruction and death on so huge a scale. He would have to go back even
further to find whatever it was, that nameless thing that troubled
him and that he would not give up searching for until he had
found it.

Someone was knocking at his door. He had been so immersed in
his thoughts that he hadn't heard the car making its way up the hillside. As he spun around, startled, he heard loud, blurred voices and
knew they came from the public address system in the park below.
Amy's meeting. He ignored it, irritated by the persistent knocking
when he wanted no visitors. Except Amy. Amy was always welcome.

He thought of pretending he wasn't in, but no, he had snapped on the desk lamp and the inside kitchen door was wide open, he was plainly visible to whoever was standing in the soft darkness at his screen door. He went into the kitchen.

Faith was leaning against the screen, one hand cupped to shade her eyes, peering inside.

# CHAPTER
## 4

Jessie and Val Sheridan sat at the table in the gleaming kitchen of their new house. The farm books were spread out in front of them, and stacks of bills surrounded the books. Val was at last going through the records with Jessie.

Jessie caught a glimpse of her reflection in the doors to the patio and saw herself as pale, badly groomed – she who was so fastidious about her appearance – and appallingly unattractive. She stared for a second, then made a face at herself, which Val failed to see. Surprisingly, given the intensity of his concern, instead of speeding up, his normally quick, assured manner and speech had both slowed. It was as if he were having trouble moving or bringing out words, as if despair had dragged him into passivity.

"At 8 per cent," he was saying, "the annual interest payment – just the interest on the principal – is about twenty-eight thousand. So . . ." Jessie drew in her breath sharply, forgetting her appearance.

"But you just said our projected annual income is less than that!"

"Drought," he said. "I gambled. I wasn't the only one, and if we'd had good weather, a few good crops, there'd have been no problem. We'd already had seven years of drought. I thought, everybody thought, it had to break."

"But did you have to borrow so much?" she asked in dismay. They couldn't make the interest payment, even if they didn't otherwise spend a cent on themselves, not even to buy food.

"Yes," he said, exhaling as he spoke, so that Jessie could feel herself colouring. "I paid Dad a hundred and fifty thousand for the farm. As it was he gave me a half section worth another fifty thousand. That new tractor was more than seventy thousand. Then I bought ten head of registered cows . . ."

"How much?" Jessie's voice was low, fearful of the answer.

"Three thousand each." Now, she thought, now he'll tell me anything I ask. They would have to go too, and in her mind's eye she saw them clustered in the field, so black and beautiful, saw the pride and satisfaction in Val's face as he watched them, remembered how proud she had been too. "Our beautiful cows," she moaned, and put her hand over her eyes. Mistaking her dismay for anger, he protested, "That was a good investment. We've got thirty-five head now."

"But borrowed money . . ." Jessie said.

"Some," he acknowledged. "But some of them are our own heifers and the ones I bought are still worth as much as they were then."

"We'll have to sell them," she said. "Then we can make some kind of payment on this incredible debt."

"No, we'll wait till fall." He sounded confident. "If we get a crop we can make our interest payment, maybe even make a little payment on the principal. Then we won't have to sell them."

"And if it doesn't rain?" she asked, although, of course, she knew the answer. He dropped his pencil, leaned back heavily in his chair.

"Then everything goes," he said to the tabletop. "Us too."

The phone rang. Jessie had taken to not answering it if Val was in the house, since it was rarely anybody but his family and they only wanted to talk to Val anyway. She knew they didn't like her much, they made no effort to hide it, and in retaliation she found them both boring and faintly stupid. Although she had to admit, in her private ledger-keeping, that the mutual hostility might be simply an effect of the fact that they spoke different languages, Val's family being wholly rural and hers wholly urban. The result was that their understanding of the world was alien to Jessie's understanding, and if it hadn't been for her all-consuming love for Val, she felt she would have left him long ago out of sheer exhaustion from the effort of trying to bridge that gap. Val glanced at her and when she didn't move, pretending to be lost in thought, he got up and picked up the receiver.

"We haven't been in town today," he said. That would be his mother then. Flora didn't say hello if it was Val on the line, just started right in talking as if she had only stopped a second ago, as if Val were still her child, camped out in her kitchen. "*What?*" he said. Jessie turned her head. "Well," sounding dubious, "it's only one letter, Mom. People will have forgotten it by next week." Another pause. "Now, you don't know that. She's not the only one with a bee in her bonnet on that subject." Another long pause while Val nodded, making fruitless efforts to speak now and then. Boy, Jessie thought, she's really in a snit about something. She was grateful she hadn't answered the phone.

Val sighed and hung up. Jessie looked inquiringly at him, seeing that his normally suntanned skin was paler than usual. Even his hair seemed to have lost its gleam and suddenly she felt her heart give a lurch. To lose Val.

"Are you coming down with something?" she asked. "Do you feel all right?"

"Couldn't sleep," he said, though she had noticed nothing, having slept soundly herself.

"What was that?" she asked, looking toward the phone.

"Mom," he said. Jessie waited. Val sat again and stared glumly at the tabletop. "Alma's gone and written some crazy letter to the paper." Which one was Alma? Oh, yes, the schoolteacher.

"What about?"

"Mom didn't say. She just said we should get the paper and read it for ourselves." Jessie doubted Flora had said anything about "we" since she rarely even acknowledged Jessie, unless she wanted Jessie to run an errand for her. "I'm supposed to call her back and tell her what to do." He laughed. "Dad washes his hands of it, whatever it is." They both laughed. "I sure hope she doesn't expect me to talk to Alma. She taught me grade four and five. If Alma's losing her marbles I'm the last one who could talk to her."

"But . . ." Jessie said, frowning. The *Letters to the Editor* section. . . . She had been about to say "is full of nonsense at the best of times," but Val interrupted.

"That much she did tell me. It's a letter to that advice column."

"Oh, my gosh," Jessie said, stunned.

"Let's put this stuff away," he said. "I've had all I can take for one day. Want to come into town with me while I get the mail?"

When they were back and sitting at the kitchen table with the small weekly paper spread out in front of them, Val was the one who exclaimed at Alma's letter while Jessie read it over and over again in silence.

"Jesus Christ!" he said. "*Somebody's* going to have to talk to her."

"But how do you know she wrote it?" Jessie asked. She could see that Alma was peculiar, different from the rest of the family, but in ways, it seemed to her, that were attractive. Alma was restrained, spoke only if she had something to say, while the other women nattered on endlessly about knitting patterns or different ways to make the latest craze in desserts and who was successful at it and who wasn't.

"This," he said, and pointed to a line. "*You do not know how you sin when you allow abortions.*" The line was out of context, made little sense in the middle of the letter. "Alma's got this thing about abortions – not just the normal dislike, she's positively nuts on the subject. Haven't you ever seen her looking at you in a funny way?" Jessie reflected. It seemed to her that everybody in Val's family

59

looked at her in a funny way. "She's never had a baby, never been married. It's like maybe that twisted her some way and now she thinks if you're over the age of nine and don't have a baby it must be because you're having abortions.

"But," Jessie objected, "what about Pastor Raven and his congregation? They're just as horrified by it. Maybe it was one of them."

"Dear Troubled: First, you are not alone in dreaming strange dreams." The phone rang and Val answered it without referring to Jessie.

"Hi, Judy," he said. Judy was his cousin on his father's side who lived in town rather than on a farm. "Yeah, I read it." Silence. "Yeah, it's Alma all right." The voice on the other end of the line, which Jessie could hear faintly though she couldn't make out any of the words, went on for a long time. "But she's due to retire in a couple of years," Val said. "All right. See you." He turned to Jessie.

"The whole town knows it was Alma wrote the letter." He quoted: "'*I think I am losing my mind.*' Judy says the school board wants to make her take early retirement or they'll fire her. She's acting pretty strange at school, too." Val was leaning against the counter, staring down at his workboots, his hands in his pockets. Jessie tried to think of something to say, but as always, she was left speechless by his family.

"Does anybody really care?" she asked. "I mean, if she's losing her marbles in public. She isn't the mayor or anything."

"You never think anything that goes on in this town matters," he said, not angrily, but pensively. She shrugged; it was true.

"Everybody here thinks Ordeal is the centre of the universe and all it is is this tiny little town in the middle of nowhere that nobody else in the world has even heard of. Absolutely nothing that happens here matters anywhere else." Val studied her, his eyes deep and thoughtful. She wondered what he saw.

"If you stay here long enough," he said finally, smiling in an almost gentle fashion at her, "you'll think the same. You'll see that's not so crazy."

"I hate it when you talk in riddles," she said sharply, turning away from him. He came and touched the crown of her head with his palm as if to smooth her hair. He bent and kissed the spot he had touched.

"It's not a riddle," he said. "Ordeal *is* the centre of the universe." She laughed at this and looked up at him, expecting him to be laughing too, but he wasn't. His eyes met hers in seriousness. "I've got to get back to the summerfallow." He left her sitting there, pushed open the patio door and went outside, speaking to her over his shoulder. "There's a few clouds building up in the west. Could be rain."

It was the perfect moment for rain, an inch right now would give the crop a good start, carry it for almost a month. God knew they were desperate for rain, hadn't had a good rain in three years, and without rain this year – Jessie shuddered. She looked up and caught Val in an expression that told her he had just had the same thought. She went outside to stand on the deck beside him.

"Would it be so bad?" she asked. "To have to live in the city?" She asked this timidly, afraid of his response. He nodded slowly, his eyes fixed on hers.

"Yes," he said. "Maybe not for you, but it would be bad for me. I don't want to live in a city." He would not say, "This was my grandfather's place, virgin prairie before that, my family claimed it from the wild, tamed it, made it into a productive place, into a home for our family."

She tried to think what this meant. Only that it was the first soil he'd ever known, that he was familiar with every inch of it, both in his own memory and the memories of all the people around him, so that it had a history that she could only guess at, that it had become something other than property to him. Or had it? If we lose it, she thought, we'll find out what it really is to him. Then sympathy for him, for the sadness in his face, swept over her.

"Don't worry, Val," she said. "It doesn't do any good." He pulled his arm away angrily.

"Don't worry," he said, his voice filled with scorn. Hurt, she thought, why did he think he had an inviolable right, with most of the world starving and homeless, to this place, when city people had to keep constantly on the move for one reason or another, so that their whole notion of *home* had changed over the generations to something that hadn't yet even been defined? Who did these country people think they were? God's chosen people?

She left him standing there and went inside, sliding the door shut on anything he might have been planning to say. After a second he went down the steps and across the yard without looking back at her as she stood watching him from inside her spotless modern kitchen.

# CHAPTER
5

In the park below Neil's house, under the shade of the tall cottonwoods and poplars planted eighty or more years before by settlers, Amy stood near the borrowed flatdeck talking to Lowell Hartshorne. Behind them a couple of men moved around setting up the public address system, and before them people were moving in groups, some carrying lawn chairs, some with blankets, down toward the grassy area in front of the makeshift platform.

"But you can support a petition," she said to Lowell. He moved carefully, shifting his stance, looking over his shoulder at the crowd that was gathering.

"Yes," he said finally.

"Then why not be the one to introduce the idea? It's not a radical one, it isn't even controversial."

"I suppose not," the minister said, studying his shoes which were smudged with dust. "Yes," he said, as Amy smiled her approval. "Yes, that much I can do." He smiled too. She saw how he was careful not to touch her, though she thought he wanted to embrace her in his gentle, comradely way. It was not that he didn't want to help them, they were his people after all, but that he had always believed that things of the spirit were everlasting, while political oppression or freedom were equally fleeting. She knew it, thought he was wrong, but loved him for his belief. His example, she thought, if only people would see it, might indeed change the world. But the fact was that they didn't see it, and time was running out. Even as she tried to persuade him, she felt guilty for doing so; even now, after he had consented.

"I'm so glad," she said. "Thank you. I know you're doing the right thing for all of us." She gave him a light hug.

"When I think it was religious leaders who largely founded this society: Reverend Lloyd, Reverend Barr, Peter Veregin and his Doukhobors, the Hutterites, the Mennonites, the Roman Catholics who came out from Quebec trying to extend God's kingdom – Father deCorby, Father Lestanc – when I look at it that way, it doesn't seem that it's going beyond the limits of my mandate as a Christian minister to help out when that very society is in trouble." He frowned though, and glanced toward the platform as if it represented something that frightened him, or that was somehow not quite the way things should be. Amy wanted to reassure him, but she was afraid she would only disturb the fragile balance he had struck with his conflicting beliefs. She suffered for him though, poor man, trying to do a job that was increasingly devalued, seen as useless by half the society he had given over his life to helping.

Mac Hicks, the postmaster, had agreed to conduct the meeting.

"Are you sure you won't lose your job?" Amy had asked. But Mac had angrily refused to listen to her, turning away, his face and neck brick-red. Amy sat on the grass close to the flatdeck in case she was needed, and waited. Women sat around her, murmuring to each other.

"I can't believe it," Rita Zacharias said, pulling her hand-knit sweater around her bosom, for it was growing dark, and as soon as the sun sank below the hills it always grew chilly no matter how hot the day had been. "I can't believe it. Here we are, right when we should be celebrating the town's ninetieth birthday, too busy fighting to stay alive to even think about a celebration.

Amy, half-listening, noticed for the first time with some surprise how the widows seemed to be everywhere, at every gathering, from wedding showers to funerals to political rallies, always unobtrusive, always polite, never seeming to change, yet, come to think of it, their alert, intelligent eyes seeming to see everything.

"I don't see why they're so anxious to get us out of here. I mean, why don't they want our little town to exist? We aren't hurting anybody," Eleanor Dumas said plaintively, not caring who heard her. On the flatdeck Mac was adjusting the microphone with a self-important air that always made Amy smile. Still, he was devoted to their cause and he was as reliable as the day is long.

"I don't believe they even think about us," Margaret Dubbing said. "Politicians only worry about things like the national debt. They aren't interested in people, unless they're people who can throw them out of office. People like us don't count, there aren't enough of us any more."

"Naw," another voice said, a man this time. "They're just stupid. Just dumber'n a sackful o' hammerheads, that's all."

"They don't want to live out here so they can't imagine why anybody would. They think everybody wants to live in the big city, where they really think everything is better," a new voice chimed in.

"Yeah, yeah," people agreed.

"Don't they watch TV? Don't they know about soup kitchens and food banks and muggings and drugs in the schools . . . ?"

"And living next door to somebody for ten years and not even saying hello . . ."

"Old people dying in their apartments, not found till they start to smell . . ."

". . . booze, porno magazines in the corner stores . . ."

"Not seeing the stars your whole life . . ." At this, heads involuntarily tilted upward, even Amy's, to peer at the few pale stars appearing through the darkening branches of the poplars and willows.

"And your family," Rita said, after a moment. "So far away from the people who mean the most to you in the world . . ."

While they were talking, twilight had begun to fall, drifting down from the hills to rest around them, softening the outlines of the trees and the buildings across the street, each other's faces, while high above them the silhouette of hills grew darker and the sky more pure, a silver-blue behind the sharp black line of the Earth. Nobody noticed Pastor Raven coming down out of the hills to stand deep in shadow at the back of the crowd, and for some reason, no barking dogs heralded his arrival, though some thought they heard the sound in the distance. Mac had straightened things to his satisfaction and had begun to speak, describing the situation which was so well known to all the people who stood or sat before him.

They stopped talking then, their few voices having grown softer and softer till they blended into the sound of the crowd, an indeterminate, voiceless hum that was two hundred hearts beating, pulsing blood through veins, lungs gently sucking in air and expelling it with scarcely perceptible sighs. In the dusky light and the lull it seemed that the crowd had become one warm, watchful being, a fluid creature at its edges, but one that held together at the centre.

"Hi," Faith said, uncertain, dropping her hand. Was she alone? He peered over her shoulder. "There's nobody with me," she said. "You can let me in. I won't stay long." She stepped back while he pushed the door open, standing aside to let her into his tiny kitchen. There was a roar from the park. The whole town must have come to Amy's meeting. How pale she was, his small, blonde wife, or ex-wife, to be accurate, how blue her eyes were still. But no, he would not look further.

"How did you find me?" he asked, looking sternly down on her.

"I asked in town," she said, peering past his shoulder. Great, he thought, more gossip. "I'm on my way to Mexico," she added gaily, a note of bravado, he thought, entering her voice.

"Alone?" he asked, disbelieving.

"Yes," she said, and moved past him to look into his living room. "What a mess," she said, and laughed that high-pitched, falsely gay laugh that so angered him.

"Just books," he said. "Well, come in, sit down. Tell me what's going on."

She sat in the very place Amy had vacated a couple of hours before, but the top of Faith's head barely reached the top of the high-backed old sofa, and now that she was seated she seemed suddenly to lose her restless bravado, her false gaiety, as if she had found herself suddenly more tired than she had realized. He saw now that her forearms were sunburned, and her nose. He sat down at his desk, swivelling his chair to face her.

"Put the light out, please," she said. There, that was the Faith he knew, always begging for something, his attention, his love, his very soul, so he said harshly over another roar from the park, "What do you want?" But he reached behind him and clicked out the goose-neck lamp. They sat in silence for a long moment while the shadows sorted themselves out, came to rest, fingers of moonlight touching this and that. He hoped Faith would leave before the meeting ended.

"I've come to tell you something." Her voice had taken on a heaviness and was oddly loud coming from her, his soft-spoken former wife.

"Yes?" he asked, keeping his voice level to keep her from thinking anything she might say could matter to him any more. Still, his heart insisted on beating a little faster, though he couldn't imagine what bad news there could be that he hadn't already heard.

"I've been diagnosed as having a breast lump." He would have spoken, but she gave him no chance, hurrying on. "I've had a biopsy and it's malignant all right. But I wouldn't let them do a mastectomy." Now she paused, but he could think of nothing to say. "I know how it goes," she said, her voice changing again, sounding as though she were talking to herself. "First the breast, then the sickness of chemotherapy, worse than the disease itself, then more tumours, maybe more operations, the other breast goes, then radiation, more illness, more tumours. Death."

"But . . ." he began.

"No!" she said, in a voice that made him drop the pen he had picked up. He bent to retrieve it, glad of something to do that would give him a moment to collect himself. "I won't be a guinea pig for the medical profession. I won't submit to such barbarous treatment. I won't." He could hear her breathing, short, quick breaths. There was another burst of applause from the crowd down below in the park. He felt himself torn; felt there was too much in the world. It was all too much.

Lowell Hartshorne had climbed onto the flatdeck and stood at the microphone hesitating as if he didn't know how to begin.

"He isn't what we need right now," Rita Zacharias said firmly, loudly.

"Shhh," several people hushed her with embarrassed hisses.

"It seems to me," he was saying, "we are losing our institutions one by one, the institutions that keep this town alive, that define it . . ."

"You'd think he was making a sermon," Rita said, her fly-away white hair forming a halo around her head, and again people hushed her and Eleanor Dumas said, "Ri–ta!" in a scandalized voice.

"We need to find a way to register our dismay and our unhappiness with these harmful decisions government is making, a reasonable and a civilized way."

"Is he saying we're not supposed to get mad?" a woman asked.

"I propose we start a petition, collect as many signatures across the province, or at least here in the southwest, as we can and send it to the Prime Minister." The crowd was silent, thinking this over.

"Can't do any harm," a male voice pronounced to the crowd around him. They were used to petitions, petitions didn't frighten them. Hadn't they signed them to keep Sikhs from spoiling the

Mountie uniform, that symbol of their history, with swords and turbans?

"Not that they ever do any good," somebody else muttered.

"You may say that it won't do any good," the minister said, still in a conversational tone, "but there are laws governing petitions too. If there are enough signatures such petitions cannot be ignored."

"What would it say, Reverend?" a familiar male voice called from the opposite side of the crowd. Martin Barrell, Amy thought with surprise. What is he doing here? He was a strong supporter of the current government. A bagman, she thought, relishing the unaccustomed word, grinning at it, thinking there isn't enough money around here for anybody to be a bagman. Then her grin died away, thinking of the poverty that had returned everywhere on the prairies where, for a short while at least, there had been prosperity. She rubbed her hands together anxiously and shivered in the gloom, though the evening was still warm.

"We'd have it properly drawn up," the minister replied. "Something to the effect that we're in desperate trouble out here in the small towns and farms of the west, that our society as we have always known and loved it, is dying . . ."

"Being murdered!" an angry voice interrupted.

". . . not as a natural process," he went smoothly on, "but as the result of careless, heartless actions by various government bodies." He paused, then rephrased. "By careless, heartless, and apparently unco-ordinated actions by various government departments."

"What a way with words," Eleanor murmured admiringly.

"We need to march on Regina!" a male voice near the centre of the crowd shouted, so that people in front turned to try to see through the darkness who it was.

"Hell!" an even angrier voice further back called, "We need to march on Ottawa!"

"People, people," the minister called in a futile effort to quieten the crowd. "You may not remember – some of you old-timers will, though – but we have an example of that very thing in our past, and I can't say that it did any good, or even that it came to a satisfactory end."

"What's he talking about?" a teenager hovering on the edge of the crowd asked another with amusement in her voice at the folly of her elders. The older people seated nearby threw the young people looks that bordered on scorn, though the kids couldn't see them in the gathering shadows.

"The On-to-Ottawa Trekkers of 1935," the minister explained, holding out his hands, palms down, as if to soothe them into silence. "Men who gathered in Vancouver and rode the rails all the way to Regina, and we know what happened in Regina."

"What? What happened?" people called from here and there all through the crowd.

"Tell them what happened," an old woman's voice called from the crowd. "It's a disgrace they don't know!"

"Yeah! Tell them!" The same angry voice that had suggested the march on Ottawa joined in the general cry. The minister extended his hands again and, although it was hard to tell in the light that had been strung up over the ball diamond backstop, his expression seemed uncertain, pleading even.

"There was a riot," he began, his voice wavering.

"There was no riot!" a new voice cried, crackling with rage. "There was no riot!"

"The police fired on the trekkers when they gathered in a town square for a meeting. One man, a policeman, was killed . . . many others were shot and wounded . . . many went to jail."

"How come I never heard about that?" another teenager asked the dark shadow that was the crowd, then turned away, not expecting an answer.

"What's it got to do with us?" Eleanor Dumas called, through the muttering scattered far and wide in the mass of people.

"That inflammatory rhetoric and confrontational devices cause more harm than good," the minister pleaded. "We mustn't even think about such measures. There's still time for reasonable approaches to government."

"Ask Jack Pritchard if there's still time! Or Amos Shaw!" Both had gone broke in the previous couple of months. Amos had left the community with his family, but Jack had been found hanging by the neck from a rafter in one of his old wooden granaries.

"The CPR didn't even send a representative to this meeting! Neither did the post office! Unless you're here officially, Mac?" This drew laughter. "Even our MP didn't show up."

"You can't talk to people who won't even show up!"

"You gotta get their attention some way!"

"A petition . . ." the minister began, but the crowd had broken up into contradictory calls. In the confusion, his worst fears realized, the minister gave up and got down from the platform. He was replaced immediately by Vera, the district's MLA.

"Folks!" she called, "Folks!" At the sound of a different voice people turned back to the platform. "You all know I'm not one to back down from a fight." There was a sprinkling of admiring laughter. She might have been in Opposition, but she gave 'em hell every chance she got. "But it seems to me that what will work best is a co-ordinated, unrelenting attack on all fronts at once. We try everything, we approach everybody, we don't quit no matter how much they try to put us off. 'It's the squeaky wheel that gets the grease!'"

"Now that's more like it!" Rita Zacharias announced, looking around at the shadows that were her neighbours.

"Shades of Nellie McClung and Violet McNaughton!" the old woman's voice quavered with satisfaction. "They got us women the vote!" Everyone ignored her.

"I think we'd better start that petition," and the crowd roared its agreement. "Then we better keep our ears to the ground and when

our Direct Action Committee here asks us to do something, we give
'em our whole-hearted support!"

It was growing late, eleven at least, and bats had come out of the
tall trees. Had anyone been looking they would have seen their silhouettes circling the dark body that was the townspeople. High
above them the stars blinked and sent out their silver light through
immeasurable space and aeons of time to anoint the heads of the
people.

"Remember that we're fighting for our rights! For our homes!
For our land!" Vera cried.

The crowd slowly dispersed, the men with their hands in their
pockets, the women with their arms folded across their breasts
against the rising chill, and they grew silent, bitter perhaps, or
perhaps only remembering, as Vera had admonished them to do,
how the place used to be when there was a town herd of cows that
the kids tended each day; how it was when everybody kept chickens in their backyards; how it was when the flu struck in '18 and
people got sick and died and nobody could do anything about it,
and old Nellie Jamieson, a tiny girl at the time, had seen the
doctor crying.

In each heart, too, private memories welled up: the time
Grandpa got into a fight with Billy Larson and would have shot him
if Grandma hadn't hidden the rifle; the days when Grandma and her
friends had a club they called the Dauntless Society; the time Henry
Dickson's boy drowned in the dugout and his mother went crazy
with grief; and all the neighbours who in the thirties had abandoned
their homes and wandered away and were never seen again.

We built the west, the people thought to themselves as they
went silently away to their small homes. We built it with our bare
hands, and they knew that this was the truth as few things are, and
that they would fight to keep what, through such hardship, they had
earned the right to call home.

The roar of voices seemed to have died away, and now Neil could hear trucks and cars starting down below, indicating the meeting was over.

"That's why you're going to Mexico," he said. They had honeymooned in Mexico, a gift of Neil's businessman father, another one of those gifts that he had wanted to refuse, knowing that it bought his soul.

"Yes," she said, in her little girl voice.

"Ah," he said. "Where?"

"You know the place." Yes, he knew the place. It was a small clinic near the resort where they had stayed in his father's condominium (and had gone back twice more, as a matter of fact). Then, they had shaken their heads at the folly of those who insisted on going to it to be fleeced and then sent home to die.

"Have you lost your mind?" he asked.

"I won't be bullied by you any more," she said, and he was surprised both that she would accuse him of such a thing and then that she would stand up to him.

"So why did you come here?" he asked angrily. "You knew I wouldn't approve." She stood then, not answering, and walked around the room, pausing to pull straight a wrinkle in the old carpet, another junkyard find, using her toe. He was afraid she was going to come to him as when they were married, putting her arms around his neck, asking to be taken on his knee. He, holding her sweetness close to him, breathing in her perfume, she sliding her small, warm hands up inside his shirt.

But she didn't come near him. Paused instead at one of the bookcases to flick on a lamp he'd set on the top to help him find a book in the middle of the night, then flicking it off again.

"Leave it on," he said, if only to say something. She turned it back on.

"I worry about you," she said. He laughed in spite of himself. She was the one who'd had the breakdowns, one during the early years of their marriage, one after he'd left her. He would never cease to be glad they hadn't had children. "I do," she insisted. "Ridiculous as that apparently sounds to you. This latest transmutation of yours is a bit alarming."

He wanted to smile again, but instead he remembered a pair of hunting eagles he had watched spiralling down the sky; how he must at first have seemed prey to them.

"You too?" he said wearily. He'd been through all this with his father, his colleagues at the university, his friends.

"You've lost weight."

He shrugged.

"Well," she said, sighing. "There's nothing I can do about that, I guess."

"Faith," he said. She put down the book she'd been holding, absent-mindedly brushing the dust off it, and looked at him. He doubted she could see him very well since he sat in the gloom across the room from her, but she acted as if she were seeing him very clearly. He had always said she knew nothing about him, but now he had, for an instant anyway, an uncomfortable sense that this might not be so, might never have been so.

"What?" she asked.

He sighed, dreading speaking. How she always found a way to force him.

"Don't go to Mexico. Go home, check yourself into the hospital. Do what they tell you." He thought she would argue, maybe even cry, but she only took another book from the crowded shelf and brushed the dust off it too. In the town below vehicles were moving down the streets, and he recognized their whine as they headed out on the grid roads, amplified and echoed by the hills.

"No," she said, almost thoughtfully. "No, I won't do that. You see, I've made up my mind too."

"Don't tell me," he said, standing. "I don't believe it. You're not doing this just to get even with me because I left you?" He could have killed her.

"You don't frighten me any more, either," she said, and set the book back on its shelf. "I'm going now."

"Why did you come?" he asked, breathing quickly, scarcely able to control his voice.

"I came to see you," she said. "We loved each other once, we lived together for fourteen years. Do you think humans can sever such connections?" She paused. "I thought you'd want to know. And anyway," she was moving to the outside door, "I've had time to think. I wanted to . . . share it with you." She sounded hopeful.

"Christ," he said. She turned away and went quickly outside where she stopped in the darkness.

"I'm going." She went around the back of her car, parked on the patch of gravel by the door.

"Wait," he said, alarmed now. "You'd better stay the night."

"No, thanks. I'll go," she repeated. "It's a long way."

"But surely you'll stay the night in town?"

"No," she said, opening her car door. "I'll stop when I get tired."

He thought now that she seemed very tired already. Sympathy stirred him, but he squelched it. He couldn't afford to feel sympathy for her or she'd have him right back where he'd been, trapped between a job he felt was useless and a marriage he hated, and still under the thumb of his father.

The interior lights of her car went on and then off as she got in and shut the door. He hurried outside, but she had started the motor, switched on the headlights, and pulled away before he could reach the driver's door.

"I'll write to you," she called out the window, then gunned the motor, speeding up, going too fast for the narrow, crooked trail down into the town.

# CHAPTER
## 6

Sandy McDonnell, a sixty-year-old bachelor, who, despite having no hair at all on his smooth freckled scalp, still kept his nickname from his days as a redhead, was on his way for morning coffee. His house on the outskirts of town had been, eighty-five years before, the headquarters of the first and biggest ranch in the region, in the long-ago times when all this high grassland had been exclusively ranching country. In fact, the town had grown up, so to speak, in his front yard, from a couple of bunkhouses to the fewer than five hundred people left today out of a peak population of over a thousand.

Although it wasn't a mile from his house down to the café, he drove. Cowboy boots with their slippery leather soles and high heels designed to hold the foot in the stirrup made walking difficult. More to the point, though, was the fact that nobody in Ordeal walked much except the women on their perpetual diets, the occasional Mountie ordered by his superiors to get fit, and the men with bad hearts whose doctors had warned them to exercise more. Once a man grew up to sixteen and got his first truck, his walking days were over.

Sandy McDonnell and Bill Peat had an unspoken competition to see who could make it down to the café first each morning. Mrs. Henwick opened at six sharp, but it was part of the agreement that arriving before she did didn't count. To win you had to saunter in as the first customer of the day and have her pour you the first cup of coffee. Sandy rarely managed to get there first. He told himself that it was because he had further to go than Bill, never willing to acknowledge that since the banker had forced him to quit ranching he had failed to adjust to the town-dweller's more precise and artificial concept of time. Sandy knew perfectly well what time he had to leave to get there at just the right moment, but it seemed he always got involved in something like sewing on a missing button or talking to his dogs or watching the crows build a nest in the trees so that he missed that time by a minute or two. Or else he would leave at exactly the right moment, but fail to reckon in the vagaries of the various clocks involved. He didn't know how he had gotten into such foolishness in the first place, but whenever he contemplated just dropping the whole thing he knew he couldn't. Trying to beat Bill gave a little spice to his increasingly pointless days.

This morning he had a plan. He left a half hour before he needed to and drove around the outer edge of town so that his truck was pointed toward the café, but from the direction opposite to the one from which he usually came. He turned down a side street, made a U-turn and pulled up with his nose hidden behind a bank of lilacs, already in bloom, that had once been old Mrs. Sharp's hedge, who was now ensconced in sublime indifference in the nursing home, rousing herself only to call for Herman, her husband who had been killed fifty years before by a runaway team when the wagon tipped, crushing him.

He waited. When he saw Bill coming down the street in his half-ton, he would step on the gas and slide into the street just ahead of him, would beat Bill to a parking spot and get into the café first. He sat and waited, his window rolled down, breathing in the scent of the lilacs.

Though it was still very early, the sun had been up for more than an hour. The night had been chilly, as summer nights usually were on the surrounding high plateau, which meant that in the valley where the town was people often woke to the last faint streaks of fog as they dissipated in the warmth of the rising sun. The street Sandy had parked on had only one house on it that somebody still lived in. All the others had either been empty for a long time or had emptied as a result of the long drought. People who had once had two houses, one on the farm and the one in town whose purpose was to save the kids the long ride on the school bus, had found it necessary to give up the house in town, since it was usually the one not fully paid for, and to move back to the free and clear, if shabby, house on the farm. Usually, though, the move hadn't served much since nobody bought the empty house in town. So Sandy sat in perfect stillness, unobserved, watching the last of the early morning fog as it began to dissolve, and listening to the trilling of the sparrows, wrens, and robins in the countless old trees the settlers had planted on this once-barren plain. The trees were dying now too, as if in sympathy with the demise of the town.

Presently he heard the neat clip of a saddle horse's hooves on asphalt. The sound seemed to be coming from behind him, up the deserted street. Who'd be out riding this early in the morning? he wondered. Especially in town. He craned his neck out the window of his half-ton and peered backward to where the street disappeared in the evanescent morning mist.

The sound grew louder, and presently a horse and rider emerged slowly out of the fog, at first a half-formed, shadowy blur, then the horse's head, then its chest adorned with a silver-studded martingale, the silver on it and the bridle glinting rose and blue, then the rider in his tall hat – they seemed almost something formed out of the wavering curtain of fog. Sandy watched, the horse and rider drew nearer, the horse's gait steady and even, that of a horse whose rider has come a long way and has a long way to go and is in no particular hurry.

"Morning," Sandy said, as horse and rider drew abreast of him. "Whooah."

The rider drew up the horse opposite Sandy's truck. It pranced a little, the rider swaying easily with him, hardly noticing, till the horse obeyed the pressure of his thighs and subsided. "Morning," the rider said, shifting to get more comfortable in his saddle.

He was a stranger to Sandy, a thin man with the thinness of the old-time cowboys who rode all day without a bite to eat, without even a drink of water, but it was tough, ropy thinness; under that worn shirt and dusty Levis, Sandy knew the man's muscles were as hard and unyielding as iron.

"Ridden far?" Sandy asked respectfully. The man nodded, looking up the street to where it crossed the main street, and on further down to where it was lined with more small, mostly empty houses. A few thin wisps of fog drifted around their blank windows and caught in the fences and hedges.

"Quite a ways," he said. "Looking for some water for my herd." Sandy reflected.

"Big herd?" he asked.

"Couple a thousand," the cowboy replied, still not looking at Sandy. Come to think of it, Sandy hadn't seen his eyes yet, the way his hat was pulled down shadowing them. The numbers sunk in. A couple of thousand! Nobody in the district had a herd that big left.

"You know where I might water 'em?" the cowboy asked. Sandy scratched his head, knocking his Hoechst cap sideways.

"Where you got 'em at?" he asked. The cowboy didn't reply, merely nodding his head vaguely toward the north or the west. "I got a dugout on my place full of water," he said, though he was a little dubious it would water so many head. "It's spring-fed. You could use it. It's over that way, on the edge of town. Can't miss it. The old windmill's still up, though it don't work no more."

"Much obliged," the cowboy said, not even looking in the direction Sandy had pointed, touching his Stetson with tobacco-stained fingers. He turned his horse which had grown impatient and was tossing its head and side-stepping again, and trotted back in the direction from which he had come.

Sandy was about to stick his head out the open window again to watch the horse and rider retreat, but just as he started to, he caught a glimpse of Bill Peat driving slowly by on the way to the café. Damn! he thought, and started the motor quickly, trying to beat Bill onto the main street. Too late. He had already sailed by and once again Sandy would be second man down to the café for morning coffee.

When he realized this he thought of the strange cowboy and jammed on his brakes, peering backwards in the rearview mirror. The fog was completely dissipated now, and the curve of the street was clear and still in the early morning sunshine. There wasn't a soul to be seen.

Well, he thought, it'd take the cowboy and his men some time to get back to the herd, round 'em up and drive 'em down to his dugout. He'd go have coffee, catch up on the news and then go back home. Probably he'd be just in time to watch 'em water and then he'd talk to the trail boss, find out whose cows they were, where they'd come from and where they were going. It made him feel good just to think there was such a big herd nearby.

By the time he'd parked in front of the café, though, he was the fourth man in: Dale Penner was there too, and Martin Barrell seated around the horseshoe counter with Bill Peat, already sipping from Mrs. Henwick's first pot of coffee. He went in slowly as if it was all nothing to him, and straddled a stool next to Dale, across from Bill.

"Word is," Dale was saying, "that the Dunbars are gone for good."

"Couldn't be," Martin said, adding more sugar to his already sugar-saturated coffee. "The kids are still in school. They wouldn't leave before the end of June."

"House is empty," Dale said. "Curtains are gone from the windows."

"What?" Martin said, setting down his cup in surprise. "But . . ."

"They left on the weekend," Dale said. "When we got up Monday morning there was nobody there. Must have left in the night."

"Why would they do that?" Bill Peat asked. "Everybody was on their side."

Martin said slowly, "You know how it is. You go bankrupt around here, you feel like you should shoot yourself or something."

Sandy said, "They haven't had their sale yet." He meant of their farm machinery. "And I ain't heard a thing about their land." Dale shook his head.

"They tried to live too high on the hog. You can't build yourself a fancy house and drive fancy cars and expect the farm to carry a load like that."

"I hear he was a half-million in debt," Bill said. "She wanted to live pretty high."

"Ah, hell," Mrs. Henwick said, emerging from the kitchen with a plate of toast for Martin. "You fellas always want to blame the woman. Wouldn't matter how many dresses she had or how many TV sets in the house, it wouldn't be but a drop in the bucket to what he owed." The men laughed sheepishly, knowing she was right. Even a thirty-thousand-dollar car was nothing compared to what a combine could cost you.

They were still laughing when the door opened and a tall, fair-skinned man with thinning light-brown hair, dressed in faded jeans and workboots and a faded red-and-black plaid shirt entered. He went to sit in one of the booths while the coffee drinkers at the counter fell silent, staring at him. Something in the stiff way the newcomer held himself told them that he was aware of their scrutiny, but he gave no direct sign and studiously ignored them. Mrs. Henwick took him a menu, then came back behind the counter.

"Who's that?" Sandy asked in an undertone.

"That Locke fella," Dale said. "The one that lives up in old Harboy's shack."

"How come I ain't seen him before?" Sandy asked, at once plaintive and indignant. It was not a good morning. Then he remembered the strange cowboy and felt a little better. As soon as he could he'd slip him into the conversation. The door opened again to admit Howard and Phil Mountain, brothers who farmed side by side and whose wives refused to get up at six in the morning, except during harvesting and seeding, to get them breakfast.

"Nobody sees him much," Bill said. "He does some kind of wildlife stuff for the government, it looks like. He's out on the prairie half the time." Sandy took a good look at Neil; no, he had never seen him before.

"Wilma says," Dale remarked, "that when she can't sleep and gets up in the night, half the time his light's still on – two, three, four o'clock in the morning."

"That reminds me," Sandy said. "I saw a stranger in town this morning. Some guy riding through town on horseback, looking for water for his cattle." In an instant he had everybody's full attention.

"Who was he? Where'd he come from?"

"Wouldn't say. Didn't tell me his name. Seemed to be coming down from the north plain." Sandy cursed himself inwardly for not having at least asked the guy his name. "Said he had a couple of thousand head to water." He dropped his bombshell casually.

"You wouldn't be bullshitting us, would you?" Martin said.

"More likely he was pulling your leg," Phil Mountain said. "Nobody around here has more than a couple of hundred head any more, and only a couple of them."

"You go on a tear last night, Sandy?" Bill Peat asked. Sandy looked around, somewhat bewildered by the reaction to his news. Come to think of it, it did sound a little farfetched, even to his own ears.

"You been watching too many Roy Rogers reruns," Dale said, laughing. "Sandy thinks he's still back on the ranch, riding herd on them dogies," Bill said.

"I seen him," Sandy persisted over their laughter. "I talked to him. Told him he could use my dugout. I got no stock any more."

"You expect us to fall for that?" Martin asked. He sipped his coffee, dismissing Sandy.

"I tell you I seen him," Sandy insisted. It occurred to him that proof could be provided. "If you fellas don't believe me, just take a drive on down to my place." He was about to specify his place on the edge of town till he remembered that everybody knew he had lost the other place. "In about an hour you can watch 'em water." The other men laughed and soon began to talk about something else.

Across the café Neil Locke chewed his toast and half listened. He rarely came into the café at all and never so early in the morning. It was only that Faith's visit had so disturbed him that he hadn't been able to sleep. He never wanted to see her again, his heart was set hard against her, but the news she brought had destroyed his defences in a second. He had tossed all night, appalled, stricken, angry, and in the early morning had felt the need to get out of his house, to hear voices other than Faith's.

"Sure it was Alma Sheridan." The voices at the stool grew louder.

"Those must be some dreams she's having."

"Doesn't appear to me it was a dream."

"How the hell do you know it was Alma wrote it? Wasn't signed."

"It was more like a vision, like in the Bible."

"What?"

"A prophecy, like about the future."

"It had to be Alma Sheridan. She's the only one got a bee in her bonnet about abortions."

"That preacher Raven has."

"Him and his people get their shirttails in a knot over just about everything. It's hellfire and damnation if you spit on the sidewalk."

"Funny how the dogs always follow him."

"I think he's got a screw loose. I think he should be run outta town."

"I heard they've decided to put up a big cross on the hill above town, over on the north side."

"They can't do that, it's private land."

"It's Mike Harboy's land and he's one of them."

"What do they want to do that for?"

"To show this is a Christian town I guess."

"They say it'll be about fifty feet high, if they can figure out how to make it stand up in that alkali soil they got up there."

Neil, who had been listening only because he couldn't help but overhear them, paid attention to this. He had bought his few acres from Mike Harboy, they were on the west side of Harboy's land, and it sounded to him as if this cross, if it were put up, would be right next to his house.

Mrs. Henwick, who was pouring everybody another round of coffee, said, "They've already started it. I saw it myself. It's in the preacher's backyard. I go right by it when I go down the lane on my way home from work. It's a good fifty feet all right. Wouldn't be surprised if they don't intend to make it even bigger. It isn't finished yet."

Neil abruptly shoved the plate away, the coffee cup too, and stood so quickly that heads turned. He walked down the row of booths to the cash register where, without waiting for Mrs. Henwick, he dropped a couple of dollars on the counter by the cash register and strode out of the café, past the "Support Local Businesses" sign, letting the door bang shut behind him.

Behind him Sandy McDonnell had surreptitiously checked his watch and got off his stool intending to leave the café too.

"I'm going out to check my waterhole," he said meaning-fully, not wanting the half-dozen men who'd come after he'd told the first four about the stranger to hear too. Bill Peat imme-diately picked up his New Holland cap off the counter and rose hastily. Martin Barrell drained the last of his coffee too, set it down noisily and followed the other two. Behind them Dale Penner hesitated for a moment and then slowly got up and went out with them.

Each of the four of them got into his own half-ton truck and fell into a line behind Sandy's as he led them toward the west edge of town. Even from a distance they could see there was no herd of cattle anywhere in sight. Martin was so exasperated at having been caught up in what he now thought was a practical joke that he gunned his truck, passed the others and turned onto the highway leading out of town toward his farm, where he should have been doing the summerfallow anyway. The others were more patient. They closed the gap behind Sandy's truck and when he came to a stop in his yard, they pulled up beside him.

"Don't see a herd," Dale Penner said, as Sandy got out. Sandy didn't reply, just led the way, frowning, toward the dugout a hundred yards behind his house and the old tumbledown barn that had once held twenty head of horses at a time. He was walking fast now and scanning the surrounding hills for sign of a herd approaching or leaving. There was nothing to see, only scarred, beige cliffs with their outcroppings of white clay glistening in the sunshine, while above a few hawks circled lazily.

"Hey, look!" Bill Peat said. Sandy and Dale turned to see what Bill was looking at, but he was staring down at the loose dry dirt around his boots. They looked down too and sure enough, where they were walking were the unmistakable hoofprints of cattle, hun-dreds of them, pounded into the ground all around the waterhole, leading down its sloping side to the water's edge. What few blades of grass there had been were trampled flat or cut off by grazing cows.

The ground was churned, pockmarked with hoofprints for a hun-dred feet in every direction.

"Funny, there's no sign of manure," Bill said. They searched the ground with their eyes, but there wasn't even one fresh, flat, and smelly cowpie no matter where they looked.

"Unnatural, that's what it is," Dale said in an awed voice.

"I can't figure out which way they came from," Dale said, follow-ing the perimeter of the hoofprints looking for what would have had to be an unmistakable trail. But there wasn't one. It was as if they had all arrived at once from nowhere, here at Sandy McDonnell's dugout, where there once had been a vast cattle ranch and now were no animals at all.

They looked at one another in wonder. Dale's face had blanched, but Sandy's fair skin had flushed red. "Look at the water," Bill said. A light breeze was rippling its surface. "The level didn't drop one inch." As if in confirmation of Sandy's observa-tion the wind suddenly picked up and would have lifted off their caps – Hoechst, Avadex, New Holland – if they hadn't instinc-tively, from a lifetime spent on the Great Plains, reached up to hold them on.

None spoke to the others, but they looked hard into each other's eyes and reached an agreement. This story would not be told; no one would believe it. Hell, they didn't believe it themselves and they were looking right at it. Yet, for some time now, things like this had been happening. Rumours spread through the community, nothing solid, no evidence, not even any certainty about who had seen what. There was an undercurrent building, though, a sense of unease, sometimes even of fear. Something big was going on, some monumental change was about to happen, and these strange events were surely portents of it, whatever it might be.

After a moment Dale and Bill walked away from Sandy, got into their trucks and, without a word, drove away.

"Haven't you been out yet this morning?" she asked.

"I went for a hike at sunrise. Oh . . ." It came to him that this had something to do with Pastor Raven and his church. She tried to pull her feet away, but he held them, cupped in his hands on his lap. "It's those religious crazies again, isn't it? What are they up to now?"

"Why don't you go look out your window," she said. "They must be nearly here by now." He stroked her feet, reluctant to let them go, then set them down gently and went back into the kitchen. In a moment he returned.

"I cannot believe it," he said, although he sounded more amused than disbelieving.

"It's not that weird," she said. "Is it?"

"Folly," he said, shaking his head. "I can't imagine what they think it will accomplish."

"To tell the truth," Amy said, "I can't help but think that part of the motive is to get a little attention, even if they don't realize it themselves." He sat down beside her again, closer this time, and took her hand in his.

"The whole thing is a measure of how desperate some people are."

"For what?" she asked, knowing what his answer would be, but wanting to hear him say it.

"For some kind of certainty." She studied him, waiting. Instead of speaking, he leaned toward her and kissed her temple.

"One thing's certain," she said. "Their bedspreads will be filthy after that climb in this heat." He kissed her temple again, sliding one arm behind her and drawing her close to him.

"Another thing that's certain is . . ." he searched for her mouth with his own and kissed her long and softly, "I want you." She pulled back from him.

"Neil, they'll be here any second, not fifty feet from your door. Can't you see us – in here making love and them right outside preaching about hellfire and damnation?" In spite of herself, she had to laugh.

Amy's truck was parked by the door when Neil drove up. He found her sitting at his kitchen table drinking a cup of coffee.

"What are you doing here so early?" he asked.

"I felt like seeing you," she said, "since I didn't make it up last night." She got up, reached for another mug, picked the coffee pot up from the stove. "Where were you?"

He bent to kiss her cheek in an absent-minded way, as if she were his wife, then pulled out a chair and sat down. She poured them both coffee.

"I went down to the café for some stupid reason. I don't know what I did that for. I couldn't stand the talk, so I left." Amy laughed and reached out to touch his cheek with her fingertips.

"Did they talk about our meeting last night?"

"If they did, I didn't hear them. Was it a success?" Not that he cared.

"We formed a Direct Action Committee," she said, serious now. "We devised a plan. I don't know how successful it'll be, but one bunch is going to travel around to the other towns that are losing their post offices and so on and see if we can't act together. Get a delegation to go to Ottawa with a petition. Another bunch is going to our MP to raise hell with him. He didn't even come to our meetings."

"I doubt it'll do much good," Neil said. He had already resigned himself to the twice-weekly drive to Crisis to get his mail.

"People even talked about chaining themselves to the post office steps when they come to tear it down," Amy said, watching Neil's face. Neil couldn't tell if she was joking or not.

"Really?" he asked, but she didn't answer him, appeared to have stopped listening to him.

"I hear you had a visitor last night," she said, looking down into her coffee cup.

"Where did you hear that?" he asked.

"Oh, you know," she said. "Somebody stopped in this morning when I was unloading the kiln." It had been Zena Lavender, not usually seen out so early, she had been surprised. Acting faintly as though she had no other purpose.

"It was my wife," he said. "I mean my ex-wife," he corrected himself. "Faith. She was on her way to Mexico and dropped in to see me."

"She's driving all that way?" Amy asked, surprised.

"I don't know what she wanted," Neil said, studiously casual. He risked a glance at Amy and found her looking intently, speculatively into his face.

"She came all this way out of her way and didn't want anything?"

Exasperated, uncomfortable, he said, "I don't have to tell you everything that goes on in my life. She came to see me, that's all." Amy flushed, but kept her tone level.

"We do mean something to each other, don't we? I mean, if she wants to reconcile with you, I think I have a right to know. We're two adults here, aren't we?" He didn't reply, angry, yet half-admitting she was right. "Your misanthropy is getting the better of you, Neil."

He looked at her then, not out of a desire to protest, but out of a hunger not to lose her, to see her steady, brown-eyed gaze and the calm in the way she held her mouth. "You love me, don't you?" she asked. "I think you do." He couldn't help but smile at her. He pushed back his chair, went around the table to her and grasped her wrist, wanting her to rise.

"Yes," he said, as she stood. He put his arms around her, his nose in her hair, urging her into the living room to the uncomfortable horsehair sofa.

"Say it," she said to him, pulling back her mouth from his. "Say you love me."

"I love you," he said obediently. Still she held her head back from him.

"Say it again." He thought at first she was teasing, but saw that she was not.

"I love you," he said, some tenderness involuntarily entering his voice this time. At this sound she opened her mouth and put it against his. After a moment she pulled back.

"I love you," she whispered into his ear.

He was startled by this, didn't think she had ever said this directly to him before. He found he couldn't remember if she had or not, yet he realized at the same time that he had taken it for granted. Yet now, when at last she said the words aloud to him, he had heard something in her voice that, instead of confirming what he already thought, made him question her sincerity. "I love you," she had said, but did she? Yet here she was in his arms kissing him with a surrender and warm passion that surely left no room for doubt.

And he was kissing her back, running his hands down her lovely long body, his desire for her rising, drowning out his uncertainty.

In the kitchen of their farmhouse eight miles from town, Jessie and Val Sheridan were drinking coffee.

"Somebody's coming," Val said. Jessie set down her cup and listened. A vehicle was approaching; in a moment she saw it to be the twenty-five-year-old white Cadillac belonging to Val's oldest sister, Marion.

"What does she want?" Jessie asked Val in a nervous undertone, as if Marion might be able to hear her out in the yard.

"She's probably here about Alma," Val said with a faint note of irritation. He got up and went to the patio doors which he slid open. Jessie didn't move. Marion was slamming the car door and moving up onto the steps so quickly that Jessie stood hastily, realizing that no matter how much she might wish it, Marion would not simply vanish. Val stood back, letting Marion in. She was a big woman, a couple of inches taller than Val, and Jessie found her altogether terrifying.

"Coffee?" she asked, offering her sweetest smile, as soon as Marion was seated.

"I'll have tea," Marion said, not looking at Jessie. Stifling her anger, Jessie put the kettle on and opened the jar of teabags.

"What brings you out so early?" Val asked.

"It isn't early," Marion said crisply. "You know I always rise early to do the Lord's work before I get to the house and garden." Val nodded, not asking what the Lord's work had been today.

"I suppose you're here to talk about Alma," Val said in a resigned tone which he tried to hide.

"Alma!" Marion said. "Whatever for?" Val looked to Jessie as if he wished he hadn't spoken.

"The letter . . ."

"Oh, that," Marion said, dismissing it with a wave of her hand. "Her usual nonsense. I'll talk to her another time."

"Oh," Val said, stymied.

"It's Mother and Father's anniversary in two weeks. I suppose you've forgotten as usual."

Val shrugged his shoulders, not indicating one way or the other. "Are we going together for a gift?" he asked.

"You know perfectly well that Mother and Dad don't accept gifts any more. We're each supposed to give a gift of money to the church. I've worked it out. We each should give one hundred and twenty-five dollars. Now, don't forget." She did not explain how she had arrived at that particular amount and when she admonished Val not to forget, instead of looking at him she looked sternly at Jessie, as if she intended to hold Jessie responsible for any of Val's failings. And what if we don't have any spare money? Jessie wondered, but declined to say. She turned away and made the tea.

"Have I ever forgotten?" Val asked in a teasing way.

"No, but you would if I didn't remind you every year well in advance." This was the first Jessie had heard of it. But there was so much about Val and his exasperating and unpleasant family that she didn't know, that she felt they kept from her deliberately so as to keep her bewildered and out of step, as if it were their revenge on her for marrying their precious Val. She set the cup and saucer in front of Marion and filled it. Marion pulled it closer. "But that's not why I'm here," she said, in a tone that had a decidedly ominous ring, Jessie thought.

"Oh," Val said, noncommittally so that Jessie knew he was nervous too about what was coming.

"Somebody has to give the anniversary dinner," she said.

"I thought you always do that," Val said. "You're the oldest daughter, after all." Jessie was beginning to feel sorry for him. Marion set the spoon down neatly on the saucer and drew in a deep breath so that she seemed to swell before their very eyes.

"Elizabeth seems to feel," she said, not looking at either of them – Elizabeth was Val's second-oldest sister – "that it's her turn for the anniversary, and when I pointed out to her that it is usually up to the oldest, she . . ." Marion's lips quivered while the end of her formidable nose reddened. Jessie watched with interest. ". . . she said some rather nasty things to me. Inferred that I am a bully." She glanced fiercely from Val to Jessie, daring them to agree with Elizabeth, but there was a suspicious moisture in her pale-blue eyes. "So, naturally, I bowed out gracefully and offered the dinner to her as she said she wanted."

"So, what's the problem?" Val asked weakly.

"The problem is, she refused to do it! First she calls me a bully and then when I demonstrate that I am no such thing, she . . ." Marion swallowed hard and glared at Jessie. Quickly Jessie lowered her eyes to the table. Val said, "No . . . kidding." His sisters often quarrelled and came to him to act as arbiter, but if he dared to offer as much as a word of advice, they indicated to him in no uncertain terms that he didn't know what he was talking about and that he should mind his own business. While Jessie watched, fascinated and appalled, Val seemed to take all this in his stride, and she saw him as their beloved baby brother, someone of no account but whom they could trust with their troubles.

"That's right," Marion said, gaining control of herself. "Would have nothing to do with it. Said she washed her hands of the entire affair. So," she shifted her gaze to Jessie, "after that I would hardly behave like the bully she accused me of being and do it myself, now would I?" Mutely, Jessie shook her head no.

"Of course not," Val said gravely. Was he trying not to laugh? "When did all this happen?"

"Yesterday," Marion said. "Yesterday I drove out to Blanche's to get her opinion." Blanche was third in line.

"What did Blanche say?"

"She agreed with me, of course," Marion said.

"So she's putting the dinner on?" Jessie asked, finally getting up enough courage to speak.

"Blanche? She can't cook to save her soul. Certainly not Blanche – though she offered." There was a bewildered silence during which Val and Jessie stole a glance at each other. "It's time Jessie took her share of family dinners." She lifted her teacup and blew across its surface while Val and Jessie sat in stunned silence.

"Sure," Val said finally.

"For how many people?" Jessie asked, dread accumulating in her throat.

"Twenty-six," Marion said. "Christmas's are worse." Jessie was beginning to feel angry. Hadn't she offered when they first got married and been greeted by an incredulous silence? Hadn't they made it plain to her over and over again that she wasn't a member of the family, and, if they could help it, never would be?

"I couldn't possibly," she said, trying to sound smooth and in control. "I've never in my life cooked for that many and besides I don't cook nearly as well as you." She thought of the exquisitely roasted beef with mashed potatoes that melted in your mouth and gravy so rich and flavourful it made her mouth water to think of it.

"You have to start somewhere," Marion said with finality.

Jessie's anger began to rise. Those goddamn so-and-sos. Her vocabulary when it came to swearing was limited to *damn* and *Jesus Christ* and if she knew any other words they shocked her too much to ever say them. For three years now they wouldn't even let her bring a salad to a family dinner and they ignored her when she was there and now they had the nerve to drop this into her lap. It wasn't even a request, it was an order.

"Well, I'm not sure," she began hotly, then noticed Val's warning look and abruptly lost steam, ". . . if I can manage . . ."

"Of course you can," Marion said. She pushed away the tea, which she hadn't touched, and stood up. "Now that's settled, I've got to be going. I've a church meeting at one and my house is a mess."

When she had gone, piloting like a queen her big white Cadillac out of the yard, Val began to laugh. Jessie glared at him.

"It's not funny," she cried. "I've never cooked a meal for twenty-six people in my life. I can't even imagine how to begin."

"Go talk to some of the other women," Val said. "They're all old hands at it."

"Like who?" she said bitterly. "You can bet nobody in your family will help me." He put out his hand to touch hers, but she pulled away. "They're a bunch of jerks," she said. "I hate them."

"Come on now, Jessie," Val said, trying to put his arms around her. "How hard can it be?" Obliquely he was admitting she was right about his sisters. "Maybe you could ask somebody to help you."

"Nobody around here has any respect for me," she said. "They all think I'm a helpless, brainless city girl. How can I ask anybody to help me?" Val was stroking her hair now, pulling her against him, murmuring to her. She guessed she was grateful he had chosen to ignore what she had said about his family. Still, at moments like this she always thought of packing her suitcase and leaving him to his family. She really did.

"I can't help you cook," he was saying, "but you know I'll stand by you." Whatever that meant. He kissed her temple, but already the pressure of his arms was slackening, and she knew in a second he would have forgotten her, would stand away from her as if he had more serious matters on his mind. This was how it had been since the rally in Swift Current when the news of the unpayable debt had come out. They no longer had a sex life; it seemed that Val had lost his desire or couldn't concentrate on it. She didn't understand it, or rather, in a way she did. He seemed to be denying himself pleasure, she thought, punishing himself because he had failed. It was no use to try to arouse him. At first he would respond, then he would sigh and turn away, forgetting her and leaving her bereft.

"I wish you didn't have to go so soon," Neil said. Amy was retying the ribbon around her hair, then she began to run the water into the sink and to splash cold water onto her face.

"I have to get back to my studio before it starts to look suspicious," she said. He laughed.

"I never figured you for a conventional person."

"I'm not," she said. "Or rather, I am. The best camouflage for a free life is a conventional surface."

"You shouldn't be involved in all this radical organizing then," he said.

"I have to," she replied. "I believe in our right to be here if this is where we want to live. I don't believe our government has the right to sell this place or give it away to business interests, to drive us out by benign neglect at best."

"I admire you for caring enough to act," he said.

She gave him an exasperated look. "You act as if all of this has nothing to do with you. What will you do when there isn't a store left in Ordeal where you can even get a loaf of bread, when everybody's gone but you and a diehard or two?"

"Perfect," he said.

"It might be perfect for you," she said, levelling her steady gaze on him so that he turned away to run himself a glass of water, "but it won't be perfect for me and it will be absolute hell for the people whose families have been here for three generations."

"The whole goddamn world's on the move," he said. "What do they want? People are leaving the land in droves everywhere – have been all this century." He sat down at the table again and Amy sat across from him.

"That's not the point," she said. "What's happening here is just one more facet of what's happening all over the world: land-based people, people who've always been rural and agricultural for the last ten thousand years are being driven off the land and out of that way of life. And the cities keep on swelling and getting more and more uninhabitable – look at Mexico City. Look at Toronto and Vancouver." Neil thought of Faith and winced. "You of all people should be able to see what's happening. Business is going to take over our food supply."

"Business already has," he said. "Business has taken over the souls of the people. When that happens everything is lost. Look around you. The farmers around here got bigger and bigger, they ruined the land with their fancy technology, they drove out and killed off all the wildlife, and now, when they're getting a taste of their own medicine, they start to whine."

Amy stared at him, silenced by his rage.

"Their time is done, it's over," he said. "Let them accept it like everybody else."

"I don't know why you hate people so much," she said. He could have told her why, felt the words rising in his chest ready to come tumbling out, but her stillness and air of weariness silenced him. Unsaid was better. He did not want to lose her over this.

"All they want is to be able to live out their lives in peace, away from the madness of the rest of the world. Is that so bad?" She asked this very quietly, but Neil would not answer her. He turned to stare out the screen door at Mike Harboy's stretch of prairie. It was covered with sagebrush and greasewood, the result of years of overgrazing on such poor quality land. Full of woodticks this time of the year, he thought idly.

Remembering the conversation he had overheard earlier that morning in the café, he thought, Mike Harboy must think God will save him. Well, God didn't save the Jews and He isn't saving the rainforests and He won't save the Saskatchewan farmer either. He thought of the rolling by of history as if it had nothing to do with him, as if he could, by living up in these hills, escape it for all his short, allotted time.

# PART
# TWO

# CHAPTER
# 7

Melody Masuria's parents, devout Roman Catholics, had been praying over her in the normal course of events since before her birth, but especially since she had reached puberty, and now that she was seventeen their fervour had increased. Her mother had even gone to the extent of speaking to the priest from Crisis about her.

It was surprising that Melody hadn't simply quit school and moved in with one of the many boys she was constantly seen with, especially late at night and in compromising situations and places, or that she hadn't at least left home. It may have been that none of the boys were ready to have her move in with them, or that there were absolutely no jobs to be had in Ordeal which would have made her self-supporting. Or perhaps there was in Melody a surprising fear of leaving home that kept her there no matter how much lying she had to do or how many narrow escapes from her father she'd had, at least to the end of her grade twelve year. The rapid approach of this event – it was only a month away – kept her mother up nights wondering what would become of her when they couldn't send her to school any more. Melody would go to the city, Mrs. Masuria knew, and her heart bled at what lay in wait for her daughter: entanglements with useless men who would spoil her sweetness and toss her aside, a fatherless baby, poverty, life as an outcast.

When Melody came home at four in the morning, her makeup gone, her mouth swollen, her hair disarranged and her blouse inside out, Mrs. Masuria wakened Melody's father. She wouldn't have done it, had colluded unwillingly with Melody a thousand times to save her from her father, but it had finally all become too much for her; she no longer had any idea what to do. She had a sense of the future being upon them already and her fear transformed itself into rage.

"You little slut!" she screamed at Melody. "You filthy thing! A child of mine!"

Stalking from his bedroom, not even speaking first, Mr. Masuria struck Melody with his closed fist. He knew about girls like her from when he was a young man, he shouted.

"They think of you as dirt! They don't care for you! They want what you can give, then they laugh! Whole town knows what you are. Don't think you have secrets."

Melody, lying face down on the floor, knew her father was right, had always known it, but had told herself that if there was some truth in that, there were other truths as well: that of all the girls, she alone had with the boys she had sex with a special communion, an intimate knowledge of them denied to other girls. She had too a sense of her own power over them because she alone could give them what they craved. She believed that though they scorned her outwardly, this was part of a private pact they had made with her. They needed her, were in a way her servants, and would go only so far with their contemptuous behaviour as not lose favour with her.

And then there was sex itself, which Melody had discovered early, had quickly learned to like very much, and at which she was, for so young a girl, remarkably skillful. In a culture that set sexual conquest as the ultimate goal in life, where on television screens all over the country night after night, models no prettier than Melody herself, and often younger, strode cheerily, sexily down the street while all the men in sight slavered after them, in those terms – and weren't they the only ones? – Melody had already acquired a measure of success. She did not think the price she paid for it was too high.

Until now, that is. As she lay on the floor, trying to move her jaw, half afraid it was broken, her father struck her with his belt across her back. He struck her again and again while Mrs. Masuria screamed and clung to his arm trying to stop him. When this was to no avail and she was beginning to be afraid that he might kill his own daughter, she threw herself over her daughter's body, taking blows that had been intended for Melody.

Mr. Masuria hadn't meant to do any permanent damage to Melody, only to give her a scare she'd never forget, thinking, in his anger and ignorance, that this would bring her home nights, would turn her chaste again. Or perhaps he never thought any of these things at all, was striking out at her only out of wounded vanity, that his daughter should be the town whore. When his wife threw herself over Melody's body, he lowered his arm slowly, blinking as if he were confused, dropped the belt on the floor, then turned away and went heavily to bed.

Mrs. Masuria got to her knees and shook Melody, wiping her own tears on the lapels of her worn chenille housecoat. Melody, after a moment, raised her head from the floor. She wasn't crying.

While under her father's blows Melody had begun to feel something beyond the pain he was inflicting. "It's all right," she said.

Mrs. Masuria, with some difficulty, since she'd grown heavy over the years and was no longer young, stood. She watched Melody roll stiffly over and, wincing, sit up. "I'm all right, Mom," Melody said, not raising her eyes to her mother. "Go to bed."

Mrs. Masuria stared at her daughter's blouse, torn now under the arms, and at the bruise turning blue along her jaw. She reached out to touch her, but Melody pulled away. "Go to bed," she said again. Mrs. Masuria hesitated, but Melody still refused to look at her or to allow her touch her, and, finally, she gave up and went into the bedroom where Mr. Masuria was already snoring.

When Melody had confronted her father she had been moving in that afterglow brought on by long and satisfying sex; she was all sensation, and the person she was had retreated to a sphere as tiny as a pea buried inside herself. She couldn't hear the words he was saying to her, he seemed no more than a noisy phantom, a dream; she thought herself impervious to him.

But that first hard blow to her jaw had cleared her head and dissipated in a fraction of a second that blurred, sex-induced spell.

"Whore! Whore!" he had shouted as he struck. It was then that a desolation had overcome her, reaching from deep inside her to spread outward even to her toes, the tips of her fingers, her scalp. She had felt the blows as they cut her flesh and the blood as it began to seep. Though the pain was appalling it gradually seemed to her to be a long way off, disconnected from her and the sense of desolation that was more immediate and overwhelming.

After she had sent her mother away she sat for a long time on the cold, vinyl-covered floor, her body throbbing with desperate pain, and let this strange misery – no, it was worse than misery – this despair, overtake her completely.

*Whore! Whore!* His words echoed as if they came from far away, from someone other than her father, a voiceless voice like the wind that rang through the centuries toward her, a voice older than time itself. Listening, she became a wisp of grass in the winter gale, a rocky chasm the wind howled through, a particle of dust floating through the endless blackness of space.

Slowly she came back to herself and to the ticking of the old-fashioned clock that had come with her parents from the old country. Unexpectedly, fear swept through her. In the light of this, she saw that the desire of the boy she had been with, his rough tenderness, meant nothing, that the pleasure they had shared was no more than the tinkling of wind chimes in a hurricane. How wrong she had been to think that sexual power meant anything at all. For a second, her fear escalated to terror.

In the light of this, there was nothing else Melody could do but turn to God.

Melody spent the rest of the night on the chair by her bed, and though her wounds ached and some of the small cuts where her father had drawn blood stung bitterly, she didn't allow herself to dwell on the pain. In the morning she waited till her father had gone to work in the garage in Crisis – he was up by six and gone by six-thirty – before she left her room.

Without speaking to her mother or even looking at her, she bathed, not touching her back, dressed in a white blouse and pale cotton skirt and chaste, white sandals, and walked out of the house for the last time, all the way across town to Pastor Raven's door and, without so much as a second's hesitation, as if this had all been fore-ordained long ago, she knocked.

Alma Sheridan had been comforted by Dear Madeleine's soothing reply to her letter. *"You are not alone,"* she had said, and, *"Return to your doctor."*

Alma didn't want to go back to the doctor, but her sense of justice rebelled at the idea of seeking advice and then refusing to take it. Tonight, the night before her appointment, she had another dream. It came at a time when she was at last beginning to feel a little calmer, had even gone to sleep in a normal way. But even in her sleep she recognized the moment when she began to move from the ordinary world of ordinary dreams into one where everything was so vivid as to seem indisputably real. When she tried to wake up, she couldn't. She was helpless against this vision.

This time she saw a herd of buffalo. They had been skinned alive. Their bodies were the yellowish colour of animal fat; their sides were marbled with blood, vertical cracks ran down them caked with dried blood. They swarmed to and fro in a frenzy like one body and they sought Alma out wherever she ran, their eyes streaming blood. They made no sound, a wind rushed around them and it wailed their terror and their rage in Alma's ears.

Their blood, their frenzy, and their pain were horrible to see, but it seemed to Alma that she could feel every cut, every bullet-wound, every broken bone. She writhed in agony.

Then she was running, gasping for breath, trying to escape them. She ran out of her house, tripping on the skirt of her long white nightgown, her grey-streaked, tangled hair streaming out behind her, screaming, "Help me! Help me!" to the darkened, empty street.

Luckily, it was the doctor who found her. He was driving home from the hospital where Old Man Paslowski, one of the last of the pioneers, had just passed away after telling him the long tale of the past of the town.

Old Man Paslowski talked of coming up from the south on horseback trailing a herd of cattle that had come all the way from New Mexico; of the owners ordering the men to stop moving when they had found this sheltered valley nestled below the grassy plains. These plains that, he claimed, a hundred and more years ago were still untouched by the white man, where the grasses were stirrup-high and you could set down your mower anywhere to cut hay. He'd been accompanied by a pack of other American cowboys, drifters, who'd drifted away again as soon as the herd stopped moving, to be replaced by Canadians coming from Alberta, or from the east, or even from faraway England.

He told again the story of the terrible winter of 1906–07, so terrible that even those who'd never lived it had it engraved on their memories, and that poets wrote verses about it, songwriters songs, and story-tellers were forever embroidering on it, as if it needed embellishment! The loss of cattle had been unbelievable; it had happened at a time when the Indians had been pushed back onto reserves, and the land had been opened to farmers. The greed of the east, of bankers and politicians – Paslowski growled with his next to last breath – had allowed farmers to cut into grazing land all over the southwest. They had ploughed up as much land as they could, destroying the rich but fragile native grasses forever, and, needing a trading centre, had persuaded the CPR to come by the very ranch-yard the owner had established. And thus, Old Man Paslowski said, Ordeal was born and the early promise of the grassland was cut short, destroyed before it had been realized.

Paslowski died cursing farmers with his last breath.

Though he had left behind two dozen grandchildren and a dozen great-grandchildren, not one of them was with him as he died. He would have said it was because they had been scattered to the four corners of the earth by that ancient decision to open land unfit for farming to homesteaders, but they would have said it was because he was a bore and a tyrant and a man who had his eyes firmly fixed on the rearview mirror.

The doctor was nearly asleep at the wheel, anticipating the warm comfort of his bed, when he saw a blurred white figure come wheeling out of the shadows into his headlights. He slammed on the brakes and jumped out of the car. The figure lay in a heap on the street. He approached gingerly, half afraid this was a hallucination caused by sleep deprivation, knelt down, and saw that it was no apparition, but Alma Sheridan, the schoolteacher.

He wanted to take her to the hospital but she begged him not to, and seeing that it was nearly daylight he took her back into her house, administered a tranquillizer, and sat dozing beside her as she babbled incoherently until she fell asleep. He called the hospital, not telling anyone where he had found Alma, but asking the night nurse to stop in on her way home.

"I had to give her a tranquillizer," he explained. "Tiptoe in, take her pulse, make sure she's all right." Then he went home, shaking his head at the foolishness of old maids, wondering if Alma was going to become a long-term problem or not – commitment even, and the relatives requiring endless explanations and reassurances.

Pastor Uriel Raven was not a native of Ordeal, but had come several years earlier, though not even his parishioners knew when or from where. One day a faded and scratched 1974 Ford had appeared parked in the back alley behind the small frame house that had belonged to old Willow Zarka. People noticed the car, but it was so old and dusty that they thought it had simply been abandoned there.

Later, pale curtains appeared in the small windows on either side of the front door. On occasion a tall, red-headed man was seen to come and go, though so seldom that nobody thought to comment on it when it occurred and by the time it occurred again they had almost forgotten the first time, so that gradually the man's presence in the house and the town seemed to the townspeople as right and as inevitable as anybody's else's. One morning when the neighbours rose, the red-haired man was outside scraping the peeling, sun-faded blue paint. After that he painted the house a sparkling white. By then his neighbours were saying hello to him and his twice-weekly visits to the grocery store were noted without comment. Slowly he had, whether deliberately or not, insinuated himself into the life of the town.

To Uriel Raven himself, things appeared quite different. He was unaware in any real flesh-and-blood sense of his neighbours at all or of himself as a stranger to all these people who had spent their lives in Ordeal. His commitment to carrying the Word of God had begun when he was still in his mother's womb; he had never seen the world as others see it but always in the light of God's word as he understood it.

He had been raised on a small farm on the edge of the northern bush, the only child of deeply religious but uneducated parents who had lived their lives adhering to what they believed to be the direct Word which the Bible was. He had never known a time when he did not pray, and doubtless he would have rebelled, as so many other children of religious parents had done before him, if this deep commitment to a religious view of life had not been accompanied by his parents' solemn belief in their son's mission.

Henry Raven, Uriel's father, had himself come from a religious background. He had been raised in Scotland in an enclave of the Plymouth Brethren, a small sect which believed itself, as had others before it, the only people chosen by God to be saved, and of which there were a few communities in western Canada. At twenty-one Henry left Scotland to pursue adventure in Canada. He obtained his father's permission by promising to settle in one of these communities. He had tried to do this, but his youthful restlessness far from his parents' eyes got the better of him. Before long he left the small ranching community where he had intended to settle and travelled north into the bush sawmills where he found work in the snowy and trackless wilderness.

Here a new vision of his life grasped Henry Raven. Coming in at night through the vast, silent forest he would look up between the branches of the trees and see the myriad stars, the pale ghosts that were the northern lights moving with mysterious beauty above him. Something – an awe – was struck in his heart, and the security he had been raised in – that heaven was his and virtually his alone – began to lose its grip on his soul. For the first time he knew fear, the fear that Jesus Christ had not, after all, guaranteed him eternal life in heaven with choirs of angels to sing to him.

He went further and further into the woods in search of trees to fell, or so he would have said if anyone had asked him, and finally the inevitable happened – perhaps it was what he had been seeking. He became lost, and when night fell he found himself alone with no idea which way to go to return to camp. He made himself a small house and bed of spruce boughs and tried to sleep. He knew he would not be looked for before morning.

It was bitterly cold, the woods were full of black bears and other creatures he believed to be unfriendly to humans. He thought of the camp, its rough log buildings, the kitchen and mess hall where the heat radiating from the cookstove at one end and the cast-iron heater at the other would be warming his twenty or so companions. He thought of their talk and laughter and he grew colder and more afraid.

He would have been all right if he had been able to make a fire, but for some reason his matches would light, would start on fire the slivers of dry wood he found, but then both the match and the wood would expire. Finally, he had no matches left.

About three in the morning, when it was darkest out, Henry heard an animal moving around outside his spruce hut. It was a bear, he was sure. It came so close to him that he could smell its dark, beary odour and feel the warmth radiating from its huge black body. This was it. He had come all this way from the land of his birth, from the wide, bearless plains of the south to meet his death here in a frozen wilderness. His remains would never even be found. He wept as the bear brushed against his hut and snow fell from the boughs, and the tears froze to his cheeks. He waited in agony for the claws, the teeth.

Moments passed. He remembered prayer. He prayed aloud. "Yea, though I walk through the valley of the shadow of death . . ."

Nothing happened. Even in the fervour of his prayer he noticed that the noises made by the bear were growing softer, that they had faded away.

In the morning he found his way back to camp by stumbling on a trail not a hundred feet from his bed. His toes were frozen; subsequently he lost three of them, and he was ill with something like pneumonia for two weeks, during which he was repeatedly delirious and saw visions of a dark angel with glittering wings, but he survived. With his survival came a renewed commitment to the God he had left behind when he first saw the canopy of stars in the black sky above the heartless frozen northern forest.

There were no Plymouth Brethren in the north, and no other church suited him, none were fervent enough, his faith burned with an unquenchable fire. Fearful that he would be contaminated by the lukewarm faith of other parishioners and by the weak words of the pastors, he thought of starting his own church but knew he lacked the gifts for organization and for oratory that would attract followers. The only person he could be sure of was the daughter of the pastor of one of the churches he had attended for a while.

He filed on a homestead on the edge of the forest. The land was swampy and stony and would never provide more than a bare living for himself and the pastor's daughter, whom he married, but they went to live on his few acres backed by forest into which he never again ventured more than a half mile.

But he never forgot that he had been saved from a terrible death by the Lord. There was no reason at all why that bear should have turned away from him that night with no more than a sniff at his half-frozen body. He remembered how the moment he had begun to pray the bear had stopped in its tracks and then had simply gone away. The other lumberjacks all agreed that it was very strange to be bothered by a bear in the dead of winter when it should have been in hibernation. But stranger things have happened, they'd shrugged to one another. Hunger pangs can wake even a hibernating bear and send him out to forage. It was not unheard of.

But Henry Raven pondered long and hard over his ordeal. At the time of his testing – that was how he had come to think of it – he had never given the matter a moment's thought. Any large animal snuffling around in the northern forest was almost certain to be a bear. It was not until he had recovered from his illness that he realized that he hadn't actually seen the animal. He had assumed that it was really there, and if it was there it had to have been a bear. But what if there was no bear at all? He had seen no tracks, but it had snowed lightly toward morning. Maybe they'd been covered up. Or maybe they'd been there and he hadn't looked, half-frozen as he was. Whatever, he concluded, God had sent him the bear to remind him of his faith.

It was his dream to have a son who would carry his message of eternal damnation or salvation to unbelievers, a son who would be so eloquent (as Henry wasn't) that he would convert them and bring them back to him. When Martha at last became pregnant he was convinced, and he convinced her, that this would be the child who would start a church here on the edge of the wilderness.

Sure that this child would be God's messenger, he and his wife combed the books of the Bible for a suitable name. At last he came across Uriel, the mysterious fourth archangel whose name means "Fire of God" and who served to bring visions to seers. So, in due course, the child was named Uriel.

Henry told this to little Uriel over and over again and urged him to prayer and to speaking in tongues. Uriel preached to the squirrels and the Canada geese and to deer in the fields. It was said later by the people who knew him that by the time Uriel was ten he could hold spellbound a flock of chickadees or cause a flight of mallards to wheel around, descend, and light at his feet.

Always Uriel was mindful of the charge his father said was his: to grow up pure, filled with the fire of God, to go out and preach, attract a following, and set up a church on the edge of the boreal forest. When he was twelve his mother died. He thought that perhaps this was the time and he would have gone and packed a suitcase, but his father said, "Soon, but not yet." Uriel waited, gathering strength and holy fire for the day when his father would judge him ready and send him out.

When he was twenty and beginning to chafe at being held back so long, Uriel came back to the farm one day after a grocery-buying trip to the town thirty miles to the south to find his father dead. He had died at the breakfast table, and one hand still clutched a piece of cold toast.

Then Uriel knew that this was what his father had been waiting for. He buried him beside his mother on a rise behind the house, facing east, packed his things, and left without looking back. He knew what he had to do. He had been wandering from town to village and back again ever since, preaching where anyone would listen to him, being driven out or starved out or leaving voluntarily because the people were too prosperous and thought they had no need of Uriel's message. But always in each small place he left behind a convert or two who would be waiting to follow him when Uriel was ready. And the year of the Millennium approached, and he decided to meet it in Ordeal, Saskatchewan.

He had denied himself a wife, a family, material goods, a place he could call home. He was waiting for a sign. He had no inkling, though his hope remained strong, that Ordeal would be different than any of the other towns into which he had driven in one old car or another and then out again. But the year of the Millennium had come at last and he extended his hours of prayer, his fasting, and preached to his few converts with redoubled vigour.

As it happened, the Church of the Millennium was to have a meeting on the evening of the day Melody Masuria knocked on Reverend Raven's door. It would be held in the two-room frame building that had been Ordeal's first school eighty or more years before and which had been boarded up until the church had taken it over. Mr. Raven had only twenty converts, but they made up in enthusiasm what they lacked in numbers, and when they got together and sang one of their rousing hymns you could hear it all over town. The volume they achieved put the Anglicans and the United Church members to shame.

Now, however, the windows of the church were kept tightly closed no matter how hot it was outside and the blinds were firmly pulled ever since the night the church members had caught five or six boys crouching in the tall grass under the windows. A worshipper had heard them giggling as she stopped to catch her breath in the middle of "I Just Keep Trusting My Lord."

After they had been chased away by Reverend Raven, who had drawn himself up to his full height and come swooping out of the church in his black gown with his fiery hair flying, the small congregation discovered that the boys had been trying to set fire to their church. The blackened ends of matches lay in the old, dry grass and there were scorch marks on the lowest row of boards. From then on Mr. Raven and his followers acquired a reputation for secrecy which increased the attitude of the townspeople that his church was indeed a very strange one.

When Melody knocked on his door and told her story, Mr. Raven felt that he had no choice but to take her in. He had no wife to object, he didn't question her, he prayed with her and then settled her into his spare bedroom. He would have sponged her wounds and put salve on them but Melody wouldn't let him touch her.

She slept away the afternoon and when evening came he roused her and took her with him the few blocks over to his church, where he instructed her to wait in a small enclosure which he used as his office until he called her in. While the singing began in the other room, Melody combed out her pale blonde hair till it was as flat and smooth as satin, and mentally went over what she would say if she were asked to speak.

When Mr. Raven opened the door and beckoned to her, she walked past him, her head gravely bent, her hands clasped humbly at her waist. As she followed him into the meeting room and stood quietly where he placed her, beside him in front of the others on a small raised platform, she heard stifled gasps as the congregation saw who their new convert was. Immediately two women fell to their knees and cried out, "Praise the Lord!" A flush rose to Melody's pale cheeks.

Mr. Raven prayed over her: "Oh, Lord, accept this woman, a sinner, among us. She comes to you in humility, overcome by shame . . ." Melody's eyes were shining. "She is our sister now," Mr. Raven told his followers.

"Welcome, Sister!" they murmured. Mr. Raven spread his large, freckled hand on the top of Melody's head as if to anoint her. Melody bore this weight silently with her eyes closed. Abruptly, she knelt.

"I was touched by the Lord's hand," she said.

"Praise Him! Praise Him!" the congregation called out and knelt too.

"Blessed Jesus has given us a great gift today," Mr. Raven began. Melody remained kneeling on the wooden platform, her head bent, her hands clasped, and her eyes closed.

"Amen," his parishioners moaned.

"He has, in his wisdom, seen fit to bring another sinner to us, one full of repentance, in a time when the world is full of sin and corruption everywhere rules. Last night Sister Melody saw the light, His light. Sweet Jesus spoke to her and her old sinning ways fell from her. Praise the Lord."

"Praise the Lord," the congregation agreed. Kneeling in front of them, Melody found her hands unclasping as if of their own volition, her arms slowly lifting, and her face turning upward toward the cobwebbed ceiling of the old school.

"I have been saved," she said, with a tinge of surprise in her voice. "I have been born again!" Tears started down her cheeks.

"Amen, Amen!" and "Thank you, Jesus!" rang through the air.

Mr. Raven took Melody's hand and helped her to her feet.

"Tell us your story," he said. "Tell us the wonderful story of how you came to let the Lord into your heart."

Events seemed remarkably clear to Melody and she began at once to speak. "Last night when my father beat me . . ." There were gasps from the people standing and kneeling in front of her as they got a good look at the purple bruise disfiguring her jaw, and then a nervous silence as she began to unbutton her crisp white blouse. "He said to me that you all know what I am – what I was." She had reached the last button. "Last night I realized that he was right. That everyone knows that I have not been . . ." She fumbled for the word, ". . . chaste. That I have had sex with boys and men. . . ." The

Reverend cleared his throat and seemed about to step forward but Melody went on. "That I have been known as a whore and a slut." She said these words with neither hesitation nor clear shame. Her voice was high and strong and the words rang in the ears of her listeners. Then she turned her back, slipped off the blouse, and showed them the blue welts that crisscrossed her back with edges of congealed blood.

At the sight some of the women began to weep with genuine shock and pity and the men flinched in shame.

"Poor child!" a woman cried and rushed to the platform to kiss Melody. Melody spun around, slipping her blouse back on and holding it shut, and stepped back from the woman, her blue eyes blazing with an unholy fire.

"No!" she said and the room grew silent. "This was my punishment for what I have been. I accept the pain. I welcome it." The congregation shifted uneasily, but nobody spoke. Beside her, the pastor's amber eyes had an intensity that would have frightened anyone who noticed it. "I love these wounds, for without them, I would not have found Jesus and my own eternal salvation." She bowed her head, quite overcome by these sentiments, for she didn't know where they had come from.

"Sweet Jesus! Bless Him, praise Him." Everyone knelt and prayed.

# CHAPTER
## 8

When Neil had gone down to the post office in the morning, reminded when he entered it of Amy's conviction that it would soon be closed, a letter postmarked "Mexico" was waiting in his box. When he saw it lying there he wanted to shut the small door and go away, but of course he couldn't do that, not when it was from Faith. He took the letter out, put it into his pocket, got back into his truck, and drove back up the hill to his house.

He took it into the living room and sat down at his desk to open it, as if sitting there might help to stave off the emotion that was welling up inside him at the thought of Faith all alone in far-away Mexico, dying of cancer. He slit open the envelope and scanned it rapidly for the worst news, then read it again more carefully.

Her treatment consisted of a strict diet. She wasn't allowed any of the things she was used to eating. She found this difficult, though she didn't miss meat. Each day she drank a potion the doctor-practitioner prepared, *especially for me, he says.* Neil snorted. *I don't know what's in it,* she went on, *he tells me anything I ask, but I can't seem to remember what he says for more than two minutes.* Stress, he thought, but she'd never admit it. *I'm sleeping well, much better than I was at home, and I feel marvellous. My tumour is shrinking.*

At this Neil dropped the letter onto his desk and put his head in his hands. Of course she would have to think her tumour was shrinking when, in fact, even if the one in her breast didn't appear to be growing, doubtless others were and worse, the cancer cells would be spreading unchecked through her bloodstream. He wondered if he would have to go to Mexico to recover her body, then stopped himself, ashamed. Her handwriting was still steady and firm; miracles did happen. But if she had been there in the room with him he would have taken her by the shoulders and tried to shake some sense into that willful, stubborn head of hers. Was it that she subconsciously wanted to die? He thought about this carefully, then concluded that she did not. No, there was something else here; he would have to think about it, for if he knew what it was that made her behave in a manner contrary to all reason, he could perhaps help her before it was too late.

Fourteen years he'd been married to her, he felt he knew everything there was to know about her. Never was there a more clinging, more dependent woman than the Faith he had married. During the first year of their marriage she had had a breakdown, part of which manifested itself as bleeding ulcers. Neil was convinced this had been brought on by the stress of leaving the safety of her parents' home where she had been raised carefully in a way that seemed to Neil to more properly belong to the Victorian era. A thousand times he'd told himself that he ought to have foreseen this since he'd known that, emotionally, she was a child.

A spasm of something like shame passed through him, for secretly he had to admit that he had loved her childlike ways and her trust in him. It had been good to be so looked up to. His tall, arrogant mother flashed through his mind, and his powerful father. I should have been happy with her forever, he thought bitterly.

But instead he had grown exasperated by the very helplessness that had at first charmed him. He grew contemptuous of her and tired of her always trailing along in his wake. After their marriage had broken up she had had a second breakdown and had spent two months in hospital. When he had tried, in the name of their four-teen shared years, to see her, the psychiatrists had refused to allow it, had even claimed that Faith wouldn't see him.

One year later she appeared at his door, telling him she had cancer and was off to Mexico all by herself to find a quack cure. And why was she writing to him now when she had refused even to talk to him? *Because I know you're worrying about me.* Well, no, he hadn't been, he insisted. It's your life, do whatever you want with it. He folded the letter and put it in the desk drawer.

He was still sitting at his desk, angry now because Faith had once again succeeded in upsetting him so much that he couldn't concentrate on anything, when he heard voices outside his house. He went into the kitchen and through the screen door saw people moving around. He had not put up a fence to define what was his land and what was Mike Harboy's, and he couldn't be sure that the people he saw were trespassing, but the sight of them exacerbated the anger already simmering inside him. He opened the door, let it slam shut behind him, crossed the driveway in front of his truck, and strode out onto the prairie.

"What the hell are you people doing on my land?"

At least twenty people were standing or kneeling in a circle on the barren, dusty ground. They were dressed in long white robes which made him, for one second, falter in his stride. They varied in age from very young – he picked out one faintly familiar-looking blonde teenager with an angelic face – to seven or eight middle-aged women and a few men, probably their husbands, and, of course, Raven, the preacher, with his startling red mane of hair. In a pile to the east of the group, definitely on Harboy's land, lay shovels, spades, crowbars, and pick-axes.

"What's going on here?" he demanded, and several of the women took steps backward. They stood in silence facing him, a light breeze ruffling the women's hair, making their robes ripple gracefully. Neil stared at their garments: they looked to him to be bedsheets and he saw that they were tied at the waist with plastic baler twine in black or orange. He wanted to laugh.

"Mr. Locke," Raven said, stepping forward to stop directly in front of Neil – he was exactly Neil's height and when their eyes met, Neil's hazel ones and the minister's peculiar burning, golden eyes – it was Neil who looked away first. "We are not on your land. Am I not correct, Brother Harboy?" Neil glanced to the group and, too late, saw Mike Harboy getting up from his knees.

"That's right," Mike called. "This is my land."

"We are here to consecrate this plot, to ask Jesus's blessing on our endeavour."

"What is your endeavour?" Neil asked, not bothering to hide his contempt.

Reverend Raven studied him without speaking for a moment. When he did speak, his voice was quiet, all histrionics drained from it.

"We are raising the cross of Jesus of Nazareth here." Neil became aware of the intensity of the heat here on the hillside. Even with the inevitable breeze, sweat was beginning to trickle down his temples and he wished he had grabbed his cap on his way out the door. But the Reverend Raven stood calmly, his red hair catching the sunlight which intensified its colour so that it looked on fire. "And by so doing, we are showing our devotion to Jesus and His Christian Church. We ask His blessing on us, on our homes, our farms, our town, all of which have fallen on such hard times."

"Amen," his followers said quietly, dropping their heads in a meek way that disgusted Neil. Yet a sensation that was almost awe was spreading through him. Truly biblical, he was thinking, yet pagan at the same time. Unwillingly he saw a stony desert hillside under the blazing sun of the Holy Land, olive-skinned people in striped robes entreating their God for deliverance from . . . who? From the Romans.

Shocked, he stepped back a little without realizing he had done so. It frightened him that for an instant he had fallen prey to the visions of others. Far beyond them he noticed an eagle soaring until it receded to a speck.

"We invite you to join us," Reverend Raven said, lifting one hand, palm up. The wind lifted and in the brief lull Neil heard song-birds twittering in the trees far below them. "But if you choose not to, allow us our privacy."

"Privacy!" Neil said, contemptuous again. "The entire town can see you up here." Nevertheless, the preacher said nothing, only gazed at him out of those strange yellow-brown eyes. Neil turned and went back into his house. But instead of closing the inside door, he left it open and sat down at the kitchen table in the cool dimness where he could both watch and hear.

The group of worshippers moved back into the circle again and held hands. The minister stood in the centre of the circle with his arms raised to the sky and his face turned upward. A sudden whirl-wind sprang up and came sweeping across the sparse grass, picking up speed as it came, tearing the grass and lifting it, gathering dust and small stones as it spun.

"Lord . . ." Raven shouted, but the rest of his prayer was lost in the whirlwind as it spun around them, whipping garments, blotting the worshippers from Neil's view, and as suddenly as it had sprung up, was gone. When the dust settled, Neil saw that they were kneel-ing. Raven's prayer was once again audible, but unexpectedly it filled Neil with revulsion so that got up and slammed the door shut.

He was a small boy at church with his father – his mother always refused to go with them – and he smelled again that mixture of dust and wax and the pungent odour of cleaning fluid. His memo-ries of church were always steeped in a sense of coercion. His father was not often violent, but he was not predictable either, and Neil never knew when something he had not even been aware of doing would earn him a blow, while sometimes his father acted as if he hadn't noticed some deliberate provocation on Neil's part. He was required to attend church and to do so with grace, and it was this that filled him with humiliation at his own helplessness, so that even as a child he had known moments of despair.

His family were Protestants, though uncommitted to any particular denomination. Neil was accustomed to his father's habit of attending one church for a few Sundays, Presbyterian perhaps, and then, for no reason that Neil could see, on the next Sunday they would turn in the opposite direction out of their driveway to a church Neil had never been to before. These churches had in common one thing: they were all failing. Neil and his father never went to the big stone cathedral downtown where hundreds of people attended services every Sunday and of which a man of his father's degree of success might be expected to be a member. Neil was grown before he understood why his father always chose small, poor churches with half-empty pews. It was his need for power. In such churches, led by a minister who was a proven failure, he could get even God in his grip and bend Him to his will.

Neil remembered one particular Sunday in one of these shabby, echoing churches. There was no choir and this minister evidently was no singer so that the resulting sound was thin and wavering and embarrassed even Neil. His father's untrained but strong baritone rose well above the other voices. Neil looked up at him and saw above his stiff white collar the way his neck tendons swelled and his face reddened. He realized then that his father was singing this loudly on purpose to show off his voice; he had appointed himself choirmaster. Neil felt himself begin to tremble in full view of his father's monstrous vanity – that he would dare such arrogance in the very place Neil had been told over and over again was the rightful home of humility.

A pale spring morning, the fresh sweet air wafting in through the open windows, in lulls, the chatter of sparrows in the bushes on the church lawn, the soft purr of a passing car, and the quick high voices of privileged children playing out-of-doors. He looked around, was at once jerked back by his father's hand on his shoulder, but not before he had seen the empty pews, the dust, the threadbare carpet, and the pale faces of the congregants. He had a sudden sense of illness, a life-sapping sickness that infected the place. He wanted only to get out of there and never return. After that, he didn't believe anything the minister said, nor his father either, and when he was old enough to act on his own, he gave up religion entirely.

And yet his hatred for his father was always mixed with an unquenchable hunger for his approval. They quarrelled often and violently, but it had taken Neil until he was in his late thirties to at last make a final break with him. Or he hoped it was final. It had been a year since he had last seen him, and many more since he had remembered that day in church when for the first time he saw what his father really was. He got up and went to the table to watch out the window.

It seemed there was no escape from the Ravens of the world and their ever-present, hungry followers. He was just in time to see the entire group filing slowly down the crooked path through the dry grass and the sagebrush to the town below.

He stood for some time seeing the spot across from his driveway where the tools still lay. There was a smoothed spot in the rough, cracked surface of the hillside where the preacher had spoken from. It was not that he did not believe in asking heaven for a sign, but that he preferred the quiet dignity of silent suffering and silent entreaties to public displays whose sincerity he always questioned.

He opened the inner door again in hopes of catching some breeze and went back to his desk in the living room.

He was still reading Butler. He read hungrily, hanging on Butler's every word, evaluating Butler's state of mind and his attitude as he read, searching for words that would reveal to him how the world had been one hundred and thirty years earlier. Perhaps

Butler could tell him whatever it was he hungered to know. He came upon a passage that held his attention:

> If I were asked from what point of view I have looked upon this question, I would answer – From that point which sees a vast country lying, as it were, silently awaiting the approach of the immense wave of human life which rolls unceasingly from Europe to America. Far off as lie the regions of the Saskatchewan from the Atlantic seaboard on which that wave is thrown, remote as are the fertile glades which fringe the eastern slopes of the Rocky Mountains, still that wave of human life is destined to reach those beautiful solitudes, and to convert the wild luxuriance of their now useless vegetation into all the requirements of a civilized existence. And if it be matter for desire that across this immense continent, resting upon the two greatest oceans of the world, a powerful nation should arise with the strength and the manhood which race and climate and tradition would assign to it – a nation which would look with no evil eye upon the old mother land from whence it sprung, a nation which, having no bitter memories to recall, would have no idle prejudices to perpetuate – then surely it is worthy of all toil of hand and brain, on the part of those who to-day rule, that this great link in the chain of such a future nationality should no longer remain undeveloped, a prey to the conflicts of savage races, at once the garden and the wilderness of the Central Continent.

*Undeveloped!* he thought. *Useless vegetation!* No wonder things had turned out the way they had if this was, and he knew it was, an example of the thinking typical of those who came here even before the first wave of settlers. He wondered, not for the first time, how far back one would have to go to find merely awe, merely joy at the sight of the Great Plains, and the true spirit of adventure for its own sake. But the ones who felt this, he realized, would be the ones who would arrive without a well-equipped party to back them up, who would come alone, would travel without set purpose or destination, would leave when they chose to, or would not leave at all. These would be the ones who would leave no record. And what was the connection, he wondered, between these unwritten lives and, two centuries later, the Reverend Raven and his bizarre mission?

Amy Sparrow was just locking up her studio to drive back out to the farm for lunch when she saw a procession inching its way up the hills to the north. Shading her eyes with her hand she stood watching, trying to make out who they were and what they were doing. A couple of dozen people in white garments that shone in the noon sun, half-carrying, half-dragging a large white cross! At first she simply didn't believe what she saw, thought it was an optical illusion that would soon resolve itself into a group of birds flying against the hillside, or somebody pulling a stock trailer.

"Crazy, isn't it?" She dropped her hand, startled. Pat McNamara and Hilda Langlois were standing beside her on the sidewalk staring up at the spectacle on the hillside. "You'd think they'd have something better to do with their time," Pat said. She turned away, looking down the sidewalk toward the café, where apparently she and Hilda had been going. A group of men, the coffee-row crowd, were standing on the sidewalk in front of it peering up the hill.

"What's going on?" Amy asked. Margaret Dubbing came around the corner, her string shopping bag bulging with groceries. She paused and peered up the hill.

"It's that crazy preacher again," she said. "They dragged that darn fool cross all the way from Raven's backyard. I hear it's fifty feet high." Amy was astonished: they must have dragged it a good half mile before they'd reached the bottom of the hill. "You'd think they'd use a tractor."

"It must be incredibly heavy," Amy said.

"I think it'd be hollow, dear," Elsa Friesen, who had crossed the street to get a better view, said. "I asked Alvin and he says he figures if a person was going to build something like that, he wouldn't use timber because it'd be too heavy. More likely it's made out of two-by-fours nailed together."

John Beim, well past eighty, who still made his slow way down to the café for a cup of hot water each morning, paused beside them.

"Two-by-fours're just as heavy," he corrected them. "They been at it since early this morning, should make her by one or two. Have her stuck in the ground by five." He laughed in his quavery old voice. "That'll be the hard part," he said. He shuffled on down the sidewalk, shaking his head in amusement. More people were gathering.

"Well, I think it's a disgrace!" Pat McNamara said, diamonds in wedding rings garnered from three husbands (diphtheria, an aneurysm, cancer) glinting as she shaded her eyes. "What will people think of this town if we have that ridiculous cross standing up there?"

"Maybe it's illegal?" Mrs. Dubbing suggested in a hopeful tone.

"They'll think we're all Catholics," a male voice said. "They'll think this is a French town."

"At least they'll know it's a God-fearing one," Mrs. Langlois said, indignant at the slur at both Catholics and French Canadians.

"A town of fools!" someone in the crowd muttered angrily.

"If you don't like it," a strong voice suggested, "tell the mayor and council."

"Private land," a man pronounced sententiously. "Private land."

In the midst of the muttering, arguments, and exclamations Amy overheard Mrs. Langlois whisper something about a meeting to Mrs. Dubbing. She was curious, wondering what the widows were talking about, but Neil was on her mind, seeing how close the procession was to his house. She began to work her way to the back of the crowd. She wanted to talk to him, but with the whole town staring up at the hill beside his house, she hesitated. It irritated her that she couldn't shake herself of caring that she, Lionel Sparrow's widow, and Neil might become a topic of conversation in the kitchens of the town and in the café and the bar. It was silly, egotistical even, but she couldn't shake her uneasiness.

Safely around the corner, she paused, thinking. She'd leave her truck parked where it was in front of her studio and walk through the deep coulee that wound its way up the hillside west of Neil's house. Where it grew shallow a few feet behind his shed, she'd simply climb up its steep side and go into his house without being seen by the people below. Pleased with herself for thinking of this, she walked quickly down the street toward the park below his house where the coulee began.

Behind her, Margaret Dubbing, Pat McNamara, and Hilda Langlois had also edged their way out of the crowd and were strolling quietly toward the café a little further down the street. If anyone had been watching they would have seen them chatting pleasantly, probably about recipes for the new dessert everybody was making called "sex-in-a-pan," or the best buy on wools for the crocheting of afghans.

"I'll report to Zena," Margaret was saying.

"She probably already knows everything there is to know," Pat said.

"Still, we have to discuss this," Hilda said. "We can't just let it pass. It's bound to disturb the balance."

"Drat it," Margaret said. "As if we didn't have troubles enough without this nonsense." They had reached the café where they paused for a moment, then Hilda and Pat went inside and Margaret strolled away in the general direction of Zena Lavender's house.

Neil was dozing on the sofa when he heard someone knocking at his kitchen door. The sound came faintly through his dream of vast prairie silences and emptiness, and as he came slowly awake, he thought of Faith and then of the people who had come yesterday disturbing his peace with their bizarre ritual on his hillside. He got quickly to his feet and went into the kitchen. Amy was leaning against the screen. He hurried to the door and flipped the hook out of its eye.

"Sorry," he said, as she stepped in. "I thought maybe . . ."

"That Mr. Raven and his crew would be around again," she said, laughing and plopping into a chair without waiting for an invitation. "Am I glad you're home!"

"What happened to you?" he asked, alarmed, seeing that sweat was running down her face, mingling with dust so that she had black trickles on her cheeks. Seeds, burrs, and grass leaves and stems were clinging to her slacks and to her blouse, and as she kicked off her sandals he saw that her feet were covered with prairie dust.

"Have you some tweezers?" she asked. "I walked into a cactus and I've still got a few needles sticking into my toes." Puzzled, he opened a drawer and brought out a set of small pliers.

"Pliers!" she said in mock alarm, drawing back. "I don't think this calls for pliers!" Laughing, he said, "They're all I have," and knelt at her feet, lifting one. "We'll have to go into the other room. The light's too poor in here." She followed him, hobbling to the couch where she sat on one end and he at the other, lifting her feet into his lap. Long narrow feet, brown from a month of sandal-wearing, elegant feet for a farm girl.

"You didn't roll your truck, did you?" he asked.

"I wasn't even driving. Ouch!"

"Sorry," he said. "One more to go."

"It was dumb," she said, embarrassed. "I wanted to come up and see you, but the whole town was staring up this way, so I decided to walk. I circled around and came up . . ."

"The coulee," he said. "For someone who's spent almost her whole life here, you sure don't know much about the landscape."

"I do so," she said, indignant. "I took it for granted there'd be a cowpath up the middle – there always is – but this time there wasn't. Nothing but animal droppings and a kind of wild animal trail."

"Why is the whole town staring up this way?" he asked. "Or is that a metaphor?" She looked away.

"Sounds good to me," he said, pulling her close again. But she resisted.

"Has it ever occurred to you," she asked him, "that we don't do much except make love? We don't go anywhere together. We don't even talk."

"You're the one who doesn't want to go anywhere," he pointed out, "and anyway, this is the most profound dialogue of all. The language of sensation. That's what we speak and it transcends all the barriers set up by words."

"Nice talk," she said, "but you know it can't express ideas. What about the language of the mind?"

"I've given up trying to talk to people," he said. "Only you, and in this language." He was sliding his hand up her inner thigh. She pulled away.

"I hate the sound of that."

"Why?" he asked, surprised.

"That you don't want to talk to me. Lionel and I had a wonderful marriage and we talked all the time. It was what, eventually, I missed the most after he died. I'd grown to need that . . . talk." Seeing her sadness, he took his hand away. "Did you and Faith talk?" she asked. He had never spoken about Faith to her, didn't want to, hated any effort to bring back the time when she had been his wife. Surprising himself, he said, "Not much. Less and less the longer we were married."

"Why not?"

"She had no ideas of her own. She used mine and called them her own. She was afraid to strike out on her own intellectually, or maybe she didn't know how. She had a very sheltered upbringing, she was afraid of everything." He turned to Amy. "That's what I like about you. You're not afraid to look life straight in the eye."

"And you spit in it," she said, then, "I didn't mean that. I'm sorry, Neil."

Stung, he would have laughed with that bitter ring to it he knew she hated most about him, but there was a commotion seeming to come from just outside his door so that both of them rose and went into the kitchen, although he noticed Amy kept well back from the door. He glanced at her, and she said, with a touch of embarrassment, "I'd just as soon not have it common knowledge that I was up here in the middle of the day." He grinned.

"Better the middle of the night?" but she didn't answer him.

Outside, the members of the Church of the Millennium had reached their destination. The long wooden cross lay flat on the hillside beside the flattened spot where they had held their consecration ceremony the day before. He was surprised by its size. Beside it, the church members knelt in prayer and as Neil studied them, he saw the film of dust on their robes and the sweat trickling off the ends of their noses and their temples. They looked exhausted, even Raven, whose normally fair skin was flushed so deep a red that his freckles had vanished.

"What stupidity," he said. Amy didn't reply. They went back into the living room and sat back down on the prickly couch.

"I don't think any of us really believe in the goodness of others," she said. "I mean, if we see somebody doing something good, we usually suspect them right away. We think up all the motives they might have for doing good that have nothing to do with simple compassion or simple faith."

"I'm surprised at you," he said. "I would have thought if anybody believed in the essential goodness of people, it would be you."

"I do," Amy responded. "I think I do." They could hear the ring of iron striking stone on the prairie outside his door.

"They must be planning to dig it into the ground," he remarked. "But Amy," he returned to her. "What they're doing hasn't anything to do with good. It's just an heroic act. All it's really doing is saying to God, "See how good we are? See how we're willing to suffer for You? But it isn't doing anybody any good. It's self-indulgence."

"Yes it is doing good," Amy said, and he was surprised by her vehemence. "That was a hard thing to do, to carry that heavy cross up that hill in this heat, and if each individual really believes he's doing it for his God, then it's doing some good. It's a purification."

"Words," he said. She was indignant.

"In a way, I even agree with them," she said. She looked at him, apparently checking to see if he'd argue with her. When he didn't speak, she went on.

"When they get it up . . ."

"*If* they get it up."

"Yes, *if* they get it up, then it will act as a reminder to every one of us down there in the town that Ordeal is a Christian town. That it means something to be a Christian."

"Let's see," Neil said. "It means slaughter of aboriginal people. It means murder of their gods, destruction of their way of life. It means the Inquisition. It means Salem. It means . . ." She was silent, saddened by the truth of his words. Outside more than one tool was at work. They heard the *thud, ring, thud, ring,* repeating itself rhythmically.

"There are good people," she said quietly. Then, "Let's go watch. We're missing an historic moment here."

Although he didn't want to, he stood when she did and went back with her to the kitchen. She watched from a distance rather than stand closer where she might be seen.

"Who's that pretty blonde girl?" Neil asked, leaning against the door frame and staring at the semi-circle of women who stood watching on the far side of the men digging the hole. Amy came and stood next to him, leaning against him, peering over his shoulder.

"Melody Masuria!" She was astonished.

"Isn't that a bruise on her face?" Neil asked. Amy looked more closely. He could feel her warm breath on his ear.

"Yes," she said. "It's probably that brute of a father who did it, although you never know, considering the life she leads."

"What life?" he asked.

"Angelic, isn't she," Amy said. "I can't imagine what she's doing here."

"What do you mean, the life she leads?" he asked again.

"You haven't heard?"

"Here we go again," Neil said, amused. "Another life history that's supposed to be a secret, but that absolutely everybody knows – except me."

"She's the town – I can't say it. She's the girl who sleeps with all the guys." She turned away. "I can't understand how something like that happens to a child. She discovered that being willing to have sex with men gives her a kind of power over them, I guess. And if the boys want . . ." She hesitated.

". . . to get laid," he supplied, soberly.

"They go find Melody. And then they call her a slut and a whore, and talk about her as if she were no better than an animal. As if it all had nothing to do with them."

"That's only the way things have always been," he said gently.

"I can't imagine what she's doing with that bunch," Amy said, frowning. Neil went back to the door.

"It's a source of constant amazement to me how everybody knows everybody else's secrets in a place like this, and yet everybody goes around pretending they don't. I suppose life would be unbearable if they didn't pretend not to know, and not to know that the other person knows." Amy laughed at this and he was relieved to hear it, felt a rush of love for her and was about to try to persuade her back to the couch when he felt her hand on his arm, her face against his neck. He held himself still as she leaned against him with the length of her body.

"I wish I could explain to you," she said. She brushed her face across his neck, then sighed and spoke into his ear. "You look out the door or down to the town and you see a landscape. So do I, but I see a different one than you do. I think of it as the spiritual landscape, that's what I see. It's what everyone who has made her home here sees. And even though it's invisible, it's the real one." He was careful not to move for fear of chasing her away from him.

"Describe it for me," he said softly.

"It's the cloud of beliefs and hopes and responses that we don't understand in others, but that they all have, every single one of them. Every one of us wants to know what's going to happen to us when we die. Even if we don't talk about it, or think we don't even think about it, it's still the biggest thing in our lives. And I see that, but on a simpler level, the spiritual landscape is the invisible network out in the whole community of the things we know about each other after a lifetime of living together. Our marriage ties, blood relationships, unrecorded incidents and situations. Each one of us is carrying a whole lifetime of experiences with her everywhere we go and they are mostly invisible, but every one of us can see them when we see another person. We see a whole landscape that you can't see at all. And so you don't understand." She added this last softly. "Our lives are continuously impinging on each other's lives. We aren't a bunch of separate people," she said. "We're a community."

Neil didn't speak. After a moment he turned to her, putting his arms around her. She was so gentle, his Amy, so clean, so purely herself, beyond dissembling. He was so touched by her, Amy Sparrow, and uneasy with the weight of his own anger, his own uneasiness with all the things she didn't know about him and wouldn't like if she did. He knew, though he didn't know why he dreaded it, that he would have to talk to her about Faith.

# CHAPTER
## 9

June turned slowly into July, another July of the long drought, and the town and surrounding countryside fell into lethargy induced by the heat and by the dreamlike paleness of the landscape. This is how it is in the height of every summer: the fields green with new crops, fading upward into the muted purple of the Cypress Hills, the unpaved roads over the blue hills standing out like dusty veins, and the walls of the distant coulees with their outcroppings of white clay lifting in the heat mirages so that they can be seen above the level of the cropland, where they aren't really, and the sky retreating higher and higher.

In the summer no one saw the sun. It was not possible to look at it, it was so huge and hot, and though its colour remained pale – creamy, tending toward white – its heat was so intense it would burn the eyes out of your face if you dared to look at it. And behind every vehicle a lengthy cloud of fine pale dust rose that hung in the air long after it had passed. Even cows lumbering slowly to their nearly dry waterholes sent up puffs of dust with their hooves, despite the fact that it was prairie they walked across. And, as always, the grass dried, turned the colour of porridge, cured, broke off, and crumbled under tires, feet, or the hooves of livestock.

Then the dust storms started. You could see them coming – a blackness to the sky, usually in the west, that might be rain or wind, the old-timers arguing, "Looks like rain," "No rain in that cloud, only wind," housewives quickly shutting doors and windows, children playing in the park running for home.

Sometimes it took only ten minutes once the cloud was spotted on the horizon until it reached the town. Then the sky turned brown, the air thickened, grew dense, the blowing dirt – topsoil from hundreds of miles away – blotted out the hills, then the edges of the town, then the other side of the street, and tumble-weeds scudded by and caught in fences and the grilles of cars and there wasn't a soul to be seen on the streets, not even a dog.

When Bill Peat rose at his customary five-thirty, he was not surprised to find the view from his front window obscured by blowing dust. The wind had been howling around his house all night, keeping him awake, knowing as he did that he had been asking for trouble when he had gone over his half-section of cropland again with his cultivator and harrows a few days before. He grunted when he saw the grey air, leaning forward, elbows stiffened, his thick hands clenched into fists resting on the windowsill. She was blowing hard enough to blow the crop right out of the ground, he thought. But he put on his torn, threadbare jacket anyway, stuck his John Deere cap onto his head, jamming it down a little harder than usual, and went outside into the gale, intending to make his usual trip to the café in time to be served the first cup of coffee at six o'clock.

He got into his half-ton, started it, backed it out of his yard, and started the three-block trip to the café, going slowly, peering out the windshield, trying to see by studying the surrounding hills and sky if there was any sign of this blowing over in the near future. Beyond maybe fifty feet down the street or to either side he could make out nothing. Sheets of dust-filled air swept by, shaking the truck. The occasional whirlwind in the midst of the general blow picked up bits of paper and pop cans and made whirling dervishes of them until they disappeared around a corner or spun slowly higher into the stratosphere.

Suddenly Bill thought he saw something in the grey a few feet
ahead of him. He slammed on the brakes, thinking they'd never
stop kidding him on coffee row if he rear-ended another vehicle at
six in the morning on an otherwise empty street. But whatever he
thought he had seen had disappeared. He gave his truck a little gas
and moved gingerly forward. There it was again, a darker grey blur,
no, two blurs, one bigger than the other. A little more gas and he
drew up slowly on the moving mass.

It was a cow. She was moving so slowly that he had to brake, he
came up on her so fast, and a small boy was walking beside her dressed
in patched denim overalls, and, of all things in this day and age, he
was barefoot. Disconcerted, Bill stopped the truck right where she was
and got out, slamming the door so that the boy turned his head to see
what the noise was about. He began walking backward, staring up at
Bill. Bill, holding his hat on with one hand, caught up with him.

It seemed as though when he caught up with boy and the thin,
tired cow, the wind lifted a little, or he found himself in a quiet
pocket, like the eye of a tornado where they say there is perfect
silence and peace, and though all around them the town was blotted
out completely by the dust storm, he and the apparition he had
come upon walked in perfect silence and stillness.

Then he got a look at things. It was a wagon being pulled by a
pair of worn-out old horses, thin and drooping like the cow, which
was tied to the back of the wagon, and even like the man and woman
who sat on the wagon seat, the man holding the lines slack in his
hands, the woman not saying anything, just staring straight ahead.

"Hey," Bill said tentatively and stopped for a second, letting go
of his hat.

"Mom, Dad," the boy said. Bill went ahead a few paces and
peered into the wagon-box behind the adults where he saw three
more children sat in places they had arranged for themselves in the
wagonload of household furniture. He made out a butter churn, a
couple of chairs turned upside-down, their legs pointing helplessly

skyward, an old metal cream can. The man turned his head, and seeing Bill, smiled with a hint of held-back suspicion almost as if he'd rather not. His lips were cracked and dry-looking.

"Morning," Bill said politely, touching his cap. "I see you're travelling."

"That's right," the man said evenly, and Bill saw how thin he was and how thin his wife was too, seated beside him so early in the morning, swaying a little with the movement of the wagon, barely bothering to glance at him. He could feel the kids' eyes on him.

"Nasty morning," Bill said.

"So it is," the man said, nodding gravely. "So it is."

Bill considered, but couldn't resist, since the man plainly would volunteer nothing. "You come far?" he asked, hurrying a little to keep up with the pace of the horses, slow as it was.

"Quite a way," the man said, considering first before he replied.

"From the south?" Bill asked, a stab in the dark.

"South," the man said, though the word didn't quite sound like an answer to Bill's question. The man's wife made a sidelong glance at Bill and he was startled at the blueness of her eyes in her lined, dust-greyed face. She had such an old-fashioned look about her that he was reminded of his mother who had died the winter of '83. It seemed the horses were going a little faster now, or the storm was closing in again. Bill stepped up his pace. The boy walking barefoot beside the cow had caught up to him, was abreast of him.

"Where are you heading for?" Bill asked, hearing the anxiety in his own voice that they might get away on him without his finding out.

"Peace River country," the man called back to Bill, who had lost so much ground that the boy was a few paces ahead of him and the cow's bony rear was on his left.

"Where there's lots of water and the grass is green," the boy said to Bill, over his shoulder, and before Bill could say another word, he had dissolved into the blowing dust, or that was how it seemed. The last thing Bill saw of them as the storm closed in again was the undulating hips of the cow as she ground her slow way into the storm.

He stopped, seeing no way of catching up with them. They were, all of them, completely vanished now in the dust and the wind and he grabbed at his cap as a fresh and fiercer gust threatened to lift it off his head and to take him up with it. Leaning into it, fighting it, barely able to make any forward movement against it, he struggled his way back to his truck, wrestled with the door, got it open, and got in.

He thought he might follow the family a little way to see where they were going, but when he started the truck and edged forward again, having reached the corner by the Co-op where he turned right to go down to the café, the wind let up a little and allowed him a dusty but relatively clear view to the edge of town. The street was empty. There was only Sandy McDonnell's pickup in front of the café, which meant Sandy had beat him to morning coffee and he wasn't going to hear the last of that, either.

So what had happened to the homesteaders? Homesteaders? Well, yes, no other word would do, homesteaders they must be, though the Homestead Act had been closed, as far as Bill knew, since the early fifties. Though, it occurred to him, it might still be open in the Peace River district.

The Peace River district; six, seven hundred miles northwest of Ordeal. That crew didn't look like it had the strength to make it another five miles. Then his head cleared and he realized that they had probably gone straight ahead down to the campground at the riverside to wait out the storm and where they could water the stock. He'd just take a little spin down that way after his coffee. Maybe in an hour or two, see how they were making out. That trek to the to the Peace was no joke. In the Dirty Thirties, he'd heard, people'd thought the Peace was paradise. It reminded him of a family he'd heard of once somewhere, who said they took five years to get there. Horses, wagon, no money, nothing but what they carried. He shook his head. What a country. Wasn't an immigrant around he knew who hadn't wished at some time or another he'd had the sense God gave him and just stayed put in the Old Country.

When Bill told Sandy McDonnell of his encounter, Sandy wanted to scoff, but there were only the two of them in the café this early in the morning and he hadn't forgotten his own experience with the phantom cowboy.

"Just now, you say?" he said. Bill nodded. "Homesteaders, eh," he said, not asking. "What's this town coming to?" He was silent for a long time. "Ghosts, more likely." Bill let out a long breath, glad it was Sandy who had said it and not him.

"Like they're taking over," he whispered. "Like when people move out, the ghosts move in."

"Maybe they been here all along and we just started to see them," Sandy suggested.

"Next we'll be running into war parties of Blackfeet on our way to morning coffee," Bill said, and Sandy shuddered.

"Or a herd of buffalo stampeding down Main Street."

"What's this business about Alma Sheridan seeing buffalo?" Bill asked. Sandy shrugged.

"I just heard she's seeing things – things that scare her half out of her mind," he said. Sandy and Bill looked at each other, fingers motionless around their coffee cups.

"There's talk of committing her," Bill said into the abrupt silence. They stared at each other, something like fear in their eyes. Behind them the café door swung open, letting in a blast of hot air, and Phil and Howard Mountain came in and straddled stools side by side.

"Better not say anything," Sandy said softly to Bill, and Bill dropped his eyes as the Mountain brothers said in unison, "Morning."

"You have to realize," Amy said to Jessie, grinning, "that they expect you to fail. They want you to fail. If you succeed in putting on a dinner as perfect as Marion's would be, they'd be mad, but if you screw up even just a little, you'll make a teeny-tiny place for yourself in their hearts."

"I never thought I'd hear anybody say that," she said. "And anyway, what I can't figure out is *why* they want me to fail." Amy set down the bamboo tool with which she had been drawing designs in the clay dust and went to sit in the chair opposite Jessie.

"Because you're one of the hated and envied city people. City people have lorded it over us country hicks as far back as anybody can remember. Gosh, Jessie, don't tell me you don't know that. Don't you watch TV? Can you think of one TV program where rural people even figure? And whenever they do appear they're portrayed as total idiots, or else in some kind of stupid, sentimental way." She crossed her legs angrily, then uncrossed them and smiled again. "Sorry, Jessie, but you have to pay the price for being raised in the city. If I were you, I'd burn the carrots."

Jessie considered.

"I'll be lucky if that's the least I do," she said. She sounded so miserable that Amy started to laugh, but seeing that Jessie looked near tears, she sobered, grew thoughtful, and spoke in a gentle voice.

"It's not easy, trying to fit in."

"It's impossible," Jessie said. "Val's family hates me and I don't really have any friends." She fiddled with her skirt, her diamond sending off sparks when it caught the light streaming in through the big window. "I don't know how to talk to people," her tone more plaintive than she had wanted it to be. "I can't seem to hit the right notes. And half the time I don't know what they're talking about." She frowned and fell silent.

"You mean all that farming stuff?" Amy asked. Jessie nodded. "That's nothing," Amy assured her. "You'll learn all that in time. All that shorthand people talk will start to make sense. Before you know it, you'll be using it yourself."

"To tell you the honest truth," Jessie said, lifting her head and meeting Amy's eyes, "I'm not really sure I want it all to make sense.

Because as soon as it does, I'll be one of you, won't I?" Amy drew back a little, her expression losing its humour, and Jessie wanted to amend what she had said, but there it was hanging between them, unretractable, and some stubborn, sorry part of her would not have taken it back if she could have. Amy reflected, remembering her time in the city and her return to the farm.

"I guess I can see that," she said slowly. "Going from an urban life to a traditional rural one is a little like being an immigrant or like marrying an Arab or an Indian. It's a whole different culture."

"But you're not like the others," Jessie said, watching Amy. "I thought you were born and raised here."

"I was," Amy said. She turned her body so she was looking out the window to Ordeal's deserted, windy main street. The sun had struck away all the shadows and the false-fronted wooden buildings had an unreal air about them, they were so vivid and precise. Jessie watched her, waiting.

"I wasn't brought up the same way as everybody else. My father was what people call a disappointed man. He came from the east, he had had a good education, and I don't know why he came out here. It was a family secret. Something ugly, no doubt." She laughed, still not looking at Jessie, her voice distant. "He married a woman from here – Mom was one of the Thorntons, the rest of them are gone now – but he always kept to himself, didn't like Mom going out much, and he tried to raise me according to some idea he must have gotten back east, from his own generation, or maybe even from the one before it." She swung her chair around and was looking now at her shelves where bowls and mugs and pots stood in various stages of completion. "I had to read to him every night from the time I learned to read. He picked out the books: Dickens, Jane Austen, the Brontë sisters, you can guess the rest. He didn't have the money to send me away to a good girls' school, but he was determined I'd grow up to be what he called a 'civilized' woman." She paused, brushed some clay dust from her knees. "So, of course, he made me different. I tried my best to erase the differences, but I guess some of

140

them are ineradicable. I'm not even aware of them." Jessie was about to speak, but Amy went on.

"Of course, I went to college. I have a Fine Arts degree. Dad wouldn't hear of me taking nursing or learning to be a teacher like everybody else around here. Anyway, not many of the women from the farms who are my age have college degrees. I could name them on the fingers of one hand. That separates me, too." Jessie was moved by the sadness in Amy's eyes. She said, "It sounds like you had an interesting upbringing."

"God, no," Amy said, finally looking at her. "It was deadly dull. I wasn't allowed to do most of the things the other kids did. And when I went away to college I nearly died of homesickness." Jessie thought of all the farm kids she'd met at college who'd never come back for their second year. "Until I met Lionel, of course. My husband." Knowing Lionel was dead, Jessie said nothing.

"He was a city boy. But he'd always had this dream of being a farmer. I tried to tell him he was crazy, but he said no, city people are the crazy ones. We got married and came back here and he and Dad hit it off. Dad was a terrible farmer, he didn't even *like* farming much, but he taught Lionel what he knew and then retired and Lionel just did the best he could. Dad left him with a terrible weed problem, so Lionel got interested in organic farming because we couldn't afford crop spray. We were always broke, but somehow it didn't seem to matter. And then he died."

"I'm sorry," Jessie said, helplessly.

"Long time ago," Amy said. "What kind of a childhood did you have?

"I'm an only child too," she said. "Val says you can tell it a mile off." She shrugged, blushing a little. "I guess I was spoiled. But my life was ordinary. Dad's a civil servant in Regina and that's where I was born and raised. I never left home till I went to Saskatoon to university, and that's where I met Val."

"We have something in common," Amy said, and she smiled at Jessie in such a frank, open way, as if she were genuinely glad to discover Jessie was like her in any way, that Jessie was for a second con- fused – she no longer expected anything much from the people around Ordeal – and then was disarmed. To have Amy for a friend! What an unexpected joy! Every once in a while Jessie's bitter loneli- ness came home to her. She would catch glimpses of her former life: her girlfriends at college, so that she never even had to walk across the campus alone, the phone always ringing for her, so that her father had grimaced and installed her own phone in her bedroom, the steady round of things to do that she enjoyed – shopping, sitting in the campus bar or the cafeteria, studying together, going to parties or dances or to listen to speakers, having supper with girlfriends in their apartments, or lying on the grass in the park at a free concert.

And now, though she had Val to herself nearly all the time, she had no one else, not even her relatives to complain about. She was no longer the centre of anybody's life, not even of her beloved Val's, because here he was pulled by his large, devoted, squabbling family and by the constant needs of the farm. Somewhere, when she had first come, at a party for her given by strangers she had expected soon to get to know better but never had, an older woman, one who was faceless to her now, had said, "What you'll find out is that the farm comes first. First it's the farm, then it's family, then it's a good hired man if you can find one, then it's a good cattle dog, then you. You'll find you come last."

Jessie had thought she was joking and had laughed.

But it wasn't even so much that she had left her family and all her girlfriends behind as it was a sense of being held apart from everyone; that sense she had of everyone watching her warily, as if she might leap up at any second and take their jugular veins in her teeth. Or being mean in that way only women seem to be, whenever they got the chance. It was as if they searched for differences and magnified them in their minds and also – yes, it was true – they got some kind of cruel pleasure out of excluding her, as if it made them feel stronger or something.

Tears suddenly poured from her eyes. "You can't know how awful it's been," she said. She fumbled in her purse for a tissue, trying to suppress her sobs but finding it impossible. She longed for her mother's arms, for the unquestioning comfort they offered her, but Amy's arms were around her, she was murmuring soothing phrases to her and patting her, so that Jessie was reminded of the fifteen or so years difference in their ages. "And now," she sobbed, "it looks like we might lose the farm."

"What?" Amy said, drawing back. Jessie lifted her face to Amy's.

"It's true," she said, drawing in deep shaky breaths and mopping her eyes. "We're in trouble too. Things are really bad."

"My God," Amy said, and turned away with a grim expression to stare out the window. "You too." She sighed. "I saw you at the rally, but I never really thought . . ."

"Please don't tell anybody," Jessie begged. "Val would kill me if he knew I'd told you."

"Never," Amy said. "You can trust me. Anyway, Jessie," she said, her voice gone gentle again, "you have to realize that there aren't any secrets around here. If people don't know for sure, they can make a pretty good guess just by doing a windshield survey. I wasn't paying attention, or I'd have known."

"A what?" Jessie asked. "Don't you go using language I can't understand, so that I feel like a moron."

"Sorry," Amy said. "I didn't mean to. You can drive past some-body's place and see what kind of crop he's got, make an accurate guess about how many bushels to the acre and multiply that by how many acres he's got, and figure out what his income must be. You can see his machinery, his cows — you can guess how soon he'll be broke." In spite of herself, Jessie grinned. Amy shrugged, smiling ruefully. "So you see, people are probably expecting bad news from the Sheridans. You built a new house, too." Jessie lowered her head, embarrassed. After a moment Amy said, "I'm really sorry, Jessie. I can see you're under a lot of pressure. I want you to know you can always talk to me." Jessie wiped her eyes again, feeling a fresh flow of tears starting.

"Sometimes I think I can't stand any more," she said, "but then I always do, because I can't even think about going back home. It would be too humiliating. And I do love Val." She turned her hands palms up on her lap, her eyes on Amy's. "I'm stuck."

"Women usually are," Amy said, her tone distant again. "They raise us up well, train us to keep our places. Teach us to feel responsible for our men's mistakes."

Jessie studied her, surprised. Assessing what Amy had said she felt the truth of it and a little surge of anger started up, at Val, at everything she had been through the last few years, at the stupidity of it. She suppressed her anger at once. How would she survive if she let her anger out? For a long time neither of them spoke.

"But what am I going to do about the dinner?" Jessie asked suddenly, her dismay returning.

"Why don't I drive out and help you get it ready?" Amy asked.

Jessie considered. "No," she said finally. "It sounds like a lifesaver, but can't you imagine what they'd say if they arrived and found you in my kitchen helping me? They'd never get over it. I'd be an object of scorn forever."

"I'm glad you see you're going to have to do it yourself, because you do. And really, Jessie, it's not that you can't. It's that you've let them demoralize you so that you think you can't. You can't let them get away with that. You're a perfectly capable woman, and you can do it. You have to remember that you're perfectly capable."

After a moment Jessie said, "It's true. For years they've been digging away at me, trying to reduce me . . . trying to make me forget who I am."

"You remember that, you'll be okay," Amy said, and Jessie said, "If I have someone strong like you to remind me every once in a while, I'll manage a whole lot better." Amy took both Jessie's hands in her own and squeezed.

When Jessie had gone, walking with a good deal more confidence then she had when she arrived, Amy remained seated where she was, thinking. There was now a good possibility that she could recruit Val and Jessie for her protest movement, or whatever it was. She couldn't think of a name that seemed appropriate. Usually she simply thought of the group of people she worked with as "us." Val especially would be useful, she thought, though who knew what lay inside Jessie that would emerge when she got a grip on herself.

She supposed she should drop in to see a few people, start planning the next step in the campaign, check up on the people doing the jobs they had decided on at the rally in the park. She frowned. How she wished she could forget all of it, forget everything, be free to devote herself to her real work. Again she looked around with deep impatience and distaste at the pots of various kinds sitting on the shelves of her studio and pushed angrily with her sandaled foot at a vat of glaze.

She did not know what the source of her discontent was and not knowing made it worse. Of course, there was always the loss of Lionel at the back of everything, but no, this was something else. She rose, stretching, feeling the discontent in every joint, itching through her muscles and lodging in her flesh, making her uneasy and distracted. She took a handful of long hair by her ear and gave it several short tugs for the feel of it, the reality of the feel: no, no help. She thought of Jessie heading back to the farm. No, Jessie's problems were not what was nagging at her. She held her hands in front of her, looking at the roughened skin, the prominent veins, the short tough nails. Her palms were tingling and she turned them toward her as if by studying them she might discover the source of her tension. Then she knew what it was, or at least what would ease it. She hadn't worked seriously for days now, at least a couple of weeks, and all that time, she knew from long experience, the tension had been building and building. Jessie's visit and her problems had toppled her tension over into the unbearable. She need to work. She needed to leave everything behind and work.

But what? She stood thoughtfully in front of her two potter's wheels, looking at them as if she were thinking hard about throwing a pot but in fact, she was not thinking at all, but feeling an amorphous blend of the sensation of throwing a pot on one of the wheels, the wetness of the clay, the tension, the steady movement, the concentration. But no. . . . She drifted away, looking at the row of small, nearly identical bowls meant for candy sitting side by side on a shelf, at the biscuit stage, waiting for her to find time to glaze them and fire them again. Nor that either.

She wandered to her high workbench, picked up a bamboo tool and dropped it, touched the dried pebbles of clay she hadn't cleaned up, then left them there. Something was growing in her mind – no, not her mind – it was in her body. Some deep shadow was coming into range, hovering, its presence growing stronger, more intense. Desire for it, for its realization, overpowered her. She felt sweat break out on her forehead, could feel her heart hurrying.

She hung onto that shadow, hung onto it, whatever it might turn out to be. Trying not to look at anything, she hurried to the door and locked it – not to be disturbed once she got started, that was the thing. She pulled the curtains tightly, shutting out the glare and the town. If anyone came and rattled the door, she would not answer. Ordeal could burn down, soldiers could come and run them all out of the district, she wouldn't notice. She lifted a large chunk of plastic-wrapped clay from its storage shelf behind her work area. She had dug it out herself, had soaked it, screened it, dried it, tested it, had been saving it vaguely for just such an occasion.

But still she hovered, her head lowered, her eyes closed, holding her breath. This was the moment; sometimes she felt it was the moment where everything was held in balance; the moment when the gods were watching and listening, when they expected homage. She felt herself weak and sullied, not ready for this act, this holy act, this act of creation. Eyes closed, she tried to clear her mind and still her heart, to hold back her growing excitement. Purity, that was what was required of her now. A moment passed: let me be pure enough for this. Let me be clean and open, so you can pass through me, into my hands.

She could hold back no longer. Dropping the plastic wrap onto the floor, she studied the clay, calmer than she had been, then, taking a cutting tool, broke it in half. She re-wrapped the remaining half in plastic and set it back on the shelf. The rest she put on the turntable. Now she could begin.

Neil arrived at her studio door at six in the morning, rattling it, determined not to leave till he was certain she was all right.

"Are you okay?" he asked at once when she opened the door, and when she looked surprised and didn't reply, he realized that he had wakened her. She was dusty and dishevelled.

"You slept here?" he asked, disbelieving, knowing there wasn't even a cot in her studio.

"I just fell asleep a while ago," she said. "As soon as I finished. I meant to go home, but. . ." Her voice trailed off, and he saw that something in the room was different. A group of figures sat on a turntable on her workbench; he knew he had never seen them before and started toward them, then stopped.

"I've been trying to reach you," he said. "You didn't answer your phone at home all night. I was worried." The figures were pulling at him, but he resisted.

"I should get a phone in here," she said, yawning. "I can't afford it." She yawned again. "Mmm," she said, and dropped onto the high stool at the counter and put her head on her arms. He saw that she must have been sleeping there.

"Hey, wake up," he said. He went to her coffee pot, emptied it, filled it with fresh water and coffee while she dozed. When he was done he went to her and stroked her hair till she woke again.

"What time is it?" she asked.

"Six in the morning."

"How did you know I was here?"

"Your truck's out front."

"Oh, yeah," she said.

"How can you do that?" he asked. "Forget about everything else but your sculpture for days at a time."

"Easy," she said. The coffee was ready and he poured her a cup and then one for himself. "It's not doing it that's hard," she said.

"The world could have come to an end outside and you wouldn't even care."

"That's right," she said, waking now. "I consider it the greatest blessing of my life to be able to do that." She laughed as if she were a little embarrassed.

"I suppose that all our great works of art have come out of that kind of active reverie."

"Active reverie," she repeated. "I like the sound of that. It sounds pretty close." She sipped her coffee. "But I always think of it as going somewhere else, into another dimension." He waited while she stared into space. "It's like a vast space in there. Huge, and the texture of . . . things . . . yes, things, life, is different than the rest of the time." She paused again, this time with her eyes on the finished group of figures, and Neil, who had been putting off looking at them because they were so compelling and would wipe out everything else, was forced to glance at them. "Time doesn't have any meaning in there," she said.

He rose, went to her work, asking, "May I?" but not waiting for a reply.

At first he saw only a group of figures in various postures, all of them working both together and against each other in their movement like a group of modern dancers. Looking closer, he exclaimed, "What . . . !" He looked at Amy but she was studying the figures from her perch on the stool. "But . . ." he said, then frowned, concentrating harder, touching the turntable so he could see all of it.

"I wanted to work in terracotta," she said, frowning, "but it began to seem that some glazes might be necessary. I think maybe . . ."

"I recognize these people, I think," he said. "This is that teenager with the blonde hair. This is Reverend Raven. This must be Mike Harboy." He saw a slyness in her depiction of them, he saw their confusion, their hardiness, the incongruity of their effort to raise the cross that seemed both to be holding them together and pushing them apart. She had sculpted their ugliness and their beauty. He wanted to say something, but a lump had risen in his throat and he couldn't speak without her knowing how affected he was.

"I'm too tired to think," she said. "I have to go home and get some sleep."

"It seems as though I never see you," he said, his voice thick. "You're always working on your protest movement or your art or when I phone you, you don't answer." She had gotten off the stool and was stretching as he began to speak. When he was half-way through she dropped her arms.

"I didn't know it seemed that way to you, Neil," she said. "I'm sorry. You know I care about you – a lot," she said, moving toward him.

"Sometimes I think you can't," he said, and was amazed to hear himself taking the role that was usually the woman's. He would have laughed if it hadn't caused him such chagrin.

"Come to my house for supper tonight," she said. "I'll sleep all day so I'll be wide awake and we can talk and . . ." She touched the side of his face with her hand, not finishing her sentence. "Please come."

"Of course I'll come," he said, gruff. "Does this mean you're getting over the trouble you have with my being there?" Ordinarily he wouldn't have said this out loud, but she had so disturbed him this morning, by vanishing for a day and a night, by the sculpture she had done that troubled him, by the way she could forget him whenever she chose.

She didn't answer, leaned forward to kiss him lightly on the lips.

"No more," she said, when he put his arm around her. "I must smell. My mouth tastes like chalk."

"I'll come tonight," he said, knowing she wanted him to leave. He turned back to her sculpture and put his hand out, unable to resist touching it. "It's very good," he said, his voice stiff. She didn't say anything. He almost hated that it was so good, seeing clearly for the first time that such a gift could do nothing but hold them apart. The fact of Lionel Sparrow, dead though he was, had the same effect. He would have given up completely right then, but the thought of making love to her that night held him back.

He went to her and put his hands on her breasts and on her hips, pulling her hard against him. She would have protested, but she saw the pain in his eyes, and held steady, passive, and after a second he dropped his head onto her shoulder, pressing his mouth against her neck, kissing it, then let her go and walked out of the studio without speaking again.

# CHAPTER
# 10

My intention hitherto had been to push on to the westward as far as the
Red River falls into the South Saskatchewan at the site of an old Blackfoot trading post of the Hudson Bay Company, called Chesterfield
House. This proposition of mine was received with universal alarm
among the men, who thought that they had done wonders already in
having gone as far as we were. They urged that the party was not
sufficiently numerous, and that to proceed any further into Blackfoot
territory was too dangerous. I was quite aware that the Indians in that
district had acquired a very formidable reputation owing to Hudson Bay
Company's having established the Chesterfield fort in 1822 by sending
up 100 men, and even then they only kept it a few years, during which
they lost a considerable number of men shot down by the Blackfeet, and
at length abandoned it as too costly and too dangerous. Our friend Mr.
McKay was on such intimate terms with us that I did not hesitate to
include him in our councils, and put the question as to the expediency
of proceeding to Chesterfield House. He replied, "Captain, if you say
the word I go, I will say hurrah, let's go; but if you ask my advice, I will
tell you plainly that I think it is too dangerous and more than this, if
you press it, your men will break up, and beyond Beads, John Foulds,
and old Hallet I could not say who will stick with you." Most unwillingly and unconvinced I abandoned the project of penetrating any further to the westward, prepared to cross the South Saskatchewan, and
direct our course for our winter quarters at Carleton.

From the west-facing window in his living room, Neil could see the hills rising higher even than his perch on the hillside. He knew they slanted north-west, always rising, till they reached the high point of the Cypress Hills fifty miles from where he sat at their extreme east end, and on to the junction of the Red Deer River and the South Saskatchewan where the Chesterfield House Palliser wrote of had once been. He had finished Butler, had been somewhat enlightened by him, but knew that he had not gone back nearly far enough. He had sought out John Palliser next.

Though it was midday and extremely hot outside, his small house caught whatever breeze there was and was still fairly cool. When he looked out the window he saw, instead of the glare of sun on the bare hills, Captain Palliser holding his consultation around a campfire in the evening cool. He thought how Palliser, even at his most daring, had never come here south of the Cypress Hills. That he had had the date wrong of Peter Fidler's establishment of Chesterfield House (it had been 1800) amused him, as did the fact that Palliser's party had been terrified to go where Fidler, more than fifty years earlier, had lived for two years.

It occurred to him that there was still no settlement at the junction of those two rivers where Palliser had finally visited in 1859. He recalled that James Butler had predicted in 1875 or so that there would one day be a great centre of commerce at the junction of the North and South Saskatchewan rivers, and that that prediction was unfulfilled and looking less as if it ever would be with each passing day. Palliser's prediction had been more accurate – that this country where he sat, surrounded by farms, was unfit for human habitation. In Palliser he felt he had come closer to finding a soul who had seen the country as God had made it. He hoped he would find in John Palliser's writings what he was searching for: that unnamed, unspoken sense of what the land was – *the west*. Palliser's account of his exploratory journey across the southern plains fascinated him. He read on:

**June 25, 1859:** . . . plains extend in all directions, where there is no grass and no fresh water; even in the river valley there is very little wood and no grass.

**July 14, 1859:** . . . After dinner pushed on to Red Deer River. Served out a little flour, this is a luxury we now seldom indulge in. A wretched soil everywhere; the horses miserably off for grass.

**July 18, 1859:** . . . I therefore determined not to take the carts and party to the forks . . . but to ride on with one or two others to the post where the old Chesterfield Fort of the Hudson's Bay Company once stood. . . . I arrived considerably before sunset, and contemplated the view with some satisfaction. . . .

**July 19, 1859:** . . . We were now halted on a salt lake, the only water we could find. The doctor had a severe spell with the carts in the sand-hills; he killed a grizzly bear. We drank a little water by digging a pit, and drinking through a silk handkerchief; the men and horses were in great want of water, and the heat was very great while travelling through miles of burning sand . . . .

**July 20, 1859:** . . . Continued our journey; found the ground very much broken and travelling very severe for the horses. Soil worthless. Found a human skull on the plains. . . .

**July 25, 1859:** . . . In the afternoon we reached a coulee, with hills and plains formed of blown sand. . . . When we were seated in the old man's tent, he told me he wanted to give me advice that I should not go further into the country, for that we should certainly get into trouble; that only two white men had ever crossed the country between the Cypress Mountains and the forks of the Red Deer and Bow Rivers, and that now we were approaching the country of the Assineboines of the plains, of whom he gave such an account that the men were very much frightened. . . .

**July 26, 1859:** We . . . halted for noon about six miles S.E. of the river, and in sight of the Cypress Mountains. . . . the Indians . . . tried to persuade us to stop, assuring us that we could not possibly reach water before nightfall; nevertheless, we pushed on; . . . we made a very long spell, and found middling water, although it was a little brackish; we camped on a dry watercourse in the outskirts of the Cypress Mountains, finding water in a few detached pools.

**August 6, 1859:** . . . Made twelve miles before breakfast over an arid plain . . . so level as to be devoid of any points by which we could continue our direction unvaried.

Only two men, Neil thought. He watched out the window again, seeing the pale, rounded hills, the washed-out blue of the sky. He wondered who they might have been and what they were after, travelling alone into this vast, desert-like south country no other white man had ever seen. What had they seen that they had never spoken or written of or reported on? In his mind's eye he saw them, two anonymous, faded silhouettes travelling south in the light of the high, hot sun: rifles, horses . . .

His reverie was disturbed by voices coming from outside his kitchen door. Exasperated, knowing it was the Church of the Millennium again, he half-rose, then declared himself too uninterested even to go look at them at their daily prayers. He sat down at his desk again, but work was impossible with the sound of chanting lifting and falling with the coming and going of the bursts of wind. He was drawn by them, he could not deny it, something about them impelled him to look and to listen though it was very much against his will. He found himself rising again and going into the kitchen, but here his stubbornness took hold and he went to the fridge, took out a bottle of beer, opened it, and strode determinedly back to the living room where he sat on his couch to drink it.

Though he would not allow himself to watch them, their presence weighed on him as heavily as if they had been in the room with him. He could not stop himself from picturing them somewhere down below donning their clean white robes, he saw them straggling up the searingly hot hillside, through the dust, till they reached their cross that loomed high above the small prairie town. Then Pastor Raven would preach. Neil leaned back against his couch and closed his eyes, and, pondering Pastor Raven preaching, he fell into a dreamlike state and things he had never seen became visible.

He saw Raven's words torn from his mouth by the hot wind, how it sent the syllables flying across the countryside, down into the town, up aloft over the prairies, chunks falling into the ears of coyotes and rabbits and the United Church minister on his way to a meeting, the town drunk hobbling on his crippled feet to the bar, the housewife rushing into the Co-op to get a litre of milk before the kids got home for lunch.

What they might have heard he didn't know: something they mistook for the distant screech of a hawk, or the purring of a kitten under the porch, or the short bark of the family dog challenged on his own territory by a robin. Or perhaps it was not a sound at all, but instead, the sudden flutter of the heart, a kink in the muscle of the thigh, an arthritic twinge in the knuckles. Or perhaps the pastor's message, broken and scattered as it was, arrived as a sudden yearning for love, a thrill of hope, or a desolation.

Neil dreamt on, listening, but still he could not hear what was said by Preacher Raven as he stood, his red hair streaming in the wind, while his flock knelt below him on the hard-packed clay, their backs curved in submission like a row of seashells left behind by the passage of the glaciers that had swept over the region ten thousand years before. He heard only phrases: blood, sorrow, and sin, sin, and more sin. That was the Pastor's refrain – sin, sin, sin, and salvation – he beat time with his arms in his flowing garment, a two-step, a foxtrot, an old-fashioned waltz, or with his fist on his chest. He fell to his knees and looked skyward, he touched his freckled forehead to the white, crumbling ground, he murmured *sin, sin, sin* – and *salvation*.

And then his flock rose, trembling, standing in the fierce sun with pale faces, eyes streaming with tears, embracing one another, or falling to their knees, or spreading their arms wide to the prairie as the preacher always did, their voices rising in shrieks and wails that sent shivers up and down Neil's back. And always, they reached their ecstasy in wind. It flapped around their robes, swirled them around the figures so that sometimes, peering around the corner of his door, it seemed to Neil that a bevy of white, shining angels might have lit in a whirlwind on the desert outside his kitchen door.

Always then, one supplicant would slowly take precedent over the others, and the others would quieten, stop their wailing and dancing, lean in to the one who now seemed to rise higher than the others. They would cluster around that one, touch him or her with hopeful fingers, and the one, in actual physical paroxysm (this Neil had seen), would speak and speak and then slump gracefully into the arms of the others.

Preacher Raven would pray, the chosen one would recover, the tribe would straighten their gowns, tighten the cords around their waists as the wind, which seemed perpetually to accompany them, would quietly die away, and they would descend in a long, zig-zagging line back down the desolate hillside to the dying town below.

Neil dreamt of all this, his bottle of beer in his hand, and waited tensely for the wails and the shrieks and the howling of the wind to die down so that he could go back to work. At last silence fell. He thought of Amy early that morning in her studio, struggling to come back to the everyday world, thought of her act of creation, one that showed up the Church of the Millennium, so Neil thought, for the hollow chicanery it was, for there was nothing at its centre that he could see save Pastor Raven's need.

He rose, intending to go back to his desk, when he was startled to hear an abrupt, too-loud knock at his kitchen door. He strode into the kitchen, hesitating in mid-step when he saw it was Preacher Raven peering in through the screen.

Neil stood on the kitchen side, not opening it.

"Yes?" His voice was cold. The pastor pushed open the door and stepped inside, stretching out his large, freckled white hand to Neil so that, taken aback, Neil found himself clasping it. Over the pastor's shoulder he saw the blonde girl with the angelic face standing in the heat on the gravel patch he called his driveway.

"Good day," the man said, tightening his grip, then abruptly letting go. He stood too close to Neil and Neil thought he saw madness in the man's bronze eyes.

"What do you want?" he asked, suddenly tight-lipped with anger. The pastor hesitated, his lips tightening too, the light not leaving his eyes.

"Our first encounter was unfortunate. It seems to me that since we worship so close to your very door, it would be remiss of me not to tell you that you are most welcome to come and offer praise with us each day." Neil imagined himself making a fist, drawing back, striking the man hard on his fleshy, freckled jaw, saw the red hair jerk and dance. He got a grip on himself.

"I am not in the habit of making a fool of myself in public," he said coldly, trying to hold in the anger that he knew could be seen by this man only as irrational. But still he said, "You'd do better to work with the sick and the poor than to stand outside my door every day, working yourselves into a frenzy."

Pastor Raven looked surprised, his golden eyes went blank and shallow and a kind of yellow burning grew in them, so that Neil was, for a second, frightened.

"The fires of hell are reserved for the arrogant in spirit," Raven said, and there was no mildness in his voice. Before Neil could tell him to leave, he had spun, the skirt of his gown flapping against Neil's legs, and was stepping outside Neil's door.

The pretty blonde girl fell in behind him as he strode across the drive in front of Neil's truck, going in the direction of his cross. Her hands were clasped at her waist now, and her head meekly bowed, but as she turned to follow her pastor, she paused and glanced at Neil over her shoulder, an unreadable, teasing look that held the faint hint of a smile. Neil was so surprised that his anger vanished, and he stood frozen to the spot watching them retreat down the hill.

He held in his hand a cluster of tiny yellow flowers. When Amy opened the door, he thrust them out to her like an awkward boy. When he saw how her face changed as she looked at them, he was glad that he had stopped to pick them. She set them in a drinking glass in a little water, holding them to her nose to see if they had a scent.

"*Potentilla norvegica*," he said. "Rough cinquefoil. Often confused with Macoun's buttercup, though they're really not much alike at all." When she looked at him over her shoulder, half-smiling, he was so embarrassed that he went on, unable to stop himself, "John Macoun, the botanist for the government, surveyed the area in 1879 and '80. He said," Neil concentrated to get it right, "that much of the southern district now considered fit only for pasture will yet be known as the best wheat lands."

Amy snorted.

"Ask the Sheridans about that," she said, but Neil went on.

"He undid the good Palliser had done. His report was just what the 'let's-open-the-land-for-farmers' people were waiting for. And now look at things."

"I see them everywhere," she said, her voice dreamy, meaning the flowers.

"Medieval witches used it in their potions that gave them the power to fly."

"No kidding," Amy said, grinning at him over her shoulder.

He pulled out a chair and sat down, and she handed him a bottle of wine and a corkscrew, then turned back to the sink where she was washing lettuce she must have just picked from her garden. "How's the protest movement going?" he asked, still embarrassed by his lecturing.

"The petitions won't be ready to go to Ottawa or the provincial government for another couple of weeks, I think. Rumour has it the Premier's coming through town, but frankly I doubt it. But if he does, he won't get out of here without a surprise." She said this last grimly, draining carrots, turning her head away from the steam.

"Surely you'd know if he were coming?" Neil asked, pouring them each wine, using the glasses she had already set on the table. He noticed that the plates didn't match, started to smile, then frowned, thinking of her poverty. Or maybe they weren't supposed to match. When he looked more closely he saw she must have made them, and they were rough and beautiful.

"No, not necessarily. Sometimes he comes to talk to the party faithful, to keep their energy up, so he can get his candidate elected. When he does that, it isn't made public, but a few people always know about it. We've got a spy in their midst." She was taking a roasted chicken out of the oven.

"I'd hate to be the Premier," Neil said, laughing.

"But you don't really believe it will do any good, do you?" she said, setting the bowl of carrots on the table next to the salad, then pausing to look into his face.

"It might keep the elevator open for a week longer, or the post office. But in the end, you've already lost the fight. Nobody around here seems to be able to see beyond the end of his nose."

"See what?" she asked, her voice tense.

He sighed. "They all want the past to come back, that's all."

"They do not," Amy said, more resigned than annoyed. She went back to the counter and lifted the chicken onto a platter. "There," she said, evidently choosing not to argue. "I think it's ready."

"They want back their hopes," he said, as though she hadn't tried to change the subject. "They want back the promise this place once held that's vanished now. The future is terrifying, the present is hopeless . . ." She stood by her chair, her hand on its back, listening. "Have you ever thought of a world where people had no plans?" he asked. She met his eyes. It was late, nearly nine, but she had slept too long and hadn't been able to motivate herself to start the meal, and then he'd been late too. She pulled out her chair and sat down across the corner from him.

"Plans?" she asked vaguely, wondering where he was going.

"Like . . . to conquer the world, or to be president of a company, or become a millionaire . . ."

"Ah," she said. "To be head checkout girl at Safeway, to move to a better neighbourhood . . ."

"To have running water on your farm, or ten acres of land instead of two . . ."

"What are you getting at?" she asked.

"What did the aboriginal people want?" he asked her. She hadn't turned on the light and she couldn't see him clearly, though the lines of age in his face and neck had softened and his eyes seemed brighter. "Who knows how long they lived here – ten thousand years since the end of the last ice age – and their lives only changed in response to the weather. But they were intelligent people; it wasn't because they were stupid that they didn't build skyscrapers or cars. They knew things we still don't know, they just didn't seem to be afflicted with the myth of progress that so afflicts us." She sipped her wine, listening closely. He paused, his eyes gone dim now, in the shadows of the room, and she felt him retreating, searching in some mental world she never entered.

"They lived in a world where each day held eternity." Another long pause while Amy held her breath. "I'm sure they never even thought about it, and maybe I haven't understood it either, because it's hard for someone like me, who was born into a world like ours – but the world must have seemed an Eden then. Even if you were starving because the game had all gone somewhere else, and you had to pray to your gods to find it. Because you knew every stick of wood, every star, every tree, and the smallest mouse tunnelling through the prairie grass was god."

They sat motionless, Amy fearing to disturb his train of thought, thinking to herself, *this is why I can't help but love him*. He laughed then, and the sound was cracked and harsh, his voice strained with bitterness, and she knew too that this was why she despaired of him.

"We call it living in harmony with nature. And we think it's charming, but backward."

"The eternal now," she said softly. He lifted his head and spoke in a louder, clearer voice, as if he would only say this once.

"Think of this: knowing what we know about science and nature, and then trying to live like the aborigines. Living a wholly creative life, one that doesn't involve acquisition or our modern idea of progress." He was silent for a moment and when he spoke again, his voice was very soft so that she barely heard him, thought perhaps she had gotten what he said wrong, but didn't want to ask. "I'd like to live like that." She thought, is it possible for us to live like that, now, today? But it seems to me that in a way, I do.

Neil raised his head and put his hand out to touch Amy's shoulder, then slid his hand till it was touching her neck. She smiled. They sat that way for a long minute.

"You and Lionel were happy here," he said. This they had never talked about, and now he had an urge to get it out in the open at last.

"Yes," she said. Then, as if she had understood and agreed with his impulse, she went on. "So happy I can still hardly bear to remember it." She moved her hands from beside her plate and set them carefully on her lap, then went on talking, looking straight ahead. "My parents had nothing in common. They'd stopped communicating by the time I was a teenager. And my mother resented my father's interest in me. She seemed to think it was stolen from her or something like that. But it wasn't, he simply no longer cared about her."

"And Lionel?"

"He was a lot like you. He loved the countryside, he loved being out of doors. And he loved me." He wanted to speak, but couldn't. "I nearly went crazy when he died," she said, and he saw that this was not hyperbole. "Lionel was my friend too," she said. "He was all I needed, at least I thought he was. And if it would have turned out any different, I'll never know, because he got hit by that car before anything bad happened between us." Again they sat quietly, the food growing cold between them. She drew in a slow, audible breath and then said, in a different voice, "Now I want to hear about Faith." Neil instantly felt irritation rising. But she was right, it was time he told her about Faith.

"We had a very unhappy marriage that lasted fourteen years, chiefly because I thought if I left her she would collapse, and when I finally couldn't stand another second of it and did leave her, what did she do but have a nervous collapse that put her on a psychiatric ward for two months."

"Why was it so unhappy?" Amy asked, keeping her voice gentle.

"I grew up and she didn't," he said shortly. Then, aware he wasn't being fair to either one of them, neither Faith nor Amy, he forced himself to continue. "She was very pretty. Small, sweet-looking. I had a tall, stern, undemonstrative mother I never got along with very well. I was attracted to Faith at once. Partly because she looked up to me, which was a new experience." His voice was tinged with unwilling bitterness. "I mistook that for love," he said. "Then, after we got married and I was in post-graduate school in the east, away from my father's long arm and my mother's . . . lack of interest . . ." He paused for a second, then hurried on. "I began to feel my own strength, my own ability to succeed on my own in my own way. And I forged ahead. But Faith, she hung onto me. She couldn't make a life for herself. She depended on me. I grew to loathe the sight of her." He was careful not to look at Amy.

"How . . . sad," she said, finally.

He had never thought of it as sad, though he knew it seemed that way to Faith. Her sadness had nearly killed her, but he had hardened his heart, he had ignored her pain, refused to think of it, or thought of it only with a fierce, wintery anger. Sitting here quietly beside Amy he knew without a doubt, though he still could not say it, that he had made Faith suffer, that he might have been kinder, that. . . . Angrily, he jerked back from his thoughts. Faith had brought on her own suffering.

"Sometimes you get such a look on your face," Amy said. It was getting very late, shadows had gathered around the room. "You're so full of anger, Neil," she said, but her voice was gentle. He had put food on his plate and now he pushed it around aimlessly with his fork.

"Sometimes I think I would like not to be angry," he said, surprising himself.

"I would like you not to be," she said, her voice sad.

They talked then about little things: the weather, the food, their likes and dislikes. They lost themselves in each other's voices and faces, weaving a nest of intimacy around them.

Later, they went into the book-crowded, dusty living room and sat side by side on an old-fashioned loveseat with a worn and faded tapestry cover. He put his arm around her, and she put her head on his shoulder. The seat faced the front window and in and around the shaggy lilac bushes they had a view of the yard, once a lawn, now shin-deep in wild grasses.

"Could you see us living together in this house?" he asked her. And immediately, realizing the implications of his question, drew back. "I was thinking how . . . I'd like to live with you and I couldn't see you happy up in my little settler's shack. So, I thought of this place."

"It's not impossible," she said, after a moment. How could he know how deeply, unreasonably she fought against the very idea, had to thrust down her dismay? Neil sleeping in the very room she had shared with Lionel.

"Maybe we could build a new house?" he asked, his tone dubious.

"Maybe," she said. Then, "No," this was too duplicitous, she must at least be honest. "I can't live anywhere else."

"But . . ." He hesitated. "But you can't imagine me here, either, can you?"

"Give me time," she said. "Let me get used to it in stages. I don't mean to be selfish . . ." Selfish was not what she meant. "To be a . . . fool," she finished lamely.

"You're not a fool," he said wryly. "There's no reason to hurry." They sat close together and held hands, watching the night sky grow darker and more filled with silver light.

"Does this mean we're going to get married?" she asked him suddenly, her voice filled with humour and excitement so that he had to laugh. Married?

"If it would make you happy," he said. He could feel the tension in her shoulders and her neck as she considered the idea.

"It would make it easier for me," she said slowly. "You know – gossip." She was silent, thinking. "But not here," she said. "Let's go away somewhere quietly and come back married."

"Done," he said. "We'll get married then," and both of them fell silent.

Herb and Flora were the first to arrive, still driving the last half-ton truck Herb had bought the year they left the farm, despite the fact they were town-dwellers now with little use for a truck. They got out slowly, ponderously, checked Jessie's flowerbed by the door, looked off to the horizon, pointed to the pasture to one side of the house, paused, considered, before they turned to the kitchen door where Jessie had been standing, waiting to greet them since the first sound of the motor had told her they were entering the yard. She was exhausted and too anxious to sit still and now so exasperated at this inevitable country ritual that she was about to slide open the patio door and call to them to come in when Val, seeing her impatience, brushed past her and went out onto the deck to speak to them first. Jessie followed.

"Happy anniversary," Jessie said, smiling, squelching her irritation. Flora looked surprised, as if she had said something impolite, and didn't reply.

"Looks like we beat everybody else," Herb said, cheerful.

"Were we supposed to bring Alma?" Flora asked, stopping on the first step.

"Marion and Alvin are bringing her," Val said.

"If nobody's here yet, do we have time for Val to show me the crop?" Herb asked, looking at Val rather than Jessie.

"Sure," Jessie said, and thought of sticking her tongue out at him. Flora had reached the top step now and she paused, puffing. She was only a little over five feet tall and had grown stout in the years since her children had grown and left home. Val went down the stairs, past his mother and he and Herb got into the truck and drove away while Flora and Jessie watched them go. Then Jessie opened the kitchen door, stood back for Flora, and together they went inside.

They had no dining room but their kitchen was large, big enough to feed a threshing crew, Herb had teased; in fact, half of it had been meant as a family room and it was in here that Val had helped Jessie put up a long table. It was already set, napkins neatly folded and resting on the bread-and-butter plates. Flora collapsed into one of the chairs.

More vehicles were driving into the yard now, first Elizabeth and her husband Mike, and their four teenagers, then Blanche and Jim with their three, then Marion and Alvin with a passenger that Jessie, peering to see, recognized as Alma Sheridan. They came into the kitchen in clusters or alone, some of the children staying outside and others who had come in pushing past the grownups to get back outside again.

"Where's Herb and Val?" Jim asked.

"Looking at the crop," Flora said.

"You kids get out of the kitchen," Blanche ordered, tying on an apron she had extracted from her voluminous purse. "Now, Jessie, I'll just toss the salad for you."

"Are there enough chairs?" Elizabeth wanted to know. "Mike, see if you can find a few more chairs. Try the bedroom," she called to his retreating back.

"Somebody's bringing stacking chairs," Jessie called into the hubbub, not moving from the stove where she was stirring the gravy. More vehicles were coming into the yard, and Elizabeth and Flora left the kitchen with the newcomers, Flora's sister Lily, her husband Frank, and then Val's cousin Judy, her husband Ed, and their four children. They went into the living room, but a moment later Judy was back, carrying her youngest.

"Jade needs a diaper change," she said. Her other little one trundled along behind, one hand in her mouth, the other dragging a dirty and ragged piece of cloth that had once been a blanket.

The women were dishing up the food now, the noise level was ear-splitting, and Judy came out of the bathroom and called to Ed who was standing in the yard with Jim and Mike, "Ed, bring those chairs in." Soon the clatter of chairs being rearranged was added to the racket.

"I forgot pickles!" Jessie cried.

"I wondered where they were!" Marion said severely.

"Here, here," Blanche said, taking a jar of dills which she must have brought herself, from the counter by the door. She opened them and began searching for a dish to put them in.

"It's ready," Marion said, and sent Shauna and Lindsay, Elizabeth's two oldest, out to the yard to call the men, and then into the living room to tell the rest of the family the meal was served.

Alma Sheridan was the first to come through the living room door and Jessie, who hadn't given her a thought since she recognized her sitting in the car as she arrived, was shocked. Surely she had lost a lot of weight? And where Jessie remembered a woman neat to the point of severity, this woman's thick, grey-streaked hair was held back in a sloppy bun from which long, untidy strands of hair hung and a loose bobby pin dangled.

"Your sweater is buttoned crooked, Alma," Marion whispered loudly.

"Where's that Herb?" Flora asked, squeezing past Alma as she fumbled with her sweater.

"I guess they haven't come back yet," Jessie said, anxious again, because the meal would have to wait and everything would grow cold and her carefully cooked food would be ruined. The other men lined up at the door to the bathroom and waited for their turns to wash their hands – they had been pitching horseshoes – and Marion instructed everyone where he or she should sit.

People were still milling around in the crowded kitchen and the last man was rolling down his shirt-sleeves and doing up the snaps at the wrist when Val and Herb drove slowly into the yard. Nobody else but Jessie appeared to have noticed their arrival and it seemed an eternity as she waited at the patio doors, before the doors slowly opened and Herb and Val got out. She could tell at once that something was wrong, and seeing the expression on Val's face as he threaded his way behind his father through the trucks and cars parked in the yard, she knew Val must have told his father about their financial problems.

As soon as Val and Herb entered the kitchen the tension between them was communicated to everyone else, and everybody sat down in silence glancing nervously at each other while they waited for the food to be passed. Judy was oblivious to the atmosphere, busy with her four youngsters, and Ed, a silent man, began to pile food on his plate without looking at anybody else. Lily and Frank, known for their meekness, kept their eyes carefully on their plates.

"Goodness!" Marion said suddenly into the quiet. "There isn't a scrap of room for these flowers and I can't see over them." This was patently ridiculous since Marion was one of the tallest people in the room and they had managed to find room for all the food on the table. But nobody said anything and Marion whisked away the centrepiece of flowers that Jessie had gone to so much trouble gathering in the field and carefully choosing from her flowerbed. She inexplicably chose one wild yellow daisy, pulled it out and dropped it into the sink. Jessie's face burned, but she was both too dumbfounded and too embarrassed to speak.

But she watched carefully and saw that no dish she had prepared was being rejected by anybody, that the beef was tender but still moist, and the vegetables nicely cooked, the potatoes creamy and the gravy dark and rich. She saw that the men carefully picked the green peppers out of the salad and left them on one side of their plates and did the same with the pearl onions in the cream sauce she had cooked the peas in, but that was to be expected, and they ate her buns even though they were heavy and some were burned on the bottom.

The colour was slowly returning to Herb's face and somebody dared to make a small joke as he handed the bowl of potatoes to him for the second time. Jessie longed to speak to him, to say something that would get rid of the sick look around his mouth, and she kept glancing at Val to see if he might be the one who could do it. At last Val set down his fork with a clatter so loud that everyone turned to look at him.

"We're going to have to talk about this sooner or later," Val said. There was a stunned silence.

"We do not," Marion said, though she couldn't have known what Val was talking about. "This is neither the time nor the place. Alma is enjoying her meal." Ah, Jessie realized now, she thinks Val wants to talk about Alma's letter to the paper. Alma blanched and began to tremble.

"Please," she said. "I've been to the doctor and he's given me tranquillizers and sleeping pills and he says . . ." She swallowed, looking down at her plate.

"What does he say?" Marion demanded, even her severity softened by Alma's distress.

"He says I should retire, then my dreams will stop. He says they're caused by too much stress."

"And good advice, it seems to me," Marion said, patting her mound of mashed potatoes with her fork.

"Yes, he's probably right, Alma," Elizabeth said soothingly. "You've done your share." Murmurs of agreement went around the table. "Forty years is more than enough," and "I don't know how the school will get along without you." Colour slowly began to return to Alma's cheeks and tears trembled at the bottom of each eye as she raised her head to meet the eyes of her family. Quickly everyone began to chatter to each other as if the exchange hadn't taken place.

"That's not what I meant," Val said loudly, and Jessie wanted to kick him for not leaving well enough alone. "I'm talking about the farm," he said. The voices dropped off one by one. "If it isn't common knowledge now that I'm in trouble," Val said, "it soon will be." The silence grew deafening. "Dad?" Val said. Herb put down his fork with a gesture so full of controlled emotion that once again all eyes dropped quickly, discreetly to plates and even the children stopped squirming.

"Don't know what there is to say," Herb said. "You're going to lose the place." The women gasped and turned pale, the men stopped chewing, set their forks on their plates, remained motion-less as if this might render them invisible, though of course not one of them would have wished to be anyplace else.

Val and his father stared at each other down the table, Herb's skin paling so that suddenly his age showed. There was an unspoken communication between them that all could see, and then Val burst out, "There's got to be a way out of this, Dad. There has to be. All I did was what everybody was doing, what the government told us to do! They were the ones who set up that loan program. It wasn't my idea. They must have thought it could work. I thought it could work!" He paused, swallowed, then said quietly, not looking at his father, "You signed the papers too." The rest of the table grew even more silent, if this were possible.

"Not much point in blaming people now," Alvin said. He was a lean, silent man, silent, everyone thought, because Marion never gave him a chance to speak, but now he directed a level gaze at Val and his calm, steady tone quietened the emotion running around the table.

"God knows I didn't want to," Herb said. "I had serious doubts. But I didn't see any other way for you to take over the farm and I couldn't stand to see the place that nearly killed my father go to somebody else. I wanted you to have it. And you were just sick to get it. Don't tell me you weren't. And Mother and me couldn't stand the thought of Fox getting it." Fox was the nearest neighbour to the north, one of the biggest farmers around and growing bigger with each foreclosure, each bankruptcy or abandonment. "I didn't really believe you could pull it off," Herb said. "I just wanted to believe it, I guess, so I signed." Flora had been motionless since Val had first spoken. Now she said, in a voice that trembled, "How bad trouble are you in, Valentine?" He answered without moving or looking at her.

"I didn't make my interest payment last year and I won't this year either if it doesn't rain."

"Sell them cattle!" Mike, Elizabeth's husband, said. "Get your cash flow going again." Mike had no cattle and Val often said to Jessie as they drove past his fields, "See all that grazing going to waste? You could feed fifty cows for a couple of weeks on that stubble, but he tore all his fences down." But Mike hated cattle, would go on about how they tied you down, made a mess, weren't worth a damn thing most of the time anyway. "Chew down the trees, kill everything," he'd say. But Val said to Jessie, "What difference does it make to him? He ploughed up every tree on the place. Even deliberately sprayed the ones that came up by the dugout to kill them."

"I thought I'd try to hold off till fall," Val said, "In case I get a crop."

"Markets might be up then, too," Alvin said. Ed remained silent. His place was so small he survived only because he had a job in town.

"You shouldn't have built this house," Marion said, looking straight at Jessie.

"It wasn't my idea," Jessie began in self-defence, seeing everyone staring at her with disapproving expressions, then thought that this was hardly sticking by her husband, and besides, wasn't the house her chief joy?

"Come on, Marion," Val pleaded, without, Jessie thought, much enthusiasm, "I couldn't ask a wife – especially a city girl – to live in that old house of Mom and Dad's. It's full of mice and nothing works in it any more. The window frames are so worn out the place is freezing in winter and full of flies in summer."

"We all started in homesteader's shacks," Marion said. "Most of us had to wait until our kids were grown before we could afford anything better. You young people think you have to have everything now."

"Let's get this straight," Herb cut in and everyone turned to him. "Nobody's likely to get a crop this year. We've had less than 50 per cent of our regular moisture so far. You saw your crop." He looked at Val. "If we don't get a good rain in the next couple of weeks, it'll be done for. It's burning already." He drew in a deep breath, then expelled it slowly. "Sell some land. I hate to say it, but it looks to me like you have to." Absolutely the last move of the desperate farmer.

"How can I sell land?" Val asked, raising his voice for the first time. "I only got two sections, and its not all farmable as it is. I'll never make a living on any less."

"You gotta do something, Val," Alvin pointed out. "You're just lucky there's still a buyer left."

Mike said dourly, "With prices as low as they are, selling won't do much good." Nobody said anything for a long moment.

"During the Depression," Herb said, "it got so bad people just walked away from their places. You didn't have to buy, you could have land anywhere for back taxes." His laugh was bitter.

The Depression, Jessie thought. The goddamn Depression. It seemed to her that she had heard of nothing but the Depression from the day she was born: how her grandfather had almost lost the farm, her father had to leave for the city because the farm wouldn't feed a family during its worst days, how he had struggled and scrounged for pennies and managed to educate himself, and then was able to get a job which, though he hated it, he'd never dared quit for fear he wouldn't get another, how his father had lost the farm anyway and died of a broken heart. She felt she'd lived through it herself it had affected her life so much. She suspected memories of the Depression in prairie people had at last become congenital. Although these last few years, people were saying, were almost as bad. Still, she did not believe, no matter how bad it got, that they would be reduced to porridge three times a day.

"But who wanted land in them days?" Herb asked his listeners. "Everybody was starving, nothing would grow, we were feeding our cows Russian thistle. We're headed for that again," he said. "This whole damn country's going to turn into a desert."

Alma began suddenly to gasp. She leaned over her plate, struggling for breath.

"She's choking!" Elizabeth said.

"Pound her on the back!" Flora called.

"Get her some water!"

"Help her up!" Chairs scraped back, people stood, crowded around Alma, laid hands on her back and head and shoulders. After a moment she raised her head. Everyone drew back; her eyes glittered, they had gone black and a strange light shone in them.

"No!" she shouted. "No!" Her dishevelled hair had become a rat's nest in her struggle for breath; her bony nose seemed even narrower and longer. "In my dreams," she said, and her voice was harsh and seemed to echo through the room. "In my dreams I see a vast desert." She put one arm out and made a sweeping gesture that included the room, the farm, the district. "Nothing but sand and more sand, blowing in the wind. The hard sun burning down. Nothing! Nobody!" Shivers ran up and down Jessie's spine. There was a long, frightened silence during which nobody moved. "You have done this!" Alma cried, pointing at them. Then she began to cough again, her shoulders slumped, her nose seemed less prominent and the unearthly gleam went out of her eyes. Tentatively, Elizabeth offered her a glass of water. She reached up and accepted it, and drank from it slowly, then set the glass down, murmuring a soft, "Thank you." It was only Alma again. Seeing this, people shook themselves from their collective hallucination, denied it, sat down again demurely.

Now Marion rose and everyone watched her with puzzled, anxious expressions.

"I am going to lead us all in a prayer for rain." She bowed her head. The silence that followed this pronouncement was startled, then obediently the adults clasped their hands and bent their heads over their dinner plates. "No," Marion announced, "that's not good enough. We'll kneel." Nobody argued. Chairs scraped, Sunday clothes rustled, joints creaked, and everyone knelt. "Hold hands," Marion commanded, but already Lindsay had taken Jessie's right hand and Ed her left. Jessie felt ridiculous. She couldn't resist a surreptitious glance to see how seriously everybody else was taking this.

But what caught her eye instead, in a gap between Marion's shoulder and Alma's, was a clear view out the patio doors across the yard to Val's crop. Heat waves rose off it, shimmering skyward to dissipate into the blue. Even with her unpractised eye she could see that the crop was burning up in the July heat.

After the anniversary cake had been cut and eaten, and the children had gone outside to play, where they could be heard screaming up and down the yard, and the dishes had been done, the women moved into the living room, where the men had already been seated for some time.

"Time was," Herb said, "you didn't even need a banker. Horses didn't cost anything to run and you could buy a year's groceries on credit. Even the feed and machinery dealers would carry you interest-free until you got your grain cheque or your cattle cheque. Nowadays nobody carries you for five minutes."

"They're all in hock to the banker too, have to make payments like us," Alvin said.

"I look around," Herb said, "and I don't recognize things any more. I don't."

"Word is the CPR will close our branchline soon," Mike said. "I can't afford to haul wheat thirty miles."

"I helped start the Wheat Pool," Herb said. "I never dreamt when I was going around talking to people about it that one day the Pool'd pull out of Ordeal and leave us all high and dry."

"It'll be the end of the town with the branchline gone, the elevator gone, the school closing, and one day soon, the post office closing too."

"The town's practically dead already," Judy said. "Two more stores closed this year."

"I don't care about that big school anyway," Herb said. "All that busing kids so they're gone from home all day. They ruined farm life."

"Riding them stubborn old school ponies back and forth kept us away from home too," Alvin said.

"At least you were outside," Herb said. "You were riding across the prairie, getting to know the wildlife, their habits, the grasses, and so on. Getting to know the way of things on the prairie."

"There was a lot more prairie then, too," Flora said. "This country used to be so beautiful when I was a child. But now there's no waterholes left 'cause the sloughs are all drained, and no grazing . . ."

"Crops everywhere, no place to ride a horse any more, even the road allowances are ploughed up and seeded."

"No birds left to speak of, no rabbits, nothing to look at but miles and miles of crop and stubble and summerfallow . . ."

The room had fallen silent again and the yearning filling the air was palpable. A collective dream was being dreamed in that room,

Jessie thought. It was so strong she could see it herself, could smell the sweet air of that magical time, could feel the breeze on her cheeks and the sun beating down on her forehead; she could feel the wildness in the air that all of them in that room had once known; she could feel their terrible sadness, their unrelenting sense of loss. She could not reconcile this yearning with what all of them had themselves done, every single one of them, to that dream. She felt her heart might break and knew it was not her own pain she was feeling.

Val spoke suddenly, vigorously, as though he had not been a part of that dream:

"I'll get a job." Around the room people sat straighter, their eyes cleared, they turned their faces alertly toward him. Jessie said, "I'll do anything I can to help, Val, just ask me." For the first time in days he met her eyes with his own, a silent acknowledgement of their solidarity.

"So," he said, and he was grinning a strange grin as if he might burst into tears or scream at any second, "So, I sell my land, I sell my cattle, I get a job. Then what? I'll still be broke and I'll have less than half of what I had when I started."

"At least it'll be yours!" Herb shouted. "It won't be the god-damned bankers'!"

It seemed to Faith that she'd been driving for days. It was perhaps three or four, she'd lost track, tried to remember if she'd stopped anywhere to sleep. She recalled only stop after stop to buy gas, have the oil checked and the windows washed, or when she felt herself nodding, pulling over to nap.

Hadn't there been a motel somewhere? Arizona? Or before that in New Mexico? With imitation wood wallboard and leaky taps and a bed so hard she felt even the none-too-clean floor would have been softer. Surely she couldn't have dreamt it if she remembered it so clearly. She must have stopped overnight. Ah, yes, the owner had been a lean, hard-looking woman who'd watched her with flinty dark eyes while the ash on her cigarette grew longer and finally fell on the counter in front of the registration card Faith was filling out.

She smiled to herself because it was night and she had made it nearly all the way to Neil's home again. The car purred on and she smiled too at the satisfyingly steady sound; such a beautiful car, her very own. It worried her that she had so much trouble remembering. Neil would say it was the result of stress – it made her smile to remember how Neil was always talking about stress, since nobody put more stress on Neil than he did himself, though he had a way of blaming everybody for it from his father to Faith herself (in the end he blamed me for everything, she reminded herself) – or else he would say it was the cancer working away unseen. She knew how he thought, but she wouldn't let him think her very thoughts for her any more. The fact was the cancer was gone, cured, and she herself knew best what it was made her forgetful.

Her attention was drawn by something on the road ahead: cattle. She was . . . where? In Montana, in ranching country. Or had she crossed the border? But no, it was antelope, not cattle, and they were gone so quickly she might almost believe she'd dreamt them.

No, she couldn't remember things because she was giving her memory a rest. All the years she had worried and struggled not to forget anything, exhausted herself keeping track of every detail of her life and Neil's, for fear of . . . for fear that if she forgot one little item her world might fall completely to pieces.

She hit the steering wheel with the heel of her hand, tears starting to her eyes. And hadn't it fallen apart anyway? Hadn't she lost everything and had to start her life over again? Now she saw the futility of trying to control her fate by sheer effort of will. It couldn't be done. And she would no longer wear herself out so uselessly. Her brain had gone on holiday – she'd sent it on holiday. Because when it came right down to it, what was the point of remembering if everything was controlled by fate?

Neil had loved her and spurned her and never understood either impulse; he'd explained his whole life since he'd left home in the wrong way and he had assigned her a place and a role that she'd done nothing to deserve. He had chosen to hate humankind and he would ruin what was left of his life if he didn't get back some balance. She would see him, whether he wanted to see her or not.

On the misty early mornings in Mexico, before the heat grew molten and the beaches filled with loud strangers, she had walked and thought, leaving her footprints in the sand to be washed away by soft splashes of turquoise water. She had thought and thought and it was plain to her that Neil might say he blamed her, but underneath he was riddled with guilt for what he had done to her. If cancer had no other virtue it at least clarified one's thinking – if you thought long enough, it might even give you a vision. She had seen the dark bulk of Neil's guilt casting his soul in shadow. It pierced her heart to think of the anguish he lived with every day and denied even to himself. She wanted to forgive him, she wanted to tell him she didn't hate him, that her heart was full of love for him, that she wanted nothing more for him but that he should be freed to love life as she had learned to love it.

Hours after he had left Amy's house Neil was wakened by footsteps crossing his kitchen floor, then whispering across the living-room rug. A voice in the doorway said, "Neil?" He tried to make sense of this, then the bed beside him sank with someone's weight.

"Amy?" he said, but the voice replied, "It's me, Faith." He struggled to wake and opened his eyes. A shadowy figure faced him, he could make out a curly-headed silhouette. Not Amy, then.

"What are you doing here?" he asked. When she didn't reply at once he fell back partly into sleep.

"I'm no longer frightened by the length of the night," she said, and he had to rouse himself again to listen. "Or by the things that make night different from the day. Maybe I'm a nocturnal animal after all. So many years I spent never seeing the darkness, going to sleep before true night settled in, waking when the sun was high. I was so frightened by the darkness."

"Darkness," Neil whispered, his tongue thick. He wanted to sit, but sleep dragged him back.

"I've seen the darkness," Faith said, and laughed a soft, little laugh with a catch in it. "It turns out not to be opaque. I thought it could hold only terrors. Oh, Neil," she whispered, "I've decided to live."

He knew there was something wrong with this, but couldn't think what it was.

"Decided?" he asked.

"I can't find my tumour," she said. "It's gone, vanished. As soon as I saw that, I left the clinic. I've been driving north ever since."

"Lie down," he said and patted the bed beside him with a clumsy hand. "We'll talk tomorrow."

"I'm not staying," she said. "I'm not tired. And the night is so beautiful."

"Sleep beside me 'till morning," he whispered. "Then we'll talk."

"I'm going on," she said. "I still love you, Neil. Don't be afraid of that."

"I'm not worth loving," he said, wanting her to know that at last, and would have said more, but sleep overcame him.

# CHAPTER
## 11

Jessie studied Val as he climbed down from his tractor cab. The sun glinted off the cab's glass and metal so that she had to shade her eyes. Her girlfriends had said when she began dating him, "But would you really like to live on a farm?" Their noses had wrinkled at the prospect. Jessie had wondered herself, but in the end Val's trim, muscular body, his crisp black hair, the way he had of gazing at her as if she were the most wonderful thing in the world, and his supreme self-confidence, as though nothing could ever shake his view of the way the world was, won her over. And now, here she was, married to him for better or worse, and whose fault was it that it was, so soon, turning out to be for worse?

She sat in the shade on the deck and tried to figure out what had gone wrong. In the time of his proudest self-assurance he had said that the days of the stubble-jumper, the country hick, were gone forever, that it wasn't possible any more to tell a farmer from a city-dweller. Farming is a business, he was fond of saying, a business like any other business. And if it was a business, that made Val an entrepreneur, like her friend Maureen's electrician husband who had started his own company. But Val had also said that farming was the only thing in the world he wanted to do, that he couldn't imagine himself doing anything else with his life. Didn't that somehow contradict his claim that farming was a business like any other business?

Surely electricians and swimming pool contractors didn't feel that way?

He was manoeuvring his tractor with the eighty-foot spread of cultivators behind it as easily as if it were a bicycle. The whole thing had cost almost $200,000, nearly all of it borrowed from the bank. She thought of old Mike Tkachuck who lived a few miles back of their farm in the same settler's shack his family had moved into around 1920 or so, who still had no electricity or running water and farmed with a D John Deere tractor that Val said was otherwise only to be found in museums. He hadn't drained a single slough or killed a single tree. He had acres of prairie grass and shrubbery where antelope, deer, rabbits, and coyotes made their homes and ducks, geese, and swans came each spring to his sloughs. Some people said he was crazy, but others viewed him with a kind of puzzled admiration. The hard labour he would have had to have done all his life without any of the amenities! And he had never married, hadn't had to support a family. She herself would abandon a life where you had to work that hard. It was what everyone had done as soon as it was possible and she refused to believe that that was wrong.

Still, something had gone wrong. Somewhere, between the old man living in his settler's shack in the middle of the wilderness and Val on his $200,000 outfit while she sat on the deck of a modern house – somewhere something had gone very wrong indeed.

She saw Val look up from his work, he was changing a cultivator shovel, and she followed his gaze. A car was coming down the road fast, a fat worm of dust rolling up behind it, still hanging in the air at the turn-off from the grid when the car was already in the yard. Val watched, his hands on his hips. Jessie went inside. She filled the coffee-pot with water, added the coffee, turned it on. She took out coffee cups, cream and sugar, spoons, and set them on the table.

In a moment she heard male voices, then the tread of heavy feet on the deck. Val opened the sliding door and held it back so the visitor could enter.

"This is Vern Galway," he said to her, sliding the door shut again. "My wife, Jessie." She shook the man's hand, invited him to sit down.

"I'll be a minute," Val said, and stepped into the bathroom where he could be heard running the water.

"I'm from the bank," the man said. Jessie froze. The uneasiness she'd been feeling since she'd wakened that morning suddenly coalesced into a ball and sank like lead to the pit of her stomach. She sat down across from him, her knees suddenly weak, and clasped her hands on her lap. He didn't look at her and she sensed it was a refusal on his part. Frightened, wondering if they might be told to leave that very day, a part of her was already planning what she would take. She studied his broad shoulders under his neat, short-sleeved white shirt, saw the light glint off his tidy blond hair as he smoothed down his tie and bent to take papers out of his briefcase.

Val came out of the bathroom rolling down his sleeves. She saw he was pale behind his sun-and-windburn and his nervousness revealed itself in the trouble he was having in doing up the snaps. She needed to touch him and she rose quickly, went to him, pushed his hand away and did up the snaps herself.

"I'll be in the garden if you need me," she said, her mouth dry, and went quickly, before he could speak, out the door. As she stepped outside she called cheerily, as if nothing were wrong, "The coffee'll be ready in a minute." She went to her garden and fell to her knees in between the rows of carrots. Her hands were trembling and she spread them out on her thighs and made herself take deep breaths.

She knew she shouldn't have run away. She thought with longing of Amy Sparrow and her words, "I don't need much," thought of her run-down old farmhouse, her potter's shop in town where she seemed perfectly content, of how she looked fine, better than fine in those cheap cotton outfits she wore. She even caught a fleeting glimpse of the beat-up old half-ton Amy drove that was the town joke.

The birds were singing in lilac bushes behind her, cheerfully, as if the creek further back were not polluted with Val's chemicals and his fertilizers or the shrubs they were perched on hadn't been stunted by crop spray. She realized with a shock that it was a wonder the birds weren't all dead too.

*Oh Saskatchewan, what have we done to you?* the lament welled up in her chest.

She rose rapidly then, dusted off the knees of her jeans, and rubbed her hands as she crossed the garden and walked into Val.

"You have to come inside," he said, in a low, tense voice, his hands too tight on her upper arms. She said brightly, blinking away tears, "I was just coming. I'm sorry, I needed a minute."

He put his arm around her shoulders and together they went up the deck steps and back into the kitchen. Inside she said quickly, brightly, "You forgot to pour the coffee." She did so and when she had put the coffee-pot back she sat down again and remained still, waiting. The banker cleared his throat gently.

"I've just been telling Val," he said, then turned to look directly at her with his pale-blue eyes and she saw this wasn't easy for him either, "that it's time we had a serious talk about things. I came out here so we could talk in privacy, informally, without having you come to my office." He cleared his throat again. "I only do this," he said, and his voice grew firmer, "when the situation is really serious." Jessie couldn't bring herself to look at Val. "How much does your wife know?" the banker asked, turning to him. Val flinched, then met his gaze.

"I've told her . . ."

"Everything," Jessie said. Galway seemed to relax ever so slightly.

"Good," he said. "You wouldn't believe how often when I make this visit it's the first thing the wife knows of the trouble." He had a thick computer printout in front of him and he began to spread it out.

"Normally when people are this far behind and there is no sign of a payment coming in, we simply foreclose. But these are not normal times and your debt is a large one. A very large one." Neither Jessie nor Val moved. He appeared to study the figures before him.

"What do you . . . do you mean you're going to let us stay?" Val asked. A quaver in his voice betrayed his emotion and he cleared his throat as if to hide it.

"Not indefinitely," Galway replied, and a hint of steel appeared in his eyes so that Jessie's mouth went dry again. "We have to see if we can work out a repayment plan so that we – the bank – can recover at least some of our money."

For the next hour they went over the accounts. They looked at the situation this way and that, they discussed it up one side and down the other. Val made suggestions, then gave them up in mid-speech. Galway was gentle but relentless and gradually it came clear to Val and Jessie that this wasn't a discussion at all, but a final humiliation, that the decisions that would make or break them had already been made, probably a long time ago, by people they had never, would never meet.

"You'll have to sell your cattle immediately. I've arranged for trucks to come day after tomorrow. That gives you tomorrow to round them up."

"But – the markets – " Val began.

"If you can't see your way clear to agreeing," Galway said, "I'll have a crew with the cattle liner to do the job for us." Jessie, to her surprise, began to suspect a hint of boredom behind Galway's uncompromising manner. How many times had he done this in the last year? she wondered. "They'll be sold in Swift Current the next day. The cheque will be paid out to the bank."

"How much time will that buy us?" Val asked, and both Jessie and Galway glanced at him, hearing the fury in his voice. The banker began to gather the papers and to stuff them into his briefcase.

"I can't tell you that," he said. "I'd say you're safe till fall. There's still the land." He stood, drawing in his breath in a way that was almost sad. Then he went to the door and put his hand on it.

"What about my machinery?" Val said, his voice flat, as if he knew the answer. In reply, Galway turned his head from them to look out into the yard. A half-ton came speeding by, screeched to a stop, was enveloped in the cloud of dust it hadn't outrun. The passenger, a stranger, jumped out, ran to Val's tractor, paused to call something to the driver, then climbed up into the cab. At once the tractor roared into life, the hydraulics went slowly to work lifting and folding the cultivators as earth fell off them in clumps.

Val jumped to his feet and started across the room but Galway blocked the door with his big body.

"Don't," he said to Val. Then, making a dismissive gesture with one hand, "They're gone." He went outside, got into his car, and followed the tractor and cultivators as they moved slowly out of the yard, led by the half-ton with its hazard lights flashing. Only then did Jessie see the Mountie cruiser as it pulled into view from beside the house where it had been waiting.

"What?" Jessie asked, rushing to Val. "What . . . ?"

"They're repossessing my equipment," he said.

"But, but . . ."

"They'll auction it, recover what they can." She put her hand on his arm but he ignored it. "I'll farm with the old stuff Dad used, I guess," he said, though she hadn't asked. They stood silently watching their machinery turn slowly out onto the grid road that led to town.

Each time he came out here it was different, Neil thought. The same grass, hills, sky, yet each time it was as if he had never smelled sage before, or felt the heat of the sun on his body, the breath of wind cooling it. Out here on the true prairie with no one else around, the world seemed perpetually new and freshly made, and its peace and beauty calmed him as if there were nothing else that mattered.

He was to marry Amy, it seemed. Why was it he could not quite believe in this? There was something in her manner – he felt she was aware of it herself and sometimes seemed to struggle with it – that told him she had doubts. He supposed they had to do with his cynicism, which she had told him so frankly she hated. He did not really like his cynicism himself (or do I cherish it? he wondered), but still wished he might learn to rid himself of it for her sake. If we marry, he thought, noting the "if," she will teach me how to hope.

He had been reading Peter Fidler's Chesterfield House journal, and he had been so upset by some of what Fidler so matter-of-factly stated that he had skimmed the journal to the end, then come out to this field where he could feel himself alone in the wild, all distractions subdued, to mull over what he had read.

Peter Fidler had recorded – indeed, the facts existed in the records of the Hudson's Bay Company – that during the winter of 1800-1801 he and his men had traded with various tribes of Indians for a total of twelve thousand beaver pelts. The figure was astonishing: twelve thousand beaver at one fort in one winter. What would the figures be at Fort Edmonton to the northwest, Fort Carleton to the northeast, Fort Qu'Appelle to the east, or Fort Benton across the border to the south? The more he thought about it, the more the implications staggered Neil.

He recalled a brief conversation he had had with a farmer he had met once when he had asked permission to set up camp on the farmer's land to do a count of foxes for a government agency. The farmer, nodding wisely, had said, "There's too many foxes this year," and Neil had been taken aback. Too many compared to what? Too many for what? If you saw one, did that mean there were too many? The spiritual poverty of such a view overwhelmed him, and then rage at the man's arrogance and stupidity swept through him. Was this not first Brother Animal's country?

They would not be satisfied till they had finished what men like Peter Fidler began, till they had emptied the country of all animals, had made it entirely and only theirs.

He had at last seen a vision of what this land must have been in the seventeenth century: teeming with wildlife, a saint's vision of heaven, a country where the lion might indeed have lain with the lamb. He thought of the endless fields of untouched native prairie grasses, of the wild, undammed rivers, the endless flocks of birds. . . .

The sun beat relentlessly down on him and he wished for shade, knowing there was none to be found for miles in any direction, unless he chose to burrow into the cool earth. He became aware that a coyote was trotting parallel to where he sat, but over on the far side of the basin at the bottom of the opposite hill. It did not appear to have noticed him and he was careful not to move. It was a big healthy coyote with a long bushy tail flowing out behind as it trotted, occasionally lowering its nose to the ground. The coyote stopped, lifted its head, stared at Neil. For a long moment the two animals stared at each other. Then the coyote began to trot again, altering its course in a curving line toward Neil, but off to one side of him.

Neil was not afraid. He had been told there was no recorded case of a coyote attacking a living human being, and the coyote was keeping a good distance between himself and Neil. Neil whispered, "Hello, Brother Coyote," acknowledging him as a figure out of myths and folktales. He thought this in the seconds it took the coyote to move gracefully around the perimeter of the basin as though he intended to continue on past Neil.

Something, a shadow maybe, or an unnamed sense he didn't know he had made Neil turn his head the other way. What he saw made the hair on the back of his neck actually stiffen. Another coyote was behind him, circling him in the direction opposite to the first.

He must have come over the hill while Neil's attention was distracted by the first. He scrambled to his feet, the knowledge that he was prey, being circled as if he were a jack-rabbit or a fieldmouse, descended on him, and a pit that was more than fear opened in him. At the same time he was curious to know what these animals would do. He stood frozen while the wind riffled the grasses before and behind him and the sun burnt down. He saw that the circle they were casting around him was growing tighter.

Steady, he told himself. Coyote doesn't attack man. He turned back to face the first, the larger coyote. The animal stopped, it was almost as if to speak to him, he was so close now that Neil could see the clear bronze eyes, the bluish fur, the stillness at the animal's centre.

A tremendous yearning swept through Neil; it had something to do with his own and the coyote's animalness. He wanted to speak to the coyote, or to follow him on foot, to run with him across the splendid, wild prairie. He might have moved, but the coyote, sitting a few feet away from him on his haunches, now lifted himself slowly, and with one last, long look at Neil trotted away in the direction from which he had come.

Neil turned and saw that the second coyote had vanished too.

The air was very still and he became aware of the heat, felt almost faint with it. It was the silence, he thought, steadying himself. There was not a sound, not the soughing of a breeze through the grass, not the chatter of horned larks, nor any cry from the endlessly circling hawks. He could feel the rapid beat of his heart in his throat. His palms were wet with sweat, sweat trickled down his neck and chest.

Then he remembered: Coyote, the creator of the world, the bringer of fire, and of death, the Trickster God himself. The sun, the grass, the sky – this is the place where words stop.

The café was packed, all the boys were in town for afternoon coffee. Bill Peat said to Sandy McDonnell, "Did you see Galway go by with that big outfit?" Sandy nodded.

"Young Sheridan's," he said, stirring his coffee.

"Poor bugger," Martin Barrell said.

"Hard to say who'll be next," Phil Mountain said.

"Not so hard," Bill pointed out and there were wry laughs.

"Almost nobody left," Sandy said.

"Impossible to get a loan these days. Credit's drying right up," Howard Mountain remarked. "You can't get an operating loan any more."

"Banks are pulling right out of agriculture," Bill Peat said.

"Except for corporate operators, big companies."

Faintly, from the hot street outside, a voice could be heard over the roar of the air conditioner that was one of the reasons the café was so popular. The glass door swung open letting in a gust of wiltingly hot air, and a short round figure bustled in followed by three or four men who all seemed to be trying to get through the door at the same time. Heads swivelled to see who the newcomers were.

"It's a hot one!" Harold Havoc shouted, and here or there someone answered him while everyone else watched in silence. "Nice to see everybody having a neighbourly chat in this nice cool place. Reminds me of the old days."

He moved further into the café and people began to murmur to each other as they recognized the men who accompanied him – local men, farmers themselves, dressed in clean white shirts and fresh denim pants with creases ironed into them. Instead of the usual caps with the names of implement manufacturers or crop sprays or chemical manufacturers, they wore on their heads brand new straw hats like the one Harold Havoc was taking off and holding against his chest. He was still dressed in the same light-blue suit they had all seen before, wrinkled and covered with food stains – coffee on one thigh, a spot of ketchup on the lapel.

"I'm here to remind you that my political party needs members. I'm here to ask you to join me in my fight to bring back old values. I want you to vote for me . . ." Mrs. Henwick came out of the kitchen where she'd been making hamburgers and seemed to be about to come down the aisle toward him. "But I didn't come here to make a speech," he added hastily, and everybody laughed knowing that was just what he had come for. "You all know what I stand for. I stand for . . ."

"The past!" somebody called out, and there were a few snickers.

"The best of the past!" Havoc shouted, raising one arm. Mrs. Henwick took another step forward, her powerful arms folded over her formidable chest, and again Havoc made a mental deviation. "I came in here because I want you all to do something for me. See these?" The men who had entered the café behind him suddenly lifted their straw hats from their head and held them high for everyone to look at. Another man came forward and in his arms he carried a high stack of identical straw hats.

"See these farmer's hats? Remember the days when that was what your grandad wore to keep off the sun? Whatever happened to an honest straw hat the farmer wore to keep the sun off his head?" He looked around the café at the men seated at the counter and in the booths. Nearly all of them were wearing caps with labels on them from some agri-business company. The men looked faintly sheepish or else merely puzzled. Even Mrs. Henwick was no longer threatening, but listening with interest.

"Throw away those caps, boys! The names on your hats spell the names of your slavery! Cargill! Avadex! Deutz-Allis! Ford! You've sold your souls to them. They bought you with their fancy, shiny, over-priced products. They told you they were your friends, that they'd show you how to farm! They sucked you in, boys! What did they do for you? They got you into hock with the banker! They showed you how to ruin your land! They gave you products that gave you cancer and killed you! And in the end, what did they do? They lost you your farm!" His face was brick-red, sweat poured down it, and in the pause the only sound was the muted roar of the air conditioner.

"Their sweet, siren song," Havoc crooned. "Profit, progress, profit . . ." His audience was mesmerized. He raised his voice. "Throw away those symbols of your slavery! Remember that once the farmer was king in this province! He owned his own place, he farmed by the sun and the rain and the lay of the land and the smell of the dirt, the good, sweet dirt under his feet!"

Bill Peat was the first to take off his Avadex cap and throw it onto the counter. Instantly one of Havoc's helpers was there to place a clean, fresh-smelling straw hat on Bill's head.

"Eight bucks, boys!" Harold shouted. "I got to make ends meet too." Up and down the aisles his helpers went trading grimy caps for clean straw hats, though here or there somebody held stubbornly onto his cap, his jaw set, his mouth thin. Wallets were being reluctantly extracted from back pockets and hard-won bills handed over. Havoc and his followers collected the discarded grease-stained, frayed caps with their Banvil, Case, and Hoegrass signs on them. At the outside door he stopped for one last rhetorical flourish.

"It's a clean sweep, fellas!" – though it wasn't – and with one last wave, rather like Santa Claus, he disappeared out the door. For a moment there was no sound in the café except the air conditioner. Then cheerful pandemonium broke out.

"I can't understand it," Val said. He hit the steering wheel with his fist, his handsome face contorted with a mixture of anger and genuine puzzlement. "It should have worked! I planned every step. I . . ." He fell silent, the anger slowly replaced by anguish. Jessie wondered for a second if she was seeing tears gathering in his eyes. Somewhat tentatively and a little too late, she said, "You couldn't plan for the weather, Val. That was the gamble."

"Or the interest rates," he said bitterly. But he had stopped talking to her now and she was half-frightened by the intensity and variability of his moods. She sometimes felt a little angry herself, thinking of the quiet security of her parents' house that she had left for Val and that all of that – she hardly dared contemplate it – was gone now, and Val was not offering her so much as a word of comfort but was wholly locked up in what had suddenly become his own personal drama. She was bewildered too, but mostly she felt that she had no one to turn to. They were reaching the edge of town and were passing down its few streets on their way to Val's parents' house. Jessie's stomach gave a lurch, and she tried to control it. She would not further humiliate herself in front of her in-laws if she could help it. They pulled up in front of Herb and Flora's house and for a second, neither of them moved.

"Come on, let's get it over with," Jessie said.

"I heard," Herb said as he opened the front door and before Val could speak. He turned away without inviting them in, leaving the door open, and went heavily into the living room. They followed slowly. Herb and Flora's living room contained the old furniture from the farm, Herb's worn brown armchair covered with a bright afghan crocheted by Flora, the old-fashioned end tables, the small hooked rugs spread at all the spots where wear was likely on the new broadloom. All of this sat incongruously in the brand new house.

There was a long silence while Val primed himself to speak. Herb ignored them.

"We've still got the land and the crop," Val said, finally. Flora hovered in the doorway between the kitchen and the living room, but neither Val nor Jessie thought to greet her and she said nothing. At last Herb spoke.

"You can forget about the crop," he said. "If there is one. They'll seize every kernel as soon as you get within a mile of the elevator." He spoke slowly, without moving, his head against the back of his chair. "From here on you can't sell a thing, but they'll seize the money." Val was pale, growing paler by the minute. "We'll get a lawyer," Herb said. "At least try to slow the bastards down. You put that half on the east side up for sale. The money'll buy you a little time. Those sonofabitches can't just walk in yet. This is still a free country."

"If I can find a buyer," Val said. "It'll have to be in secret."

"If somebody wants it, we'll find him."

"Nobody'll want it if it's got a lien on it," Flora said from the doorway. "And anyway, '*Woe to those who add house to house / and join field to field / until everywhere belongs to them / and they are the sole inhabitants of the land.*' Isaiah, 5:8."

They all looked at her, but she turned and went back inside the kitchen where they could hear her rattling china. Jessie looked to Val for some rebuttal or confirmation of what she had said. He was still not moving, not looking at her, keeping his eyes on his father. Herb leaned forward, his fine, papery skin suddenly flooded red.

"If that's the way it is," he said, rage rendering his voice guttural, "we'll borrow from the credit union so you can make a payment. I'll put up this house for collateral. It's free and clear. It'll bring us thirty, forty thousand." Jessie began to cry quietly, her tears sliding silently down her cheeks. Neither man paid any attention to her.

"You can't do that," she said to Herb. "You already bought the farm once. It isn't fair."

"Be quiet, Jessie," Val said, and had Herb not been there, she would have hit him. "You could lose this house," he said to his father. "If this drought keeps up. Then where'd you be?"

"We've got our pensions," Herb said. His voice rose, got louder and louder. "I was born on that place. I'll be damned if I'll let some sonofabitching banker have it!" Flora had entered the room carrying a tray with cups and saucers on it and now she set it down with a bang that made them rattle.

"Herb Sheridan!" she said. "There is no call for language like that. You should be ashamed." Herb ignored her. Flora sat down and began to pour coffee, her mouth set in a hard line which, Jessie suddenly realized, was to hold back the tears.

"We'll sell the car," Jessie said. She hated the way they were ignoring her as if none of this had anything to do with her, and at the same time, she could feel it, they were blaming her. She wanted to show them she was not afraid to do whatever had to be done. Val looked at her in surprise and for a second she thought he would tell her again to keep quiet. If he did, she *would* hit him – as hard as she could right in his stupid handsome face. She glared at him. After a minute he said, "It isn't worth much," in a dismissive way.

"We could get ten thousand for it," she said loudly. "It may not pay off our debts, but it'll give us some . . . cash flow," she said, bitter to find herself using his language. "And I'm going to get a job."

"She's right," Herb said. "You could get at least ten for it. Sell it." Jessie, still furious, drew in a deep breath through her nose, her lips set as hard as Flora's. She had never in her life been so angry. The absurdity of blaming her! But it was the country way, she had been here long enough to know that. Unless you were a saint and a martyr, everything was always the woman's fault. She felt like walking out.

"But what'll we drive?" Val said, stalling.

"Drive the truck," Flora said abruptly, and Jessie could feel him letting their beautiful new car go too.

"I don't like the idea of my wife working," Val said, sullen now.

"I don't like the idea of starving!" Jessie said. As soon as it was out, she was sorry. Val, who had been pale as a ghost since afternoon, had flushed a bright red. "Oh, God, I'm sorry," she said. Val blinked rapidly and looked away.

"The trick'll be to find a job," Herb said, as if he had not witnessed what had passed between them. "The town's practically shut down. And it's getting worse every day."

"I can drive to Crisis," Jessie said.

"In what?" Val said.

"Stop it, Val," Flora said. "She's trying to help. And don't tell me you can't get something running for her to drive. That old '65 Chrysler is still in the shed. Not a single thing wrong with it. Right Herb?" Herb nodded. Val moved, rubbing one hand roughly across his face, clasping his hands together, then letting them go.

"I'll start looking for a job right away. To tide us over till we get out of this mess." Herb stiffened, but Flora kept pouring cream into her cup, carefully, as if her life depended on doing it right.

"Listen, and you listen good, Valentine," Herb said. "The good times are over. If you think in a few years you'll be right back were you were a year ago, driving a fancy car, living in a new house, spending money like it was water, you forget it. From here on in it's gonna be a fight to the end just to hang onto whatever you got left." He paused, staring hard at Val with eyes that burned so that Val couldn't look away. "If you can't live with that, you walk off that place tonight. You hand over the keys to the banker. Because you'll farm like we did fifty years ago and more, or you won't farm at all."

And Jessie, who had at last begun to understand that what went on between Val and his father was something she could safely ignore since its roots went back to homesteader days, was thinking ahead to her next step. She could still leave Val and the farm. She pondered while the talk went on around her.

She would give Val plenty of time to come back to them as a couple, the way it had been before and to the promises they had made to each other, whether spoken or not. And if he did not, she would leave.

But staying, she would fight. She would leave the financial manoeuvring to Val and Herb who understood it, who had it bred into their bones from generations of struggle to stay on the land. But she would stand by the bargain she had made when she married Val.

# CHAPTER
# 12

Melody Masuria lay on the white chenille cover on the double bed in Pastor Raven's guest bedroom. The blinds were pulled and although it was another brilliant summer day outside the house, the room itself was in darkness except for the streaks of light that stabbed their way around the edge of the blind. At the foot of the bed a small colour television played silently.

Melody lay in perfect stillness, her arms extended by her sides, palms up, legs straight, thighs and calves touching under her long white gown. Her hands were covered with small squares of white terrycloth and a white terrycloth towel lay under her small feet and was folded over to cover them. She lay with her eyes open, gazing upward into the shadows that bound the ceiling. Now and then the blind lifted, allowing in more light, then sighed and fell back against the window frame. A basin of clear water sat on the night table beside Melody, and beside it more small white towels were neatly folded in a pile.

The door opened quietly and Mr. Raven entered, carefully dressed in a crisp white shirt and neatly pressed beige cotton trousers, his long red hair brushed back and resting down his back in a shining swatch. He clasped his hands at his waist and bowed his head slightly. Melody didn't move.

"How are you, Sister?" he asked.

She watched him take the few steps from the open door to her bedside.

"Is it time to make the pilgrimage up the hillside?" she asked, stirring.

"There will be no pilgrimage today," Mr. Raven said hastily. "My – our followers are spending the day in prayer in their own homes. We will perhaps meet here tonight to determine what our next step should be."

"Someone should know," Melody said vaguely. She was not sure who, but someone should know. She frowned. "Have you called anyone?" she asked. The pastor made a perplexed face and shook his head no. "What about the head of our church ?"

"I am the head," he replied gently, modestly. "There is no one else." They were silent for a moment. "Perhaps the Catholic arch-bishop?" he suggested. "Or all the ecclesiastical heads in the province?"

"I think so," Melody said vaguely, her voice feeble.

"My dear," Mr. Raven said, bending toward her as if to touch her. Melody, though she remained lying down, drew away from his touch, so that he pulled back his hand as quickly as he had extended it. "Would you like a glass of cold water?"

"Water?" Melody said with a hint of irritation. "Lemonade," she corrected him. "Fresh lemons." Her voice grew firm. "And lots of sugar. I cannot stand sour lemonade."

"Lemonade," the pastor said, as if he found this request a little out of order. "Certainly, Sister." He hesitated, evidently trying to see Melody's eyes clearly in the darkened room, then giving up. He backed away toward the door, bowing his head again.

"Look!" Melody said abruptly. He looked up quickly, alarmed. She lifted her head from the pillow and for the first time her eyes gleamed blue. "Look!" He followed them to the TV screen. Phone numbers ran continuously across the screen below a close-up of a man's face. "Clyde Leroy!" she said. The pastor returned quickly to her bedside where he stood watching the screen. "It's perfect!" Melody exclaimed. "He has an enormous TV audience, and all kinds of money for publicity! He's famous all over the world."

"He receives money to spread the word to the faithful, to carry out his mission in the world," the pastor said, keeping his voice gentle, though with a hint of admonition.

"Of course," Melody said, her voice drifting back into weakness. "Of course. How better? You probably don't know much about the Catholic church, but I do. And it takes years, practically centuries, before they'll . . ." Her voice trailed off. The blind lifted, letting in a shaft of light that revealed Melody's pallor, before it fell back with a smack. "I can't wait," she said. "Jesus doesn't want me to wait that long."

The pastor was silent, thinking, as he peered down at Melody stretched out on the bed.

"You're all right?" he asked, still gentle.

"Oh, yes," Melody said. For a long minute silence held again. Then Mr. Raven turned in a way that was almost absent-minded and walked slowly, thoughtfully, to the door.

"You'll phone Clyde Leroy?" Melody asked, her voice suddenly shrill. He hesitated, his back to her, then gave a nod. "Don't forget the lemonade," she said. The pastor went out, shutting the door quietly behind him. Melody turned her eyes back to the television, watching with a new intensity.

The Messenger of God went to the kitchen and began to squeeze lemons. He went about his work methodically, as he might have done had he been given the task of cutting a precious jewel or solving a difficult problem in mathematics. Still, for all his appearance of deep concentration, it was not his work his mind was on and he sprayed a jet of lemon juice all over his clean white shirt without even noticing.

He was deeply troubled. He could not understand how this child, ignorant of God's ways, this sin-ridden female defiled by the touch of men, could have been given the sign he himself had desired all his life. Hadn't he led as clean, as pure a life as a man could lead? Hadn't he given over his very life to Jesus, not asked for a wife or a child knowing Jesus had said, "*And everyone who has left houses or brothers or sisters or fathers or mothers or children or lands, for my name's sake, will receive a hundredfold, and inherit eternal life.*" This pill was almost too bitter to swallow.

Humility, he well knew, was what was required of him, but humility was a concept he had not fully understood. However, he was unaware of this shortcoming. He knew himself humble in the gift of eternal life promised him, but he had never questioned his assumption that there had indeed been a gift. But now, no matter how he struggled with the question, it seemed clear to him that he was required to care for the one who had been given what he had, all his life, believed was to be his.

Abruptly, not even turning off the gushing tap, he dropped to his knees. Overcome by a paroxysm of sorrow or pain at the mystery he had in so unexpected a fashion become part of, he bent his torso till his forehead touched the cool vinyl. He clenched his fists and rested them on the floor on each side of his head.

"Beloved Jesus," he prayed, "I humbly beseech you, tell me how I have failed you. Or if this is something I have yet to learn, and the task you have set before me is indeed the one that I must do, I beg you, give me the wisdom to know what I must do. And the courage, Dear Jesus, to do it." He was forgetting the language of the Bible in which he was accustomed to couch all his thoughts and prayers. Indeed, he found himself as prostrate as an Arab. A deeper strain of desiring writhed inside him, billowing and twisting, formed of his disappointment, his irrevocable knowledge that he had no right to desire anything, even as he struggled for understanding and for peace. Words came into his head: "Go, *weigh for me the weight of fire, or measure for me a measure of wind, or call back for me the day that is past.*"

He knew these words well. His mother had read them to him over and over again when he was a child. Second Esdras, Chapter

Four, Verse Five. They were the words spoken by the archangel Uriel in a vision to the seer Esdras. And when the seer could not answer these questions, Uriel had gone on: *"You cannot understand the things with which you have grown up; How then can your mind comprehend the way of the Most High?"*

All his years of training in the ways and the words of the Most High began slowly to return to him, calming him. How indeed to understand the Lord's Way? Patience, he counselled himself. He lifted himself to a kneeling position, wiped his eyes and smoothed down his electric, unmanageable hair. With trembling fingers he clasped his hands to his chest as if to still the rapid beat of his heart, and prayed.

Often over the last while, Pastor Raven had been on his knees praying hour after hour at the same time as Alma Sheridan, only a block away, had been kneeling in prayer by her bedside. Though, of course, neither of them knew of the other. Had they known, they would have been distraught, despairing even, to realize that while one of them was praying earnestly for a sign, the other was praying with as great a degree of seriousness to have a sign taken away.

Meanwhile, Melody, who had also been given a sign, or so it seemed, lay on her bed and watched, with the sound turned off, Reverend Clyde Leroy preaching his vision of eternity to the multitudes.

Alma had been persuaded to write a book. She never knew this had been the doctor's idea, but her fellow teachers at her retirement tea urged her to, saying that with so many years experience with elementary pupils and so much success at teaching them, it would be foolish, selfish even, to retire without leaving behind a compendium of her wisdom. Alma never doubted that she knew what she knew, nor even that she could write a book. She doubted, rather, that it would be read; especially not by those very teachers who were most in need of its advice. She was glad, though, to find something to do that would fill the long evenings and keep her up far into the night, for she had come to dread the fall of darkness and the moment of sleep. Her nightmares had not gone away with retirement as she had hoped, but had instead become even more persistent and terrifying.

She had dragged out all the boxes of papers she had collected through more than forty years of school-teaching and was organizing the contents: samples of work done by pupils long since grown whose faces she could barely remember, memos and messages from principals many now gone to their final rest, papers issued to teachers by experts in education, packages of letters held together with rubber bands, that had come from parents and from grown-up ex-pupils writing to tell her of the course of their lives. At ten each evening, the time she usually retired, she would instead brew herself another cup of tea, drag out a fresh box and dig into it with determination.

On this particular night it was almost two when Alma finally went to bed and her head was spinning with the pictures and voices out of her past. She was beginning to find that it didn't do to struggle too hard to pin down a memory precisely, because the harder she struggled to clearly delineate its boundaries the more amorphous it grew, until the shape of memory shifted and changed, became unrecognizable, and she was no longer sure the event had happened at all.

She thought of all the years she had taught children about the past, about La Vérendrye and Henry Kelsey, Samuel Hearne, Peter Pond, and Peter Fidler. When it came right down to it, how did she know these men had ever existed? Night after night she sorted history into piles, saw it stacked up around the room. Push a pile over and the pages slid across the room, lost their order, mixed with other piles. She was beginning to doubt the existence of history. It's all dreams, she whispered to herself as her head touched her pillow, only dreams.

From beyond the place of dreams, a new vision welled:

"Forty per cent of the Earth's surface is grassland," she heard her own crisp, disembodied voice instructing. Her vision cleared and from her vantage point high above the edge of the boreal forest she saw the lonely splendour of the high plains, the thousands of square miles of virtually empty rolling grassy land with only a few farms·and ranches sprinkled across them. Settlers had divided the Earth into squares and set buildings neatly onto them, they had cut straight roads across it, and ploughed it up with long furrows. They thought they could own nature, harness her like a horse, and drive her to do their bidding.

Now, inexplicably, the past and the present co-existed and, moving across the Earth's grassy surface, she saw small bands of people with brown, weathered skin, clear eyes, and taut, strong bodies covered with the skins of animals. Then she felt keenly her own disconnection with the ground she had lived on all her life. Sorrow swept through her and she would have been overcome but she found herself swooping out over the plains as the people vanished into tiny, distant dots and she was surrounded by a countless horde of creatures all importuning her in a hundred different languages, their arms, made gaunt in wars, famines, floods, and droughts, stretched out to her. They keened their misery to her, clutching at her with stumps made bloody in the torture chambers of the world. They cried out their hunger and their need to her, she felt she would drown in their burning eyes, while the endless wind blew across the prairie and the grasses rustled and whispered.

A new sound was growing. It came rolling across the plain, shivering the grasses before it, a thunder that was not thunder, booming and rolling, drowning out all other sounds. It was the voice of God.

Alma was consumed by His voice, she vibrated with it like a tuning fork. God lifted her in His teeth and shook her, then set her down gently, turned inside out. She awoke overcome by terror and in her struggle she fell beside her bed in a tangle of blankets and sheets.

Time passed, but Alma could no longer measure time; time had deserted her forever. The quaking of her body slowly reduced to trembling, but the trembling was to remain forever; it had been caused by the current that was the voice of God flowing through her body, it would never again be turned off. All her beliefs learned in a lifetime of church-going turned to ashes in an instant as when a white-hot flame is put to paper. Now she saw how it was – that God was, simply and clearly, of another realm – mighty and terrible, and she smaller than the tiniest mote in His eye. If she had not felt her bones pressed apart by Him, her sinews stretched past breaking, her brain sent reeling out into the stars, she would have wept at the sheer silliness of the things she had been taught about God.

She waited.

GO AND TELL THE PEOPLE.

He had ordained her a prophetess.

The emptiness inside her was filling with sounds, they were milling around, arguing among themselves, pushing and shoving each other, forming into ragged ranks, then falling out again.

She would wait. When the time came to speak she would be filled with His power and the words would marshal themselves into ranks of brave and shining soldiers of the Lord, and she, Alma, would speak at last.

From then on, wherever Alma went – to the post office, where she stood quivering on the steps looking into the faces of the people who came for mail, to the grocery store, where she stood inside the door watching, up one street and down another – she mumbled softly to herself.

"Alas – " or "Thus says the Lord . . ." she would begin, but the sounds that followed weren't right – "regab . . . minterha . . . kilar . . ." – or were from languages she didn't know – "*sanguinaire . . . sueno . . . fod-sünde. . . .*" When the time was right, she would speak.

She hurried along, muttering to herself while the people of the town spoke kindly to her or watched her with worried eyes. Something would have to be done, they knew, but not just yet.

Strange how Alma was in the thoughts of many in that community. Rigid, judgemental, unpleasant often, there had always been a strata of personality just below the surface that seemed, to those who had noticed it, faint bewilderment. It was as if in her heart Alma was not nearly so certain about things as she gave the appearance of being, or as if, if she relaxed for even a second, all her uncertainty would drown her. Those who had a vein of this in themselves recognized it in Alma and suffered for her at the slow disintegration of that hard, clear surface that had protected her from the terror of her own doubts. Jessie Sheridan had seen it, although she had no name for what it was that stirred her sympathy.

She was leaning against the counter in her spotless kitchen thinking about Alma's dreams and about her suffering. She was herself, for the first time in her life, actually suffering too, and she felt utterly alone. In the midst of the disaster that threatened both of them, Val had turned away from her. He had become morose and sullen and had withdrawn into himself. He lay asleep on the sofa in the next room, lying on his side with his back to the room, his head scrunching the gold velvet pillow her aunt had given them, his shirt wrinkled and stretched tight across his back, his knees drawn up and his hands pressed palm to palm between them. As soon as she stepped into the living room she could smell the flat, salty smell of his unwashed body.

It was useless, dangerous even, to try to wake him. If he woke he would stare uncomprehendingly at her with red-rimmed eyes and shout, "What! What!" not in any enquiring way, but in a rage at something that wasn't there, and when she persisted so that he finally came to himself, he would not even apologize. He would only grunt and turn his back on her again.

Jessie had stopped sleeping except in shallow passages that did not feel like sleep. During the day her world, previously full of the brightest primary colours, had turned grey and she had begun to carry with her at all times a pain that sometimes centred itself in her chest and sometimes in her gut. It was barely endurable, and it blighted and shrivelled everything she looked at or touched that might have brought her the barest second of happiness.

She didn't know what to do about Val. She had talked to no one about their disaster, no one who was close to her, and everyone in their world seemed to view it as Val's disaster and not hers, as though she had no right to any suffering of her own. And she was appalled and ashamed by what had happened to her clever, confident husband, appalled by his collapse. She didn't want anyone to know, not even his mother. Yet things couldn't go on this way. She had to do something, if only she knew what.

She would have cleaned the house while Val slept, but already it was painfully clean. She couldn't concentrate to read and there was no one she wanted to talk to. Restless, unhappy, she put her hand on her solar plexus and took a deep breath, trying to alleviate the pain. She crossed the room to the patio doors and slid them open and stepped out onto the deck. It was so hot, incredibly hot; it was not to be believed how hot it was.

She crossed the little patch of yellow-green lawn, the gravel, and was soon beyond the farm buildings and out on the strip of prairie at the edge of the field of wheat. Durum it was, too short and burning up, the heads crested white which meant they weren't filling as they should. The inevitable wind was blowing and she knew it would brew thunderclouds later in the afternoon that would be dry of rain.

The heads of wheat rustled against each other and the insects the field was full of hummed in a higher key. As far as she could see in any direction there was nothing but the pale cream of the wheat bending and shivering, rising to sway, bending again, reaching, whispering. But wait: far out, beyond anything she could clearly make out, near the edge where the Earth curved gently away, something was moving. She stood very still, the ache in her chest forgotten for the moment, and watched. A moving streak, dark against the sea of ivory. It was a coyote.

Standing in the field of short, sparse durum, the heads empty of kernels, she felt mocked by the coyote, she and Val and their dreams of comfort and wealth. Standing in her failed crop, her shoes filled with dust, the sun withering everything it touched, it came to her.

She saw herself and Val as part of an endlessly long line of farmers who had stood just so: she saw this in countries all over the world – she saw crops withering, dying; she saw ragged people, their eyes dark with suffering, she saw them leaving with nothing but what they could carry, turning their backs on their homes. She saw more: she saw big landowners or companies driving them off their own plots of land, turning them into serfs in their own countries; she saw growers of rice, potatoes, bananas, cocoa, corn, and more. She saw it was true of fishermen, hunters, trappers, miners. She saw that she and Val were nobody, nothing in the scheme of things. Their success meant nothing, neither did their failure.

Rage filled her, that this was not how things had to be, but that they were this way only because those who could help, would not. Not governments, not churches. They were doomed; she saw it clearly.

Better to run with the coyote, she thought bitterly, and was confused. She became aware of the sweat pouring down her temples, making her dress stick to her chest and back, her hair press stickily to her neck. She was made dizzy by the sun and by what she had seen. Its hopelessness appalled her. She turned and ran for the house, the wheat whipping against her shins and catching in her skirt, her shoes striking hard lumps of dirt and throwing her off balance.

There was something about praying inside his house or the drafty old school he used for a church that left Uriel Raven unsatisfied, especially when he was particularly troubled or wrestling hard with a difficult spiritual problem. At these times, if he had no other pressing matter to attend to, he would go out at night to walk among the hills that surrounded the town, watching the stars, listening to the night sounds carried on the clear, sharp air, and smelling the distinctive scents of the prairie.

Often in these directionless wanderings he would kneel and pray, but instead of closing his eyes and bending his head, he would raise his face to the sky's infinite blackness, and to the light of the distant stars coming to him over unimaginable distances. Then he felt in touch with God, or at least he felt the possibility of being in touch grow stronger. He prayed for strength and for wisdom and he felt the stars probing his tormented soul. Sometimes he prayed till he fell asleep, waking at the first rays of light to go slowly home, his clothes marked with bits of grass and twigs and burrs from the wild licorice, his unruly hair blazing up around his anguished face, gathering barking dogs as he went.

Now Melody, the fallen angel, had come to him in repentance and had been rewarded with a sign. She had begged him to call the television evangelist Clyde Leroy. Today he had done that very thing, and now, sleepless, he strode along, stumbling in gopher holes, catching his pantlegs on greasewood bushes, stepping on prickly pears, hardly feeling their needles. He had called Clyde Leroy and after an hour or more of explaining to disembodied voices he had finally spoken to the great man himself.

He would send someone, Leroy had promised him, soon. Raven had an image of Leroy's silk-clad minions, his painted, amazingly coiffed women. Someone would meet the girl, examine her, pray with her and would report back to him. He and his advisers would confer, and would get back to Brother Raven.

Raven had set down the phone with his head ringing from pressure that had been building all the time he was speaking to the officers of the Clyde Leroy Evangelical Mission. He had left the triumphant Melody and gone to his room to pray. But prayer eluded him; try as he would he couldn't get rid of the pain that was a writhing knot in his gut.

He was being asked to give up his own quest for glory in favour of helping Melody achieve hers. He knew he must humble himself before her for her sake and for the sake of his own soul. This was his task, he knew it, yet he doubted he could do it. She was a child. She was impure, having violated the first law all women must obey. And there was something in her he didn't like, was uneasy with, something on which he couldn't quite put his finger. He listened hard to her every utterance, watched her mouth and her eyes and the gestures she made with her hands, but no matter how hard he tried he couldn't discover what it was that bothered him. He knew that no matter what, God was testing him. He would not fail Him.

Thus tormented, he had come out into the hills seeking solace. He skirted Neil Locke's house, noting but not caring that a soft yellow light was still blossoming in the window though it was three in the morning. He knelt only briefly and without joy at the cross he and his parishioners had erected with such travail, then rose and went on again, climbing higher toward that pure line where the black edge of the hills met the crystal sky. He kept his eyes on that glow as he walked, as if he might, if he went far enough, walk into that clarity.

Unexpectedly, he felt himself descending. His first step down woke him from his reverie as his jaws crunched together, and he spread his arms to break his fall, knowing he had stepped into the deep coulee that ran on an angle across the hills from the town below and that formed a boundary between two ranges of hills. He couldn't stop himself, and he descended the coulee's crumbling clay sides, sliding now and then, catching hold of a clump of sage or skunkweed growing in the hillside, trying to stop his fall.

It grew darker as he descended and he could see nothing below his feet, couldn't even see his feet. Only inky blackness and the smell of animals all around him, for he knew it is in coulee bottoms hidden among the wild roses, the saskatoons, the chokecherries, the creeping juniper, the badger bushes, and the occasional timorous willow that the animals of the plains find shelter from the heat and the cold, from predators and the never-ending encroachment of men.

He fell past an eagles's nest without knowing it and slid right by a massive granite boulder covered with lichen the colour of the sun during the day that turned black in the darkness. He felt the gathered warmth of the sun as he passed the rock and then the cold where sometimes a spring seeped upward to dampen the clay, and still he descended into the implacable blackness below.

The air grew colder, the scents stronger, he grasped a rose bush to slow his fall and felt its thorns enter his flesh. Dirt rose up and slid inside his shoes, the Earth's smell was strong in his nostrils. Bible verses tumbled through his head:

> If anyone comes to me and does not hate his own father and mother . . .
> . . . and do you think you can comprehend the way of the Most High . . .
> to one is given through the Spirit the utterance of wisdom . . . to another is given the working of miracles, to another prophecy . . .
> If I speak in the tongues of men and of angels, but have not love, I am a noisy gong or a clanging cymbal. And if I have prophetic powers, and understand all mysteries and all knowledge, and if I have all faith, so as to remove mountains, but have not love . . .

His mother's gentle face rose before him in the darkness, her pale eyes and faded, red-gold hair. "We have given you the name of the fourth archangel, the one not yet heard from . . . "

"Uriel, one of the holy angels – for he is of eternity and of trembling. . . . "

He slid further, having lost his footing entirely, and felt the wet clay dampen his trousers and shirt, then his feet struck more wet clay and cold air struck him in the face. He knew he had reached the bottom.

He could see nothing, but he struggled to his feet, his hands muddy from digging into the clay, mud on his face and his feet coated with mud and slipping in the wetness. He turned and turned but there was nothing, only impenetrable blackness every way he looked. He moved and his foot slid on a small rock and he fell, planting both hands in a sage bush, which he recognized by its dusty, pungent odour. And the wind was rising, must be, for he heard it loud in his ears like the rushing of giant wings.

He clambered to his feet again and saw ahead of him in the velvet blackness a faint glow. He was entirely disoriented and couldn't think what the light might be, but it was moving toward him, a floating glow, and hairs rose on the back of his neck. It came closer and formed itself into the shape of a man which glowed all around its silhouette, particles of light rested on the surface of its garments like dust on the wings of a moth. For a second Uriel was paralyzed with fear, then he dropped to his knees in the mud and tried, through chattering teeth, to pray. He heard a voice.

"Uriel, rise." Terrified, Uriel did so. "You wish a sign from God," the voice said, gentle now. "You believe the Holy One has chosen you to prophesy for Him." Uriel felt himself grow calmer, though he couldn't have said why, but a force emanated from this being that stilled his fear. He felt power coming from it, but no danger. Slowly his teeth stopped chattering and his breath came less quickly.

"So I have believed," he acknowledged, wishing to say more, but feeling silenced without knowing how.

"Has God given you a sign?" the voice asked.

"He has not," Uriel admitted, lowering his head, then spoke over his own desire to be silent. "But I have prayed. I have followed the Lord's commandments." The angel laughed, amused.

"Good works," he said, still laughing, though more gently.

"No!" Uriel interrupted him, "I have not done good works. I have carried instead the Word of the Lord to whoever would listen and to some who would not. I have been spurned and scorned and driven out. I have believed making converts to the Army of the Lord is the one great work. . . ." Uriel trembled again, waiting, but the angel was silent. "And I have believed," Uriel ventured, "that one day He would reward me for my work in His cause, that one day He would give me a sign before He would lift me up to join Him in paradise." He paused. "But now . . ."

"He has given the sign to someone else." Uriel was silent. "Uriel," the angel said, "Fire of God . . . how do you know the Word of the Lord?"

Stunned, Uriel couldn't speak.

"How do you know you are chosen?" The angel's voice had risen to thunder and Uriel heard small animals skittering away from them in the bushes around their feet. Weakness sped through him, rushing like wind. He almost fell, but out of his years of training, words came.

"The Bible . . . it is the true Word. . . ."

"Have you seen the tablets Moses brought down from the mountain?" the angel asked, closer to his ear now. "Have you seen the waters part? Have you seen Him walk on water?" As these words pushed their way into his heart Uriel felt himself gripped as though in a vise. The grip was neither hot nor cold, it neither burned nor did it freeze, nor did it cause him pain. It was merely inexorable. He struggled, trying to free himself of the grip of the angel. The glow vanished as the angel's grip on Uriel grew stronger and stronger while the night grew blacker and blacker and he felt himself sinking further into a dark, bottomless, silent realm.

# PART
# THREE

# CHAPTER
# 13

There is in Ordeal a hotel, a bank, a town hall, a lumber yard, a school, a hospital, a lodge for old people, two grocery stores, a feed store, a café, a post office, and several dozen small, tidy frame houses, most of which are painted white or, in response to the craze of fifteen years earlier for "natural" things, sided over with varnished cedar or pine which, though attractive in its own way, rather spoils the romantic, old-fashioned look characteristic of the towns first settled about the time of the First World War.

The streets at the heart of the town are paved, but out toward its edges the pavement narrows until where the town dissolves into prairie there is no pavement at all, only a thin sprinkling of gravel, then only hard-packed dirt trails with pale ghosts of dust scudding down their surfaces, and the occasional tumbleweed skittering along.

In summer the town is racked by storms, the lightning cracking and sizzling down the sky, the thunder booming and rolling, making dogs cower, while on dry days the town sits in the centre of its valley as quiet as it might be if no one lived there at all. On hot summer days the asphalt grows sticky with the heat which it radiates back into the air far into the night, not cooling until just before dawn. And when the heat grows unbearable and the wind blows hard and constant so clothes can't be hung on the lines for the dust, and hairdos are ruined, and even the dogs won't come out from the shade, everyone remembers that this is how it has always been every summer, far back into childhood, sighs, and goes inside to wait it out.

In the bitter winters the same wind whips up snow that burns the face with cold and drivers have to pump their brakes to stop on the ice-coated streets. Blizzards whip the town, obscuring it from view in the howling white, freezing everything to a standstill, or burying it under hills of ice and snow. And when the snowfalls are over the grader pushes up a long, narrow bank of snow and ice down the centre of the main street where the yellow line is in summer.

Trees sixty to seventy feet high, mostly cottonwoods and poplars, shade the streets, though in the early days of the town there were no trees at all, only bald prairie with a stream meandering through a valley. Now, on many streets the homeowners have chopped down the old trees, leaving only stumps, mutations ten feet high, and on others, spruces planted many years before have grown so thick and high that the houses in their midst have all but disappeared.

Winding around the edge of the town is the river, a narrow, shallow stream with tall grass growing along its banks, and shrubs – different kinds of willows, rosebushes, and chokecherries – and in a wet year, wildflowers – wild morning glories, fireweed, wild anemones, brown-eyed susans, milkweed.

Overlooking all of this is the graveyard. It is far from full, this hillside where the people of the town go to their last resting place among the dry, yellow prairie grasses. In winter their graves are buried under snow, in summer, despite the vigilance of the living, tunnelled into by gophers. There are three or four impressive granite headstones – red, black, sparkling grey – but most of the graves have small flat stones or white wooden crosses or nothing at all to mark them. The graves tell of the lives and the deaths of the people: in fires, from smallpox and diphtheria and pneumonia, in childbirth, from heart attacks, cancer, pneumonia, by falling off horses, or overdosing with drink, or by suicide, or peacefully departing in extreme old age.

Every farmyard is a long-fingered extension of the town, or the town of it, and even the heart of the town is a part of the heart of the prairie in which it sits, and which a piece of also sits in the heart of each man, woman, and child who lives in it.

It is possible that the town itself lives, that some mornings early it groans and stretches and the hills move back a shade to make room for it; or other times, in the light of the moon, it rises higher, breathes in the sharp blue air and hums to itself, a thin, high tune. It hears talk of its dying and knows that it is growing weaker, but it revives when children play along the river's banks, or when its people gather to celebrate anything at all, from the harvest to a wedding. This is the town built of memories, dreams, phantoms, where the future, too, hangs about, waiting for incarnation.

At its heart are the widows. They are the ones who know Ordeal best, who daily feel its pulse. It is thought by the townspeople that these women are without power, that the deaths of their husbands have rendered their lives meaningless and without purpose. Yet they are the ones who hold the town together, cutting across so many families as each of them does, reaching into every corner of the small community, knowing collectively all that takes place and guessing the rest.

Zena Lavender had been a widow for twenty-eight years. She knew when her Alden died of pneumonia – the result of the night he struggled home with their few cattle to keep them from freezing to death in a blizzard – that she would not marry again, no matter who asked her. Alden had been a handsome man, he had grown handsomer in the years since his death, and Zena had never been able to imagine herself as somebody else's wife. She wore the mantle of her long widowhood with dignity and an air of noble suffering, as if, as the more unkind said, she were better than other people. After Alden's death she had sold the farm and moved into town with her four children, long-since grown and gone.

She was always cleaning the windows or sweeping her sidewalk or down on her knees clipping stray blades of grass to exactly the right height, or watering her flowerbeds, or inside her small house she was dusting, polishing, vacuuming, wiping, sweeping, rubbing, or straightening. This was how she worked out her pain, her sorrow, her loneliness. Her house gleamed. Her yard was perfection itself.

And she did not go out much. People came to her.

This very morning she was expecting someone and when she heard the knocking on her front door she hastily untied her apron and hung it up, and patted her hair as she passed by the mirror on her way to answer the knock. She opened the door. Rita Zacharias stood on the step along with Ava Bound. They had been invited by Zena and everything was in readiness. They went at once into the sitting room and sat down on the uncomfortable brocade-covered loveseat under an enlarged and elaborately framed photo of Alden Lavender in his Second World War soldier's uniform. He looked serenely down on them, nobility in his gaze. Zena served tea and the exquisite little cakes she was famous for iced in pink and green. The subject of Ava's recent widowhood came up.

"You have to develop interests of your own," Zena said. "Ways of passing the time or it will be very hard for you in the years that are left." Ava nodded.

"It's been several months now," she said, "and I still can't sleep. I'm not used to being alone at night."

"None of us were," Rita announced without a trace of sympathy in her voice.

Cirrhosis of the liver had taken her husband away, and as for marrying again, well, I guess not. Once was enough for some people. "You just have to ride it out. That's what the rest of us did. Get a pill from the doctor if you have to." Rita was a small, plump woman with a halo of fly-away white hair and a tendency to sloppiness that the other women deplored. But she had a good heart, they knew, and she was irrepressible, nothing would ever change her.

"Whatever you do," Zena said sternly, "do not touch sherry. It's too easy to become a habit."

"If you keep busy," Rita said, "you'll be too tired to lay awake nights."

"Or call One Of Us," Zena said, carefully spacing her words and leaning forward to look significantly into Ava's eyes. Ava knew she had been invited here for some good reason, and guessing that she was about to hear what it was, kept silent and sipped her tea.

"Do you think any of us can sleep?" Zena asked wearily. She glanced up to the portrait of her husband and let her eyes linger on his. Ava followed Zena's gaze, and suddenly began to cry. She covered her eyes with one thin hand while the china teacup resting on her knee trembled and tinkled. Quickly, with a matter-of-fact air, Rita reached out and took it away. Zena offered Ava a box of tissues.

Though Dennis had had a heart condition since middle age and had been slowly deteriorating over the last few years, Ava had never adjusted to the imminence of his departure, and now that he was gone she was devastated. Since he had gone and left her, whole swatches of her thick, dark hair had turned white.

"I'm sorry," she said, lowering her hand from her face.

"If you need to cry," Zena said, "you can cry with One Of Us."

Ava wiped her eyes and managed to gain control of herself.

"You sound like an organization," she said. "Like the Lion's Club or something."

Rita and Zena exchanged a look. Zena smiled.

"It does look that way, doesn't it? But more like the Masons, you might say. We do not advertise ourselves." She set down her teacup on the lace doily on the table beside her chair and placed both hands on her lap. "You can't go on this way, Ava," she said sternly. "Look at you, thin as a rail. You need something to occupy your mind with. There are enough things going on in this town that you should have no difficulty finding something."

"But Zena," Ava said. "The town is dying. They say the post office is going to close and everybody will move away . . ."

"Precisely!" Zena said, suddenly fierce. She sat even straighter in her wingbacked, tapestry chair and some of her long-vanished, youthful beauty reappeared in the firm line of her jaw and the graceful tilt of her head. "Rita and I have much to talk to you about before the others arrive."

"The . . . others?" Ava asked.

"Margareta, Beata, Pat, Hilda, Nellie . . ."

". . . Eleanor, Elsa, Sarah, Beth . . ." Together, Rita and Zena named every surviving woman who had been widowed over the last fifty years in the town: by drowning, cancer, heart disease, alcoholism, Alzheimer's, hunting accidents, car crashes, mangling in farm machinery, goring by cows or trampling by bulls, or by turning their faces to the wall or worse, their guns on themselves, after a farm loss.

"A secret society!" Ava breathed, her eyes wide with excitement.

"Together we represent the history of this community," Zena said. "We gave birth to the last two, sometimes three generations; we worked on the farms and the ranches to build them up, and we ran businesses in town; we were volunteers in the hospital guild, the cemetery society, the arts council, the museum association; we ran the church groups, we cooked endless meals for weddings, funerals, family reunions. We . . ." She stopped and, clearing her throat, rearranged her skirt over her still-shapely knees. "We built and maintained this town," she said with finality. Ava looked to Rita to find her staring back with a mischievous grin.

"So we aren't going to let it go without a fight," she said.

"Drink your tea, Ava," Zena said gently. "The others will be here in a minute and we have plans to make."

Another hot afternoon and Jessie parked the truck in front of Amy's shop expecting to find the street deserted in the baking heat.

Instead, it was busy. When she got out of the truck she noticed that the truck parked next to her had Montana plates and that a little further down the block a man and a woman, smartly dressed strangers, were coming out of the café and getting into an expensive-looking, shiny dark car.

"Hi," she called, into an empty shop. Amy emerged, looking, as she always did, calm though slightly rumpled, from the back room where she kept supplies and her electric kiln.

"Hi, Jessie," she said, dusting her hands off on her slacks. "Got time for coffee?"

"That's why I stopped," Jessie said. She shut the door on the heat and came around the counter to her usual chair where she sat with her back to the window. Amy was pouring coffee.

"Lucky I just made a fresh pot," she said. "What was in here would have melted a spoon." She grinned over her shoulder at Jessie, then hesitated. "Jessie, what's the matter?" she asked. She handed Jessie a mug of coffee, then sat down across from her.

"I suppose it's written all over my face," Jessie said ruefully. "I had to talk to somebody," she said. "I thought maybe you'd have some idea . . . I mean, I'm afraid to tell anybody . . . it's just that . . ." She gave up.

"Tell me," Amy coaxed.

"It's Val," Jessie burst out. "He's . . . I think he's having a breakdown and I'm scared to death. I was almost afraid to leave him alone this afternoon, except that . . ." She lowered her head.

"What?" Amy asked. "Except what?"

"He sleeps all the time," Jessie said.

"I'm not sure what you mean," Amy said slowly.

"I mean, he just sleeps all the time. I can't wake him up."

"Isn't he eating?" Amy asked.

"Not really. A little coffee now and then, or I'll get him into the kitchen for lunch and he'll eat two mouthfuls and go back to the couch and back to sleep again." She looked away. "And when I do wake him he's always . . . angry. I'm half afraid of him."

"That's terrible!" Amy said. "That's pretty serious." She thought for a minute. "Have you talked to his parents?"

"I don't dare," Jessie said.

"They might not know how to handle it either," Amy said, "but still . . ." Some people passing by had stopped to look in the window behind Jessie at Amy's display of pottery. Their voices could be heard in the room, but the words were indistinct. "I hope they don't come in," Amy said. Jessie turned to look and saw the couple she'd seen coming out of the café, the woman tall and slender, wearing a thick coating of expertly applied makeup and her pale blonde hair so perfectly arranged, Jessie at once wondered if it was a wig. The man was shorter, dressed in a shiny grey suit – silk? – and a white shirt with a subtly patterned tie in a deeper grey.

"Strangers," Amy remarked. "Come to think of it, there seem to be an unusual number of strangers around the last few days. Summer holidays, I suppose. Tourists, though what tourists would want to come to this place for is beyond me." The couple was already opening the door. Amy sighed and stood to greet them.

"Afternoon, Ma'am," the man said in the softened speech of an American from the south of his country.

"Good afternoon," Amy said, smiling.

"I wonder if you could help us," – actually he said "hep," Jessie noticed – "since we're the proverbial strangers in your beautiful little town."

"It's very hot," the woman remarked, "almost as hot as home."

"Though a different kind of heat," the man agreed.

"I'll be glad to help if I can," Amy said.

"It's the Pastor Uriel Raven I'm inquirin' about," he said gently. "Do you know where we might find him?"

"I can tell you where his house is," Amy replied. "I don't know if he's there or not. Actually, I haven't seen him in days. Not that I usually do," she added hastily.

"We'd be much obliged to you, Ma'am," he said, his voice growing softer and his smile more artificial by the moment.

"Though I am not used to such wind," the woman said. She had trailed away to look at the vases and jars on the shelves.

"We do have . . . a . . . lot of wind," Amy said to her, but the woman didn't acknowledge having heard Amy. Amy went to the window and pointed. "Go that way three blocks, turn right, and it's three blocks down, either second or third from the corner, I forget which."

"I'm sure we can find it, Ma'am," the man replied. He put his hand on the doorknob. "Coming, Roseanna?" he asked. The woman turned from the rows of pottery and went slowly to the door.

"I do hate to go out in that heat," she remarked as she went out through the door he was holding open for her. Jessie and Amy watched through the window as they walked by. A rush of wind whipped the woman's skirt and lifted the man's tie over his shoulder.

"Who were they?" Jessie asked, round-eyed, forgetting why she had come. "You should see the car they're driving." Amy leaned toward the window.

"I see it," she said. "What is it, anyway? A Lincoln?" She went back to her chair. "Something's going on," she said, "but I don't know what it is." She observed Jessie again, seeing how downcast she was and remembering why she had come.

"I think you have to go to his parents," she said. "It's the only thing to do." Jessie frowned.

"Val will hate me for it," she said. "But I have to do something, and I guess they're the only ones. . . ." She stood slowly, reluctantly, as Amy watched. "I guess there's no use putting it off." She set down her coffee mug on the counter and went slowly to the door where she turned. "Thanks, Amy. I feel better just talking to somebody."

"Let me know how it turns out," Amy said, smiling.

Jessie went outside, shutting the door quickly before the wind could catch it, and squinting into the glare and the heat. She was opening the door of the truck when a voice called to her. A man was leaning out the window of a small, smart new car.

"I wonder if you could tell me how to find Pastor Uriel Raven's house, or else his church?" He was young, no more than thirty-five at the most, and extremely neat in his light summer shirt. There was something flat about his eyes that chilled Jessie. Surprised, Jessie repeated the directions she had heard Amy give the other strangers. He thanked her and as he backed out, she saw that his car bore California plates.

She went straight to Herb and Flora's house and was pleased to find Flora alone in the kitchen.

"Lemonade?" Flora asked. Jessie shook her head no. They sat opposite each other at the kitchen table. Flora studied her, then grew pale. "What is it?" she asked finally. "What is it now?"

"I've come about Val," Jessie said. "I don't know what else to do."

"What's the matter with Val?" his mother asked, not looking at her, and Jessie saw that Flora was not surprised, had perhaps even been expecting this news.

"He hasn't – it's – he won't stop sleeping," she said finally. "He won't do anything. He lies on the couch all day and half the night and sleeps and I can't wake him – " She hadn't meant for it to come out like this, all at once, and garbled as well, but she couldn't . . .

"All the time?" Flora was alert now, watching Jessie intently, as if she intended to leap up immediately and put things to rights. "Does he eat?" Why was everybody so worried about whether he was eating or not?

"Not much," she said.

"How long has this been going on?" Flora demanded.

"A week, ten days," Jessie said. Flora thought for a moment, not looking at Jessie, still in that alert pose, as though she just needed a minute to figure out what to do.

"I'll have to go see him," she said. She looked around her spotless kitchen once as if to make sure everything was in place before she left. "I'll just leave a note for Herb," she said, as if to herself. "No, he'll think I'm over at Marion's. Better leave it alone." She looked at Jessie then and Jessie saw in her eyes a strength and purposefulness she hadn't seen there before, and that comforted her. "Let's go," Flora said.

When Jessie pulled up onto the gravel driveway at the farm she watched vainly for signs that Val was up or had been out, but the house looked as closed and deserted as it had when she'd left a few hours before. She went slowly up the stairs, waiting for Flora and holding the door open for her.

"Where is he?" Flora asked in an undertone. Jessie pointed to the living room. Flora stopped just inside the doorway with Jessie behind her. She stared at Val's back. He lay on the sofa with his knees drawn up and his arms across his chest. A faint snoring filled the silence. Flora crossed to him and bent over him. She shook him gently.

"Val, wake up. It's your mother." There was no response. "Val!" She shook him harder, and her voice grew louder and more firm. "Now you wake up, Valentine, this minute! It's time you got up!" To Jessie's astonishment Val stopped in mid-snore, lifted one arm, straightened his legs, and swivelled to a sitting position on the side of the couch so suddenly that his mother jumped back. Jessie saw years of Flora waking Val every morning for school, for farm work.

"What?" he asked, yawning and stretching. He lifted his head to look uncomprehendingly from his mother to his wife and Jessie saw that he had thought he was a boy again in his parents' house. "Whassa matter?" he mumbled.

"You!" his mother scolded him. "Look at you! Now you get into that bathroom this minute and take a bath. I could smell you the minute I walked into this room." Val's expression changed to one that hovered between resentment and resignation, but he stood up slowly. There was an instant when his eyes began to clear and remembrance of his situation began to dawn, but Flora didn't wait for the refusal that was sure to come next. "Go on," she said, and gave him a little push so that he went toward the door and into the hall with his mother on his heels. Flora's voice went on, then she heard water gushing from taps and the bathroom door slam shut. In a moment Flora was back in the living room.

"Caught him by surprise," she said grimly, and Jessie almost laughed. "Put some coffee on, will you, Jessie? He'll need some when he gets out of the tub." Obediently Jessie went to the kitchen and was surprised to find Flora following her. "Now when he comes out of there," Flora said, "he's going to be hopping mad."

"Better than sound asleep," Jessie said.

"That's the thing," Flora said. "I've got to get him while he's wide awake. So I want you to go for a walk." Jessie was taken aback, angered. She was about to refuse but the look on Flora's face made her hesitate. "I know he's your husband now," Flora said, "but I'm still his mother and I know things about him you don't. I know what I have to say to him." Jessie couldn't think what to say. Flora said, "He was like this once before, in high school, when that Griffith girl threw him over. He was expecting to marry her." This was news to Jessie. What Griffith girl? "She was a silly twit," Flora said. "He didn't know when he was well off. Anyway, it was never as serious as this time. Now will you go?" Jessie nodded, swallowing.

"That's right," Flora said. "I'll get him moving for you." Jessie went reluctantly to the door and opened it. As she stepped outside she heard Flora call, "And when you get done in there, you shave, Valentine! You look like a bum with that beard! You hear me, Val?"

Zena Lavender's living room was crowded with women. Chairs had been brought in from the kitchen and the bedrooms and every one of them was occupied. Despite the afternoon heat and all the warm bodies crowded into the room, it was surprisingly cool. But Zena always kept the curtains pulled tight, and for years she had lavished loving attention on the old trees that surrounded the house, keeping it cool and shaded in the summer heat. Their business done, the women were chatting quietly among themselves. Teacups tinkled and delicate transparent napkins rustled. Outside in the trees a flock of birds sang loudly as if to provide cover for the meeting inside, for the women had arrived on foot, one by one or in groups of twos and threes, arriving separately at the front door, or slipping in quietly through the back. The outside of the house gave the appearance of one in which nobody lived. In the midst of her guests, Zena sat in alert silence, watching the others.

Beata Morgan had been silent for some time, and now she sat looking back at Zena. Beata had once been a beauty – as Zena had been – and as they were the same age and had both been born in the countryside, they had known each other all their lives. In high school they had competed for boys and as young mothers, for social leadership. Now at last, as widows the competition was over and Zena had won and had become the acknowledged leader, a fact which Beata accepted with all the grace she could muster, which was considerable. She set aside her teacup, folded her napkin, set her ankles primly against each other, and spoke.

"Everyone here is aware of the problem with Melody Masuria?" The murmuring around the room came to a halt and then several voices indicated that they knew about Melody while heads – white, silver, gold – nodded. "The question is," Beata said, "how should we react?"

"There are starting to be quite a few strangers in town," Hilda Langlois said. "Today an emissary sent by Clyde Leroy arrived and went to Mr. Raven's house."

"Aahh," the women said, a collective sigh of relief.

"She'll be gone soon, then," Zena said.

"But in the meantime," Elsa Friesen remarked, "we're in for an awful time."

"Total strangers everywhere you look."

"We'll have to start locking our doors."

"Not leave a thing out in the yard overnight."

"Oh, come on," Rita interrupted. "These are religious people. They're not thieves."

"What about members of the press who are bound to come too?"

"And hustlers from Lord knows where the minute they get wind of our little miracle-maker."

"Girls, girls," Zena called. "It won't last. When the worst is on us remind yourselves that it will be over in a couple of weeks, a month at the most." There was a lull while the women considered Zena's advice.

"What do you make of the reports about her?" Pat McNamara asked. "Do you think she's a fake?" Contradictory opinions filled the room till the women began to laugh.

"There'll be those who'll believe no matter what is proven," Rita said.

"And those who won't, for exactly the same reasons," Pat said.

"What a thing for Ordeal to become famous for," Beata sighed.

"Well, she may or may not be a saint, but that cross is real enough," Margaret Dubbing said sharply. Normally religion was a forbidden topic in this group since there were representatives here of every one of the town's churches. Beth Mustard spoke for the first time. She was the only one present who was a member of Mr. Raven's congregation, and though she'd been as welcome as anyone to the group (right after Zachary Mustard had died falling through the ice one spring on the South Saskatchewan when he'd gotten drunk and bet he could still cross), there was a slight, but undeniable distance between Beth and the others.

"I hear the cross singing sometimes," she said. A total silence fell over the room. "I mean," she went on, colouring slightly, "that sometimes, especially at night, if you stand outside and listen, you can hear it. I believe it is speaking to us." A woman tittered. As a group they did not approve of mysticism. "And sometimes when I wake up, I have a feeling in my head that it's been talking to me." She paused. "It makes me very uneasy," she said in a low voice.

"It's the year," Sarah Paddock said into the silence. "You can't end two thousand years of Christianity without peculiar things happening. It's only to be expected. She said this authoritatively, as if she'd been through it before.

"It's that blasted wind," Zena Lavender announced, and everyone was amazed at the ferocity of her language.

"One of these days the blamed thing will blow down and that'll be the end of . . . it," Rita said, remembering in time that in this group nobody was ever to speak disparagingly of anyone else's beliefs. Another silence followed. Zena straightened herself again and all eyes turned to her.

"Is everyone clear as to what she is to do?" she asked, looking around the room. The women nodded or murmured yes. "Well," she said, and all of them recognized by the note of finality in her voice that the meeting was over and they were to slip out in ones and twos and go quietly back to their homes.

# CHAPTER 14

The Mountain brothers were sitting side by side on stools at the counter in Mrs. Henwick's café. Sandy McDonnell, Martin Barrell, and Dale Penner were there too, arranged around the horseshoe, each with a cup of coffee in front of him.

"If you ask me," Phil Mountain was saying, "a person can starve to death here as well as anywhere else."

"If you still had a young family you'd feel different. Harvey's still got three kids in school," Dale pointed out. "He's gotta go where he can feed 'em."

"Is it true he's moving to Saskatoon?" Martin asked.

"I heard Swift Current," Sandy said.

"His wife's related to my wife on their father's side," Dale said. "It's Saskatoon. He got a job welding in a plant up there. He's a damn good welder."

Phil said, "It's a damn shame to lose another family. Anybody buy his place?"

"Hah!" Sandy said. "It's Farm Credit land now, like most of the province. Maybe it'll go up for bids one of these days, but there's nobody left to bid on it."

"Might be old Fox will. Some of it borders on some of his land."

"He's got so much land now some of it borders on everybody left in the township. I can't figure out why he's buying up all that land."

"Or where he gets the money to do it."

"Land's never been cheaper, and it's getting cheaper all the time."

"Could be Fox is buying it for a German maybe, or a Japanese."

"There's laws against foreign ownership."

"Always a way for a smart man to get around the law."

"That land's not earning a cent of profit. Why would anybody want it?"

"Just to hold on to, maybe, 'till things change."

"Great big corporate farms with nobody living on them."

"I bet the Hutterites'll buy it."

"They'd take over the countryside if they had half a chance."

"Naw, they're as broke as we are. I'll tell you what I heard. I heard one of the biggest multinationals around has made an offer to the government for all the land in the province that Farm Credit owns." There was a stunned silence.

While they had been talking, the door had been repeatedly opening to let people in or out. Each time it opened, a wave of hot air engulfed the men at the counter and they all glanced at the door to see who was coming or going.

"What's all the fuss about?" Anders Soren interrupted before anybody could comment on such disturbing news. He was seating himself on one of the last empty stools, and his arrival – he was never seen in the café – made them half-forget what they'd just heard.

"What brings you in?" somebody asked.

"You mean you haven't heard the news?" somebody else asked.

"That's why I came in," Anders said, his voice wry. "To find out what's going on. Coffee," he said to Mrs. Henwick who was already handing him a steaming cup. Anders looked from man to man, waiting for somebody to break the silence and explain to him why the town was full of strangers.

"It's that Masuria kid," Mrs. Henwick said. "And that crazy Raven and his crew."

"Now what?" Anders asked, spooning sugar into his coffee.

"She's gone and started bleeding on them," Mrs. Henwick said, wiping the trail of sugar on the counter and not looking at him. Anders, a bachelor, coloured. "From her hands," Mrs. Henwick added hastily, "and her feet, too, I heard."

"What?" He was so startled that he knocked the spoon out of his cup, and Mrs. Henwick had to wipe the counter again.

"You never heard of the . . . stigmata?" Sandy McDonnell asked. He himself had only heard of it that morning, but Anders didn't know that.

"Yeah, I heard of it," Anders said slowly. "It's some Catholic thing, isn't it?" He was a Lutheran. "Are you trying to tell me . . . ?"

"That's right," Sandy said, smug because he'd been the first to know.

"How do you know?" Anders asked, sounding a little belligerent, if not outright disbelieving. "Did somebody see her or what?" He looked around the horseshoe again. No, none of them had seen her.

"That's what we hear, that's all," Mrs. Henwick said. "And I figure it must be true, because the town's filling up with strangers and I don't know one other reason why that would be."

"Summer holidays?" Anders said. "Tourists."

"You ever seen this many people in my place when there wasn't a school reunion or a family reunion or a wedding or a funeral?" Mrs. Henwick asked.

"That Henderson reunion," Anders said.

"Next weekend," Howard Mountain said, and Mrs. Henwick, her tone confidential, told him, "Go down to the campground and take a look at the licence plates there. There's everything from Texas to Ontario."

Jessie had driven into town with Val in their truck to buy groceries while Val picked up the mail and went to settle a bill at the feed store. After his mother had gotten him back on his feet, Jessie, afraid to let him sit still for fear he would relapse, had rushed him off to Medicine Hat where they had sold their car. Though parting with it had been hard, it at least gave them the feeling they were doing something about their situation and it felt good to have some money in their hands again.

"It sure as hell hurts me to do this," Val remarked, as he pulled up in front of the feed store. "The cattle gone and I'm still paying for feeding them last winter."

"We," Jessie corrected him. "We'll feel better if we don't have to walk around town embarrassed because our bills aren't paid."

"Yeah, I guess," Val said, resigned. He opened the door. "You might as well take the truck and get the groceries. When I'm done here I'll go over to the café and you can pick me up."

"Okay," Jessie said, "but I want to stop in and say hi to Amy."

"No hurry," Val said. "What are all these people doing in town?" There was activity everywhere, surprising for a hot day in July when usually the town was quiet as a grave. Behind them, three campers approached in succession, moving in the direction of the camp-ground. Val had to wait while a family passed by, the biggest child holding the hands of two of the smaller ones. Jessie waited till Val had disappeared inside the feed store and for the last of the campers to pass, then backed out into the street. She put the presence of so many people down to one of the many school or family reunions that were held all summer long and to which she was never invited since she was related to nobody and had gone to school elsewhere.

Even the grocery store was crowded, not like a supermarket on a Saturday, but unusually busy for Ordeal. And the shoppers were nearly all people Jessie had never seen before, and who, she thought, had a faintly peculiar look about them, were different even from the prosperous-looking city relatives of local people who strangers usually turned out to be. Was it something about the way they dressed? she wondered as she waited at the freezer for her turn to look over the packages of frozen fish and the cut-up chicken. It wasn't so much that they were unfashionable, nobody in Ordeal worried much about fashion either. It was something indefinable in their manner. . . . She bent at the dairy cooler to pick up a litre of milk at the same time as a woman, another stranger, did the same. As the woman straightened, holding her carton, she wobbled, almost dropping it, and Jessie put out her hand to help her. But the woman said, dismissing her dizziness, "It's the heat. I'm not used to such heat, and then coming into this air conditioning."

"It *is* very hot," Jessie agreed. "Where do you come from?"

"Northern B.C.," the woman said, and gave Jessie a brief, shy smile over her shoulder as she set the milk in her cart and pushed it away. When Jessie started up the last aisle where the barbecue supplies and charcoal briquettes were, she encountered three nuns in long black robes, apparently discussing insect sprays. She was so startled that she stopped and stared. The nuns rotated their heads from their contemplation of the cans of spray and smiled at her.

"Good afternoon," they murmured, smiling. "We seem to be in your way."

"Not at all," Jessie said hurriedly. "Excuse me," and wheeled past them as if she were merely distracted by having so much to do. Then at the checkout she had to wait behind a family who she recognized as the ones who had passed in front of Val when he was going into the feed supply store. Yes, the oldest girl in her faded cotton sundress was certainly the one Jessie had seen, with her pale hair in neatly crossed braids pinned firmly into place at the base of her skull. The children's mother was checking her groceries as the clerk pushed them past the till. When the last of them was through, the husband took out his wallet and paid while his wife stood quietly beside him, looking thoughtfully at her five silent children with the same pale freckles on their noses that she had, and the children stared soberly back at her out of her own light-blue eyes. Jessie couldn't interpret the look the children and their mother exchanged.

She had paid for her groceries and was loading them into the truck when the husband leaned out the window of the crew cab truck he was driving, which had a homemade camper on its back, and asked, "Can you tell us how to find the road that takes us up to the cross?" He gestured to the north where they could see its tip between the treetops. "From here you can see a road right beside it," he said, "but we haven't been able to find the way into it." He was younger than she had thought and he kept combing his thin, light-brown beard with his fingers as he spoke to her.

"I don't think there is a road," Jessie said. "I think you have to walk. I think that road you're thinking of goes up to somebody's house." The man hesitated, irritation crossing his face.

"I'll ask in the café," he said. "Bless you." As he drove away Jessie saw that the truck's plates said *North Dakota*. Maybe there's some kind of a church meeting going on, she thought.

Before she could back out she had to wait till a mini-van with CRMQ painted on its side drove by. She wondered what it would be doing in town. When she turned onto the main street there wasn't a single place left to park and she had to find a spot around the corner. Inside Amy's studio strangers were handling the coffee mugs, vases, and pitchers while Amy answered questions in a polite and calm way as if she did this every day. Jessie hesitated, thinking maybe she should go away and come back.

"Come on in, Jessie," Amy called around the woman she was talking to. Jessie went behind the counter and sat on the dusty wooden chair she always sat on when she dropped in for coffee. Amy began to wrap the set of coffee mugs, but Jessie jumped up, took the newspaper Amy was crumpling from her, and wrapped them herself while Amy went to the next customer, a middle-aged man wearing a neat, short-sleeved cotton shirt and chino pants, which marked him at once as coming from elsewhere. He handled the blue-glazed bowl he was buying with some care.

"This is lovely," he said to Amy, "very skillfully done, an unusual glaze." He reached for his wallet. "You don't charge enough for such fine work," he scolded her. When the bowl was wrapped and he had gone out with his wife, leaving the store empty of customers, Amy cast Jessie a jubilant look, went to the door, turned the lock, and flipped the "Back Later" sign so it could be read from the outside.

"How's Val?" she asked.

"Pretty good," Jessie said. "Going to his mother was the right thing to do. She knew what to say to him. I don't know why I waited so long to go to her."

"Wouldn't have done any good any earlier," Amy said firmly. She poured them each a cup of coffee. "I made two hundred dollars already today!" she said. "Everybody wants souvenirs!"

"That's wonderful, Amy!" Jessie said.

"My house is in desperate need of shingles," Amy said. "If this keeps up, I'll be able to afford to have it done, instead of climbing up there with a hammer and sticking on a patch or two myself." She laughed and sipped her coffee, then set her cup down and stretched happily. "I can't tell you how happy it makes me to have somebody come into my studio and tell me that I'm talented."

"I thought you knew that," Jessie said. Amy had, in the short space it took Jessie to speak, grown thoughtful. She looked away from Jessie and her eyes grew distant.

"I work here alone day after day, year after year. I sell a little, things I know people can use. Nobody says anything more to me than, 'That's nice,' now and then. I know half the people who say that to me would say the same thing to Rembrandt or Henry Moore. They don't see the difference between what's 'nice' and what's original and beautiful. They don't have the training." She sighed deeply and moved her gaze to the dusty wooden floor. "I get so discouraged, working away here, never having anybody who really knows look at my work, never getting a word of praise that comes from real understanding. It's so hard for an artist who lives out in places like this. People don't know how hard it is."

"I think your work is beautiful," Jessie said soberly. "Did I never say so?" Amy lifted her head and slowly she seemed to see Jessie again.

"Don't pay any attention to me," she said. "I choose to live here. I shouldn't go begging for sympathy." They sat in silence for a moment.

"Who are all these people?" Jessie asked. "I even saw a TV station van. What's going on?"

"You haven't heard?" Amy asked, surprised. "Well – Melody Masuria has gone and developed the stigmata . . ." Jessie gasped. "I'm not kidding," Amy said, sitting up and looking straight at Jessie with a glint of amusement or amazement in her eyes. "It's supposed to have happened a week or more ago and somehow all these people heard about it. Through their churches, I suppose."

"It must be a hoax," Jessie said. A couple of women stopped at the door, read Amy's sign, and went on down the sidewalk, chatting to each other.

"I don't know if it is or it isn't," Amy said thoughtfully.

"But they're just a bunch of crazy . . . fanatics," Jessie said.

"I've always thought," Amy said, frowning, "that answers come to the people who need them most if they're willing to put themselves on the line to get answers. Doesn't matter who they are." Seeing Jessie's bewildered look, she went on. "I mean, why should a Catholic martyr or a . . . Sufi saint . . . get enlightenment and not a Christian fundamentalist?"

"Because they're so incredibly ignorant about theology and because they're so rigid and judgemental," Jessie said, after a moment's thought.

"True," Amy said. There was a silence. "But – their need is just as great, isn't it? I mean, they're just as desperate. They give up their good name for their religion . . ."

"They're horrible people," Jessie said. "They're cruel and vindictive." She blushed bright red and put her hands to her face. "I'm sorry!" she said. "I didn't mean to be so . . . vehement. I . . ." Amy laughed.

"You're only expressing what most people think," she said. "But God works in mysterious ways . . ."

"His wonders to perform," Jessie said, and they laughed quietly together.

"Melody does strike me as an unlikely saint," Amy said.

"What will happen, I wonder," Jessie said. "Will somebody come and take her away to a hospital? Will she die? Will . . ." She paused, out of possibilities. "Or maybe one day she'll just levitate to heaven."

"Search me," Amy said. "Doesn't the stigmata just go away eventually?" Jessie shrugged. "I keep thinking of Bernadette and Lourdes. It makes me nervous. We have such serious problems to deal with right here in this community and this has to happen – it sidetracks everything."

"Maybe they're connected!" Jessie suggested, laughing, but Amy gave her a surprised, serious look. "I hear everybody is praying right now," and she involuntarily cast a glance heavenward thinking of all the prayers, involuntary and otherwise, she had cast upward in the last month or so. But Amy appeared to be lost in thought.

"It is the end of the world as we've known it," she murmured.

Jessie didn't care to pursue this. "How's your protest movement going?" she asked. Amy was suddenly more animated.

"We've just found out the date the Premier is coming here for a private meeting with some of his supporters. This election coming up is starting to make ripples. This is all a secret, Jessie, so don't say anything to anybody. We've decided to organize a big rally here for that day. But we have to do it without scaring off the Premier, because if he knows that's going to happen, he simply won't come." A couple of children peered in the window, noses pressed against the glass, hands cupped around their faces, but when they saw the two women they ran away, their laughter hanging in the air behind them. "We'll call a meeting and talk it over, I guess," Amy went on.

"Val and I want to come," Jessie said. Amy looked so surprised that Jessie could feel herself flushing.

"Great. We need all the help we can get," she said, lowering her eyes. Jessie said, "I didn't even know what must have been obvious to the whole countryside, but now I do, and I'm not going to sit back any longer and let things happen. And Val needs to feel he's doing something."

"Nobody's going to help us but ourselves," Amy said, sighing. "I wish I could persuade more people of that before it's too late." Again some adults stopped outside and looked in at the clay figures Amy had arranged among the bowls and pitchers.

"I suppose I should let them in," Amy said.

"Make hay while the sun shines," Jessie said, laughing.

"Hey," Amy said, "before you know it, you'll be one of us."

"When you lose your farm," Jessie said, standing and shaking out her rumpled cotton skirt, "you're one of the community whether the community wants you or not."

"Yeah," Dale Penner said, using the firm tone of one in possession of the truth, "the Doc saw her. Her mother took him over to Raven's, but Melody wouldn't let her mother see her. But she let the Doc in. He won't tell anybody what he saw. Says it isn't any of his business if anybody asks him."

Bill Peat came in and took the last empty stool, between Howard Mountain and Val Sheridan.

"Have you seen what's going on out there?" Val asked. "The place is choked with strangers." Bill Peat looked over his shoulder at all the newcomers filling the booths. He spoke in a hushed voice.

"That ain't all. Drive down Raven's street," he said. "That's all I'm saying. You won't believe your eyes." He closed his and set his lips in a thin line so everybody knew he'd say no more on the subject.

Jessie entered the café then, looking for Val, and when she saw there wasn't a single empty place to sit, she beckoned Val, who had already seen her and was pushing back his coffee cup and rising. They left the café together behind three local women who had apparently stopped in for an afternoon chat and a cup of coffee away from their own kitchens. They were grouching indignantly about not being able to get a booth.

"I'll be glad when this nonsense is over," one said, and another replied, "With any luck somebody'll soon come and take that little idiot away."

When they were out on the street, Jessie asked breathlessly, "Did you hear about it?"

"Let's drive down Raven's street and see what's going on."

In a minute they were driving down the main street in the direction of Raven's street. Val turned the wheel at his corner and suddenly braked hard. The street was a sea of cars, campers, and trucks and vans, and threading among the vehicles were dozens of people on foot, both strangers and local people. They stared, too amazed for a second to say anything.

"Come on," Val said, after a moment. "We'll have to leave the truck here if we want to find out what's going on." He shut off the motor, put the keys in his pocket, and they got out, moving into the crowd zig-zagging among the vehicles toward Raven's house.

As they drew closer they began to hear, wafting gently over the heads of the people and the shiny chrome of the cars and motor homes, weaving its way through the dusty leaves of the trees, riding on the heat waves, thin singing. It was hard at first to distinguish it from the breeze that carried the sound, but as they drew closer a word or two came clear and they knew it was a hymn that was being sung. They rounded the snout of a van with Ohio licence plates and saw, standing in front of them in a semi-circle eight or ten deep, a crowd of people. Some were kneeling, though most stood, and a few with admirable foresight had brought lawn chairs and were seated on them. All faced a house with a low picket fence boxing a small square of grass with a crabapple tree off to one side.

There was no one in the yard and people pressed against the fence. Some of the women waved fans made of newspaper slowly back and forth in front of their faces. A young woman who knelt off to one side clutched the picket fence with both hands and swayed awkwardly back and forth while tears streamed down her face. Another pushed herself out of the crowd, made her way to the front and fell on her knees just behind the picket fence. She began to pray aloud and then to grasp her long hair in her hands and to pull. Jessie was torn between horror and fear. As she and Val watched, two men called, "Out of the way, please," making their way through the crowd as people moved back to let them pass. They carried between them a stretcher on which someone lay, though who it was couldn't be seen since the person, male or female, was covered with a blanket.

This was too much. Jessie clutched Val's arm, looking frantically around, stretching onto her toes, struggling to see above or around the crowd to some way of escape.

The elderly women seated on their folding chairs stood and pulled them back to make room so the stretcher could be set down between them and the picket fence. The praying women moved over too. The hymn had died out and there was a lull. The crowd, as if bothered by the sudden quiet, shifted restlessly, and Jessie noticed a television crew at work photographing them from the far side of the street. There was a low moan from somewhere at the back of the crowd, causing people to turn their heads in that direction as it grew louder. Someone was blowing on a pipe or striking a drum with a deep voice. But no, it was chanting.

The crowd parted and a cluster of men in thin and ragged saffron robes, their leader beating a slow rhythm on a conical drum that hung suspended from his shoulder, advanced through the people. The crowd suddenly surged in all directions at once, and the picket fence wavered and groaned at each end. Val was at last alarmed. Jessie could tell it by the way he suddenly put his arm around her shoulders, applying pressure to make her go back in the direction from which they'd come.

"Hurry," he said, directly into her ear, or otherwise she'd never have heard him over the agitated rumbling of the crowd and the chanting and the beating drum punctuated now and then by the tinkling of bells.

Together they began to struggle back to their truck, sidling between the surging crowd and the parked vehicles. Abruptly Val was boosting her up onto the hood of a car – the owners were still seated inside, unable to open the doors against the crowd, and they shouted and the driver shook his fist at them – and she was down the other side with Val behind her, holding her close against him, yet pushing her forward.

He used all his strength, not caring who he shoved out of the way, to open their truck door, and held it open with his body while Jessie scrambled in and across the seat to the passenger side. It was stiflingly hot inside, and the noise from the crowd was so loud now that when Val started the motor Jessie couldn't hear it. She looked out the back window as he put it in gear, but all she could see behind them were other vehicles and a steady stream of people still pushing their way forward.

"You'll run over somebody!" she cried.

"No, I won't!" he shouted, his voice grim, and she realized with surprise that he was enjoying himself. He began to sound the horn steadily: *beep-beep, beep-beep*. Frightened, Jessie leaned out the open window and shouted, "Look out! Move away! You'll get run over!" Most made an effort to get out of the way when they heard her, and she saw a big motor home parked behind them start up too. It began to back up slowly with people peeling out of the way from behind it, and between Jessie's shouts and Val's horn honking, a space was gradually created between the two vehicles. They made steady progress, and in a moment had backed out of the street and around the corner onto the main drag.

Val held the truck steady before he edged into the stream of traffic moving up and down, and Jessie saw sweat trickling from his hair down his neck. Suddenly the screech of a siren nearby filled the air, and Val abruptly jerked the wheel back again. They edged over to the curb and waited.

In a moment they saw two police cars racing down the hill from the direction of Crisis. Cars pulled over to the curb to let them past, and as they reached the corner where Val and Jessie were, they screeched to a near-stop and turned onto Raven's street. Almost immediately the last police car backed up, turned, and went screaming down the main street, evidently intending to approach Raven's block from the other end of the street.

The car at their end blocked the entrance to the street and one of the Mounties inside jumped out, ran into the main street, and began directing traffic away from it. The Mountie inside the car got out too, holding a microphone which was attached to a public address system on the top of his car. Everywhere people were halting to listen, but the Mountie in the street had motioned to Val to drive on, so he put his truck into gear again and joined the stream of cars.

In his house high up on the hillside Neil, stretched out on his sofa reading while Bach played softly in the background, set down his book to listen. Through breaks in the incessant wind that buffeted his house, he could hear a low keening that he was beginning to think must be made by human voices. He listened. There! It sounded like chanting. Impossible, he thought, Protestants don't chant, but still. . . . He listened again. Singing too, he thought.

He threw his feet to the floor, knocking against the bottle of beer and catching it before it fell over. He rose, carrying it, and went into the kitchen where the noises were louder. Without pausing there, he went on, pushing back the screen door, stepping outside onto the gravel patch in his bare feet, skirting his truck, and stopping dead as the panorama on the other side appeared before him.

Triple – no, four times the usual number of worshippers were on their knees below the cross. Straggling up the hillside on the path that was now a well-worn one were more supplicants, many of them approaching on their knees. He couldn't believe his eyes.

The wind rose and howled, then subsided, tossing fragments of prayers at him in many languages, together with the hysterical sobs of women, the loud pleading of men. He surveyed the crowd sharply, not wanting to miss a detail: a child being fed Coke by its mother; a man, his head lolling against the headrest of his wheelchair, being pushed by a teenager across the bumpy prairie; a crippled boy, thin and pale, rocking past on crutches: all labouring under the blistering afternoon sun.

Neil stood, his anger fading in the face of his incredulity, the frayed edges of his shirttail flapping in the wind, rubbing his thinning, dishevelled hair with one hand, his bottle of beer still in the other. He had meant to shout at them, to drive them away, but saw it was hopeless. There were too many and more were coming up the hillside. He didn't notice that the people closest to him were glancing at his faded, ragged clothing, his bare feet, his lined face, and were edging away to find other places to worship.

After a moment he turned and went back inside, closing both doors and slumping against the inside door. He had chosen this place because of its very isolation and the few people who lived here. He grimaced, closing his eyes and throwing back his head against the door. Images of the prairie swept past his eyelids: the coyotes approaching him, their eyes gleaming while the far-off hills shimmered in the heat haze and the hawks above dipped and soared. Himself standing alone breathing in the sweet scent of prairie – sage and grasses and earth mingled. He thought for a moment that his heart might break at what he now saw himself losing.

Where to go now? he asked himself. There was no more grassland left in Canada where a man could be alone with the gods of the wild, there was no place left where he could go. If he had had a gun, for one second, he might have gone out there and killed one of them; he would have killed the woman crying hysterically, or the crippled boy, or the nun prostrated on the ground. But his rage passed, and propelled by its passing, he went back into the living room and sat down on the couch again. He tried to think what might have happened to bring such a crowd of strangers to this isolated little town in the middle of nowhere. Lourdes and other famous shrines passed through his mind. That was it: a miracle, or something the foolish chose to think of as a miracle must have happened. For a moment he was so astonished he didn't even scoff, but only for a moment; then his customary scorn overcame him and a wall of depression fell over him. He felt himself giving up at last on humankind.

Then he thought of Amy, her smooth, tanned skin, her clear eyes, the huskiness in her voice when she said his name. Longing suffused him and in the midst of it, a flash of insight came and left again: he would leave here; Amy would refuse to come with him. He would lose her.

Talk about ironic, Amy thought to herself, looking out the spotted kitchen window to the parched garden beyond as she washed lettuce for her supper. A multitude of the faithful – pilgrims – setting themselves down to worship not ten feet from the biggest cynic who ever lived. If she hadn't cared so much for Neil she would have laughed. But, she thought, taking a tomato out of the fridge, where did all this confusion leave them in their fight to save the town?

If Melody's wounds were proven to be genuine – were the wounds of a stigmatized person ever proven to be genuine? – then what would happen? For a time the crowds arriving would swell to huge numbers, especially if Melody remained in Ordeal. But even if she went away the town where she had been born and raised would be considered a holy place by believers, Amy supposed. There would be new restaurants, new hotels and motels, an industry in souvenirs.

Whether Melody stayed or not, in time, the number of people arriving would become a steady, predictable stream and the town would settle down – those who could would make a living in the tourist industry. Those who couldn't would leave.

But the industry probably wouldn't be big enough to accommodate everybody who wanted to be part of it; some would leave. There would be those who couldn't bear living in a circus atmosphere; they would leave. Any farmers who couldn't cash in on the steady supply of visitors to the area would still lose their farms. And all of this only if Melody was not shown to be a fraud.

On the other hand, if it turned out to be a hoax concocted by Mr. Raven and Melody (and privately Amy thought this was what would happen), it would all be over in a week or two. Could they afford to give up their plans – the meeting with the Premier, the protests – on the not-too-likely chance that Melody was a genuine saint who had been anointed by God?

No way, she told herself, pouring dressing on her salad. But this wasn't up to her alone to decide. She'd have to call a meeting immediately.

And then there was Neil. She took her bowl of salad into the living room and sat on the old couch that faced the front window. She ought to call him, find out how he was making out with those pilgrims praying a few feet from his kitchen. She put her hand on the cool plastic of the phone that sat on the low table by the couch, then paused, looking out the front window past the ragged bushes with their leaves curled with drought and the knee-deep grass cured to a pale yellow by the unrelenting heat. She frowned without realizing she was doing it.

Why was it that no matter how she tried, she couldn't seem to fully accept Neil as her lover, as a mate for her lonely soul, as a potential husband? She had no doubt of her love for him, nor any doubt that he loved her, yet there was this urge in her at every moment of intimacy to withdraw from him, this not-very-becoming hesitancy. She struggled to keep him from finding out about it because it so upset and embarrassed her. She was no teenager, she didn't hate men. Still, she couldn't put her finger on whatever it was that held her back from wholehearted acceptance of him.

She let her hand drop from the phone onto the worn fabric of the sofa, remembering for no reason when it had been new, when she was a little girl and her father had ordered it from the catalogue for her mother who, having come from the poorest of Depression-poor families, had no experience of beautiful things. How she had yearned for them.

Amy sighed, thinking how she and Lionel had been more like her father, caring mostly for books, music, and the countryside in which they were lucky enough to make their home. She mused on in the silent house, not noticing that dusk had come and she was sitting in near-darkness. The old room, shabby and dusty, seemed filled with ghosts tonight, not frightening ones, but the shadows of her dead husband and of her younger self. She loved this room. It was part of the only home she had ever known and where she had lived as a bride with her beloved Lionel.

Lionel. She closed her eyes. She could see again his thick dark hair, the look in his eyes as he bent to touch her, could hear again the whisper of his voice as he fitted his body to hers, and feel his warm breath in the hollow of her neck. Tears slid down her cheeks. Five years. Five years and she was still overcome by his absence. She tried to think of Neil but his face wouldn't come. If Neil were here now, she knew, she wouldn't be able to let him touch her. She shivered at the thought and a wave of nausea swept through her. She bent over, caught between longing and revulsion, and realized that she could not possibly ever marry Neil.

# CHAPTER
## 15

Amy was half-heartedly scrubbing the messy side of a vat of glaze, trying to make at least some difference in her shop. She heard the door open and for some reason thought it was Jessie.

"I'll be there in a second," she called, without looking. "Pour yourself some coffee." She gave the vat another wipe and then gave up, rising and turning, pushing her hair back from her face. When she saw her visitor, she put her hand down and stared. Something told her, she didn't know how she knew, but surely this was . . .

"I'm Faith," the woman said, "Neil's former wife." Amy's heart gave a quick little flutter and instinctively she tried to brush away some of the dust on her blouse. Unexpectedly, Faith laughed.

"Don't worry," she said. "I envy you, having something important to do with your life." She looked around the shop, even walking over to one of the shelves with a display of pitchers and touching one of them while Amy studied her. She was a small, very pretty woman with fine, naturally curly hair in a halo around her face. Her cotton sundress was crisp and spotless, her sandals looked as though they'd never trod on earth. Amy had a hard time imagining this creature, wholly feminine in the old-fashioned sense, as Neil's wife.

"What brings you here?" Amy asked, to say something, trying to sound casual and friendly, noticing for the first time how unnaturally thin Faith was.

"The very question," Faith said, laughing and turning back to Amy. "I came to meet you." Amy wanted to ask, *How did you know about me? Nobody knows about me.* But Faith was going on in her soft voice. "I felt sure Neil must be involved with somebody, so I asked in the café. The woman who runs it said Neil's girlfriend runs a pottery shop right down the street, so I came over."

"Why?" Amy asked, flushing with embarrassment and annoyance. Faith studied her quietly.

"I told her Neil wasn't in and did he have a friend who might be able to tell me when he'd be back," she said, but this only made Amy blush harder. Seeing this, Faith appeared to decide that ignoring it was the best course. "I wanted to meet you, get to know you. I'm worried about Neil."

Amy considered. "I had the impression he's worried about you," she said, having just realized it.

"Oh, that," Faith said. "That's over."

"What?" Amy asked.

"My cancer." Amy gasped. "I had a breast lump, but it's gone now. I'm all right."

"I – that's wonderful."

"Yes, it is," Faith said. "I wanted to see if Neil had found someone who could help him, since I no longer can."

Amy went to one of the wooden chairs and sat down carefully, looking at Faith, who was staring out the window.

"Help him," she said slowly. "In what way?"

"In the very way you're thinking," Faith said lightly. "I can see you understand. He's wavering on the brink of hermithood and I don't want that to happen to him."

"Nor do I," Amy said quickly, "but I'm not sure . . ."

"One can't be sure," Faith agreed. "One can only try."

"But I still don't . . ." Amy began.

"Because he was my husband," Faith said. "I loved him more than I loved myself. You don't stop loving somebody just because he thinks he doesn't love you any more. It's true I was wrong to love him the way I did – I've moved on to . . . a new understanding – but he remains the single most important person in my life."

"I love him too," Amy said, but she could hear herself sounding worried and uncertain.

"I know," Faith said. She smiled as if she recognized something in Amy she knew well herself. She moved as if she were about to leave, and Amy, seeing this, stood, trying to think of something else to say to this strange, pretty little woman who so interested her. Faith reached the door, but she came back, and, to Amy's surprise, suddenly embraced her gently.

"I can see what you are," Faith said. She went to the door again. "Goodbye," she said, and let herself out still smiling a secret, inward smile.

Early afternoon and a stiff prairie wind was flattening the grass, tossing the birds like crumpled paper against the sky, whipping the skirts of the women worshippers at the cross, making the cross itself creak and groan, and next to it, rattling loose boards and shingles on Neil's small house. His old truck was parked between the house and the worshippers, and behind it, Amy's beaten-up and worn-out old truck, and behind it, Faith's new little red car, its shiny chrome trim blazing in the burning sun.

Faith, Amy, and Neil were seated around Neil's kitchen table, the remains of their lunch still between them. They were curiously still and silent, as if someone very ill were in the next room, oblivious to the faint sounds of prayer wafting in over the roofs of the vehicles and to the ominous snaps and creaks of the cross and the whistling of the wind past the guy wires. Or so it seemed.

*"The wind bloweth where it listeth, and thou hearest the sound thereof, but canst not tell whence it cometh, and whither it goeth: so is everyone that is born of the spirit."* It was Faith, speaking softly.

"What?" Neil said, startled, then without waiting for a reply, spoke to Amy. "These things do no good." He meant marches, rallies, confrontation. Amy took her eyes from Faith to say, "I think history proves you wrong."

"No," Neil said. "History proves me right. Revolutionaries have a way of settling in to become the oppressors." A gust of wind dipping in through the open window lifted a torn envelope from the counter and tossed it to the floor. Nobody moved to pick it up.

"So we should let this community die on its feet." Amy said this quietly, studying him to see if he truly meant what he had said or if his cynicism was only a disguise for a profound and unendurable hope.

"It doesn't matter what you do. If the forces that shape the economy and the sociology change, so will the community. It will adapt itself in whatever way."

Amy was tentative, believing herself not to be a match for him. "What about this? That we are the sociology and the economy of this country."

"I don't know what you mean," he said, lifting his head suddenly as a paper bag smacked against the screen door and then was whipped away as abruptly as it had come.

"Like the Brazilian rain forest," Amy said. "If you kill all of it, you kill the planet. It's the same with the traditional way of life. Kill it, you kill the soul of the country." Neil laughed, lifting his head. The sound had an artificial ring to it, and the wind sang a derisive reply. "You have to admit the country is in desperate shape." Faith turned her head to look out the door to the truck and over it to the section of the cross that was visible.

"I think it doesn't really matter," Faith said. They turned to listen carefully to her. "Each of us has the job of looking after our own souls. Living here, living there – it doesn't matter. You can do the work of the soul wherever you are."

"And what does that mean?" Neil asked, exasperated. Amy was touched by Faith's words and angry with Neil for the note of contempt in his voice.

After their visit in Amy's shop, Amy, thinking Faith had left town, at lunchtime locked her shop and drove up to Neil's house to tell him Faith had come to see her. Faith had come in on them while they were sitting close together on Neil's decrepit old sofa. Neil was angry at her sudden appearance, but Amy had been deeply embarrassed. Faith had materialized in the doorway and, seeing them, had slumped against the frame as if what she saw was too much for her. She had gone so pale that Amy, afraid she was about to faint, jumped up to help her.

"I'm all right," Faith had said. "It's the heat and the constant sound of wind in my ears." She paused, straightened. "Like the sound of giant wings beating and beating," she murmured.

"What are you doing here?" Neil had asked, barely containing his anger.

"The usual," Faith said, smiling, but her voice trailed off and she went into the kitchen and sat down. Amy glanced warningly at Neil behind Faith's back and he had quickly glanced away, chastised.

They sat in embarrassed silence till Amy said, "I'm starving. Have you anything to eat, Neil?"

"Cold meat," he said. "Bread, lettuce."

"Good enough," Amy said. She rose, found the food, and set it on the table while Faith found plates and cutlery and put them out. Neil brought out three bottles of beer from the fridge and three glasses from the cupboard. They made sandwiches and ate them and sipped the beer, even Faith, though she had hesitated at first.

Neil could feel some kind of powerful current between the two women, the one he loved now, the one he had once loved. He couldn't see why Faith hadn't immediately gone away when she'd seen them together. He knew (and was surprised to realize it) if she had brought a lover with her he would be angry, would go away, would want to know nothing about their relationship. Amy and Faith sat across the table from each other looking into each other's eyes as if each could read the other's thoughts. It made him both angry and uncomfortable. The wind rattled something on the wall below the window. It clattered erratically, then fell into silence while the wind soared onto the roof to whistle eerily around the chimney.

"*The ungodly are . . . like the chaff which the wind driveth away,*" Faith murmured. Amy frowned, trying to tell if Faith was mocking the people outside the door or not. Neil moved his beer bottle irritably.

"Since when did you start quoting the Bible?" he asked. Faith frowned.

"It's the strangest thing, but lately all these quotations from I don't know where keep popping into my head." She gave a short laugh that had the undertone of a sob. "And the only way to get them out of my head is to say them." She looked away from the other two to the cross that towered over the house.

"Are you . . . all right?" Neil asked, softening at last.

"Oh, yes, very well," Faith said quickly. Her skin in the shadowy room had taken on an unnatural transparency that made it seem to glow with an inner light. She had lost more flesh, her small hands were thin, the bones like those of a songbird, and her eyes – even Amy could see it – held a measure of torment in them.

"Have you been back to the cancer clinic?"

"Of course not." Neil was suddenly aware that her voice had changed. It had always been light, breathless, a small girl's voice. Now it was heavier, darker in tone, lower in pitch. "I'm winning this battle myself," she said, and there was such firmness in her tone that Neil let it go. Faith pushed her nearly full bottle of beer in a small, wet circle. "Are you going to make a life with Neil?" she asked Amy.

"Faith!" Neil scolded. Amy coloured and looked at the tabletop. Neil was surprised by her response, a little offended. Wasn't it settled? Faith ignored him and leaned toward Amy.

"I hope so. He needs another human being close to him or we'll lose him for good. I'm not the right person, though it hurts to say so." She smiled at Neil when she said this last.

"I'm not crazy about being discussed here," Neil said, and both women laughed, not in the least embarrassed.

"Once when I came here you were at a meeting in the park. Neil and I were up here on the hillside and could hear the crowd and the speakers."

"I spend quite a bit of time organizing for political action," Amy said.

"I wish she wouldn't waste her time," Neil said.

"It does take a lot of time," Amy admitted.

"And does no good," Neil put in.

"When I got sick," Faith spoke, "when I realized no one could help me, that God had chosen me for this trial, I knew it was up to me to control my own destiny, that a fate had been chosen for me, but that I could act freely within it. At first I thought I was just another victim, but eventually I began to see that . . . some of us are chosen for special purposes." The cross creaked a soft lamentation.

"*They have sown the wind and they shall reap the whirlwind,*" Faith murmured irrelevantly, and Amy involuntarily shuddered.

"I don't mind the cross so much," Neil said, "as the damn people it attracts." Amy stretched to catch a glimpse of the crowd. The Mounties had erected barriers to prevent the people from spilling over onto Neil's land. They had stopped hawkers from selling cold drinks, ice cream, and religious medals from virtually Neil's doorstep and the town had hastily enacted ordinances that kept people from camping overnight by the cross. After sundown Neil at last got a little peace.

"Do you still want to meet our town's holy woman?" Neil asked Faith.

"Yes," Faith said. "I think it would be wonderful to talk to her. Do you know her?" she asked Amy. "What's she like?"

"I told you," Neil interrupted. "She's no better than a prostitute."

"Better than!" Amy and Faith said in unison.

"She isn't genuine," Neil said. "She can't be. And she's an anachronism. Wrong country. Wrong faith."

"The last stigmatic died only in 1968," Faith said.

"Frauds, every one of them," Neil said. "Or hysterics."

"But," Amy pointed out, "she comes from an old-fashioned eastern European household. She was raised a Catholic – a real Old Country kind of Catholic. *I* suspect her because she went to Raven instead of to the nearest Catholic priest."

"I didn't think you agreed with me," Neil said.

"I don't know if I do or not," Amy said. "But there's no getting around the fact that she was an outcast, an unclean woman. I mean, what does Christianity revere most?"

"Virginity!" the two women said in unison again.

"So here we have a very sexually experienced girl. And what is she likely to want most? To be pure again."

"Let's not forget the uplifting story of Mary Magdalene," Faith said, and Amy studied her to tell if she was being sarcastic or not. "Maybe her virginity's been restored again."

"She's a fake," Neil said.

"Or maybe . . ." Faith said, slowly, so that they both watched her. "Maybe she's a fake in the way you mean. Maybe she did will these marks herself – out of her own pain at being one of society's outcasts. But that doesn't mean that God didn't take pity on her. He allowed her to will this. And by so doing she has become holy – she has purified herself."

"It's a waste of time talking about this," Neil said, angry again. "She's probably using chicken blood – if there's any blood at all."

"How will we ever know?" Amy asked.

"It doesn't matter if we know or not," Faith insisted. "I choose to believe that she's been genuinely blessed by God."

"It matters a lot to me if she's genuine or not," Amy said. "St. Francis of Assisi was genuine, but since then there hasn't been one who was." She fiddled with her glass. "But it does bring up the question of what's genuine. I mean, how many of us will nail marks into our hands and feet? It isn't an easy thing to do, obviously, or there'd be a stigmatic on every corner. Yet . . ." she paused. "Yogis could probably do it if they wanted to, but they don't because it isn't part of their tradition."

"They lie on beds of nails instead," Neil said, sourly.

"It doesn't matter," Faith interjected. "It's the suffering that counts."

"What are you talking about now?" Neil asked in exasperation. The wind gave a sudden push, opening the screen door and then slamming it shut loudly. Instead of replying, Faith bent her head low so that the white of her scalp showed through her fine blonde hair. Nobody said anything for a long time.

"Are you well?" Amy asked at last, her voice gentle.

"I am well," Faith said, as though she had been far away, thinking of something else. Her blue eyes seemed larger when she looked up and the other two caught a glimpse of anguish which passed as quickly as it had come, so that neither of them was sure of having seen it.

Abruptly Neil pressed the heels of his hands against his eyes.

"Faith, Faith," he moaned. "For Christ's sake, go back to the cancer clinic."

"So you can feel less guilty?" she asked. He dropped his hands and stared at her while his face flushed a deep red. Amy looked away quickly.

"So, that's it," he said.

"No, it is not," Faith said, her voice strong. "I've thought long and hard about this. I am doing this for myself. Not for you, not for anyone else." She stood up. "I'm going now." She walked out while Neil and Amy stared after her. They were about to follow when they heard the soft purr of her car as it moved away from the side of the house.

"Why does she keep coming?," Neil asked, his voice cracking with pain. "She won't let me help her."

"She comes to help you," Amy said, touching his hand. Then she too got up and left.

Eight of them sat in Amy's kitchen in the half-darkness of the summer evening, nobody bothering to rise to put on the light, moths batting softly against the door and the first late-summer trilling of the crickets as background to their deliberations.

"No moon tonight," Vera, the MLA, remarked, staring out the screen door to the soft shadows that were shrubs and bushy overgrown perennials that hadn't been cared for since Amy's mother's death. Amy liked them that way.

"Be easier to get in and out of here without anybody seeing us," Val Sheridan said.

"Can't get used to being a radical, eh?" Lowell Hartshorne said with a grin, sounding faintly uncomfortable himself. Out in the yard a nighthawk was swooping low over the shrubbery making his rusty call into the darkness. Its sound faded as it flew into the night.

"Somebody better call this meeting to order," Mrs. Henwick said. "I got a café to look after."

"I'm just an interested bystander," Vera said, throwing up her hands in denial, grinning, so that everybody laughed.

"Okay," Martin Barrell said. "I call this meeting to order. Mac, you gonna take the minutes?"

"Don't need no goddamn minutes," the postmaster said, then, turning to Jessie and Amy seated side by side, added, "Excuse me."

"Notice he doesn't apologize to me," the MLA said, grinning.

"Hell, Vera," Mac said, "I heard you use language so bad it made *me* blush." He nudged her and they laughed together.

"I'll take the minutes," Jessie offered. Amy pushed a notebook over to her and handed her a pen.

"I call this meeting to order," Martin repeated while backs straightened, elbows came off the table, and throats were cleared. A truck droned down the highway a mile away, the sound dwindling as it passed. "It seems to me that the main issue here tonight is whether we ought to go ahead with this protest rally or not, in view of the fact the town's full of strangers on account of the Masuria kid."

"I think we should go ahead," Mrs. Henwick said when nobody else spoke. "The town's full of reporters right now, TV cameras too. We'll get plenty of publicity."

Lowell said, "The town's getting lots of publicity as it is."

"All the wrong kind," Val interrupted. "'This dying little prairie town . . . ' It's all about the holy woman and Raven and his congregation. It isn't about the town's problems."

"As soon as Melody and Raven go," Amy said, "the reporters will go too."

"The point still is," Martin said authoritatively, "that the Premier will be here on the tenth. Everybody knows he's going to be here – will somebody just snap that light on – and if we roust him out, make enough noise, he'll have to listen to us. He'll have to respond."

"I wouldn't be surprised if he jumped at the chance," Lowell said. "Free publicity for the election. He won't know we intend to confront him." He glanced to each of the others in turn, looking for agreement. Amy had risen, but instead of putting on the electric light, she had struck a match and was lighting an old kerosene lamp that was sitting on the counter. She brought it forward and set it by Jessie's elbow so she could see to write.

"I use this in the summer," she said.

"Reminds me of when I was a kid," Vera said.

"These things don't attract insects quite so badly," Lowell said. Behind the circle of their backs there was a soft shadow that melted into a darker one at the edges of the room, and then into the greater darkness outdoors.

"It's as if the light holds us together," Lowell remarked. Nobody spoke.

"Okay, a rally it is," Martin said, speaking loudly to cover his embarrassment. "The problem is, how to get people to come to the rally if what we're really up to is a secret, so that we don't scare off the Premier."

"What time's he due in town?" Vera asked.

"Two."

"Won't your friends be suspicious if you don't show up for the meeting with him?" Mac asked Martin.

"I'll tell them I'll be a little bit late." He shrugged. "They'll go ahead without me."

"When all this is over they could make things hard for you," Vera said.

"Things couldn't be harder than they already are," he said. "Unless we all move to Bangladesh. "That's the least of my worries."

"What if we organized a concert on the street?" Jessie suggested. A moth that had somehow found its way into the room batted against the lamp and died.

"We could go to our supporters, some of the people who went to the rally in Swift Current, tell them what's really going on, tell them to spread the word. A concert seems like the perfect thing. Wouldn't even attract suspicion."

"I'll get them out," Vera said.

"I'll get the coffee-row crowd out," Mrs. Henwick said.

"We can tell everybody right at the start that the Premier's coming. That way he won't be able to back out. We'll catch him by surprise." Vera looked around the faces, pleased with herself.

"Perfect," Lowell said. "But what about the program? Who can we get to sing?"

Jessie said eagerly, running over his voice, "I heard Connie Kaldor sing one of the saddest songs about a dying prairie town . . ."

"I've heard that," Amy said, pleased.

"How would we get her to come?" Jessie said, as deflated as she'd been eager a moment before.

"She has relatives south of here," Amy said. "I know them, and I just happen to know she'll be here visiting them right about that time. I'll drive over and pay them a visit. I'll let you know what happens."

"We'll need speakers, too," Mac said. Murmurs of agreement, followed by suggestions, ran round the table. Outside in the night a pair of owls were hooting from down at the abandoned barn, and as the night cooled the air, fog drifted in, though nobody at the table noticed.

"I think we should dwell on the destruction of our heritage," Val said. "I think that's important. I move we ask Mrs. Art Corrigan to say something."

"Is she still right in her mind?" Amy asked.

"Drifts in and out," Mac said. "She doesn't mind what she says."

"When the time comes," Martin said, "I'll tell the Premier that the people are having a street concert and that it'd be the perfect moment for him to drop over and say a few words. Point out to him how much publicity he can get."

The meeting moved on. Jessie scribbled away. It was agreed Val would chair the program, Vera would speak, certain others would be asked to speak.

"It's a simple matter of survival out here in the country – never mind farms or small businesses. How can we live out here? That's the question. We want to save rural life," Martin said. The meeting closed.

"Well," Vera said. She reached behind her and picked her cap up off the counter where she'd tossed it when she sat down. Using both hands she set it carefully on her head, pulling it down tightly over her dishevelled, grey-streaked hair. She looked around the room at the others as they rose and went to the door. "We have to do this," she said, in a voice so serious that everyone stopped whatever he or she was doing to listen. "But I have a funny feeling right here." She hit herself in the solar plexus with her fist turned sideways. "This is going to be a big one. I can feel it."

Lowell was the last to leave Amy's kitchen. Amy thought he had seemed melancholy and yet uneasy or tense, and she wasn't surprised when he seemed to be hanging back, pretending to finish his cold coffee, using the bathroom while Amy said good-bye to the rest of the committee. They left silently, shutting the doors of their vehicles soundlessly, starting motors without any roaring. Then the gravel crackled softly under their tires as they drove away.

She turned to Lowell, about to remark on the fog, which had grown quite thick, when he spoke. "Are you all right, Amy?"

Surprised, she replied, "I'm a little worried, that's all."

"I feel the tension mounting too," he said. They stood side by side at the door and gazed out into the night. Lowell moved restlessly, laughed unexpectedly, in a sheepish way. "I had the strangest dream last night," he said. Amy leaned against the door frame waiting for him to go on. He didn't look at her, kept his eyes on his shoes, until the story itself lifted his head, and she found him gazing into her eyes, yet seeming not to see her at all.

"I was driving down the highway from one town to another like I've always done, year after year out here. I wasn't thinking about anything at all. I was looking ahead at the highway when suddenly, there in front of me at the end of the road – no, at the place where the road and the sky meet – there was this town! It was the strangest thing!" He lifted one hand and brushed back his non-existent hair. "There's no town there, and it looked as if I would drive right up the road and into it, up into the sky, I mean. It was that real."

"A mirage?" Amy suggested. His eyes cleared, and she saw him seeing her again.

"What? Oh, yes, a mirage," he said, and his eyes grew distant once more. "I can't tell you how beautiful it was. Like a town in one's dream; it was perfect, somehow. A jewel. And it seemed that it rose up out of the heat waves on the horizon, sort of – was made out of them, as if they'd for an instant in time and space coalesced and made what we've all always known in our hearts was there if we could just strain hard enough to see it. It was . . . it was a phantom town. It – there were all these neatly painted wooden houses and the false-fronted stores, you know? And they seemed to oscillate gently up there in the sky, almost as if they were . . . beckoning. The streets were pale and looked parchment-thin and clean, as if nobody had ever walked on them. And you could see between the buildings these tall, lush old trees, and the sun was shining – every once in a while the sun would strike a leaf – you know the way it does? And the leaf would send off light like a diamond." He had lifted one hand while he was speaking, his eyes shining. Now he lowered it and looked at Amy again. "And the strange thing was, Amy . . ." She waited. "It was that it looked exactly like Ordeal."

He had finished speaking. The silence in the room grew and blended with the amorphous humming of insects outside and with the other soft night sounds. They stood motionless, looking into each other's eyes. Amy couldn't think of even a comment. He had seen a vision, that was plain, and she was in awe of it.

"And the funny thing is, I have this sense that I've had this dream before, sometime, but I can't quite . . . you'll think I've lost my mind."

"Of course not, Lowell," she said. "These strange things happen sometimes. Nobody knows why or how. I think it's beautiful. I envy you for having seen it." He smiled and then sighed, turning back to the lamp on the table as if he, like the moths, was also drawn to it.

Amy said, "Sometimes I ask myself, what are we doing all this for? What are we going to save the town for? For what? History moves on."

"We have a right to live here if we choose to," he said. "Or maybe what moves us to fight is the way some of us are drawn to a life in nature. That need is still alive in us and we recognize it for what it is – a human truth – the need to live within nature."

In her mind's eye Amy was seeing a farmer riding high above a dusty field in his massive tractor, a rancher riding slowly on a horse through his herd, children pouring off a school bus, a woman shaking a rug out her kitchen door toward a field of wheat. When it came right down to it, what did she care about farming? What did she care about a failing café, or a bankrupt hardware? Nothing.

"Something big is going on here," she said. "If I could only grasp exactly what it is . . ."

"People have to make a living," Lowell said, and now there was resignation in his tone. "Does anybody ever mean it when they say, I'll starve before I'll do that?" He sounded so sad, Amy thought. She hated to see him going out alone into the foggy night, thought of his dead wife, how lonely he must be even though he spent his life in the midst of crowds.

"Do what?" she asked.

"Oh, brand cattle or de-horn them, or plough up grassland. . . ." Then he laughed, dismissing everything he had said. Amy couldn't think of anything to say to make him feel better.

"People will do anything," she said.

"The season's turning," he remarked. "Soon everyone will be harvesting whatever crop there is."

"Harvest always make me sad," Amy said.

"Why?"

"Lionel died in the fall. I spent that winter alone. Sometimes I think I'll never get over it. What happened to me during that long winter."

Lowell put his arm around her, tentatively at first, and when she didn't resist, he drew her to him and stroked her hair. In a moment, Amy drew back.

"Soon I'll be retiring," he said. "Who will I comfort then?"

"I'll come to you for comfort," Amy said.

As he moved slowly down the highway toward town through the thick white fog, Lowell's mind was on Amy, her sadness, which he now saw to be ineradicable. Suffering, the Book of Lamentations, there would be no permanent end to anyone's sufferings on this Earth. The weight of all the years of listening to the sorrows of his people lay heavily on him. His car purred softly through the white so that it seemed to him it was borne up by it, that his wheels were no longer touching pavement. He couldn't see beyond a foot past the hood of his car, but he drove on, thinking. What good had he ever done them? he wondered. Often he had forgotten or not understood himself that suffering was to be the way for everyone. If he couldn't remember it, how could he expect others to?

He could tell by a sixth sense honed by years in the community that he was approaching the town. Dimly he thought he heard the ringing of the railway crossing's warning bell, but he wasn't sure. It had been such a long time since the last train had gone down the track, probably there hadn't been one since harvest the year before. People were muttering that the CPR had already closed the branch-line and had forgotten to tell them. He braked carefully and waited. There was nothing to see but soft white light in each direction, yet he thought he could hear the distant rushing of the train and its melancholy whistle trailing away. He peered ahead and thought he could see a rhythmic pink glow that would be the flashing of the warning lights, but he couldn't be sure.

He listened again, uncertain whether to go ahead or to wait, half-wondering if he wasn't experiencing an aural mirage, a trick of the fog. But wasn't that it again? The rhythmic clack of wheels against the track? But the sound faded again, if he had heard one at all, and the fog thickened and grew whiter. He put his foot gently onto the accelerator and inched forward.

He was out on the track, feeling the front wheels bump over the rails when on his left a pale circular glow appeared that was denser than the light surrounding it. It spread indistinctly, growing larger as it hurtled in silence toward him. And then he knew. This was how his Maker would appear, silently, out of fog, growing ever brighter, until His light was blinding.

# CHAPTER
# 16

"But why a concert in the middle of the day?" Hilda Langlois asked the group of women standing around her as they read the poster taped to the window of the grocery store. Beth Mustard, standing beside her, had stretched on tiptoe to be able to read it.

"Does Zena know about this?" she asked Hilda in an undertone.

"Ssshhh," Hilda hissed, indicating Alice Waldham, who was not a widow, standing on her other side.

"Why in the middle of the day?" Alice asked briskly and tapped her knuckle once against the glass sharply, as if to make the poster disappear. "It'll be so hot then you'll be able to fry an egg on the sidewalk." She pushed her way out of the group, shaking her head.

"Why on the post office steps?" Rita Zacharias demanded to know, pushing her frizzy hair back. She turned to Beth and Hilda, a light of understanding appearing in her bright little eyes. "The — post — office — steps," she said with heavy significance. Hilda pursed her lips in disapproval and would have hushed her too, but just then old John Biem came out of the grocery store, tottering a little as he shifted his bag of groceries to his other arm so he would have a clear view of the steps. The women waited to see if he would make it himself or if he would need help.

"Big day today, ladies," he announced, having reached the side-walk without incident. The women waited to hear what he was talking about. "Coyotes," he said in a loud whisper, stretching his long neck to come closer to them. "First light . . ." He paused, look-ing at each one of them in turn. "First light heard them singing. Looked out my window," he paused again, "and there they were, could see 'em plain as anything. Right down there at the end of my street. A pack of 'em. They was sitting on their haunches." He demonstrated. "Their heads was raised high and they was howling out a warning."

"Have you been drinking your horse liniment again, John?" Rita asked him sharply. Since Old Man Paslowski's death, he was the oldest man in the district and therefore everybody's property. "Coy-otes don't come into town."

"I heard them myself," Hilda said stiffly. "I didn't mention it, that's all. I thought they might have been attracted by that pack of dogs we got running around town these days."

"I heard them too," Beth Mustard put in timidly. "It gave me the shivers, they were so close." She turned to Mr. Biem. "What do you think it means?" she asked, while Rita rolled her eyes in disgust behind John's back.

"Premier's in town today," he said. "Big doings going on. I can't tell what. You ladies ought to know," he said, turning to Rita so quickly he almost dropped his groceries. He shook his head slowly, teetering dangerously as he did it, so that Beth and Hilda both reached out a hand to steady him. "Mark my words," he said. He wandered away, still shaking his head, out onto the street, where Sandy McDonnell, who was passing by in his truck, almost hit him, and Grant Voth had to brake hard to avoid hitting Sandy's truck.

In the meantime Mrs. Lou Kelly had come up carrying her poodle in the crook of her arm.

"A meeting!" she said. "Connie Kaldor singing! Well, well! I wonder what the occasion is." She looked around at the older women, smiling cheerfully at them as if this was the best news in the world. She set her poodle down on the sidewalk where he promptly began tugging on his leash. Mrs. Kelly was always cheerful, to the general annoyance of just about everybody. "The woman's feeble-minded," her husband had been known to say more than once. Nobody answered her. "Guess I'll just have to wait to find out," she sang, fastening the leash to the garbage bin outside the door of the store. The poodle yipped in annoyance at her, then subsided with an air of resigned exasperation, as if there wasn't a thing you could do with Mrs. Kelly, who stood smiling down at him.

"Seems to me," Beth Mustard said disapprovingly, "that we shouldn't be having public gatherings of any kind with Mr. Hartshorne still warm in his grave."

"It gives me the shivers to think of it," Rita admitted.

"I believe the cross had something to do with it," Beth whispered.

"What are you talking about?" Hilda said, apparently scandal-ized. "There you go again. It's only a chunk of wood, you know. And anyway, the man was hit by a train. There was a fog. We all saw it."

"Some train!" Beth said, indignant for once. "On a closed-down branchline. In the middle of the night. First train in more than a year. John Biem's right. It's some kind of a warning."

"Warning about what?" Rita demanded.

"Who knows?" she whispered. "It's the Millennium – anything can happen."

"The what?" Mrs. Kelly asked, but her poodle was yapping again, looking up at them with its bright little eyes, making such a racket they couldn't hear themselves think. Rita threw her hands up in annoyance and went into the store. Beth watched her go, frown-ing, then turned, crossed the street, and went into the post office. Hilda remained a moment longer staring at the poster with her finger to her chin, then hurried away too in the direction of Zena Lavender's. Mrs. Kelly, ignoring her poodle's insistent racket, fol-lowed Rita into the grocery store.

The poodle sat on its haunches, quiet now, and watched the people come and go, some stopping to read the poster before they moved on. After a while he put his snub nose down on his curly white paws and went to sleep.

The crowd had been gathering since before noon, at first only a cluster or two of men standing on the steps of the Co-op and in front of the filling station, as if their being there was an accident, and a group of women outside the hairdresser's. A few children played on the bench next to the barber shop and slightly more cars than usual were parked on Main Street. By twelve-thirty enough people had arrived that there was no room for all of them on the sidewalk and many of them were standing on the street. Val Sheridan and Mac Hicks, who was on his lunch break, were setting up yellow barriers they had borrowed from the municipality to stop vehicles from passing in front of the post office, and this drew more people who didn't want to miss anything. Next, Val and Mac had set up the public address system on the speakers' platform, which was the wide space at the top of the post office steps in front of the main doors. Jessie, who thought of the balloons, had had them inflated, and hung them from the railings, together with a few yellow and red paper streamers. Amy had arrived with her arms full of a dusty red rug that had once been a prized possession of her mother's and which, with Val's help, she had spread up the steps to the microphone, anchoring it in place with bricks placed neatly on each step. The gathering crowd offered suggestions and, when she was done, murmured its approval.

One o'clock came and the crowd grew thicker. Promptly at five minutes to two Mac Hicks emerged from the post office and, with a flourish, drew a key out of his pocket and locked the outer door. There were a few audible gasps at this unprecedented act – closing the post office in the middle of the afternoon! – and a buzz of conversation from the crowd over what this might signify. Val and Jessie stood together at the bottom of the steps, Jessie frowning nervously, Val checking his watch every few seconds. Near them, on the small square of lawn to one side of the steps, Amy and Vera stood together watching the crowd as it gathered and began to press close. They saw Martin Barrell make his way through the people, speak briefly into Val's ear, and then disappear as quickly as he had arrived. Old Richard Corrigan came around the corner pushing the wheelchair containing his tiny, shrivelled mother, people moving aside to let him pass. He paused in the shade behind Vera and Amy and leaned with his back against the wall of the post office, resting. His mother appeared to be asleep with her chin dropped against her chest. Mrs. Henwick came striding around the corner, late, not even having bothered to take off her wide white apron.

"Connie Kaldor's here," she said to Amy and Vera. "She's sitting in her car around the corner. She'll wait there till we give her the signal."

"Better let Val know," Amy said. Val was slowly mounting the steps to the platform. Mrs. Henwick called up to him, he nodded, and grasped the microphone. Mac hurried down the steps and stood beside Amy, Vera, and Richard Corrigan. Jessie slid in beside them too.

"Good afternoon." It was the pastor, Mr. Raven. He bent his head as he spoke, and in the harsh sunlight his skin was unnaturally pale and the red-gold of his hair, which was neatly tied into a ponytail, seemed to give off sparks. Amy noticed at once that instead of wearing his cleric's black gown, which he often wore as he strode about town, he was dressed today in an ordinary pale-grey suit. When he straightened Amy saw that the suit hung on his gaunt frame as if he had recently lost weight. "I've come to offer a blessing in Mr. Hartshorne's place," he said.

"That is kind of you," Amy said soberly.

"His death is a great loss to the community," he said, and, since he had never in the past shown any interest in the community, they were all too startled to reply.

"Indeed it is," Vera said. "And a peculiar death it was," she added, as if to herself.

"The Lord works . . ." Mr. Raven began, but Val's amplified voice drowned him out.

"We've invited you here today to listen to some music . . ." Val began. Amy glanced at Jessie and saw that though Jessie's eyes were fixed on her husband's face, that faintly worshipful expression with which she used to look at him was completely gone. It soothed Amy to see that calm, open expression. Abruptly Mr. Raven moved from beside them and went slowly and unostentatiously up to Val. Val glanced at him, then, realizing his purpose, gave the microphone over to him.

The crowd stirred a little impatiently and muttered. They didn't appear to like the idea of being addressed by someone many of them regarded as at the root of the community's trouble, as if they had forgotten all about drought and economic hardship the day the cross went up. But Pastor Raven looked calmly out to the crowd, and they were silenced by his gaze and waited quietly for him to speak. He clasped his hands loosely above his waist, lowered his head, and began.

"I am glad to be here to offer a prayer this afternoon," he said. He spoke quietly in a conversational tone. "It gladdens my heart to know that people like yourselves, country people, haven't forgotten that no matter how badly our world seems to be going otherwise, it always behooves us to offer prayers to the Power which governs our lives at the beginning of any enterprise, and especially to ask a blessing on our small attempts at righting our world." Amy was stunned. "*Our* world! *Our* efforts!" Somehow Raven had always held himself aloof from others, even from his own parishioners. She was sure he had never said "our" anything before, but always "your," as if he knew that the Lord had reserved a special path for him alone. He paused; there was neither a movement nor a sound from the huge crowd that had gathered. "Even the native people whose home this was before we came, and who we liked to think of as savages, were humble before their Maker and would not have dreamed of trying to do anything without first offering prayers to their God." Not a fly buzzed, not a bird twittered. It struck Amy as she listened that surely no God could fail to listen at such a moment as this – a people in dire straits, its priest full of humility.

 She saw then, looking out over the bowed heads of the crowd, that even the Hutterites from the nearby colonies had come to the meeting. They clustered together, the bearded men in their black suits and hats, the women in their brightly coloured long cotton dresses with their dotted kerchiefs tied securely over their hair. Near them she saw that the *Rebekahs* must have broken off from their meeting to come because they stood, a group of grey-haired women in their long white dresses ornamented with brightly coloured satin sashes and badges of office that shone in the bright light. A contingent of teenage girls in light-coloured shorts and skimpy blouses lounged against the wall of the post office on the opposite side from where Amy stood. Next to them were a group of tanned and muscled teenaged boys. Women who must have left their homes to pick up a loaf of bread, not even stopping to take off their aprons or remove their curlers, were sprinkled through the crowd, and mixed in also were the men of the district: ranchers in tight, faded jeans and western-cut shirts, the sleeves rolled down to the wrists and the snaps carefully done up despite the intense heat, their big hats shading their faces. And farmers, broad-shouldered and tanned, wearing caps or straw hats stood shoulder to shoulder. Kids came and went; those who couldn't walk yet were held in their mothers' arms or rested in front of them in their canopied strollers while older kids sat together on the curbs or played together in the shade in front of the stores. A mechanic had come from his shop still wearing his grease-stained coveralls, and next to him stood the two hairdressers, still wearing their plastic gloves from perms they were giving. Even the men who operated the graders that maintained the district's roads had climbed down from their machines and stood in the crowd in their dusty work clothes. Everyone had come.

"I want also to offer a prayer for Lowell Hartshorne, who gave up his life for all of us." Amy lowered her head this time too as tears sprang to her eyes.

He had done that, she thought, it was as if he was to be the ritual offering before the great undertaking.

When Pastor Raven was done, she watched him move away from the microphone and, thinking of the way he usually strode about town with his head up, his jaw set, and a hard light in his eyes that seemed half-crazy to her, she was surprised to realize that all of that was gone, that he seemed in every way an ordinary man. And where were the dogs that had always accompanied him?

She noticed then that Jessie had slipped away. Val was back at the microphone now and the crowd was stirring again as heads turned to one side. Connie Kaldor, led by Jessie Sheridan, was making her way to the steps. Val put his hand out and she ran up them, a tall, smiling blonde in a brilliantly coloured pink-and-green silk coat, dazzling in the bright sun. She carried a guitar, and when she turned to face the crowd light flashed from its polished silver trim that was blinding. The crowd clapped and cheered — she was practically a hometown girl.

But Mac Hicks had thrust himself forward before Val could say anything and had taken the mike. He was waving a piece of paper. The singer backed away, allowing him full sway. He offered no preliminaries.

"I have here a letter from the post office officially notifying me that this here post office of ours that's been in this town one way or another for over eighty-five years is going to be closed next month. Come winter there won't be a post office in Ordeal any more." There was a stunned silence, then murmurs, then cries of outrage. "Now listen, neighbours!" Mac shouted. "Our Premier is here in this very town this very afternoon and we're going to bring him over here so

271

he can explain to us how the hell his government could let such a thing happen!" Mac had run out of words, his indignation reddening his face and making veins in his neck stand out. Val took the mike from him. He had to shout to get back the crowd's attention.

"Someone's gone to get the Premier and you can address your questions and remarks to him. In the meantime . . ." He couldn't be sure anybody was listening, so he repeated it, louder this time. "In the meantime, we are lucky enough to have our own Connie Kaldor sing for us!" He stepped back and threw his arm out in a theatrical gesture toward the singer, who came forward and stood quietly at the mike waiting for the crowd to settle down.

"Friends," she said softly, and people stopped muttering and turned their attention to her. "It saddens me to be here in the face of such bad news, but I won't comment. I'm going to sing a song instead." She settled the guitar strap on her shoulder, touched her guitar, and looked out over the crowd, which was motionless again, listening.

> *A town dies slowly*
> *Like an old pioneer*
> *the heart goes*
> *the eyes go*
> *but the mind stays clear*
> *It remembers how it was a long time ago*
> *a few little houses against the blowing snow*

Her voice grew stronger, rose above the heads of the crowd, floated across the rooftops and up the hillside till it reached Neil Locke's ears as he sat reading in his living room.

> *But you learn to pace your life*
> *by the changes in the weather*
> *changes in the time*
> *people learned to build this town together*
> *proud of their spot on the railway line*

Tears glistened on many cheeks of the listening people.

*but when they think that you can't work anymore*
*they want to leave you alone*
*they take out your railway*
*let your curling rink fall*
*make granaries out of your homes*

*A town dies slowly . . .*

Connie finished her song and there was dead silence. She leaned into the mike and said, "I have to go now. Thank you." The audience remembered itself and began to clap and cheer but she was gone, had slipped through them so quickly they had hardly noticed her departure, and then she was leaping into a car at the far edge of the crowd, the door shut, she was gone.

Vera was speaking.

"You've all heard me talk plenty of times about what's happening . . ." Another stir was disturbing the crowd far to the back and everybody in the middle and at the front turned to see what was going on. Three long, shiny cars pulled up, and who else but Harold Havoc stepped out of the middle one. His arms went up as soon as his foot touched the street and his mouth opened and words were coming out before he'd penetrated the crowd. The people parted, grinning, as he made his way to the platform, bounded up the stairs, and as Vera stepped aside to allow him the mike said, "I don't need no mike, Vera. I guess I can be heard without one."

"Just don't go on too long, Harold!" Vera shouted so everybody would hear. "We still plan to hear from the Premier!" The people shouted their agreement. Amy turned to Jessie.

"Where's Val?" she asked, having just noticed he was missing from the platform. Jessie nodded across the crowd. Val was far out at the edge talking with Martin Barrell. As she watched they each strode away in different directions, Val back into the crowd and Martin, presumably, to get the Premier.

Harold Havoc was in full oration now, gesturing flamboyantly, his straw hat slipping to the back of his head and that silver belt buckle of his shining in the centre of his belly like a moon.

"I told you this before," he shouted. "I asked you to listen. Farm foreclosures, businesses going bankrupt, people moving away, elevators closing down, branchlines getting tore up, and now the post office closing! It's time for action, folks, and we got to take that action ourselves!" There were shouts from the audience, it was hard to tell if in agreement or disagreement, but Harold out-shouted them all. "No! Government won't help! And you know why government won't help?"

"Tell us why, Harold," a few voices shouted mockingly.

"I'll tell you why!" he responded. Sweat had begun to streak down his cheeks and his neck glistened with sweat. "Because what's happening to us is natural! It's inevitable! It's what since biblical times has happened to a people that's lost its way – a people that's forgotten prayer! A people that's forgotten Nature is a gift the good Lord gave us – not so we can exploit her and get rich and to hell with our fellow man!"

"Whose side you on, Harold?" a man shouted, and people laughed.

"The side of the Christian way of life!" Harold thundered, his voice bouncing off the walls of the buildings and echoing back. " . . . Christian, Christian . . . Christian . . ."

"Why won't you listen to him?" a woman wailed.

"We don't listen," a deep, powerful voice said, and all heads turned to see who it belonged to, "because he is sunk in the past. Because this is the future and we have to learn how to live in it." The voice was coming from a man standing at the back of the crowd. His dress was indistinguishable from theirs and his face was hidden by a hat that was pulled down so that its brim cast a shadow over his features.

"Who is he? Who said that?" people asked each other.

274

But nobody knew who is was.

"He looks like that John Palliser," somebody said. "His picture's in the museum."

"He's been dead for years," somebody replied.

"Is it . . . could it be Tommy Douglas?" a teenager asked.

"Long dead," an adult replied.

"The old prophets are dead," the man said in the same voice that commanded attention even though he didn't seem to be shouting. "A new prophet must appear." On the platform Harold Havoc shouted, "And I am that new prophet! And if you . . ." He froze, one finger pointed heavenward, looking off in the opposite direction to the one where the stranger was.

Everyone turned to see what he was looking at.

A double row of people was making a smart turn at the corner apparently heading for their gathering. Every one of them was dressed in a long white robe with a blood-red tie at the waist and the group was led by a young blonde girl whose robe was so long in the sleeves that her hands were hidden in its folds. It was Melody Masuria leading the members of the Church of the Millennium. Amy glanced quickly at Raven. She saw him straighten abruptly and a surprised look appear on his face. The marchers were singing, and as they reached the edge of the crowd, they grouped themselves in a semi-circle with Melody at their centre and fell silent, looking up at the platform.

Harold Havoc stood in confusion. He appeared to have shrunk, and Val, seeing his uncertainty, quickly took the microphone.

"Is she bleeding, Mom?" a child was heard to ask into the silence, and people laughed and hushed each other. Val spoke.

"The Premier has said he'd be delighted to come out and say a few words to us," he said, and everybody's attention was turned back to the platform. Encouraged, Val went on. "The person who has lived longest in the town, Mrs. Ava Corrigan, has a few words to say to us." Mrs. Corrigan was sound asleep in her wheelchair, but she woke abruptly and began to struggle with claw-like old hands to get herself to her feet. The crowd waited politely as her son helped her up the stairs. At the top she turned to face the people and tottered so violently that Val caught her on one side and her son on the other.

"Leave me be! Leave me alone!" she scolded them, slapping at their hands. She wavered, looked as though she might fall, was steadied by her son, and began to speak.

"I never made a speech in all my life," she said. "And I ain't going to now." People waited, grinning at each other. The teenagers by the post office rolled their eyes at the folly of adults.

"When I got married I was just sixteen. Had my first baby when I was seventeen and a half. Richard here. I started a raspberry patch the summer he was born. First year it was too dry and the canes all died. Second year the deer came in and killed them, and what they didn't the horses trampled during the rodeo when a bunch of 'em somebody was trailing spooked and got away. Dick, God rest his soul, drove a team and buggy to Crisis and got me some more canes and I put them in the third spring. The next year they flowered and the year after that they grew a nice crop of berries.

"Now I wanted to save them precious berries from them birds – all the fruit we got in them days year in and year out was saskatoons and chokecherries and buffalo-berries and cactus berries – so I covered them all with mosquito netting. So then them little raspberry bugs got so bad the bushes were just swarming with them, sucking out all the juices so them berries were just white, and you couldn't hardly get any berries for yourself."

She paused, then put both hands on the mike and closed her eyes while her lips worked as if she might be adjusting her false teeth or chewing on a piece of toffee. The silence grew interminable and Val was about to move forward again when she opened her eyes, let go of the stand, and went on.

"So the next year I decided not to cover the bushes, and when the bugs came again and started eating the berries, all the little birds

276

that couldn't get at the bugs when I had the bushes covered flew in and ate all the bugs, and that was the first year I got raspberries." Her voice grew louder at the end of the sentence as if she were making a point. The people who had listened carefully to her looked at one another uncertainly. Was this a parable like in the Bible? Had the old lady lost her marbles? She had waved her son forward to help her down the steps and the people, seeing this, began to clap, at first only a spattering of applause here and there, but soon everybody had joined in and there were even a few cheers and whistles.

"What was that all about?" Jessie asked, laughing. Amy, who hadn't clapped, was frowning. She said to Jessie, "I think it was about how our attempts to tame nature only make things worse." Then she laughed too, looking at Jessie's puzzled expression. "Oh, she had a message all right," Amy said.

But the Premier was coming! The crowd could feel his presence, could sense him walking smartly up the main street in double-quick time, knew in a moment he would round the corner, waving and smiling and so smartly dressed in a trim, dark suit with a shirt so white it would be blinding and a classy maroon tie knotted in the smoothest of knots directly below the centre of his chin and maybe a little bit of maroon hanky peeking out of his breast pocket, the way he looked on television.

And there he was, the crowd parting to let him through, the Premier shaking hands or touching people on the arm or shoulder as he passed them, smiling, smiling all the way through the huge crowd to the steps, up which he sprang like a boy of twenty, and spinning around to face his constituents. Photographers snapped his pictures and TV cameras whirred. He raised both hands above his head, still smiling, and waited for the cheer that always greeted this gesture.

But nobody cheered, except two or three of his party faithful who had accompanied him from their meeting, and when nobody else joined them, they fell silent too. The Premier frowned and lowered his arms.

"People of the beautiful town of Ordeal!" he called. "I'm delighted to be here at this gathering today to say a few words to you . . ."

"We don't need any crap from you!" Martin Barrell yelled. "We want to know what you're going to do to help us!"

"We need help, not talk!" people shouted to the startled Premier.

"My government . . ." the Premier began, recovering his confidence and ignoring his hecklers and for the first time grabbing the microphone so as to drown them out. "You know we will assist you in any way . . ."

"Keep our post office open!" Mac Hicks suddenly shouted. He had run up the steps and had shouted into the Premier's ear. The Premier pulled back, knocking his beautifully knotted tie askew as it caught on the microphone. He had begun to sweat and this reminded everyone how hot it was and how annoying it was that they had to stand out in this incredible heat to listen to a politician tell lies.

"We want our post office!" they began to chant.

"As you know, Ladies and Gentlemen, the post office is under federal jurisdiction. . . ." The shouts and cries of "Boo! Boo!" drowned him. "Federal jurisdiction . . ." he shouted.

"Bullshit again!" Bill Peat shouted.

"Federal jurisdic . . . My government . . ."

"Thus says the Lord . . ." A shrill voice cried from somewhere near the back of the mass of people. "Alas! Alas! Alas!" The words cut through the muttering and shouts of the crowd, through the Premier's abortive attempts to speak, and made everyone turn and stretch to see who was doing the caterwauling. A collective shiver ran down the spines of the people, scalps crinkled in dismay with each cry. They began to push and shove each other, trying to get out of the way of the newcomer with the terrible voice. *"The Lord has spoken! Thus sayeth the Lord!"*

It was Alma Sheridan.

The Premier, who had looked like he was about to try to make his escape, stood frozen to the spot with terror written on every line of his face and body. Alma's long grey hair looked as it it hadn't been combed in a year. Some of it hung in clumps down her back and some was caught up one side of her head above her ear. Her dress was a shapeless black bag-like garment with the hem hanging down and long threads touching her ankles and the tops of the men's bedroom slippers she wore in the place of shoes. Despite the staggering heat she had thrown a wool shawl over her shoulders. She advanced up the steps to the platform and tore the microphone out of the frozen Premier's hand. Then she threw it down the steps where it bounced, making horrendous screeches and crackles and abruptly falling silent like a beast killed.

"Thus . . . sayeth . . . the . . . Lord!" she cried, and her voice was so loud it seemed it might be heard over in Crisis twenty miles away. At just that moment eight or ten crows flew over the crowd and drowned her out with their harsh cries. They coasted low over the heads of the crowd, and as they sailed over those standing on the post office steps, one dropped a large white mass onto the shoulder of the Premier's perfectly tailored dark suit before they landed in a fierce-eyed row on the edge of the flat roof of the post office, facing the crowd in front of and below them.

An electric hush had fallen over the people.

"I have seen the Lord," Alma shouted. "I am commanded to speak. You have been listening to false prophets. The prophets of progress, the prophets of technology. You would have been better to have turned away! LISTEN!" Her cry was so loud it might have pierced the heavens. Mothers put their hands over their childrens' ears and strong men's knees gave out. "I gave you the Earth to husband and you have killed or driven away the birds and animals I gave into your hands for protection! I gave you a vast land to live in and you have refused entry to the poor of the world! I gave you . . ." The people, getting over the initial shock, were moving now and beginning to complain bitterly and loudly to each other. Someone picked up a stone from the circle of gravel that surrounded the row of trees that grew out of the concrete and threw it. It missed Alma and sailed so close to the Premier that he jumped back, looking frantically for an escape, but the crowd was pressing closer and closer so that the stairs were no longer passable.

"You have desecrated the soil . . ." Someone else threw a stone and it hit Alma hard on the shoulder. She lifted her face to the sky and raised her hand as if to grasp it. "Alas!" she cried, and the sound fell down the sky and echoed and re-echoed all across the town and up into the hills where Neil raised his head from his book, dropped it, and fell to his knees, his face buried in his hands. Another stone struck Alma, this one on her forehead, and drew blood. "I curse you!" she cried. "Drought! Pestilence!" A hail of stones struck her and she fell to her knees. "Hurricanes! Fire!"

As soon as she had appeared on the steps the doctor, who was part of the crowd, had scurried away to the hospital two blocks over. Nobody had noticed him go and by the time he returned, moments later, they were so agitated by Alma they didn't see him drive up in the ambulance. But now Alma was suddenly surrounded by him and the two nurses in their white uniforms that he had brought with him. They were bending over her, someone was handing up the stretcher, they were forcing Alma onto it and strapping her in, taping her mouth, and then she was being handed, stretcher and all, from man to man over the heads of the crowd to the ambulance.

The Premier had finally extracted his hanky and was wiping away the bird droppings on his shoulder. The crowd was shifting and re-shaping itself, its mutterings giving way to a confused roar of voices. The Premier, his confidence returning, raised both hands again and stepped back to the centre of the platform. He began to shout, but nobody could hear him. Out in the crowd, at various points, six or seven grey-haired women were pushing their way to the front.

"We want a moratorium on foreclosures!" a farmer shouted, and the cry was taken up and repeated. "Save our farms! Save our farmers!" people were shouting.

The grey-haired women were closer to the steps now, but nobody was paying them the slightest attention, and nobody had noticed that each of them was carrying a shopping bag.

"Give us back our elevator!"

"Give us back our branchline!"

The women simultaneously reached the bottom step. Far off to one side a long, silver limousine whispered around the corner and drew up beside Melody, who still stood there in her white gown with her followers with their blood-red sashes arranged behind her. One of the doors opened on silent hinges and a small, round man with a smooth cap of silver hair stepped out and began to speak to Melody. It was Clyde Leroy, the television evangelist.

"Save our farms!"

"Save our post office!"

The chants grew louder and more and more confused, out of rhythm and contradictory, and the crowd began to surge back and forth. The Premier was sweating profusely, still struggling to make himself heard, when suddenly he was surrounded by a squadron of stout, grey-haired women who dropped their shopping bags to reveal chains, handcuffs, and padlocks. The chains rattled and clanked as they fell to the cement and were lifted as each woman wound them around herself and around the iron railing of the platform. Val, Vera, and Martin began to grapple with the women in an effort to stop them from chaining themselves to the steps.

Someone shoved the Premier and he would have toppled off the steps except that — to his horror — he had been handcuffed to the rail by one wrist.

Val had given up trying to stop the women. He had retrieved the microphone and was trying to make it work.

"Calm down everybody!" he shouted, but nobody was listening, the mike wouldn't work, and to make matters worse a strong wind had come up and it blew his words away as fast as he shouted them. Behind him, the Premier was cursing and shouting orders to which nobody was listening. The women, now securely chained, had begun to sing "We Shall Overcome."

The wind was rising now, whooping around the corners from both directions at once, whipping up skirts so that women had to hold them down, and lifting men's hats from their heads so that everywhere they could be seen chasing them. Everybody was squinting hard, trying to see through the cloud of blowing dust that was rapidly obscuring the whole street.

"Who did it? Who handcuffed the Premier?" people shouted to each other, laughing and covering their faces with their hands to keep the dirt out of their mouths and eyes.

On the platform the Premier was shouting soundlessly into the wind, jerking so hard at the handcuffs that it looked as if he might tear his arm out of its socket. The crowd was thinning, chasing hats, shopping bags, scarves, hair ribbons, and sundry other items. Women bent to shield their children from the wind and turned to point up to the sky where a black cloud bank was rapidly approaching from the west. Melody and her people had fallen to their knees and were praying aloud, while the wind whipped their gowns up over their heads and made them look like a posse of angels which had swooped down from heaven to light on the street. The silver-haired man in the silk suit kept talking to Melody as she prayed. She pushed him gently aside so she could see what was happening on the platform.

Later, people said it was as if she had been drawn by a magnet, as if she couldn't have stopped if she had tried. She stood, walked slowly, her gown hanging in graceful folds to the street so that it looked as though she had no feet, through the remains of the madly scurrying crowd straight to the post office steps, mounted them, went right up to the Premier, who stood writhing and shouting incoherently, his tie whipping in the wind, still handcuffed to the rail.

There was disagreement about what happened next: some said none of this happened at all, while others swore they had seen it themselves with their very own eyes. Out of the many differing and confused accounts the consensus emerged that Melody had reached out one small white hand neatly bandaged in white gauze, touched the handcuffs that held the Premier, and instantly, they fell away to the cement. Then Melody turned and walked away, back to the waiting evangelist who took her gently by the arm and ushered her into his car, got in himself, and the long, silver limousine whispered away, and neither the car nor the people in it were ever seen again in Ordeal, Saskatchewan.

But accounts were conflicting and confused because the advancing black cloud was doing something funny to the air. It had turned the air brown and the sound of the wind was a deafening roar louder than an approaching freight train. The sound struck terror into the hearts of everyone and sent them running for cover. Even those who had never seen a tornado before knew its sound instinctively. Mac Hicks made his way back up the steps and, fighting wind, got the door unlocked and open and disappeared inside. Val grabbed Jessie and helped her into the post office too. Amy had rushed to help a mother holding her infant while she struggled to get her toddler out of its stroller and into the arms of its father, who was rushing down the street toward them.

The noise had accelerated to a high-pitched screech, like a jet taking off. It blotted out all other sound and the day grew dark as night. The tornado was on them, swooping over the town, uprooting trees, sucking up buildings and cars and whirling them away.

High up on his hillside Neil Locke had seen the tornado coming long before the townspeople had. He had been warned by the truly alarming creaks and groans coming from the cross by his house.

Realizing at last that it was a tornado, not at all sure by then he would even have time to scramble to safety, he opened the trapdoor under the kitchen table and dropped down into the dirt cellar below his house. The trapdoor fell into place with a crash, and he was in blackness.

Then he remembered that Amy was out on the street below. He reached for the trapdoor to hoist himself back out again but it was too late, the storm had hit; even from the safety of his cellar and even over the roar of the wind he could hear the giant cross give a horrendous groan, followed by an earthshaking C – R – A – C – K that split the air and that told him that the cross erected in the name of Christianity by the Pastor Raven and the Church of the Millennium had been destroyed by none other than Mother Nature.

# CHAPTER
17

What was left of their crop after the tornado, followed by hail, had swept across it stretched out all the way to the horizon from where Val and Jessie stood in the flattened yellow grass at its border. A couple of crows flapped by cawing raucously so that Jessie shuddered.

"It wasn't much of a crop, but at least it was something," she said. Val said, "It wasn't ours anyway, Jess. The bank would have taken it all." Behind them the sun was low on the horizon so that their shadows stretched out long over the land and their backs were bathed pink.

"It would have helped pay our debt," she said ruefully. Val dropped the handful of straw he was shredding between his palms. He brushed them against each other.

"The cattle are gone, the machinery's gone, the crop's gone, and now the land is too. There's no earthly way we can pay. There's nothing left they can do to us," he said.

"I can't believe how much it hurts to lose everything, how awful it feels to know everybody knows you're a failure, that you have nothing." She kept her eyes on him, saw him flinch.

"Are you going to leave me?" he asked, his voice low.

"No," she said. "I've learned that much at least. *This* is the world. And anyway, I love you." He smiled, slid one arm around her shoulders. Insects hummed monotonously in the still air and the sun slid lower down the sky. She found a rock nearby, a small red granite rock with flecks of mica sparkling in it. She sat down on it, stretching out her legs. Val stood above her, toeing the loose dirt with one boot, his hands easy on his hips.

"It's like this," he said. "We can't afford a lawyer, but the Homestead Act says they can't take the home quarter on us for three years, so we still have a place to live. We've got three years' grace. A lot can happen in three years." Jessie hugged her knees, observed an ant crawling past a stunted sagebrush, sighed.

"Your mom and dad will lose their house."

"They can move back out here. We'll let them have the new house and we can fix up the old one to live in – like they wanted us to do. Could you stand that?"

"It would be a relief," she said with feeling. "I could stop feeling so guilty." Though she would miss her beautiful new house more than she could ever say. Val raised his head and looked off toward the faintly pink haze beyond the ruined wheat where the horizon was supposed to be. In the fading light the field was smoothing out and starting to shine again.

"What a time to get pregnant," she said.

"As good a time as any," he said. He sat down on the dusty grass beside her.

"All those rallies didn't do much good, did they?" she remarked.

He reflected. "It turns out that we're the only ones who really understand this rural world we live in, so it's no use going to the government. We have to save ourselves."

"We had the fun of seeing a bird poop on the Premier. We saw him handcuffed to our post office." They began to laugh. They laughed so hard that Jessie fell off her rock and put her hand on a cactus and still laughed so hard she couldn't see to pull out the needles. Val took her hand in his and gently pulled them out, then daubed the dots of blood with a dirty tissue he pulled from his pocket. They sat side by side in dust in front of their devastated crop and held hands.

"They say," Jessie said, "that soon there won't be any more farming like this. That these wheatfields are already a thing of the past. All our food is going to come from greenhouses and factories and laboratories."

"What will happen to the land?" Val wondered.

"Maybe it will go back to the wild — be full of animals and the grass will grow again and people will come to see it and walk on it just because it's so beautiful."

"I can't get a grip on that," he said. "This farmland turned into so much . . . scenery."

"That must be the exact reverse of what the first ranchers said, 'I can't get a grip on what's happening to all this scenery — it's turning into farmland.'"

"How will we live?" Val asked, tipping his head up to look into the deep blue of the descending night.

"We have to find a way to stay on the land even if we don't farm it," she said.

"So, our kind of farming is dead," he said. "But not because of vanishing wildlife or polluted air and water and destroyed fertility — though that would have killed it in a few more years."

"Ah, yes," she said bitterly. "It's gone because it was . . . bad business."

Neil stood on the patch of gravel beside his house and watched the few remaining members of the Church of the Millennium as they worked at cleaning up the site where their cross had been. It was early evening and so still as to be unnatural. It seemed to Neil that the stillness magnified sound, that he could hear each footstep, each grunt and expelled breath as they moved slowly across the grass, bending to pick up splinters and chips of what had been the cross.

Curiously, all the members of the church were dressed in ordinary work clothes, jeans and shirts and running shoes or boots instead of their robes, and even stranger, Neil thought, they were almost completely silent. They crisscrossed the site without speaking or looking at each other, and if there was a chunk of wood too big for one person to lift, someone would speak a name in a dull, uninflected tone without even looking at the person being spoken to. Even the air felt dead, and if the birds were singing, they were doing it somewhere else. Sounds rose up to them from the town below with a startling clarity – the roar of a chainsaw as it bit through a tree broken by the storm, a raised voice, the loud hum of a motor as a truck manoeuvred into position to pick up debris.

Uriel Raven was there too, Neil saw. For some minutes now the preacher had been bending and rising, rhythmically working his way toward where Neil was standing. He hadn't raised his head once, and as he bent, picked up paper, and half-rose to stuff it in the garbage bag he was dragging, he caught a glimpse of Neil and halted.

Neil couldn't take his eyes off Raven, for something was missing, had gone wrong or changed in the interval since their last encounter. As they faced each other a breeze came up and fluttered the tail of Raven's shirt where it had come untucked. It was as if the Earth had sighed – a breath of cool air in the stifling heat. Neil cleared his throat.

"Good evening," he said finally. Raven didn't respond for a second. "Evening," he said quietly and seemed about to turn away, to go back to his work, but Neil stepped forward to hold him.

"It's a lucky thing nobody was hurt," he said, tossing his chin to indicate the places around the cross where the worshippers had gathered. It seemed that Raven's responses had slowed somehow, because it took him a while before he responded.

"Yes," he said. "It was very lucky," and Neil was surprised because he hadn't attributed this to God.

"The Lord works in mysterious ways?" Neil found himself prompting. To his surprise, Raven laughed.

"So He does," he said, and laughed again, as if he were surprised.

"I don't see the girl," Neil remarked. Raven sighed.

"She's gone," he said. "She's become part of a television ministry. She'll never come back." Neil frowned, searching the preacher's face for some clue as to his feelings.

"Did she really have the stigmata?" he asked.

Raven's gaze turned inward. He dropped his eyes to the ground beside Neil. "Well," he said finally. "In any case, she's gone." He looked briefly into Neil's eyes. "She can do much more good as part of a big ministry than she can do here." On impulse Neil said, "Why don't you come in and have a cold drink with me?" Raven seemed about to refuse, reconsidered, then said, "All right."

Neil led the way into his kitchen and even pulled out a chair for the preacher to sit on. He went to the fridge and, without thinking about it, took out two bottles of beer and handed one to Raven. Raven took it from him and held it at eye level, studying it, then set it down on the table in front of him. Neil put a beer mug down beside it and Raven filled it inexpertly, pouring it straight down so the beer foamed up and spilled over onto the table.

"You've never drunk beer before?" Neil asked. Raven was like someone waking from a long sleep and still groggy. Finally he said, "No. I came from a religious home. I've spent all my life, one way or another, with people who are religious."

"One way or another?" Neil prompted him. He sat down across from him.

"They prayed, they waited for signs . . ." He lifted the glass and sipped. He gave no sign whether he liked the taste or not, it was as if he simply hadn't noticed. "As I have," he finished.

"Signs?" It occurred to Neil that he, too, waited for signs. Maybe everybody did. "Have you ever received a sign?" he asked.

"Yes," Raven said. He spoke heavily. Neil waited.

"I would have thought you'd be . . . joyful," Neil said, adopting Raven's language.

"Joyful?" Raven asked. He sounded surprised. "Once I would have been," he acknowledged. "But when it actually happens . . ." He shuddered, feeling the cold, damp air, smelling the wet clay and the grip of the angel hard on him. He closed his eyes, opened them, rearranged his feet under the table. "I think I've been wrong all my life."

Now Neil saw what had changed. Raven wasn't sure any more; Raven was groping, like everybody else. His simplicity of manner, his rock-bottom honesty, as though subterfuge and ostentation had left him forever, cut through Neil's disdain and his anger departed.

"Wrong about what?" he asked gently, although he thought he knew. He raised his eyes to Raven's and found the preacher looking into his face. He saw depths in Raven's face and in his eyes, echoes and shadows that had never been there before. Raven spoke again.

"You spend years praying. You build up a picture of choirs of angels singing gloriously, in silver robes, light streaming down, joy everywhere. Then God – whatever God is – sends you an Angel and the Angel shows you His might. He gives you a glimpse of the unutterable power and mystery." He sat without moving and Neil was motionless too. They sat for a long time. Then Raven lifted his hand; Neil looked again into his eyes and saw a hint, a tiny spark of the fire that had burned in them before.

"And that," Raven said, "is a place from which to begin."

Neil said, "I'm leaving," and was surprised at himself, because he hadn't even thought of doing this.

"Why?" Raven asked. Neil thought of Amy, her gentle eyes, the curve of her soft flesh under his hand, and anguish tore through him. He steeled himself against it.

"Everything I tried to leave behind is here too," he said, through gritted teeth. Raven watched him with eyes that were tender. "In wilderness there is purity," Neil said.

"Have you no ties?" Raven asked.

"None," Neil said, then remembered Faith. That she was dying he knew with certainty. He would go to her and stay with her until she was gone. Then he would be free. "And what about you?"

Raven smiled briefly, stirred like someone waking from a dream and said, "I will remain. There are always things that need doing and someone to do them. Once I would have turned away from them as unworthy of my gifts. Now I know that I am barely worthy of the things that need doing."

After Raven had gone Neil began to pack his few things. Night had fallen and coyotes were crying sadly in the wilderness of the hills. He stopped and listened. Visions of the grassland he loved swept past his eyes. The grass was dying in the long drought, there was almost no wildlife left. Once the plains had been rife with antelope, herds numbering in the hundreds, swift foxes, coyotes, deer, jack-rabbits, and before that, the great herds of bison. He brushed a thick layer of dust off each book as he took it down from the shelf. Dust storms were not new. They had been reported by the earliest explorers long before there was agriculture here. They were a natural part of prairie ecology and had changed the land, as had the prairie fires that periodically swept the grassland, especially in fall, and that fed the natural erosive process.

Streams caught the run-off that was filled with soil. They trickled and then swept on to the seas at each edge of the continent. The tramping of the buffalo, the wind, the fires, the washing effect of water, the churning up of the soil by gophers, badgers, and other rodents, all had served to keep the grassland in constant flux since the time of the last ice age.

Even the glaciers had been nothing more than an event. They had come and gone five times in the last two million years. Seventy-five million years ago this place had been a sea; fifty-five million years ago it was savannah; thirty-seven million years ago it was open forest and sabre-toothed tigers and crocodiles lived here; by the mid-miocene period fourteen million years ago it was open savannah again; sheet after sheet of ice had covered it, when suddenly, ten thousand years ago, the grassland had at last appeared.

Constancy was an illusion, he thought; nature itself was forever in flux, and nothing was inevitable, or permanent.

Amy Sparrow stood in the doorway of her potter's studio, leaning against the frame enjoying the sunshine. Across the street a couple of workmen were standing, gloved hands on hips, surveying the old service station that had been shut down for years and that the tornado had torn apart and deposited in a pile in its lot.

Old John Beim on his morning constitutional had paused and was pointing with his cane at the broken, splintered lumber. Amy could remember when the service station had been one of the gathering spots where people stopped in for a chat or a friendly game of cards.

"Seems a shame, don't it?" a voice said, and Mrs. Zacharias stood beside her, shading her eyes with her hand and watching across the street.

"Lucky nobody was killed," Amy said.

"That was some meeting, wasn't it?" Mrs. Zacharias said, straightening her glasses and brushing ineffectually at her unruly curls. "I thought I'd die when that crow dropped on the Premier's good suit."

"Weren't you one of the women in chains?" Amy asked.

"I was," Mrs. Zacharias said.

"Need a payloader," a passer-by shouted at the workmen across the street.

"I been here all my life," Rita said, "and my parents before me. All my kids were born here, and Linda's buried here. Seemed worth fighting for."

"They'll take our post office anyway," Amy said.

"Then somebody'll have to drive to Crisis and bring back our mail," Rita said, stubborn. "Was only the tornado that made Zena unlock us. We'd still be there if it weren't for it." A big yellow pay-loader was roaring up the sidewalk and onto the lot, where it stopped. The driver jumped out, but all conversation became impossible because of its roar. "People managed here when there wasn't nothing at all!" Rita shouted into Amy's ear. Amy nodded. Rita marched away.

Amy was about to go back into her shop when she saw Neil's truck coming slowly toward her. As he approached and then passed her she saw the cartons in the back that she knew would contain his books. She caught a glimpse of him at the wheel, but if he had seen her he gave no sign. For a second she felt the full shock of his loss, put up a hand to attract his attention, then dropped it and turned away. It was better this way.

She closed the door to her shop and began to stroll down the street, moving toward the edge of town, with no destination in mind. At the corner where the two main streets intersected, she paused. Two workmen from Crisis were replacing the shattered window in the grocery store, and further down the street Martin Barrell was up a tree, sawing a limb that had been partially broken and would drop on the head of some unsuspecting passer-by in the next wind. And there was Zena Lavender in her front yard picking up shingles and other bits of debris on the grass and in her flowerbeds. Amy strolled over to her.

"The storm certainly made a mess," she remarked.

"Dreadful!" Mrs. Lavender agreed. She straightened and her eyes met Amy's. Amy was taken aback by her penetrating gaze. It was as if she had bored into Amy's heart and had seen everything there was to see. Embarrassed, hardly knowing what she was saying, she said, "Lucky nobody was killed." Mrs. Lavender had turned back to her flowerbed. She reached into it, thrusting aside the purple petunias and pulled out an object that gleamed white.

"What's that?" Amy asked. Mrs. Lavender held it in the palm of her hand and Amy bent to get a better look at it.

"It's a piece of the cross," Zena said disapprovingly. "Tsk, tsk." She tossed it onto the pile of scraps and dusted off her hands. She seemed about to turn away, then looked at Amy again. "I do hope you'll drop in for tea one of these afternoons," she said. Amy hesitated, was about to reply politely, when suddenly Mrs. Lavender interrupted. "Or, perhaps not," she said. "You have your art. Mustn't take you away from it." Amy stood silent. Mrs. Lavender didn't speak again, but knelt in the flowerbed with her back to Amy and began weeding furiously. Amy wandered away.

Ahead of her, far to the west, thunderclouds were building up along the horizon and a couple of hawks circled something on the other side of the river, screaming as they went. The fields were silent, there was no crop to harvest.

She sat down on the grass at the edge of the river. So many of the neat, pretty houses that were still occupied would be abandoned in the coming months. Soon you would have to go to Crisis for even the most basic items. There would be no farmers left. She wondered what would happen to their land and was afraid it would be farmed by multinationals. But no, she thought, the land is all but dead. It's too late for that.

A breeze shook the tall grass around her and rippled the surface of the murky stream below where she sat. The willows on the far bank rustled. She knew the little river was full of silt from the farmlands and polluted with crop spray and chemical fertilizers. What a mess we've made, she thought.

She looked back to the small, dying town where she had spent her life, thought of Zena Lavender in her flowerbed and Martin Barrell sawing off a tree limb and herself in her shop making pots. She thought of other civilizations, much greater ones, that had died. Greece. Neil is wrong, she thought. It is not the aboriginals' dreamtime to which we must return. That dream, too, is gone. It is the idea of progress that has killed us. We were whole the way we were, but we dreamt of progress and our dreams destroyed us. It has always been this way.

We will go on; we will find new ways to live; the gods expect it of us.

Restlessness assailed her and she stood shakily, examining her unease. She knew what it was: a new sculpture. It had been hovering all morning just below her consciousness, dark and shapeless, and now it rose a little. She felt her power gathering: knew that neither thunderstorms nor tornadoes nor the greed of others would stop her. She would carry on trying to express this compelling vision she had until she died. She allowed it full sway, standing there in the wind before the opaque green stream, and it clutched at her like a colossus and shook her. I will, she thought. Yes.

She thought of Paris and New York. She thought of art galleries, theatres, concert halls. Her heart ached for all the wonders they contained, even as she relinquished them. She relinquished them for the sky, for the sweet, hot smell of the earth in the spring, for the steady warmth of the sun on her skin, for the stillness and for the birdsong. She relinquished civilization for the power that dwelt silently inside her that now and then gathered itself, leapt upward and pushed itself into clay. She would give up all but that power for the distant, eerie melody of the coyotes as they sang their ancient, wild song of the prairie.

# ABOUT THE AUTHOR

Sharon Butala is the author of *The Gates of the Sun* and *Luna*, two novels in a loosely connected trilogy completed by *The Fourth Archangel*. Her other novels include *Country of the Heart*, which was nominated for the Books in Canada First Novel Award, and *Upstream*. Her first short story collection, *Queen of the Headaches*, was short-listed for a Governor General's Literary Award in 1986. Her most recent short story collection, *Fever*, was nominated for a Commonwealth Award in 1991, and one of its stories, published in *Saturday Night* magazine, won a Silver National Magazine Award. Her short fiction and articles appear frequently in Canada's best magazines and newspapers.

She lives near Eastend, Saskatchewan with her husband Peter.